The Stars Shine Bright

The Stars Shine Bright

Alice Townsend's story

Julia Parker

PIATKUS

To the memory of Rudolf Valentino
and Rudolf Nureyev, named after him

Copyright © 1996 by Julia Parker

First published in Great Britain in 1996 by
Judy Piatkus (Publishers) Ltd of
5 Windmill Street, London W1

The moral right of the author has been asserted

A catalogue record for this book is available from the British Library

ISBN 0-7499-0360-0

Set in 10·5/11·5 pt Times by
Datix International Limited, Bungay, Suffolk
Printed and bound in Great Britain by
Butler & Tanner Ltd, Frome & London

Author's note   Some of the great stars of the silent screen appear in my story, as a tribute to their work and with thanks for the considerable pleasure they have given, and will always continue to give me.

Prologue

The Times, Friday, August 17, 1900:
   Birth. TOWNSEND On Wednesday August 15, to Robert and Elizabeth
   (née Newcombe), at Queen Charlotte's Hospital, London, God's gift of
   a daughter, Alice Caroline.

1912

Chapter 1

June, 1912

'Just *how* many sharps are there in the A major scale, Alice? Surely you know by now.'

'Three, Mummy.'

'Then *why* are you only playing two? What about G sharp?'

'Sorry, Mummy, but it's so boring.'

'Boring? How can you say such a thing! The piano's the most beautiful instrument ever created, and you, my girl, are extremely fortunate to be learning on such a beautiful one.'

Eleven-year-old Alice Townsend heaved a sigh, and slumped over the edge of the keyboard.

'Yes, *I* know . . .' she sighed.

'Don't drop your wrists like that! Now look, I must see to Philip and get my books together for third form English. Daddy's almost ready, and we have to leave in fifteen minutes, otherwise we'll all be late. Meanwhile I want you to practise that scale over two octaves – *with* the G sharps. I'll hear you at five o'clock before tea – yes, and that second section of "Für Elise" as well. So get on with it now, please.'

Lizzie Townsend left her daughter at the piano while she hurriedly said goodbye to her young son, leaving him as usual in the charge of his nanny, Molly. Then she gathered together everything she needed for her day's teaching.

Left on her own, Alice, with a heavy touch, knocked out the notes – very fast and very inaccurately. Ten minutes later her father popped his head round the door of the drawing room.

'Ready, Alice?'

'I suppose so, Daddy,' she replied glumly.

'That's my girl – got your satchel?'

She nodded. As she made her way to the door and passed her father, he affectionately ruffled her hair.

'Daddy . . .'

'Yes, I know. You don't have to tell me. But you know music *is* wonderful, and it's only natural Mummy wants you to excel at it.'

'But I'll never be as good as she is.'

He winked.

'Well, we'll see. I'll get the car, and the three of us must get on with our day.'

Robert Townsend went out into Edwardes Square and unlocked the Wolseley sixteen. Lizzie and Alice joined him for the short journey east, along Kensington High Street for about a mile to Queen's Gate where Alice's parents taught in the two schools they owned jointly with their life-long friends Eustace and Emma Beaumont, who lived on the premises.

By five o'clock Alice was dutifully back at her mother's beautiful piano, and not at all happy to be there. To her the instrument was anything but beautiful. It seemed to grimace at her. The keys looked like menacing black and white teeth waiting to snap. And snap they did – every time she hit a wrong note – so much so that when she was learning something new she would very quietly 'test' the note first to see if it sounded right. If it did that was fine, and she would strike it so that the sound was louder, but if it did not she would shrink or simply get angry and thump it to try and *make* it sound right.

On this particular day she managed to get the scale right, and was told that her rendering of the first two sections of 'Für Elise' was just a little better.

Her mother's words cheered her to a certain extent, but as soon as she was released from the piano stool she rushed up to her room and closed the door. Once inside her mood changed. She went to the top shelf in her wardrobe to take out everything she needed for the following morning. Tomorrow was Saturday – her favourite day of the week. It was not that she disliked her general lessons at school, it was simply that she adored Saturdays – and Saturday mornings in particular. In fact she decided that she lived for Saturday mornings! And tomorrow would be very special. Among her jumble of tights and old ballet shoes was a long narrow paper bag with

Porselli's Famous Italian Ballet Shoes.
West Street, London W.

printed on it in decorative lettering. With the greatest possible care she took out her very first pair of pink satin, blocked toe ballet shoes. They were her greatest treasure. Now, with their ribbons sewn in position and the toes carefully darned in precisely the right way by the patient Molly, they were ready for her first lesson in pointe work on the morrow. She held them to her cheek, feeling more and more just how beautiful they were. She smelt them. Surely there was nothing on earth more lovely than the smell of new satin ballet shoes?

'Right,' Mrs Stedman, her teacher, would say tomorrow, 'girls, put on your toe shoes,' and she would be on the way to becoming a real ballerina.

She would be taught how to tie them correctly, and then helped to make her first steps on pointe. It was very exciting. But before all that could happen she knew that she would have to do an hour's piano practice before leaving for the ballet school.

Chapter 2

Charlie Cook took his bicycle from its place in the area and went out into Queen's Gate. He mounted it to ride west to his Hammersmith home, where he would tell his parents his good news.

He noticed a group of Rosamund Academy girls saying goodbye to each other, and one of them began walking in the same direction as him. Recognising her, and seeing that she was limping very badly, he drew up beside her and dismounted.

'Hello, Alice, what's wrong? Have you twisted your ankle?'

'Charlie . . .' She began to blush, delighted to have been noticed by such a senior boy. 'Oh, Charlie! No, I've not twisted my ankle, but I've got awful blisters on my toes.'

'Blisters on your toes! Why, are your shoes too small?'

'No, you see it's my dancing.'

She went on to explain that she had started pointe work (and had to describe what it was), and that she had been practising too much.

'And Mummy came up to my attic where I do my practice, because she'd heard a lot of thumping about, and she was cross with me. She said I was disturbing Philip – you know he's my brother – he's in the first form.'

Charlie knew.

'She said I was making too much noise and would make my toes sore, and that it would be my own fault. I should have listened to my dancing teacher who said not to do too much. Anyway, she said, instead of making my toes sore I ought to have been practising piano – awful, boring scales.'

The older boy smiled.

'Well, I know how you feel. I sometimes pull muscles when I try to do too much practice for athletics or cricket. So you play the piano too! I didn't know you did such a lot.'

Alice looked up at him and bit her lip. Tears came to her eyes.

'I say, you look jolly sad – are your toes that sore?'

She did not want to appear babyish.

'No, it's nothing, really, I'm alright.'

They were quiet for a while as they made their way along the busy, crowded Kensington High Street. Then Charlie said, 'I've just been with your father and Mr Beaumont.'

'Oh, why? How awful! – did they tick you off? What have you done wrong?'

'No, I thought I must have at first, but, well, I'm to be Head Boy of Creswell from September.'

'Congratulations! That's lovely. You'll be jolly good I know you will.'

Alice glanced shyly at him, then rather nervously enquired, 'Have you decided what you want to do when you leave school? Your parents own several shops, don't they? I've heard Aunt Emma telling Mummy about them. Will you work with your father?'

'No, Alice, I've always wanted to go into the army. I've just told the Heads that, and they've suggested I go to Sandhurst. I'd like that.'

'Gosh! That's really exciting! But won't your parents be disappointed that you'll not work with them?'

'No, not really. You see, there have been quite a few chaps in Mother's family who've been in the army – there was my Uncle Charles, who I'm named after . . . so I'll be carrying on a family tradition.'

'And I expect one day you'll visit us in your army uniform.'

'Yes, I certainly will.'

'That's wonderful, Charlie. Your parents'll be so proud and pleased.'

'I hope so. I think they will. Look, I'd better ride on – I do want to tell them. 'Bye, Alice – take care of your toes.'

'I will.'

It was the first time Alice realized how nice it was that a boy could be so kind and understanding. She had not had a lot to do with boys – apart from her much younger brother, and Stephen Beaumont, who was Emma and Eustace's son; because the Beaumonts were 'Aunt Emma' and 'Uncle Eustace' to her and Philip, both Stephen and his two-year-old sister Rose, were like cousins.

It was a considerable compensation for having to walk home. Her parents had an important staff meeting, and her mother had insisted that she get home early to do her piano practice. But she had lost her bus fare, and so had to hobble along. While she had been walking and talking to Charlie, she had hardly noticed the pain, but once he left her it returned, and by the time she got home and torn off her shoes and long white socks, she discovered that her blisters had been bleeding, and the blood had dried, sticking her socks to her toes.

Molly was sympathetic.

'You shouldn't do so much dancing, Alice, you know you shouldn't   your poor little toes are a mess. Look, I'll wash them and wrap them up. Surely ballet isn't worth it.'

'Oh yes, Molly – yes it is – I don't care about the blisters, they'll soon heal!'

*

9

The house-lights dimmed, the curtain went up revealing the stage crowded with Arab men and women in flowing robes, whirling Dervishes, Bedouins, Chinese jugglers and acrobats, and a group of slave girls with bare midriffs who at once started an exotic dance with little bells attached to their ankles and miniature brass castanets in their hands. The plot, an amalgam of several Arabian Nights stories, was dramatic, and involved a host of colourful characters; beautiful Princesses, beggars and slave girls – the latter much talked about because of their sensational dancing and revealing costumes. The show was a delight. No-one who had any inclination for the theatre wanted to miss seeing it.

The Townsends, sitting in the front row of the circle of the Garrick Theatre for a performance of the successful musical play *Kismet*, looked down on the spectacular scene. Alice, leaning well forward, was totally engrossed in the dancing, and throughout the evening longed for the girls to return to the stage – either to make sinuous, exotic oriental movements or to step and glide and form lovely patterns with their arms and hands when they came alive as the Sultan's jewels. She knew that she would not find it at all difficult to move like them, and in spite of her mere twelve years, she just knew she could – and would in due course – take a place on that stage.

The evening had also revealed to her that there was far more to dancing than just ballet and the more fashionable 'fancy dancing' which was taught to most girls simply to give them grace and social standing. She now instinctively knew that it was possible to express thoughts and feelings in movement. She became fascinated by the idea, and in the privacy of her attic studio created sad movements, happy movements and funny movements. She found library books and read about dancing in other countries. Remembering the slave girls' dance, she made up her own version. She slipped into another world when she was dancing. She had learned mazurkas and European dances with Mrs Stedman, but she was certainly not taught the sort of movements the slave girls had made in the wonderful colourful and exciting production of *Kismet*, and somehow felt almost guilty as she tried to reproduce them in the attic.

As Alice's passion for the dance grew so did her determination. She knew this was the only thing she wanted to do – or would *ever* want to do. At the same time her loathing of the piano increased. Her father pointed out that to be a dancer one had to be musical – which she naturally was – but the only reason she had to put up with the hours of practice her mother insisted upon was that once it was done she could either go to her dancing classes or retreat to her attic studio where, some time previously, Robert had fixed a large mirror and a barre along one wall.

Lizzie rather thought that her husband was far too sympathetic towards his dancing daughter but he reminded her that, after all, Lizzie herself was no mean dancer – they had waltzed in a very spectacular fashion in their youth, and she had always loved it. He tried to impress on her the fact that Alice had inherited this talent from her, but had not inherited any serious ability for the piano. However, it was to no avail. Robert was fully aware that his wife was an enormously talented pianist, but because of her youthful determination to study and become a teacher, her own progress as a concert pianist had been thwarted. She continued to regret this – in spite of the fact that she loved teaching. She very much wanted her daughter to follow in her footsteps and achieve the international fame she did not; she secretly longed to see her Alice, one day, come onto the platform in the large Queen's Hall to perform piano concertos under the baton of Sir Henry Wood at his famous Promenade Concerts.

At present, her disappointment and even anger when she saw her dream beginning to flutter away as Alice became more devoted to dance, was something that Lizzie could not control. The further from reality her dream slipped, the more determinedly she pursued it. Alice had taken two piano examinations, and had done reasonably well, though Lizzie knew that her daughter's marks were not as impressive as her own had been when she was twelve.

'Work on that Czerny study today. It's not difficult, I don't think you'll need any help with it now we've been through it.'

Lizzie left her daughter alone to go and give instructions to Mrs Wilson, their elderly housekeeper. She was soon out of hearing range of the first floor drawing room.

Alice was furious. She hated Czerny. She loathed his dull repetitive studies, which they always seemed to make her fingers ache which was far more intolerable than the sorest of toes or aching limbs after too much dancing practice. She looked up at the music in front of her – a series of chords with a lot of black notes which changed every so often. She placed her fingers on the keys, but unfortunately on a number of wrong notes. The noise was dreadfully discordant.

She did not care and defiantly continued playing the wrong notes. As she did so she started shouting, 'I hate the piano. *I hate the piano!*' She thumped more wrong notes, then slid her fingers up and down the keys in long *glissandos*, slapping the keys to the continued accompaniment of her shouting: 'Hate, hate, hate!'

Philip heard her, and apprehensively popped his head around the drawing room door. Seeing his sister in such a fury frightened him and he rushed down to the kitchen, where he pulled his mother from her conference with the housekeeper.

'Mummy, come up, come up – I think Alice has gone crazy. She's making a dreadful noise, you can't hear her down here.'

Lizzie hurriedly climbed from the basement and rushed into the first floor drawing room.

'Stop it *at once*! You'll ruin the piano.'

11

Alice continued thumping, shouting, 'Good! Horrible thing! Horrible thing!'

In her fury, Lizzie caught at the piano lid and slammed it down, catching Alice's fingers. Alice screamed and ran tearfully out of the room.

Lizzie had succeeded frightening herself and terrifying her daughter.

1915

Chapter 3

April, 1915

Emma Beaumont, having finished her usual administrative duties, was having tea with Lizzie at the end of the school day.

'I just can't believe it, Emma. Arthur Silvester – and Iris – both gone. She was killed at Menin, you know, and he was a brilliant cricket coach – I saw several of his team biting their lips as Eustace read out the roll of honour this morning.'

'Yes, it's unbelievable. And I doubt if Robert will have time to take over this season.'

'He says he'll do what he can, but only after school, so the boys will just have to put up with what they can get. Then Iris . . .'

'Dear Iris . . . she was my star pupil, before she joined the staff. No wonder the clerical division snapped her up – it was a joy to teach her shorthand, she was brilliant at it from her first lesson and soon became faster than me, such a nice girl.'

The two women fell silent. Nearly every month they had news that an old boy, or occasionally an old girl, had been killed or severely injured.

Emma sighed, 'Eustace is all too often very depressed these days.'

'Yes, so is Robert. But we all are, aren't we? I even caught Alice crying the other day. But, Emma, even if our husbands are in reserved occupations they are doing a marvellous job in their own way. Oh! I don't know how I'd cope if Robert . . .'

'He wouldn't, *surely*, He really *is* needed at the schools.'

'Sometimes I think that in spite of everything, and even considering Alice and Philip, let alone all the work he's doing, he might enlist; but I don't mention it – and as you know I couldn't stop him if he said he was going to. I don't want to sound unpatriotic, but I don't think Eustace would pass his medical, do you . . . his eyes?'

'Yes, Lizzie, his eyes *are* very weak – they always have been.'

Emma fell silent, remembering those many years ago when Lizzie had first introduced them – how Eustace had looked at her, face to face, through his very thick pebbled spectacles, and how rude she had thought he was! Flicking herself out of her momentary day dream, she stood up.

'Now I must go over to Harrods to collect all that knitting wool for my girls' "Comforts for the Troops" club.'

'I've had a letter from Charlie-boy.'

Emma at the other end of the phone was delighted to hear her old friend's voice.

'You must be so relieved. How is he?'

'He's well, Em, thank God. He tells me a lot of news – I'm surprised it wasn't censored – but what he says does worry me.'

'What does he say?'

'He says the other day they noticed lots of yellow smoke rising up and coming towards their trenches, and it made all their eyes sting and run, and he and his men were ever so sick afterwards. I saw in the newspapers something about poison gas. So I'm sure he's had a dose of that from Fritz, damn him.'

'Katy, I'm so sorry – but you know they are developing . . . gas hoods, I think they call them, and he and his platoon will be issued with them soon.'

'I do hope so, Em. Horrible, isn't it? I do so worry about him, but at least he's alright so far.'

'You must be very proud of him too, Katy. To think that right from the beginning of the war he was taken out of Sandhurst to command that platoon. He's a thoroughly professional soldier – not like most of the boys at the front.'

'Yes, we are proud of him. I've had another photograph of him – in his Lieutenant's uniform. He looks so handsome, though I says it as shouldn't. I sent a copy to Jim, he's down at Dover overseeing victuals for France. At least they are using all his grocery trade knowledge. I'm just about managing the shops, though I might soon employ one of your girls to do the books for me, if she doesn't want to go off to the front. I do miss Jim, Em, it's so lonely without him. Like you four, we've always worked together, you know. Thank goodness I have the other three. Must go now. Come down to tea soon, though I doubt if my carrot cake will be anything like what we used to have at your place in the good old days.'

'They will return, Katy, they will return.'

As she slowly and reflectively hung the ear piece of the telephone back on its hook, Emma had serious doubts about her last statement.

The garden in the centre of St James' Square was looking its best on one sunny, May morning. Eustace, Robert and Alice were leaving the London Library laden with books for work and pleasure reading. They were on their way to join Emma and Lizzie for a rare, relaxing morning coffee in Fortnum and Mason's. Their thoughts and conversation had, for once, been unconnected with the schools or the war, and Alice, who was reading *Barchester Towers*, had remarked just how vile she thought Mr Slope. Eustace responded with a particularly shrewd remark which made father and daughter

16

laugh. As they were about to turn from the Square into Duke of York Street, two women walked abruptly up to them.

'Cowards, cowards!' one bawled at them.

The other grabbed her friend by the sleeve and in a rough Cockney accent said to her, 'Don't bovver wiv' them, they're too old.'

'Oh no, I *will* bother with 'em. Cowards! You ought to be ashamed of yerselves, you with yer books and yer smart suits. Why aren't you at the front like real men? Afraid of gettin' hurt? Or are you a pair of nancy boys, eh? Is that it?'

She pulled a face at Eustace as she spoke, then, turning to Alice ranted on, 'And you, girl, aren't you ashamed to be out with two grown men who aren't doin' their bit?'

Alice was furious and ready to attack the woman. Seeing her reaction, Robert put a firm restraining hand on her arm.

'Madam, I beg your pardon, we don't deserve . . .'

Eustace attempted a reply, but was too shaken to be really effective.

'Look, I don't know who you are, and you know nothing about us. Please leave us alone or I'll call a policeman.'

Robert too was trying to keep his temper.

'Go on, then, do just that – but 'ere you are, 'ave this first, both of you, *cowards!*'

And with that the young women thrust white feathers into Robert and Eustace's hands, and ran off down towards the Square.

'Well, I knew this happened, but I never thought we'd be presented with those,' sighed Eustace.

'Daddy, this is awful. They just assumed . . . they don't know what good and vital work you and Uncle Eustace are doing. Oh, I really felt I wanted to hit her.'

'Well, dear, you very nearly did, and that wouldn't have been at all a good idea. Do try to calm down.'

After a pause, while the three of them recovered from the outburst, Robert said, 'I think I'll have to go, old man, I really think I'll have to go. Could you possibly manage Creswell without me?'

'But, Robert, why? There are so many who can do what you could do at the front, but so few who can do what you do at the school,' said Eustace. 'Of course, it *is* a question of conscience, and if you feel you really should go, well, yes, we'll get by. I know one or two very elderly retired teachers who would help out. But, Robert, what if the worst happened? Do think of your darlings . . . Lizzie's a tower of strength, but would it be fair on her? Besides, you're not as young as you used to be – neither of us are.'

'I've been thinking about it for some time, you know. I can contribute a great deal because of my special subjects.'

'Languages, you mean?'

'Yes, my fluent German and French would be an asset. This bloody feather just seems to be the last straw!'

17

He had to smile at his statement, in spite of the gravity of the decision he had just taken.

Alice had been quiet while this exchange was going on. Now she opened her mouth to speak, but before she could utter her father had turned to her.

'Alice, do you understand how I feel? I'm sure you do – you're so grown up for your years. But all this tension between you and Mummy is awful, so I really need to know that you will smooth things out between you while I'm away. Will you promise me that you'll try to do that, and do your best to look after her and Philip?'

'Yes, Daddy, I'll try – though it won't be easy. But your work at school, that's important too, as Uncle Eustace says. I don't see how the others will cope without you. Oh, Daddy, please, *please*, think again – it's so dangerous.'

Robert took his daughter's arm in his own and patted her hand to reassure her, both realising deep down that it was probably right for him to use his skills for the war effort.

They turned into Jermyn Street. Eustace bought the first edition of the *Evening News* from a newsboy who was shouting excitedly about something. He took the paper and as he walked along glanced at the bold headline: *LUSITANIA SUNK, 1,195 LIVES LOST. MANY WOMEN AND CHILDREN PERISH.*

'Oh no, Robert, look! Dreadful, dreadful!'

'Bloody Germans. That makes me want to enlist even more!'

The tranquillity of the morning had been totally disrupted.

As it became more and more obvious that the war was not going to end as quickly and as decisively as everyone had thought at its outset in August 1914, life became increasingly less colourful. It was considered not just bad taste for women to wear elaborate clothes, but downright unpatriotic, and so – especially in the summer months – there was much less colour in the city streets. Sadness and depression, though along with great patriotic fervour, was everywhere.

One evening while Alice was doing her ballet practice in the attic, Philip knocked on the door. Alice liked to be quite alone at this time so that she could concentrate and discover why she might not be holding her arabesque as steadily as she should, or correct her position if she stumbled off pointe.

'Can I come in, sis, please?'

'Yes, Phil, of course. Come and sit on that cushion. I'll do a few extra barre exercises, if you want to talk.'

Philip, now nearly nine, came in and sat down, elbows resting on his knees, and sighed deeply. Standing at her barre as she corrected her fifth position, Alice asked him what was wrong.

'Do you think it's right for Daddy to leave us like he's going to?'

'Yes, I think so. You see, he's pretty clever, and I'm sure he'll help to catch lots of horrid Germans, because he'll know what they're saying.'

Philip was quiet for a moment.

18

'Yes, but he'll have to *be* with Germans to do that, won't he? And that'll mean he'll be caught by them.'

'No, I don't really think so. He'll probably listen out on the wireless for messages and all sorts of secret plans and troop movements, or perhaps make prisoners talk about where the enemy lines are . . . He told me he thought it would be quite exciting. Well, that's what he says.'

'So he'll not be firing guns and things like that or, or . . . you know, what the soldiers do when they go into battle . . . what is it?'

'You mean jump out of the trenches?'

Philip nodded.

'Go "over the top" – that's what they call it? No, I wouldn't think so. Besides, Daddy will be a Captain, not just a private, so he'll not be in any real danger . . . Not like Charles Cook. He has to command a whole platoon of men.'

'Was that Charles Cook who was Head Boy?'

'Yes, Phil, he's at the front. Aunt Emma tells me that Mrs Cook says he's very well. Oh, Philip, I do hope Charles will *always* be alright.'

She stopped, sat down on the floor, and started absently to untie her ballet shoe ribbons.

'Now go, I must change. Done your homework? Feel better now we've talked?'

Philip had done his homework, and he did feel better.

The Inner Circle train drew to a halt at Kensington High Street station. Robert walked slowly westward along the busy High Street, thinking that he would all too soon be parted for many months from his beloved Lizzie and their two darling children. He tried to work out in his mind how he would break the news to them. It was not going to be easy, but they would want to know how the interview at the War Office had gone. He knew that he was doing the right thing, both for himself and for his King and Country. But he wondered now, as he had wondered so often in recent weeks, whether he was not acting selfishly. He didn't *have* to go to war; yet he knew he must. He didn't want to leave his wife and children – and his all-engulfing and satisfying work – but knew, somehow, he had to. He thanked God that he had such a supportive family.

He arrived home to find the younger generation with several classmates from Alice's form and her friends from the ballet school all enjoying a happy tea party in the back garden. The atmosphere was extremely jolly. Alice was about to cut a birthday cake cleverly shaped in two figures – a one and a five. It was the fifteenth of August, and her fifteenth birthday. With the help of a delicate August breeze, the young girl blew out her fifteen candles.

He watched from a distance, studying his daughter with love and admiration. Here she was on the brink of womanhood, yet still able, without embarrassment, to enjoy the simple pleasures of childhood. As he looked at her his thoughts ran on a year to her next birthday. She would by then be more of the woman than the child. Her body, already perfectly formed, would have developed further. Her attitude to life might well have changed, and her determination, which had always been a marked quality, could be either an asset or a stumbling block – as it had certainly been where her attitude towards the piano was concerned. That troubled him. The clash had already caused a serious rift between her and her mother; all too often he had to take on the role of peacemaker – not always successfully. He doubted if Alice would ever really conform and accept authority or the conventions of the time, any more than his Lizzie had done when *she* was young. He also knew he would always admire her for her strength of character. He noticed her long blonde hair with a touch of chestnut as it caught the brilliance of a sunbeam. He smiled to himself at its beauty and its subtle likeness to her mother's.

The children's voices were joyful, and excited laughter rang out all over the compact and pretty garden, its mid-summer flowers adding colour to the scene. Emma and Lizzie were looking on admiringly, and Eustace, sitting on a stool nearby, was playing his guitar – something he did tremendously well, but all too infrequently in these busy times. Molly and Tabitha, who was Charlie's sister and Stephen and Rose's nanny, were serving ice cream and jelly, and little Rose was presenting Alice with a daisy chain she had just completed.

If only the world was as peaceful and as happy as this scene . . . And I'm to leave it all behind me . . . all too soon, Robert thought. He quietly slipped back into the house, went into the study, and drew the blinds.

'Look, Alice, we must have a very serious talk.'

'Daddy?'

It was the second time within the last few days that Alice's precious dancing practice time had been interrupted. She sat down on a large cushion as Robert settled into an old armchair.

'We must think very carefully about the way you and Mummy clash and argue over your piano lessons and practice.'

'Oh, Daddy, you know I hate . . .'

'Yes I do know. How could I fail to know! It's very sad. Tell me, dear, do you love Mummy?'

'Oh *yes* – of *course* I do. And she plays so beautifully. But I'm hopeless by her standards, and as much as I know it would make life easier if I could be as good as she is, I know I never shall – I'm just no good at it, and that's that. I simply don't want to waste all the time I have on practising and practising and practising, when I know I would get more out of going to extra dancing classes. Daddy, I really do *not* want to be a concert pianist, I've *no real talent*.'

'But Mummy thinks you have, and you know she knows a great deal about it. And she's so keen for you to become one. I can't understand why you hate it so much. Are there other reasons? Even if you don't think you're good at it, surely it's fun to play? And it complements your dancing. Besides, you love music, and you're a very musical dancer – Mrs Stedman has said that time and time again. Do you know why you hate your lessons with Mummy? All her other piano pupils at school love her as a teacher, and when there's no real problem when she takes you for English and Geography at school . . . in fact I'm sure you'll do well in your national examinations next year. So why do you and she clash so badly over piano lessons?'

Alice was quiet for some time.

'Well, do you know why?'

She looked up at her father, tears in her eyes.

'Yes, Daddy, I do.' Sobbing she got up and rushed into his arms.

'Tell me, then – if you can.'

'Oh, Daddy, it's awful – it's always been awful. At first I honestly couldn't understand what it was I hated so much. I thought it was the piano itself, and it wasn't so long ago that I really realised that . . . that . . .'

'Go on.'

He stroked her hair.

'That when Mummy gives me piano lessons she become someone quite different – not the Mummy I know and love. She becomes, well, fierce and much more strict than when she's teaching me English – really hard and horrible. She sounds different and her face changes, there's a hard line between her brows, and she frowns. She hardly ever really smiles and she makes me nervous . . .'

'But surely she praises you too? After all, I know you do try very hard to please her – that is when you can both keep your volatile tempers.'

'Well, yes, she does, sometimes; but it's somehow never as if she really means it. It's always, "That's not too bad, dear" – then she'll go on to tell me what's wrong. Then we both get angry and I glare at her and thump the piano and, and well, you know what happens.'

Robert sighed.

'Darling, do you think that after I've left you can try very, very hard not to upset her? Not to thump the piano, or shout how much you hate it, as you do all too often?'

'I'll try. It won't be easy, Daddy, honestly it won't, but I will try.' She paused again, then drew away and went back to her cushion. Robert was about to get up and go.

'Well, I'm going to talk to Mummy. We really must sort this out – we've tried time and time again over the years, but as I'm going away . . .'

'Daddy, is there any way we can compromise? Do I really have to spend what amounts to three times more time at the piano than at dancing? Couldn't I have more than one dancing lesson a week? You know that's what I *really* want to do. If I could, say, go after school even once more a week, then I might find pleasing Mummy just a little easier. Please, please ask her for me.'

'I'll see what she says.'

21

Robert kissed his daughter on the forehead. Concerned and extremely puzzled he went downstairs to find Lizzie. What Alice had told him contradicted everything he knew about his warm-hearted, loving wife. How could she become such an ogre when teaching her daughter? Her daughter, whom she loved just as much as he did? It was totally uncharacteristic – and he knew that she would deny that it happened.

Her reaction was just what he expected.

'It's total nonsense, Robert! Of course I don't treat her any differently. She's just trying to get round you, you know how she can exaggerate. Yes, I do get cross with her from time to time – but that's simply because she's so lazy and her playing is so careless. I have to din things into her if she really is to develop her considerable talent.'

'Well, she's not one to invent or tell lies about things like that, you know. Anyway, that's what she's said. I doubt if she would like you to know I've told you. So give it some thought. She suggested a compromise.'

'Indeed. What?'

'She says she would find it easier if you would allow her to go to one more dancing class a week. I think you should. After all, we don't know that she really *is* talented as a pianist – that's only your opinion. We've never let her play to someone like ... well, I don't know – your old Professor for instance.'

'I *know* she has talent. There's no need for confirmation from anyone else. As for her dancing – that's just a part of her general education.'

'Don't be quite so sure, and, Lizzie, darling Lizzie, I don't want you and she to be at loggerheads once I'm away. So I say she should have that extra class. It will keep her happy, and if she is happy I think she'll be more willing to keep up her piano studies.'

Reluctantly, Lizzie capitulated.

The station platform was crowded with men in uniform and women and children saying last goodbyes. As the four of them, standing close together outside Robert's first-class compartment were doing their best to keep cheerful, another train with a red cross painted on it pulled in at the next platform; but at that moment there was the slamming of doors and a great hiss of steam from the engine of Robert's train.

'Darlings, this is it. I must go now.'

'Of course you must. Take care, take care always, my only love.'

'And you too.'

Robert and Lizzie kissed for the last time. In a very grown-up way Robert shook Philip's hand, then smiling, his father picked him up and hugged him, while Alice threw her arms round her father's neck and said her goodbye, promising that she really would try not to upset her mother. It was a moment that touched them all very deeply, but the women somehow managed to give their beloved Robert all the support he needed.

The carriage doors slammed. There was a whistle from the guard as he raised his green flag and, among hundreds of other womenfolk of all classes, the three of them stood waving on the platform until the train disappeared out of sight.

They turned to leave the station. As they did so, they saw a line of men standing one behind the other, their eyes bound, each with a hand on the shoulder of the man in front. They were slowly making their way towards a waiting bus. Many more, some on crutches, others on stretchers, their cigarettes lit for them by V.A.D nurses, or drinking cups of tea from a mobile canteen, were waiting to be taken away in ambulances.

Lizzie stopped and stared at them for a moment or two. Alice noticed a tear falling down her cheek.

'Don't look, Mummy, please – that won't happen to Daddy. As he says, he'll not be near the front line. Look there's a taxi, let's grab it and go home, *please!*'

She tugged at her mother's sleeve. Lizzie responded with a heavy heart.

1916–1917

Chapter 4

Summer, 1916

'No, Alice, not until you've taken your music exam, I absolutely forbid it. For weeks now you have had to revise for the College of Preceptors National school exams, and you're dreadfully behind with your music. You hardly know the studies, your scales are uneven, and your pieces lack any kind of expression or feeling. You've simply masses of work to do in the next few weeks, so put the dance classes right out of your mind.'

'But, Mummy, I *always* go to Mrs Stedman's summer classes. They're the best of all. We watch professional dancers and often meet ballerinas and dancers with big parts in musical shows. Please, please don't tell me I can't go. I've worked hard at school – you said so yourself.'

'Yes, you have, and that's exactly as it should be. But your music practice has been pitiful – just like your playing. You simply must get your Senior grade. So, from the end of term it'll be two hours in the morning and two in the afternoon, and then your lesson with me at five o'clock every day; and between times you can catch up on your theory – at least until the exam. Then we'll see.'

Alice was furious. All the dancing she was able to do was a few barre exercises after the evening lesson with her mother, by which time she was very tired and soon felt pain in her limbs and back, which she knew was a danger signal and that when she felt it, she must stop.

She spent some sleepless nights thinking about her situation, and eventually came to a decision – one that would, she hoped, make her mother see sense. She started to work hard and stopped throwing tantrums, though she found it extremely difficult to control outbursts – especially when practising; and *how* she practised the dull scales and exercises! The studies were not quite so bad, and she made herself come to terms with the two set pieces. One was a lyrical Chopin Nocturne and she found that as she played it, she worked out in her mind dance steps to fit it.

In this way she tolerated some of the long hours, and her mother's extremely critical comments. And very gradually Lizzie became less hard on her. She realized that Alice was making progress, and that resulted in a considerable easing of tension and a previously unknown calm – albeit an uneasy one – between them while they were both at the piano. From time to time Lizzie managed the odd smile, and the occasional, 'That was very nice, dear', in a tone of voice virtually unknown to Alice at lesson times.

'Come in, Miss Townsend. Alice – that's right, isn't it?'

The examiner smiled kindly at her. Alice nodded.

'Get settled, then in your own time play the first two pages of the exercises, please.'

Alice started off quite well, and felt a little sorry for the examiner, who seemed to be such a nice man. But she knew she had to put her plan into action.

'Now E major, over four octaves.'

She looked at him and feigned nervousness. She wrung her hands and made them shake.

'Don't be nervous, my dear. I know this is difficult for you, but try to forget I'm here.'

She smiled weakly, and hesitantly began. First she missed a G sharp, then having reached the top E, on her return down the keyboard turned the major into the minor. Having covered two octaves she slowed to a halt. The examiner was still kind, and asked her to attempt a different scale – D major. This she decided to play quite well. She began to perform the studies and purposely made endless mistakes. She stopped, started again, and constantly repeated notes.

The examiner asked her several theory questions – to all of which she knew the correct answers, but to all of which she gave entirely wrong ones. She played her pieces without any expression and often out of time, and when she ought to have been *pianissimo* she was *forte*. The slow Chopin Nocturne she played so fast that she stumbled over every note . . . and so it went on until the end.

The examiner looked at her over his spectacles.

'That will be all, Alice, thank you.'

Pretending to cry she rushed out of the examination room.

Lizzie was waiting for her downstairs in an ante room of the Trinity College of Music where Alice had taken her exam. She was feeling relaxed and pleased, because she knew that Alice would do extremely well.

'How did it go?'

'Oh, Mummy, it was wonderful! I really enjoyed it. He was such a nice, kind man, and he smiled at me and kept saying "good, good, good". I really think I've done quite well. It's all so much better now you like my playing so more than you used to.'

'Well, Alice, you have worked hard, I must admit – and I really do think you'll become a lovely concert artist.'

Lizzie hailed a taxi and as they rode back to Edwardes Square Alice said, 'Mummy now that I have worked hard – and I *think* I've done well in the exam – could I possibly . . . please could I go to Mrs Stedman's summer classes? You did say you would think about it.'

28

'Well, of course, we don't *know* that you've done well, and we won't for two weeks or more, until I get the result of the examination.' Alice felt her heartbeat increase as her mother spoke. 'And I suppose five hours a day piano practice *is* a lot. But you must still do two hours before going off to class. We don't want your technique to slip, now you've made such good progress. If you promise to do that – then why not?'

She promised, thanked her mother, and felt very smug.

Alice, on the top deck of the bus, making her familiar journey to ballet class, felt quite pleased with herself. She had persuaded her mother to allow her to go to Mrs Stedman's every weekday. She was able to mix with professional dancers, who specialized in classical ballet and all other forms of dance.

At this particular moment she had drifted off into a little reverie about her future, and saw herself in a magnificent tutu being partnered by a handsome, strong, male dancer and acknowledging rounds of tumultuous applause. Then she was thrust back to reality by the crowded bus suddenly coming to a halt.

'Cor, look at that, Bess!'

The loud Cockney voice of a young girl talking to her friend in the seat in front attracted Alice's attention.

Squinting slightly at a large poster on a nearby wall, the girl read on, '"National Service. The Women's Land Army. God speed the plough and the woman who drives it." I wouldn't mind that would you, Bess? Better than bein' bossed around by ol' fussy tindrawers, eh?'

Her friend was quiet for a moment then replied, 'Oh I dunno, all them cows . . .'

The lively girl turned around and glared at Alice.

'You – what are *you* doing for the war effort, eh? That's what I'd like to know!'

Alice blinked at the confrontation.

'Well, I've just done my school exams,' she said, and remembering she had once danced at a concert for wounded soldiers she added, 'but I also entertain the troops.'

At that the two girls burst into laughter, got up and made their way to the exit.

The girls' remarks were food for thought for Alice.

What *am* I doing for the war effort? she thought. Should I go and join the Land Army, should I go off and work in a munitions factory? I really ought to do something, she mused to herself.

It was after class that day that, in the changing room, she found a copy of the theatrical weekly newspaper, *The Era*. Thumbing through it while eating an apple, she came across a report saying that a new musical comedy was about to go into rehearsal. *Chu Chin Chow* was to open at the end of August at His Majesty's Theatre. Plans for the production were lavish, and it would prove the biggest spectacle of its type that London had ever seen, expected to be especially popular with recuperating servicemen and those on leave.

Alice was fascinated. Turning the page she saw an advertisement announcing that dancers and singers for the chorus were to be auditioned the next day, Tuesday, at eleven.

She read the details of the audition. Fortunately, it was called for precisely the same time as her ballet class, so attending it would prove no problem. She need not say a thing to her mother, or anyone else.

Alice arrived in good time, to find queues of hundreds of young men and women outside the theatre. Just before eleven o'clock the doors to the auditorium were flung open and they all filed in – everyone eager for a chance to appear in such an important show. Eventually male and female singers were seated on one side of the orchestra stalls, while dancers of both sexes were on the other. The theatre was packed, and soon Alice discovered that the circle was full of hopefuls as well. A large man and another beside him, who looked small and rather like a monkey, sat at an improvised table in the fourth row of the stalls. Very soon a menagerie of animals trooped onto the stage. There were several camels, two men holding snakes which twisted round their bodies, some chickens, a horse, four donkeys and a couple of bullocks. Two women sitting near Alice remarked that they thought they were going to audition for a musical, not Smithfield cattle market.

The fat man, Alice was delighted to realise, was Oscar Asche, who they had all so admired in *Kismet*, and who was to be the producer and star of this show. He started to select the animals he wanted, while a stage hand was kept busy mopping up the stage after those who had relieved themselves. After about half an hour they were led off – the fortunate ones being sent one way, the rejects the other. Then they made a start on the dancers, who were asked to do a simple step in groups of about twenty at a time. Alice was told to stand on one side with about eight from her group. A secretary came up to them.

'There's no point in your waiting around any longer now. We'll have to short-list you all. Can you come back tomorrow at the same time?'

The eight young women said they could.

Alice took her usual bus home, arriving just in time for lunch as if nothing untoward had happened. Keeping as near to the truth as possible, she artfully told Lizzie that she had met a lot of new dancers, her class was interesting, and added casually that Mrs Stedman had congratulated her on the strength of her pointe work – something her ballet teacher had said the previous day.

The following morning she went straight to the theatre as requested. Again Alice was short-listed, and asked to return on the next day – she had been chosen for final selection. Again she went home as usual, and rushed upstairs to her attic studio to practise the sort of movements she had been given at the audition.

On the third day of auditions the hopefuls entered the theatre by the stage door. The singers were the first to be chosen. Their reactions as the final selection was made was quite startling: some started to sob, some looked furious and tossed their heads as they were told to leave, others hugged the person standing next to them as they heard good news.

There were only about thirty dancers left. They were told that the production needed eight smaller girls and eight tall ones who could also act as mannequins to show off elaborate costumes. This time they were given a more complicated step to perform, making sinuous movements with their bodies and arms and performing a lot of waist bends and graceful hand movements. Alice enjoyed executing the short dance, which she picked up quickly – it was considerably easier than what she was used to doing.

'Thank you. Stand over there with those young ladies.'

Alice did as she was told, and smiled nervously to a much older young woman standing next to her.

'Don't look so nervous, duckie, we're in. Look at the others, they're going back to pick up their things, just like those they didn't want yesterday and the day before.'

Alice, wide-eyed, could hardly reply.

'You really think we've got the job?'

'Yes, and I should hope so too, after all this messing about – three days of it, no less. It had better be good pay.'

Alice suppressed a squeak of excitement by cupping her hands over her mouth.

'Miss Townsend, come this way, please.'

She walked down a little flight of steps over the orchestra pit to Mr Asche who, as usual, was sitting at his table with the monkey-like man, who she learned was a Mr Espinosa.

'Miss Townsend, Alice.'

She nodded.

'We like your dancing – you move really well.'

'I can do pointe work too, in fact I'm very . . .'

'Yes, well, we don't want toe-dancing in this show,' he said quite brusquely. 'As I was saying, you move well. We could use you as a slave girl and in the dancing chorus generally. Would you mind being a slave girl?'

'No, I'd love it!'

'Sure about that? The costumes will be, shall we say, somewhat revealing, but I take it that you're not shy, eh?' Oscar Asche chuckled.

'No, I don't think so.'

'How old are you?'

Alice hesitated. 'I'll be sixteen in two weeks' time.'

'Um . . . bit young but we like dancers that way – if they're good enough, and you are. But at any rate you'll be sixteen before we open. Go up to the office and my secretary'll make out your contract. We're paying two pounds ten a week, but can't manage anything for rehearsals – is that alright with you?'

31

'Oh yes, Mr Asche, thank you so much!'

The excited Alice was about to leave but decided to say, 'Mr Asche, I saw you in *Kismet*, I thought it was wonderful – will er, our show be like that?'

Oscar Asche grinned and looked at Mr Espinosa.

'Yes, Alice, you can bet it will – and much more so. Our show is going to be sensational!'

Alice, her voice breathless with excitement, repeated her thanks, and went upstairs to the office, where she shakily signed her contract.

Lizzie flicked through several letters. There was the monthly account from Harrods, a letter from an animal charity, and then she saw what she thought might arrive that day or perhaps in the following day or two.

The letter had '*Trinity College of Music, 11 Mandeville Street, W.1*' printed on the back of the envelope. Tearing it open, she eagerly read Alice's result. The letter informed her that her pupil had gained twenty-eight marks out of a possible hundred in the Senior Grade examination.

Lizzie could not believe it. She then read the breakdown of marks. Alice had been awarded six out of twenty for her scales and exercises. The comment was that her work was totally inaccurate and uneven. Her technique was extremely poor in the execution of her studies, and the interpretation of her pieces was inaccurate and very careless. The examiner added a footnote.

'I am sorry that Alice Townsend has performed so badly. She is a very nervous pianist, and while it is evident she has worked hard I believe that she has no real ability or talent for piano. As she has a pleasing personality I would suggest that she should follow some other interest.'

Stunned, Lizzie read the report through again. She could not believe it. Disbelief turned to anger. How could Alice have played so badly – how *could* she? Shaking with anger she looked up the telephone number of Stedman's Dancing Academy and dialled it. Mrs Stedman herself answered.

'Mrs Townsend, what a coincidence. How nice to hear from you. I was about to telephone you, to ask after Alice. It's three days now that she's not attended. But perhaps she's ill? There are rather a lot of summer colds going around . . .'

'She's not with you. Are you sure?'

'Why, yes, quite sure. She's so keen, Mrs Townsend, and so thrilled that you're allowing her to come to summer school . . .'

'And you don't know where she is?'

'No, I'm afraid not. We've been missing her. I do hope . . .'

'Well, I'll have something to say to her when she gets back.'

Lizzie hung up the telephone receiver abruptly. At first she was perplexed and worried; but then her fury mounted again. She knew Alice was not nervous during examinations. She also knew that the girl could play all that was required of her very well indeed. Alice *must* have done badly on purpose. It was one-thirty. Alice was always home by one, and had been these last two days. She rushed out to the front gate and looked up the road towards Kensington High Street. She waited there impatiently, but Alice did not appear. She returned to the house and tried to eat a sandwich lunch, but her anger made her extremely restless. She rushed to the front gate time and time again. It was almost twenty to three when she saw Alice turn the corner.

When she saw her mother's expression Alice knew she was in for a great deal of trouble. Naively, she had hoped that just when she told her good news her mother would be proud, and could be won over – after all she had been chosen against very severe odds. But the confrontation about to take place was far, far worse than ever she could have imagined.

As she approached the gate Lizzie rushed out to meet her. Pushing her into the house she said, 'Go in at once, into the study. You've got a great deal of explaining to do!'

As she entered the study Alice saw the examination result on Lizzie's desk.

'Now, in the first place where have you been these last three days? I know you've been absent from Mrs Stedman's, so I need to know what's been going on.'

The terrified Alice, stammering, sobbing and hardly coherent, told her mother her news.

'*What*? You've done *what*? I can't believe it! You've actually got a part in a common musical comedy? You have been deceiving me these last three days, but that's not all, my girl. Look at this – go on just look at it!'

Shaking with anger she thrust the report into Alice's hands. Trembling even more than her mother Alice read it. It was her turn to be angry.

'There you are, see what the examiner says. He's quite right – I *don't* have any talent for the piano. I've always said so, and Daddy seems to think that way too. Now here it is in print. Look: "Alice should follow some other interest." Now do you believe it? Mummy, I just have *no talent* for the piano. Not like you. Why can't you see that? I'm not cut out to play. I was born to dance, and dance I will – so there. I start on Tuesday.'

'You'll do no such thing. In fact you'll not even have any more ballet classes until you have passed your Senior Trinity College Piano. And, young lady, you will take it again in November. I've seen through you, Alice, I know you're not a nervous pianist – you've never been nervous in your previous exams. In fact, you did badly on purpose.'

Alice's heart sank. She denied the statement.

'You're lying. You *did* do badly on purpose! You can't fool me. You planned to do badly so that the examiner would say you were no good and that would prove to me that you are not talented. Well, it's just not on. I'll telephone Mrs Stedman and tell her not to expect you any more, and I'll give your ballet things to the church jumble sale. No arguments.'

Alice gave way.

'Yes, alright I did do badly on purpose, but I won't take my piano exam again. I won't. You can't make me. And I *will* go to ballet class. Don't forget I'll be earning so I can pay for my own lessons!'

33

'You'll do not such thing. Give me that contract – where is it? In your bag?'

Alice had put her bag down by the door and Lizzie rushed over to grab it, but Alice was quicker.

'I won't let you have it, so there.'

'You will, you will!'

Clutching the bag, Alice ran upstairs to her room, with her athletic mother close on her heels. The young girl made for her bedroom and slammed the door. Lizzie caught her up, but as she turned the handle, Alice turned the key in the lock.

'Go away, Mummy, go away. You won't tear up my contract. I've got that job, and I won't need your money – no, nor Daddy's. I'm going to be a famous dancer whether you like it or not.'

'Let me in, Alice. *Let me in!*'

'No – I won't.'

Lizzie hammered away at the door for some minutes. At last in despair and fury she went downstairs leaving Alice sobbing on her bed. But Alice's tears were not just tears of regret. Yes, she was crying – but her heart was not breaking. She was angry, determined, adamant and she had plans to make. She was very much her mother's daughter. Meanwhile downstairs Lizzie's mood was equally adamant. Mother and daughter were locked in their own stubbornness. There was no room for compromise.

For a long afternoon there was no communication between them.

Around five o'clock there was a knock on Alice's door.

'Go away. I don't want to see you. I don't want to talk to you.'

'It's me, Alice.'

Sighing and relieved, she let Philip in.

'Look, I thought you might be hungry – I pinched this from tea.'

He handed her a plate with a cucumber sandwich, some fruit cake and a scone. And from his pockets produced a banana and an apple.

'Sorry there's nothing to drink, but you've got the tap-water. Mummy's in a dreadful mood. I asked her what was wrong when I came in and she said you had been very, very naughty.'

'Well, as she sees it I have – but I don't care, Phil, I think I'm doing the right thing.'

As briefly as possible Alice told her young brother what had happened.

'What are you going to do?'

'I'm going to leave home.'

'*Leave home*? How can you? How can you?'

'Well, rehearsals start on Tuesday, and I'm determined to be there. But how can I live through the weekend? You see, I'm sure someone in the show will put me up – I've made a friend there already and I think she would help. But, Phil, I'm not staying here – I just can't. I'm *not* going to be a pianist, I don't care what Mummy says.'

'If she finds your contract she'll tear it up, I bet she will.'

'Well, we'll have to hide it, won't we?'

'I'll take it, sis. I've got several really secret places in my room – she'll never find it.'

'Thank you *so* much, Phil. Look, put it under your blazer and go, and I'll say that I've burned the contract; I'll burn some old comics in the grate here and show her the remains.'

'But what about everything you've said about not wanting to play piano any more?'

'I'll climb right down. Then I'll go early Tuesday morning.'

'I expect she'll write to Mr – Mr Asche.'

'Oh, I hadn't thought of that.'

'Well, Molly always takes the post. Sometimes I go for her, so every day from now on I'll offer to go, and simply tear up Mummy's letter to him. By Tuesday it'll be alright because you'll have started work.'

'I'll need all the money I can get. We don't get paid for rehearsals. I've got two pounds three and eight in my post office – how much have you got?'

'One pound four and seven.' Philip was good with money. 'You can have it. I'll draw it out when I go to the post.'

'Phil, you darling! Thank you so much for everything.'

Brother and sister hugged each other.

The following morning, Alice re-appeared at breakfast and put on an act. She said she was deeply sorry, that she would try to pass her piano exam in November, and that she had burned her contract.

'So you've come to your senses at last?'

'Yes, Mummy, I *am* sorry – really sorry, and I don't min . . . well, yes, I am sad about missing ballet until November, but . . .'

'Alice, you *say* you've burned your contract – how do you expect me to believe that?'

'I burned it last night in the grate in my room – I lit my emergency candle then caught the paper, there's probably some ash still there. Go and see for yourself.'

Doubting her daughter, Lizzie swept out of the breakfast room and went up. All the while Philip had been sitting noiselessly eating his porridge. Once they were alone they grabbed each other's hands.

'Do the remains look convincing?'

'Oh yes – shush – she'll be back soon.'

'Well, that seems alright,' said Lizzie. 'Now I must write to Mr Asche at His Majesty's Theatre.'

A sad Alice replied, 'Yes, Mummy,' and glanced at Philip.

'And you, young lady, will write to your father telling him everything that's happened. I don't know what he'll say. It will just add to all the troubles he's having to bear at the Front.'

*

35

Alice and her mother had calmed down, but Alice had a great deal of planning to do. She did not want to involve Philip more than necessary, but she knew she had to, to a certain extent. On Monday afternoon she had thrown herself into her scales, her studies and her pieces and after a long session, Lizzie gave her and Philip permission to take a neighbour's dog for a walk around the communal garden in the centre of the Square.

'Look, Phil, you can always find me at the theatre. There's the telephone number. I expect I'll have to find an hotel for tomorrow night – that is if no-one can put me up. I've packed a case and I'm going to slip out before anyone is up tomorrow morning. I don't want to leave home, but I simply cannot make myself do what I don't want to do. Phil, are you sure you'll be alright?'

'I'll miss you dreadfully. And heaven knows what Mummy and Daddy'll say, and then there's Uncle Eustace and Aunt Emma when you don't come to school next term.'

'I'll miss you too. But at least I'm almost sixteen – just a few days now, so I've not done too badly, and my school exam results were very good . . . Phil can you bear it?'

'Yes, sis, I think so—'

'I'll be alright! Now you must always say you know absolutely nothing. You must not get any blame – is that clear?'

'Yes, Alice. We'll keep in touch, somehow.'

They returned the dog and went in for dinner knowing it would be the last meal that the three of them would have together for sometime.

And in a peaceful, calm atmosphere Alice kissed her mother goodnight, telling her how much she loved her.

Chapter 5

Alice left her mother plumping the cushions before she herself made final preparations for bed. Unseen by Lizzie, she looked back at her mother, and weakened. If only they could compromise . . . But she knew it would be impossible, that if she stayed at home she would be thwarted in what meant so much to her. She knew she had to strike out alone. If her father had been home, things just might have been different – perhaps they would be, after the war . . . 'After the war . . .' – that was on the lips of everyone with their own special hopes and desires. But Alice knew she could not wait that long. This show had come along at precisely the right moment, even though her immediate future was in so many respects dreadfully uncertain.

She climbed the solid staircase to her room – her dear room, warm and familiar, with so many contents she loved. She lit her bedside lamp and looked around. She wanted to take a lot of things with her, but she knew she had to say goodbye to them – at least for a while, maybe for years. Her dolls, her toy dogs and teddy bear, all seemed to have sad expressions, but Alice told them to cheer up. She pulled her medium-sized suitcase from where she had hidden it under her bed and looked at the bear again. Grabbing it, she stuffed it and another dress into the bulging case. After she had been to the bathroom she turned down the beautiful antique crazy patchwork quilt and got in bed.

She could not sleep, afraid that if she did she would not wake up early enough; but eventually she drifted off, and her own inner alarm, which so often worked as well as an automatic clock, woke her. Lighting a tiny torch, she saw it was five-fifteen. She got out of bed, put on three pairs of knickers and three petticoats, her stockings, two skirts under a summer dress, and her light weight summer coat. Carrying her warm winter coat she carefully added the last-minute things to her case – sponge bag, brush and comb and nightie – and slipped out onto the landing. The tiniest hint of daylight was starting to glow through the fanlight over the top of the front door. Molly and Mrs Wilson were still asleep, as were Phil and her mother. Carrying the heavy case she made her way downstairs, taking care not to step on the third from the bottom, because it creaked. She let herself out of the front door and, leaving an envelope on the doormat, slipped into the Square.

She turned right, made her way to Kensington High Street, and soon picked up an early morning bus that would take her to Piccadilly, whence she could walk quite easily to His Majesty's Theatre and her first day's work as a professional dancer.

She arrived at the stage door, her arm aching due to the weight of the case, but the theatre was still locked up. By now it was six-thirty, and she knew she had time to fill before her call, which was for nine o'clock. Trudging around, she eventually found a workmen's café, where she ordered tea and toast and tried to make herself as inconspicuous as possible in a corner seat. A young lad came and sat at her table and, flirting with her outrageously, managed to cheer her. But all too soon his boss called to him, 'Come on, Alf, those flowers'll be dead if we don't get back to the market.'

Thumping down his mug of tea, her breakfast partner had to leave.

She decided that she would return to the stage door, only two streets away. As she did so she noticed a man unlocking it.

'Morning, miss, you're bright and early – must be keen! But before I lets you in I must make sure you're on me list.'

He produced a clip-board with several sheets of paper. Alice gave him her name.

'Oh yes – there you are. Right up them stairs, your dressing room's at the top. You'll find yer name on the door, love. Want some 'elp with that case?'

'Oh yes, please,'

'Arthur – come 'ere. You carry this young lady's case up to her dressing-room.'

'Right, Fred!'

'Cheeky blighter, it's Guv'ner to you, m'lad!'

The spotty-faced fourteen-year-old winked at Alice. The stage door-keeper noticed and thumped him in the back.

'You behave yourself, my lad, otherwise I'll throw you out.'

Climbing the seventy stairs behind the boy, Alice was taken to her dressing-room, which she saw she was sharing with three other dancers.

'Thank you, Arthur.' She gave the boy a penny.

All she could do now was to wait and hope that Elsie, the girl she had spoken to at the audition, would come soon. She desperately wanted to talk to someone and she had seemed so kind and understanding.

She looked around.

The dressing-room was bare and rather bleak. It was long and narrow, with a wide shelf and a long mirror attached to the wall. This was the communal dressing table. Four rather battered chairs were placed alongside the table and a row of harsh electric lights ran right along the wall. There was a long rail on the opposite wall, which to hang costumes. She saw another shelf above the rail, where she presumed hats and head-dresses would be kept, and there was one battered old armchair in the opposite corner to the single washbasin. She decided to take one of the places – the furthest from the door, and the nearest to the washbasin. This would be her place for the run of the show. Settling herself in gave her something of a sense of security – at least she belonged somewhere – even if the space was but three or four feet square. She looked at the clock on the wall. She wondered if her mother had read her letter by now. She thought of Phil, knowing he was on her side, and hoped that he would take notice of what she had said, that he must try not to become involved. It would not be easy for him, until he was paid his next instalment of pocket money he was decidedly broke. Alice had to make four pounds twelve shillings last until the show opened, and she had already spent fourpence on breakfast, twopence on her bus fare and had tipped the lad . . .

'Here's the letters, Mrs Newcombe.'

Mrs Wilson handed Lizzie four envelopes. Glancing at three of them, she was delighted to see one from Robert. Excited, she said, 'Oh, do give Alice another call – tell her there's a letter from her father.'

The housekeeper shuffled out of the room. Lizzie gave a gasp as she looked at the envelope at the bottom of the pile. It simply had, '*Mummy*' written on it in Alice's sprawling, flamboyant handwriting.

What on earth . . . she mused to herself – then went into deep shock as she read,

Dear Mummy,

As much as I love you, I know that the two of us are never going to agree. I will never *ever* play as well as you – no matter what you think. Now I have this job I will be able to support myself quite well. Do not come after me. Do not ask me to come home because I will *not do so*. Give my love to Aunt Emma and Uncle Eustace. I am sorry that I will not be Head Girl of Rosamund, and that I have let them down by not spending another final year at school. But now I will be doing what I am best at, and what I want to do more than anything else in the world. Goodbye. My love to you, Phil and to Daddy when you write to him again.

Alice

Lizzie screwed up the note, shaking with anger. Reactions crashed through her mind. Fury at her daughter's defiance and stupid impulsiveness, terror at what might happen to her, and an overwhelming sorrow that they should be splitting up – especially at such a time when the world itself was in such turmoil.

'Robert, oh, Robert, if only you were here,' she cried aloud.

Philip came in for breakfast.

'Mummy, what's wrong, what's wrong?'

Lizzie showed him the letter.

'This is awful. What are you going to do, Mummy?'

Suspiciously, Lizzie glared at her son.

'Do you know anything about this? Do you, Phil?'

'Why no, Mummy, honest I don't.'

'You two, you're so close that I thought . . .'

Philip hated telling lies, but he knew he must, for his sister's sake. He managed to convince his mother, then very hesitantly asked again, 'What are you going to do, Mummy?'

'I'm going after her – at once. It's simply a lot of nonsense. She's not sixteen yet. I'll drag her out of that theatre by the roots of her hair if necessary. Heaven knows what your father will say.'

In her haste Lizzie even forgot to read the rare, cherished letter from Robert, who was on the Somme.

'Alice darlin', lovely to see you. Ready for work, then?'

'Oh, Elsie, I hope so.'

'Are you alright? You look a bit peaky. What is it? Got grandma?'

'No, that's not due for another two weeks – but, Elsie, I've had to leave home.'

'That's a bit drastic, isn't it?'

Alice started to tell her tale.

'Look, lovie, the others are coming. Soon we'll all have to go on stage, so tell me everything in the lunch break. They'll break at one – Oscar always does. It'll be just like *Kismet*, all over again.'

The door opened.

Elsie got up to hug Dot and Madge – both of whom she had worked with in other shows. It was a happy reunion. She introduced Alice, who felt very young and inexperienced, but full of admiration for the older girls.

'Look, girls, our Alice here's got a spot of trouble – we'll all have to help her.'

'What's wrong, dearie?' asked Dot.

'Parent trouble, Dot – Alice has left home.'

'Cor, that's brave of you. Got a boyfriend you can go to?'

'Er, no . . .'

'All cast on stage please – at once!'

The croaky, half-broken voice of young Arthur was heard at the top of the stairs.

'Tell us more later on. We'll do what we can to help, won't we, girls?'

'Yes, of course – don't you worry, dearie.'

The taxi drove off, turning right down into the Haymarket. Lizzie rushed across the pavement and hammered on the stage door.

Fred, the stage-door keeper, came out.

'Look, there's no more jobs going in the show. Everything's cast – you're far too late.'

'Do you really think I look as if I want a job – here?'

'Well, Madam, that's all anyone comes to the stage door for when a show's in rehearsal . . .'

Lizzie tried to push past him.

'Let me in! Let me in!'

'I can't do that. The public's not allowed in – no matter who they are. I'm sorry, Madam, but that's my instructions. I'll lose my job if you pass me.'

He was physically restraining her.

'I want my daughter! She's in the . . . the show. She has to come home *now*. Please call her. It's Alice Townsend.'

'No, I can't do that, either. She'll be on stage.'

'I'll wait.'

'You'll have a long one. And you can't wait here – so I must ask you to leave – and at once, if you please, Madam.'

Unwilling to be put off, she asked, 'What time will they break for lunch?'

'One o'clock sharp. Mr Asche always breaks at one.'

'Right, I'll see my daughter then. Please tell her I must see her.'

Oscar Asche had just finished telling his cast the story of the show.

'Right, that's all for now. Dancers, you'll work with Mr Espinosa in the downstairs bar. Singers in the circle foyer. Principals on stage, for the first read-through. Be back by two, please. Thank you, everyone, you are all going to be part of the most lavish, spectacular and tuneful show ever to be seen on the West End stage.'

As the huge man lifted himself to his feet, the cast broke into a hearty round of applause.

'Come on, let's go back up, Alice.'

The four dancers who were sharing the same dressing-room started to remount the stairs, and Fred bellowed out, 'Miss Townsend, there's a woman here – she wants to see you at once.'

Alice stopped dead. Her new friends looked anxiously at her.

'Your mother, Alice?'

'Yes, Dot.'

'Do you *want* to see her?'

'No! She knows perfectly well how I feel.'

'Well look, she won't be allowed in – you have to give permission for anyone to come past the stage door, so just tell Fred.'

Shaking with fear, Alice called down the stairs, 'Tell Mrs Townsend that I won't see her. She's not got my permission to come in, Fred.'

Grimacing to himself – he was used to stage-door dramas, but usually with over-persistent young men – Fred delivered Alice's message.

Lizzie shrugged her shoulders, now even more aware of what she saw as Alice's stupidity.

41

'Let her get on with it,' she muttered to herself, 'I don't care. She'll learn the hard way. She'll be crawling back in a day or two.'

'Here you are, have one of these.'

'Thanks, Madge.' Alice munched her bully beef sandwich. The four girls, having moved their chairs into a group, had pooled their packed lunches. They encouraged Alice to tell them what had happened and she began to feel a bit better after she had unburdened.

'So where are you going to live? Have you got somewhere to go tonight?'

'No. I've a few pounds – well just four, actually – so I'll have to find a hotel for the time.'

'Oh, no, you'll not be safe unless you go to a smart one – and that'll be too expensive.'

'Dot's right, Alice. If you go to a cheap one, who knows what'll happen to you? – a drunk soldier on leave . . . It don't bear thinking about. What about your dancing teacher – could she help?'

'Don't think so.'

The four of them were quiet for a moment. Then Elsie said, 'Look, there's a sofa at my place. You can stay there until you find somewhere. We haven't got much space, but you're more than welcome. I know my sister won't mind. My older sister's with us, too. You'll like them, and we can't have you spending that money on a cheap hotel.'

Alice's eyes glistened. She hugged her new friend with relief. Then they all changed into their practice clothes and went to the downstairs bar to start learning the first routine, where they made friends with the other dancers from different dressing-rooms, and the male dancers who were to work with them as partners in some of the numbers and the crowd scenes.

All afternoon they learned a dance for the first act, and during the last hour were joined by the singers. Then Mr Asche plotted the opening crowd scene, and the rehearsal ended at six.

Tennyson Street was a turning just off Queenstown Road, Lambeth. Elsie put the key into the lock of number twenty, and it reluctantly turned. On opening the front door they almost tripped over a baby of about ten months who was squatting on the strip of worn carpet, crying heartily.

'Sal, I'm back, I'm back. Where are you?'

A youngish woman wiping her hands on a thick apron appeared. Her face was flushed and her hair dishevelled.

'I've got a friend here. Alice, this is my sister, Sal.'

Sal smiled warmly, and pushed past Alice and Elsie to pick up the crying child.

'Don't mind her, I'm just about to give her a bottle. Dolly'll be home in a minute. Come into the parlour.'

Sal noticed Alice's case. Not unkindly, she asked, 'Oh, have you come to stay?'

Alice was embarrassed. Elsie hurriedly explained to her sister, then turning to Alice said, 'As you see, it'll all be very cosy! There's Dolly's three kids – two of 'em still out to play – and this little 'un. Dolly's at the Woolwich Arsenal munitions factory, she'll be home soon.'

Alice glanced around at the tiny parlour, noticing a faded old print of Queen Victoria at her Diamond Jubilee hanging crookedly over the fireplace.

'It's tremendously kind of you. It'll only be for a night or two, until I find somewhere more permanent.'

'Welcome, anyway. I'll go on getting the tea – I'll do some extra potatoes for Alice. There's toad-in-the-hole tonight, by the way. You tell Alice a bit more about us!'

Cheerfully, Sal went back along the corridor to the kitchen.

'Dolly's husband, Sandy, is in France, and since they were bombed out over in Hackney she's moved in here with us. This was our Mum and Dad's place 'til they died. Sal used to be a singer – well, I expect she will be again after the war, unless she gets married herself. For the time she's doing all the housework and child-minding while Dolly's earning some money for the kids – a soldier's pay's not much.'

'You're sure it's alright?'

'Of course it is, ducks, don't you worry. We're not short of bedclothes, you'll sleep fine here.' She patted the sofa on which they were sitting.

'Elsie, can I go to the lavatory, please?'

They got up and walked along the narrow corridor and through the kitchen where Sal was busy with the potatoes and sausages. Elsie opened a dark brown door which led onto a small back yard.

'Second door on the right, the first one's the coal house.'

Alice went in. She could hardly believe what she saw. It was just a boxed in compartment with an oval hole. There was a chain to pull, but it was not what she was used to. Afterwards she wanted to wash her hands.

Returning to the kitchen she smiled at Sal and noticed a single large brass tap over a large sink. Obviously there was no hot water, and she would have interrupted Sal who was at the sink. She offered help with the potatoes – she was quite good at peeling them, having been taught by Mrs Wilson – but the kindly Sal told her to go in and rest, as she knew she and Elsie had had a busy day.

She returned to the parlour.

'I'm afraid you'll just have to keep your case under the sofa,' Elsie explained. 'Look, I'll hang your coats in the hall. Just as well you left some of your best frocks at the theatre.'

On Elsie's earlier warning of lack of space, Alice had taken the liberty of hanging quite a lot of her clothes on the rail in the dressing-room.

They heard the front door being flung open, and the thump of hob-nailed boots in the passage.

'I didn't, I didn't start it!'

'Yes you did, you did.'

There was further scuffling and noisy arguing. Sal told the boys to shut up. They continued. Alice tried to smile, and said, 'Boys will be boys!'

A little later she was introduced to Dolly, who did not shake hands because hers were filthy from her work at the factory. The evening meal – tea, as Alice soon learned to call it – was chaotic. She had never seen anyone fall on their food like the two boys who, having settled their quarrel, sat with chins almost on the table and scoffed their food in a slobbering instant.

Alice had thought there must be an upstairs to the house, but it turned out to be just a ground floor flat. Elsie and her two sisters slept in the one bedroom with the baby in a cot, while the two boys, who were twins, would normally have had their camp beds put up in the parlour, but now had to make do with them in the kitchen, where the family spent most of their time. They were good-natured people, and once Dolly had explained that Aunt Elsie's friend had nowhere to go, the twins grinned and nudged each other in the ribs.

The family went to bed early. Alice was settled down on the sofa, which was upholstered in leather and was placed under the window. Because there was no garden to speak of, only the thickness of the wall separated her from the street. She tucked herself in and was lying on a feather tie, but the sofa was rather narrow. Try as she might she could not sleep. She was disturbed once by a woman screaming and obviously throwing crockery at her drunk husband, and then by a noisy motorbike. At last when she drifted off she dreamed that she was sliding down a grassy slope, waking to discover that still tucked into all her bedclothes she had slipped off the sofa and landed wrapped in feather tie, sheet and blanket on the floor. This made her laugh as she got up and re-made her improvised bed, making certain that at least on one side the sheet and blanket were very firmly tucked into the back of the sofa.

She woke up when she heard the front door close, and looked at the clock. It was six o'clock. She assumed that Dolly was going off to the Woolwich Arsenal to work. Soon the baby started to cry. Then she heard the twins arguing in the kitchen. She lay there for about an hour when Elsie popped her head round the door.

'How did you sleep?'

'Very well, thanks. Do you think I could have a bath, Elsie?'

She realised as she spoke that she had said something very silly. There was all too obviously no bathroom.

'On Friday nights the family goes out, then I have a bit of peace and I heat up water for the tin bath we keep in the yard. Can you wait 'til then?'

'Oh, yes, of course,' replied Alice.

'But they're out of the kitchen for a while. There's hot water in the big kettle and a bowl under the sink – it's all yours for a few minutes.'

Alice was grateful, and said so. She made her way to the kitchen. She managed to pour some scalding hot water into a chipped enamel bowl and

44

cool it (rather too much) with cold water. She gave herself an all-over wash as quickly as possible, nervously expecting to be interrupted any moment by two inquisitive eight-year-old boys whose behaviour bore absolutely no resemblance to her brother's.

She was fast realising just how differently people lived. This family were so kind, but obviously life was hard for them, with so few facilities and space. But they seemed to take no notice of the restrictions of the poky flat with its dark passage, worn bit of carpet, harsh leather sofa and worst of all, the dreadful lavatory and the lack of privacy. What if she wanted to go in the night? She would either have to ask for a po or step over the boys in the kitchen and unlock the back door to get to the yard. She just hoped the situation would not arise. All this went on through her mind as she dressed in the parlour, taking a clean blouse from her case to wear with her light-weight cotton summer skirt. Soon she joined Elsie and Sal at the kitchen table.

'There's some porridge if you'd like some,' said Sal.

She took a plate and dished up spoonfuls from a huge saucepan and handed it to Alice. It had been made with water and tasted awful, but Alice was polite and ate it thankfully.

'Look, I've not much money, but I simply can't go on living off you like this. I'm sure I'll find something more permanent in a few days, but please let me contribute something towards your housekeeping.'

'Don't you worry, Alice, we're alright for today and tomorrow, but I might get a bit short on Friday morning before Dolly gets home with her wages.'

'Yes, of course.'

Alice drank strong tea from a thick mug advertising 'Rowntree's Elect Cocoa', after which she and Elsie left for their rehearsal call at nine, picking up a bus in Queenstown Road to take them part of the way to the West End.

'Now, in this scene I want the boys and girls to work together, so let's line you all up for height. Boys first – tallest at the right. Yes, you, Alex, then George, then . . . er, let me see . . . Mike . . .'

Mr Espinosa was matching the men and girl dancers. Having arranged the men he started to line up the girls. Alice – at all but five feet six – was the tallest.

'Now, Alice, you stand in front of Alex . . . Elsie in front of George, and yes, Dot go with Mike.'

The selection went on for some minutes, with the choreographer making a few minor changes here and there, where two dancers were virtually the same height, then having finished he said,

'Now you have your partners, and you will be with them in any scene or situation where boys and girls have to be together. We're all good friends, and I hope you can build up good working relationships. I suggest that when we have our next break you get to know each other – if you don't already, because I see several *old* faces here! Meanwhile we'll make a start on the cave scene.'

Alice glanced over at Elsie, who seemed to know her partner – no doubt from previous shows. She turned towards Alex and introduced herself.

He said, 'I saw you at the auditions. You move very well. I'm Alexander McIntyre, by the way, nice to meet you properly.'

They shook hands.

The rehearsal went reasonably well. Quite early in on the ensemble dance Mr Espinosa required the boys – as he always called them – to lift the girls. Alice was thrilled. She jumped just at the right moment and to her surprise she found herself almost floating above Alex's head. Blushing with delight and surprise she said, 'Oh, that was marvellous!'

'Och, y'poor wee lassie, have y'not done any pas de deux before?'

'Well no, actually.'

'Oh well, we'll have to put that right.'

Over lunch Alice discovered that her partner was from Edinburgh and had been trying to get work in London for several months. They talked about their training. He was impressed when he learned who her teacher was.

'But I don't think I can go there any more.'

She explained that she had quarrelled with her mother, and until she was earning she could not afford to go to class.

'Perhaps then, it's time you went to a new teacher,' he suggested.

All too soon the lunch break was over. Back at work a great deal of Alice's unhappiness melted away as she learned the routines and had her first experiences of pas de deux – even though the work she and Alex were doing together bore little or no resemblance to classical ballet.

Elsie and Alice discussed their day going home on the bus.

George was a good dancer, but Elsie was more impressed with Alex.

'Yes, he is strong! I don't feel at all nervous when he lifts me. I like him a lot. He seems very kind. He's goodlooking too, don't you think?'

'Oh, yes, Alice, but if I were you I'd try not to think about that.'

'Why? Er . . . is he dangerous?'

'No, duckie, far from it. He's probably very safe as far as you're concerned.'

'I don't understand . . .'

'Come on, here's the church, we must get out.'

After a noisy but lively supper of bubble and squeak Alice spent her second night in Tennyson Street.

The first week of rehearsals passed very quickly, but by Thursday Alice, who had coped as well as possible with her hurried all-over washes in the kitchen, was feeling in dire need of a nice long relaxing bath. She did not want to upset Elsie or Sal, but the thought of sharing a galvanised bath of water with Elsie on Friday evening appalled her. She needed to shampoo her hair –

she had not dared spend money at a hairdresser's – she would still not get paid for over three weeks; and she did not like to ask for more time in the kitchen to do some washing. She knew that if she did Sal would willingly do it for her, but she felt she could not impose, although she was fast running out of clean summer dresses and blouses, and had only two pairs of clean knickers left in her increasingly untidy suitcase. She mentioned this to Dot, who at once came up with the solution.

'Look, Alice, every two or three days I go to the Marshall Street Baths in Soho. I do my washing – and you can dry and iron too – and have a wonderful deep hot bath. The old biddies in charge pop their heads round the door every so often to see if you're alright, and bring lovely towels, and you can use as much water as you like. I'm going tomorrow morning, really early, before rehearsal. It's very nice, want to come with me?'

Alice agreed, and because of the crush at home Elsie joined them. They got there as the place opened, and bustled in with about twenty housewives loaded with washing. They did their laundry among the steam, smell of soap, lively chatter and grumbles of the women. It was an experience that dazed Alice. She knew how to wash clothes – Lizzie was not the sort of mother to allow her daughter to grow up in luxurious innocence of such things – but the colourful language, the thick accents, and a fight that broke out between two women arguing over an extremely old pair of bloomers were scenes that would stick in her memory.

The bath was huge, the water was deep, and although the surroundings were clinical and without a trace of luxury, Alice felt much better for it. She knew she would come regularly even if it meant, for the time anyway, getting up at least two hours earlier to do her washing and keep clean.

She was fast realising that her determination to do what she wanted was giving her the resilience to cope with what she had to admit were dreadful living conditions – the state of the lavatory made her feel sick every time she used it – but she would just have to cope with it until she started earning. She thought about her lovely home and just how much she missed Philip. She so wanted to get in touch with him, but if she telephoned there was only a very slight chance that he would answer. If she wrote to him their mother would see the letter, and she dare not attempt to contact Molly or involve her.

On Friday morning she gave Sal ten shillings. Sal was extremely grateful, and they had mutton stew for tea as a result. Alice would always be indebted to this family for their kindness. It was arranged that she should stay with them until the show opened and she was earning. She worked out that if she gave Sal ten shillings a week she would have just about enough money to buy the odd pie, apple, bread and cheese for her lunches and her bus fares. She also decided to ask some of the girls if there was anyone with whom she could share a flat.

Chapter 6

'Say, girls, listen! As you know, it's our little Alice's birthday today!' Elsie called to the others.

'Ah, lovely! What is it? Sweet sixteen and never been kissed? Never mind, darlin', you'll soon get over that!' laughed Madge.

Alice could feel herself blushing and was totally unable to do anything about it.

'Come on, everyone, charge your glasses.'

Elsie produced a bottle of Tizer, and went round to each of them pouring it into their grubby glasses.

'A toast – to our Alice! And now I'm getting her surprise.'

She disappeared under the long bench and brought out a box. It had the name *Leichner* emblazoned on its lid.

'And now for Alice's initiation! Come on, duckie – sit you down.' Knowing that this was Alice's first engagement, and that her birthday was imminent, the three of them had clubbed together from their meagre savings to buy her a set of stage make-up.

Elsie, who had organised the whole thing, proceeded to make her up, giving her a somewhat swarthy complexion by mixing two or three different shades of the thick sticks of greasepaint, then adding blue eye shadow from a much thinner stick and mascara from a solid block, which, before rubbing the little stiff brush onto the colour, she instructed Alice to spit on, so that the thick black would collect in the brush. She completed her task by applying 'Carmine Number Two' to Alice's lips, turning them to a bright, glowing red.

While all this was going on the other girls crowded round making suggestions and silly jokes. The atmosphere was very lively.

'You can look now – you're a real slave ready for the market!'

Alice looked at herself in the mirror and gasped – she could have been born of Asian parents! Squealing with delight, she thanked them all so much. It was a wonderful birthday present.

There was no card or present from her parents, and on such a day as this she missed them dreadfully. She wondered if they were thinking about her. She knew that her mother did not know where she was living, or with whom.

She also wondered what her father had said when he learned of their dreadful quarrel. She wished that she could see Phil – if only just for a minute . . . Nevertheless she had made her choice, and apart from the new and very different problems she was facing, she loved the hard work and the strong bonds of friendship that she was building not only with the other girls who shared her dressing room but with the rest of the cast, who were also friendly – even if they were very much involved with their own contributions to the show. She was also cementing a good friendship with Alex, who she decided was somewhat mysterious, but so very kind, and a stunning dancer.

'Elsie Arnold! Miss Elsie Arnold, wanted on the telephone!' Arthur's unmistakable voice called from outside the door.

'What, who wants me? Cor, girls perhaps it's one of them Dukes we hear so much about!'

Breaking up the little birthday celebration, Elsie rushed off downstairs to the stage-door keeper's office.

'Wonder what that's all about? Hope her nephews or the baby's not ill,' said Dot.

'They were fine this morning,' Alice said.

There was a hush in the dressing room. After a few minutes Elsie returned, looking pale. She went straight over to Alice. The room was even quieter – everyone knew how often in these sad days families suddenly heard bad news of their menfolk at the Front.

'Oh no, it's not bad news – in fact, it's lovely for Sal – Sandy's got ten days' leave. He's just arrived home, and I'm afraid that . . .'

'That you can't put me up while he's at home.'

'Oh, what a shame. Poor old Alice, and on your birthday . . .'

The other girls were sympathetic, and the formerly jolly atmosphere became quite glum.

'Well, I wish I could help, but we're crowded out too,' sighed Madge. Dot was in the same position.

'You can't go to an hotel. I suppose we could ask Mr Asche . . .'

'No, that won't do at all – but thanks. Look, I'll curl up here and sleep – I'll be alright.'

'Well, it's against the rules, you do know that.'

'Yes, but I don't see what else I can do.'

Alice moved over to the old armchair.

'If I turn this chair round like this . . .' The heavy chair, with a caster missing, was difficult to move. 'And curl up in it, like this . . . I don't *think* I can be seen from the door – go and see, Elsie.'

Elsie did, and found she could not see her friend.

'So when Fred does his rounds, if I keep very still he won't notice, specially if we throw some clothes over the back. Once he's gone I'll have the whole theatre to myself – until morning. Then when you three arrive someone can go out with me so it won't look as though I've been here all night, and I can get some breakfast. What do you think?'

'It'll be alright provided no-one tells on you – and *we* won't, will we, girls?'

They swore secrecy, and the rehearsal resumed at two o'clock as usual.

By just before seven Alice was alone, but she dare not move from the dressing-room for fear of encountering Fred, who she knew would be around until dark. She did not have anything to do, and time dragged – and the more time dragged the more miserable she felt. She tried to think of other things, what she could do to fill the lonely hours while she was stuck in this dreary dressing-room perhaps for a week or more. She decided to join Westminster Public Library and catch up on some reading, and when she had her case from Elsie she would sort her things out, and tidy it. But for the present she was dreadfully bored. Has anyone ever been bored on their sixteenth birthday? she asked herself. Then she suddenly remembered she was about actually to take part in the biggest and most spectacular show ever produced in the West End! And that made up for a lot.

Around eight-thirty she heard Fred's heavy footsteps on the stairs. She heard him open then close the door to the dressing-room next to hers. As an extra precaution she covered herself completely with a selection of her friends' rather smelly practice clothes. The handle turned. She held her breath. His heavy footsteps come closer.

He hung around for what seemed like ages, but it was probably only a few seconds, then, satisfied, he left, closing the door behind him. She heard him visit the other two dressing-rooms on the top level of the theatre before, eventually, his footsteps died away as he made his way downstairs. After a while she crept to the door and, having listened for a while, heard him slam the stage door itself.

She was now alone – totally alone – in the vast, fascinating building so she decided to explore, and made her way down to the stage. The smell of paint permeated the whole theatre. The elaborate scenery of Kasim Baba's palace and harem was taking shape in the roomy scene docks at the side of the stage. Alice gazed up at the flats, the very realistic caves and palace buildings in child-like amazement. She was not allowed into these areas while rehearsing, and the sight thrilled her.

But it was now almost dark, and she saw less and less. She returned to the stage and stumbled over a heavy chair. In the near darkness she saw an electric light switch labelled 'working lights'. She switched it on, and to her amazement the auditorium came alive, the heavy sheeting covering the seats in the stalls and circles reflecting the bare, cold light of the un-shaded bulbs. The stage was lit, too. She walked to its centre and looked out over the auditorium. Her imagination leapt into the future . . . She was wearing a glorious tu-tu, and having performed some beautiful classical ballet was standing with her partner behind her, acknowledging storms of applause and showers of flowers from her adoring audience. She made an elaborate reverence. But the vision faded. Here she was, yes, in this marvellous theatre – but alone and with no home to go to, just a very uncomfortable armchair to sleep in.

50

She returned to her lonely dressing-room, took off her frock and hung it carefully. She wrapped herself in Madge's Spanish shawl and curled up on the chair. In half an hour she had cried herself to sleep.

During the days that followed the show began to come alive, and as it did so, rehearsals got longer. By the end of the second week the cast was not released until seven or eight o'clock. Sometimes the dancers and singers finished before the principals, and Alice was left alone in her dressing-room hearing music and the sound of spoken instructions wafting up from the stage.

She had settled into a dreary routine. Her back ached because of the unnatural positions she was sleeping in, and sometimes when Alex lifted her she felt considerable pain, which she tried to ignore. But Alex noticed her wince.

'You mind your back, my girl. We don't want you off with injury on the first night, do we?'

She reassured him, and asked her friends if she could borrow cushions to make a sort of mattress on which could sleep on the floor once Fred had done his rounds. That was sensible, but even so the floor was terribly hard. In spite of the growing excitement of her work and her costume fittings – she and her friends had several changes of beautiful costumes, each more elaborate than the last – she knew she was not at her best, and this depressed her. She made certain she ate well, and went out into the fresh air as much as possible during the day when she was free. She walked in St James's Park, hoping not to see anyone she knew. She looked at the shop windows, but her money was dwindling – in spite of the fact that as she was not at Tennyson Street she had an extra ten shillings.

She knew she could go back there once Sandy's leave was over – but did she want to? She took regular baths at Marshall Street, and could wash her face and feet in the dressing-room as and when she wanted to – and she did not have to use that ghastly lavatory. Perhaps after all she was better off as she was, though if she were found out ... That was the real difficulty. She knew she would be heavily fined – and that she simply couldn't afford.

But as the first night loomed ever nearer, her excitement, her enjoyment of her work, and the help she was getting from her supportive friends seemed to lighten her problems, and she decided to make herself concentrate on all the good things. She told herself that she had already achieved what many girls of her age and older were longing to do. All the same, the fact that she wanted her family to share her success was always in her mind. The last thing she really wanted was to defy her mother. Yet she knew that the step she had taken was the right and only one for her.

One night – it was just two days before the first dress rehearsal – when her friends had left the theatre but there were still quite a lot of people around, she flopped down in the now all too familiar old chair, physically exhausted. Her mood slumped as her unhappy feelings got the better of her. She could

51

hear lively chatter from the dressing-room next door, she could hear singers still practising scales and a lot of theatre life going on around her, but she felt lonely, so desperately lonely.

She burst into floods of tears, sobs came gushing out of her and she buried her head in her hands. Try as she might she could not stop crying. Hard physical work and all her emotion had lowered her resistance. Her inner strength, determination and ambition seemed to desert her. Her stomach heaved as she sobbed.

The door opened.

'Och, what's all this? What's the matter, wee one?'

She recognised Alex's soft Edinburgh accent. Red-eyed and stomach aching because of her sobbing, she looked up at her on-stage partner.

'Oh, Alex, it's nothing – really it's nothing.'

'I don't believe you. You're not the type to sit bathed in tears like this. Now come on, tell your Uncle Alex what's wrong.'

Although he was only just twenty-one he was remarkably kind and fatherly towards her. He picked up her face flannel, went to the washbasin and wrung some fresh cold water through it.

'Come on – look up.'

As she did so he gently sponged her face as if he were a nurse attending a patient.

'Well, I'm waiting, lassie. What's it all about?'

The story tumbled out of her. From time to time Alex told her to slow down, so that he could take in all the details of her story.

'So, you're in a fix, aren't you? Parents! They really do so much damage. I've had dreadful problems with my father, so I know, believe me!'

Sadly, Alice nodded. 'You too? But, Alex, you won't tell on me, please? *Please* don't tell I've been sleeping here.'

'Of course not! But you can't sleep here much longer, can you? No wonder you've been having problems with your back when we do the lifts, now I understand. Dancers must always look after their backs – far more important than feet.'

'But I'll have to stay here until the show opens, and I . . .'

'Start earning some money, yes I know.'

He paused thoughtfully for a moment.

'Alice, don't get me wrong, will you? I'd never harm you, er, in the way a lot of fellows would – or take advantage of you. My flat – it's a basement in Tryon Street, just off the King's Road in Chelsea – has a spare bedroom and a nice bathroom with a *proper* lavatory, not just a hole down the back, dearie. Would you like to come and see it? Then if you liked it perhaps you would care to move in with me.'

'Oh that's so kind, but I couldn't possibly, it wouldn't be er . . . proper.'

'Alice, you will be quite safe – I've just said so. You've no worries on that score, I assure you. I think we could be such good friends, look how well we dance together!'

'But you're a young man, I can't live with a man!'

'Alice dear, there's something you'll have to learn. It's not all men who want to er . . . make love to women. I'm one of them – so you will be safe in that respect.'

'You mean you don't like girls – ladies – in that way?'

'Yes, that's what I mean.'

Alice was totally confused, but pretended not to be ignorant and tried to understand.

Alex went on, 'Just two months ago my boyfriend, Bunny, joined a cruise ship as a steward. Now he has to live in Southampton when he's in England. I was sad about that, but he has his career just like me. So I'm alone. It would be lovely if you could see your way clear . . .'

'I would like to live in Chelsea. It's always sounded fun.' Alice paused. 'Yes, Alex, I'd love to come and see your flat – but I can't move in until I get some money.'

'You can and you will. You can give me some money when we start getting those nice regular pay calls on Thursday mornings. Come on, gather up your things – let's go in style! I'm fairly broke, but we'll take a taxi. Here, let me help you pack your things. Even if you hate my place you mustn't stay here another night!'

The basement flat was charming. Alex had hung the walls with posters of past shows he had been in, and there was one frame which consisted of a large montage of autographs of theatre folk. The atmosphere was friendly and Alice at once felt at home. The bathroom was civilised, with a huge copper gas geyser at the end of the bath which once lit, produced plenty of hot water. Everything looked as if it worked well, even if nothing was luxurious. Her bed-cover was deep red velvet and trimmed with a heavy gold fringe. Alex told her that he had re-made it from a section of an old curtain that had hung in the Globe Theatre. She noticed a treadle sewing machine in the corner of the living room, and assumed that he made good use of it.

'Well, what do you think? Do you like it?'

'Oh, Alex, it's lovely, it really is. Do you mean I could actually move in, right away, and, er . . . you won't mind having a girl around the place?'

'I'll love it. After all, Alice, I really do *like* women – it's just that I . . .'

She feigned worldly wisdom and replied, 'I understand,' gently patting his arm as she spoke.

Chapter 7

August 31st, 1916

'Are you sure you've got everything?'

'Nothing much to bring. Everything I need is at the theatre already.'

'Come on then, let's go. Nervous?'

'I would be, if I had that dreadful skinny Frank for a partner and not you!'

Alex slammed the front door and they hurried out into the street, turning into the King's Road and making their way to Sloane Square Underground Station, to travel back one station to South Kensington and pick up the line that would take them to Piccadilly Circus – the stop nearest to His Majesty's Theatre.

Alice had settled down in her new home and was increasingly happy. Alex was such good company! She had never met anyone quite like him. He made her laugh, he made suggestions about her clothes – all of which were most unsophisticated – showed her how to tie a scarf differently, how to wear her hat at a different angle . . . He gave her confidence and made her feel a lot more grown-up. Though it was rather dark, she loved her room, in which Alex had painted a proscenium arch on one wall, with curtains swinging back over old-fashioned footlights.

Now, they were on their way to the theatre for the first night of *Chu Chin Chow*. At the stage door, they saw Fred's office piled high with bouquets, the letter-rack bulging with envelopes and telegrams for members of the cast. Alex went to his pigeon-hole.

'Oh, lovely, there's one from Bunny. Anything for you?'

'Doubt it.'

'No, you're wrong – there're two. Here you are.'

Other members of the cast were pushing by them and also picking up their mail, all nervously laughing and wishing each other 'break a leg'.

'See you at curtain up, eh?'

'You bet. Thanks for everything, Alex – you're a real pal.'

They went their separate ways – dressing-rooms were on opposite sides of the theatre. Alice mounted the stairs and joined her three friends.

Dot and Madge had already displayed their good luck cards around their section of the long mirror and Elsie, having just taken off her hat, was opening hers.

'Ah, that's nice – it says "all love from all of us". Look, Alice, isn't that sweet? They're in tonight – everyone of 'em but Sandy, pity he had to go back to France. You've got two there, I see – who are they from?'

'I don't suppose there's one from my mother,' Alice sighed, opening the first. But then she let out a little cry of glee.

'Oh, look, Elsie, and you two – it's from my brother. He says he's been following all the reports on the show, and one day he'll sneak out and see it, and he wishes me all the best. He's missing me.'

'Well, I expect he is. But isn't that lovely of him.'

Alice felt a lump in her throat.

Seeing her suddenly saddened expression Elsie said, 'Cor, look at that other envelope, Alice. "International Cable", it says!'

Puzzled, Alice opened it.

The message read, I KNOW JUST HOW YOU ARE FEELING AND WISH YOU EVERY SUCCESS TONIGHT AND ALWAYS STOP WAS DELIGHTED TO HEAR OF YOUR BEING CHOSEN FOR THE SHOW STOP ALL MY LOVE AUNT SARAH.

'Good heavens, how did she know? How *could* she know?'

'Aunt Sarah' as Alice had always referred to her, was Emma's sister. She just remembered her from the occasion when, years ago, she had visited England with her husband, Lionel Maitland, from the Caribbean island where he was Governor General. She had always wished she could have got to know her properly, because she had been a dancer at the end of the nineteenth century. She had married when Alice was a baby.

'She's not really my aunt – but she was a dancer too when she was young – I wonder what she danced like.'

'What was her surname?'

'Cooper.'

'Sarah Cooper?'

'Yes, why, Elsie?'

'My old woman used to see her and rave about her, *beautiful* worker – bit flighty, and daring, though, she said. Old King Teddy liked her, you know!'

Elsie winked. What she said confirmed in Alice's mind what she had heard hinted at when her mother and Aunt Emma had talked about Aunt Sarah. But she was still puzzled about how she could know about the show and her part in it.

'Well, you know, love, there's been a lot of reports about us in the newspapers and magazines – your brother said that, didn't he? And I expect she gets them all. Nice of the old duck, anyway!'

Alice was delighted that someone of the older generation was encouraging her.

After about an hour of preparation the call 'Overture and beginners please!' boomed up the stair well. They made final adjustments to their swarthy make-up, and trooped down the stairs to the stage, catching up with the rest of the cast as they went.

The programme told the audience that *Chu Chin Chow* was roughly based on the Arabian Nights' story of 'Ali Baba and the Forty Thieves', and there was delighted applause as the curtain rose on the spectacle of Kasim Baba's Palace. Alice and her group were first seen in silk drapery which clung to their figures, gold headbands low on their foreheads, helping to keep elaborate black wigs in place. Later in the show they represented jewels in the cave scene which was revealed to the audience when a huge stage rock, at the command of 'Open, sesame!', was rolled back to display all manner of riches; sacks of crowns, piles of necklaces, and trees – the 'fruit' taking the shape of rubies, emeralds, topazes, some of which came to life as they began to move into their number. It was at this point when Alice danced with Alex for the first time, as a pair of emeralds.

An elaborate slave market scene closed the first half. Here Alice was able to show off her acting skill as well as her dancing ability. She was chosen to be hurled by the wrist towards the footlights, and had to attempt to escape, terrified at the possibility of what might happen to her as she was auctioned to the highest bidder. As the tallest of the eight dancers she also joined with the eight mannequins for a scene which displayed the hero and heroine's great fortune. She had to walk on stage with bare feet, trying not to stagger under the weight of a huge costume which consisted of three tiered and hooped skirts, each fuller and wider than the one above it, and a draped georgette top. On her head was a crown as wide as her shoulders, supporting a very fine gauze veil with a heavy gold fringe. She also had huge circular earrings and harem trousers, with a bare midriff. The colours of the costume, and of all those used throughout the show, were mostly turquoise, lemon, orange, bright blue, silver and black and the eight girl dancers with their bare-chested partners performed a Javanese dance in the first act, as well has having several entrances as townspeople, servants, slaves and entertainers.

Storms of applause broke out as the curtain fell at the end of the first half of the show, and the dancers, panting and excited, hurriedly made their way back to their dressing-rooms for a short break before changing into their second act opening costumes. The show was obviously going even better than had been expected. Spirits were extremely high.

The second half was even more gorgeous and spectacular than the first; and while from time to time Alice felt sad that most of her family were ignoring her and her personal success, she tried hard to put her personal feelings behind her and enjoy the occasion.

It was past two in the morning when Alice and Alex arrived home after a night they would not forget. The audience had kept the cast on stage for well over twenty minutes after the first curtain call. The stage was deep in flowers and Mr Asche gave a curtain speech which was cheered uproariously, both by audience and cast.

Back in the dressing-rooms, the buzz of the young women's voices became more and more excited as they discussed their work and the way the principals had stunned the audience. They knew that the love duet 'Any Time's Kissing Time' and Ali's 'Cobbler's Song' would soon be whistled and sung in the London streets, and by everyone who loved the theatre. When at last, the audience left, the cast went to a celebration party and now, full of food and just a little too much to drink, the two friends staggered down the steps to Alex's front door, happy and very exhausted, having decided that Mr Asche's prediction that they would be in work for many months would come true.

'Miss Townsend, there's someone at the stage door who wants to see you. He says it's very urgent.'

It was the first Saturday of the show, and between matinée and evening performances. Alice, who had put her feet up and was eating an apple, suddenly tensed.

'What's his name, Arthur?' she shouted to the messenger who was just outside the door.

'Says he's your brother, Phil.'

Thrilled but nervous, she shakily replied, 'Tell him to wait there. I'll be down.'

She flung on her dressing-gown over her underwear and rushed down to find Phil by the stage-door keeper's office. She was in full make-up.

'Phil, it's wonderful to see you! How did you manage to get away?'

'Alice!'

They hugged each other. Alice realised that she had not seen her brother for over a month.

'Mummy thinks I'm at a cricket match on Wormwood Scrubs, but, sis, something dreadful's happened.'

'What,' she asked anxiously.

'It's Daddy . . .'

'Oh, my God – surely he's not . . .'

'Oh, no, he's not been killed, but he's been horribly injured.'

'Phil, no! Where is he? Tell me? And how's Mummy?.'

'Well, it was pretty ghastly, really. We heard on Thursday evening.'

Thursday evening, on our first night, thought Alice.

'Yes – go on.'

'Well, the front door bell rang, and it was a telegram. Mummy nearly fainted. Mrs Wilson was out, so I called Molly, and she and I helped her to the sofa. It said Daddy had been injured at Beaumont Hamel. He's been sent back to London and is in Moorfields hospital.'

'Heavens, then it's his eyes! Oh no, Phil, that's dreadful. Has he been gassed?'

'No, but a shell exploded near him. They say that he won't lose his sight permanently, but he's all bandaged up, and will be for some weeks, I think.'

The ten-year-old boy blinked back a tear.

They hugged each other again.

Alice did some quick thinking.

'Phil, do you think I could see him? Do you think he'd want to see *me*?'

'I dunno. When I mention you at home to Mummy she always changes the subject or simply says nothing at all. Oh, sis, it's not been easy for me either, you know.'

'Poor Phil, I'm so sorry. But what do you think?'

'Well, why don't you go and see him when you absolutely know Mummy won't be there? She goes twice a day now, of course, but we'll be back at school quite soon, and I know she's got one of those endless staff meetings on Tuesday – do you think you could go then?'

'Why, yes, of course. Phil, I'm so glad you've told me all this – I really am. I do hope you won't get into trouble.'

'No, I've plenty of time before I know the match'll be over. I'll have to make up the score, – she's bound to ask me! But where are you living?'

Alice told him, and wrote her address down in the notebook he always carried with him.

'You living with a *fellow*?'

'Yes, Phil, but please believe me, he really is just a friend.'

'You're not lovey-dovey with him?'

'No, absolutely not, honest, cross my heart!'

'Well, alright.'

'But you can always contact me there, I'll be around for ages.'

'Look, I go to the hospital most days with Mummy. If she talks to a doctor or a nurse then I'll try to tell Daddy that you'll be coming to see him.'

'Thanks, Phil. Gosh, I do hope he'll be alright.'

'So do I and he's only heard Mummy's side of your story so far, don't forget.'

'I won't! And, Phil, it was lovely to get your note last week. Thank you so much!'

'Goodbye for now.'

They hugged each other yet again.

'Am I doing the right thing, Alex?'

'I think so. After all, as you say your father's always been more understanding than your mother, so why not tell him your side of the story?'

They were walking in Regent's Park. It was Sunday afternoon. The Band of the Grenadier Guards was playing in the nearby bandstand. While autumn was in the air, the sun shone and it was good to be well away from the theatre on this, their one free day in the week.

'Yes, I think you must go, and you know, it may well not be as bad as you think,' said Alex, 'though try to be strong enough not to tell him where you're living.'

'I'd thought of that. Phil knows, but I know he'll not let me down.'

58

'That brother of yours sounds a real sweetie.'

'He is, we're very close!'

At that moment they turned and smiled at each other.

'Oh, *no*! We can't get away from it, can we?'

The band had struck up 'The Robbers' Chorus' from the show.

Cheered and amused they strode off quietly singing 'For we are robbers of the glen . . .'

'He's down in the end bed, Miss Townsend.'

She thanked the nurse and walked the length of the ward. Blinds were pulled down over the long, tall windows, giving a shaded, eerie light, re-flected from the white tiled walls. She recognised her father at once, though she knew he could not see her, because, as Philip had said, his eyes were swathed in bandages. And – Phil had not told her this – one leg was heavily bandaged, and supported in a sling raised above the bed.

For a moment she stood horror-struck to see her alert, athletic father in bed motionless, unable to read or do anything. She stood a short distance away from the bed for a while, bracing herself for the encounter.

Creeping forward, she spoke to him very softly, as if he were asleep. Not daring to touch him, she quietly murmured, 'Daddy, it's me . . .'

'Alice!'

He stretched out his arms in the direction of her voice, and she readily fell into them, bursting into tears.

'My love, it's good to see you.'

The words made her cry even more.

'Don't worry, I'm making good progress.'

She examined him more closely as he spoke. She could see that there were scars on his face which were exposed to the air and obviously healing quite well.

'Darling, I'm so glad you're here. But you do have a lot of explaining to do. Your mother's worried sick about you. Why don't you come home?'

Alice knew she had to be firm.

'Daddy, I can't. It's impossible. You don't know how awful life with Mummy was before I left. I just know I've done the right thing – and I'm doing really well. I get more money than the other dancers – not much, but some – because I'm acting as well as dancing. The show's beautiful. I wish you could see it!'

'Alice, I'm afraid you're being very stubborn and very wicked.'

'Yes, and so was Mummy,' she replied crossly.

'That's rather different,' said Robert. 'You won't come home then?'

'Absolutely not.'

'At least tell me where you're living, so that we can keep in touch.'

'If I do that Mummy'll come round and try to force me to come home. No, Daddy, I won't; but I live very comfortably, you know – I'm not short of money, and . . . I'm *happy*.'

'You don't know just how like your mother you are!' said her father, wistfully.

'Well, Daddy, I can't help that, can I? I've just got to live my own life.'

'But you're only sixteen! You should be still at school working for your final exams, and perhaps going to Mrs Stedman's once week, for at least another year. Then, well . . . we could see.'

'No, Daddy, no. I won't give up my job. It *is* a *job*, you know. And if I left I'd be letting Mr Asche down. And besides, I love it so. You'll just have to accept it. It's final.'

She was amazed at how firm she was being.

'Alice, believe me, I do understand – more than you realise, I think. If this is the way you want it, well, I'll try to placate your mother.'

'Daddy, if you can, that would be lovely; but honestly, I've just suffered too much at home. I'm making my own way now, and you and Mummy will have to get used to the fact that I'm not going to come home again.'

Seeing her father look so sad, she had almost weakened; but in her heart she knew she must not. She changed the subject, and Robert told his daughter how he had been wounded. He had been well behind the lines, but when he was outside his office a stray shell had come over and landed close to him, shrapnel had struck him in the face, and also severely injured his leg.

'Will you have to go back to the front, Daddy?'

'I don't think so. I'll be at the War Office here in London until it's all over, then back to teaching.'

'So you'll be living at home once you're better.'

'Yes.'

This was good news for Alice. With her father at home her mother would be less likely to have time to think about her; and he would, she knew, put in a good word for her, knowing in his heart that she was doing what she wanted, and indeed what she did best.

It was getting close to the time when she must be at the theatre for the evening performance.

'Behave yourself, Alice, I mean that. Don't be led astray by anyone – especially any man. Keep yourself to yourself. I think you know what I mean. I'm sad you're acting the way you are, but I do see your point of view.'

'Thank you, Daddy, and I do understand that you can't go against Mummy. I'll come and see you again, as soon as I can.'

'Perhaps it would be better if you didn't.'

His voice was cold, and what he said hurt her, though she realised his remark was because he did not want to cause a rift between himself and her mother.

'Do you mean that?'

'Yes, Alice, I'm afraid I do – though I sympathise with you and your ambitions.'

She lightly kissed him, said goodbye, turned and left the ward.

*

60

The show settled down to what they knew would be a very long run. Bookings were excellent, and *Chu Chin Chow* was particularly popular with servicemen home on leave.

Alice and Alex got on extremely well. He was a good cook and made all kinds of dishes after the show. They seldom went to bed much before one-thirty – it always took a long time to relax after the rush of energy and exhilaration of the performance. There were evenings when Alex went out with friends after the show, and on these nights Alice travelled home on the underground and often took a taxi from South Kensington Station. Sometimes she went out with her own special group of friends, with some of the singers and their partners, for a cheap supper in one of the many little cafés near the theatre. Alice started to learn more about wines – she already knew a certain amount, because she had been brought up to taste them from quite an early age. On more than one occasion – usually on a Thursday or Friday night when they had more money – parties of the cast would go into Soho and eat late at the Italian 'Quo Vadis' restaurant in Dean Street.

> 'Surely 'tis so – you ought to know,
> Any time's kissing time!'

The lovers were coming to the end of the first chorus of their beautiful duet when the musical director put down his baton. There was a sudden silence, and the stage manager walked onto the stage.

'Ladies and gentlemen, the air raid warnings are being sounded. The performance will cease while the raid continues. You may leave the theatre if you wish.'

The audience, which had been so enthralled, groaned at having been brought back to reality. Most got up to leave, to assemble in the nearby Royal Arcade or anywhere close by which they thought reasonably safe.

'Come on, girls – let's go into the street to see the fun.'

At Elsie's suggestion, throwing coats over their flimsy costumes, they rushed to the stage door and into the street.

'Isn't it exciting? Just like firework night! Look, Alice, up there, a Zeppelin. Isn't it huge?'

'Dot, is it going to blow us all up?'

'Shouldn't think so. It's probably lost its way!'

The Zeppelin moved slowly towards the west. They saw several flashes and heard gunfire which they thought came from Hyde Park.

The girls were excited but frightened, and put their hands over their ears. Some young officers saw them from across the road, and catching a glimpse of bits of chiffon below the hemlines of the girls' coats, realised they were in luck. They rushed over to offer comfort and protection.

'I say, girls, are you alright?'

'Don't be cheeky, young 'un, we're *ladies* to you!'

'Jolly frightening though, isn't it? Not for us, of course!'

'Of course not!'

The four dancers giggled. There was a flash of light momentarily brightening up the whole blacked out scene, in which Alice caught sight of a familiar, smiling face.

'*Charlie*, it *is* you, isn't it?'

'Alice, I was coming to see you after! I saw your name on the programme, and couldn't think there were two Alice Townsends. I say, this is stunning. Chaps, I've known this young lady . . .'

As he spoke policemen on bicycles appeared blowing their piercing whistles and turning huge wooden rattles to inform the public that the raid was over. As they did so the street lights came on again, and Alice could see Charlie more clearly as he smiled down at her.

'Must go now!'

'I'll see you after the show – at the stage door!'

She was thrilled at the prospect.

'Let's go to the Carlton for supper – now, before the rest of the crowd take up all the best tables.'

'What a lovely idea, Charlie. But first let me tell Alex, otherwise he'll wait for me.'

'Oh.'

Charlie sounded glum.

They were given a table in a pleasant corner.

'Now tell me . . . well everything. I thought you were going to be Head Girl of Rosamund – at least that's what I last heard. Mother told me in a letter several months ago, so imagine how surprised I was when I saw your name on the programme. I say, Alice, the show's simply ripping, isn't it? Far more exciting for you than being still at school, eh?'

Over supper Alice told her story. She then learned that Charlie was home on leave from the Somme – not very far from where her father had been injured. She was delighted to be spending time with him again as she had liked him for a very long time, and even more since they had their *tête-a-tête* on the day he had been appointed Head Boy of Creswell.

But that was a long time ago. Since then she had seen him only once or twice, mostly at tea parties Emma had given for her family and friends and their children. Then with the coming of the war and his being taken right into the army before he had finished his course at Sandhurst, they had drifted apart. Now she decided that he was a really charming young man – handsome, upright and tall with a lovely fresh complexion. However, behind his dazzling smile and bright blue eyes there was a sadness which he disguised, but which was nevertheless obvious to Alice. Quite correctly, she assumed that it was the effect of the ghastly battle scenes which she knew he must be witnessing.

'Gosh! I can't tell you how delighted I am to meet you again, what tales I'll have to tell when I get back to my unit! Being friends with a girl in *Chu Chin Chow*! – it's unbelievable! Everyone'll be fearfully jealous!'

Alice smiled.

'When do you have to go back?'

'On Monday morning. I've had ten days' leave. Mother's arranging a family party on Sunday, and I went down to Dover to see Dad. But at the moment – well, here I am, and with a star of the biggest and best West End show ever staged!'

As he spoke he reached across the table and took her hand. Her heart thumped at his touch.

They finished their meal, and outside he hailed a taxi.

'Where do you live?'

'Charlie, because of all my problems at home no-one apart from Phil knows where I live. Can you promise faithfully not to tell your mother? She and Aunt Emma are such good friends that it would be bound to slip out, one way or another. Then Mummy would be told, and that would make life impossible for me.'

'My lips are sealed, really, Alice. But . . .'

'But what, Charlie?'

She had been expecting this kind of query all evening.

'Yes, Charlie?'

'Look, I say . . . I don't want to pry, but do I take it that you're . . .'

She felt his embarrassment, so spoke for him.

'That I'm living with a man?'

'Well, er, yes – that was what I was getting at. If you are, well, I say that's not exactly pukka, is it? Er, if you see what I mean!'

'No, Charlie, it wouldn't be. But though, yes, I do live in Alex's home, we're not lovers, and never ever will be – I assure you.' She paused. 'You see, Alex doesn't like the ladies . . . in that way . . .'

'Oh, I see. So he's a – well, one of those.'

'You could put it like that. But please, Charlie, don't hold it against him. He's *so* kind and looks after me just like an older brother.'

'If you say so. I don't approve of all that sort of thing – just isn't manly. But I can see you're safe with him.'

By now they had reached Tryon Street, Charlie had paid the taxi driver, and they were at her front door.

Teasingly, she asked, 'Am I safe with you?'

He made no answer, but took her in his arms and lightly, rather shyly kissed her on the mouth, holding on to the tender embrace for a few delightful seconds.

She smiled up at him with all the admiration a young girl could possibly give a brave hero.

'Goodnight, Charlie.'

'Goodnight, Alice. I say, though, let's have tea together tomorrow while you have a break between the two performances, that is if you'd like to.'

'Yes, please, Charlie.'

The exotic sounds of the tango began to filter across to them from the far end of the hotel lounge, where the trio of musicians were just starting to play.

'May I have the pleasure?'

As Charlie spoke he stood up and with old-fashioned formality offered Alice his hand.

They moved to the open area of the dance floor, where two or three other couples were already dancing, and began the long, sensuous movements and sudden turns which characterised the dance, and so explicitly expressed its passionate rhythm.

She soon began to enjoy herself, and Charlie, too, initially apprehensive as he took his very special partner out onto the floor, relaxed and led her into yet more complex movements.

'You know, you really are a most splendid dancer – but I'd expect that, with all your training.'

The praise brought a flush of colour to her cheeks. She was quiet for a moment then managed to reply, 'Well, you see, the only ballroom dancing I've done was what we learned at those classes after school – you know the valeta, and the Gay Gordons . . .'

'Oh, yes, and the Lancers and the Viennese Waltz. I remember; but that didn't do us much good, did it? It's all so old-fashioned!'

'The girls in the show taught me this!'

'They certainly did a good job!' And he turned Alice, supporting her back as she leant almost to the floor as the music ended. They were returning to their seats when she saw a young woman nudge her Naval Officer boyfriend. The couple walked up to them as they returned to their table.

'Excuse me, Miss . . .'

Alice looked up at the girl, who was a couple of years older than herself and very plain, and smiled.

'You're in *Chu Chin Chow*, aren't you? You're the slave that runs across the stage. We saw you from the front row of the stalls just now, didn't we, David?'

Her boyfriend agreed, and the girl handed Alice a somewhat crumpled programme.

'It would mean so much to us if you signed this for us. We have some of the principals, but your signature would complete our afternoon for us! My name's Alice.'

Charlie, glowing with pride, handed Alice a beautiful Waterman fountain pen.

Smiling, she rather shakily wrote, 'To Alice and David with best wishes from Alice Townsend.'

'Thank you so very much. You've really made our afternoon, hasn't she, David? Oh, you're Alice too! How nice!'

As they went on their way, the young man muttered to Charlie, 'Lucky blighter!'

'There you are, you see – I said you were a star last night, and now you're really famous.'

Charlie was grinning to himself with pride and self-satisfaction.

'Well, it was a surprise, that's never happened before! Here you are, here's your pen.'

'Keep it, I don't want it back. You must have it, and when you use it you'll think of me and a wet, chilly autumn afternoon when you were asked for your autograph for the first time.'

'I can't, not possibly!'

'You must. I want you to!'

She was so thrilled that when she attempted to say thank you hardly a sound came out. She just smiled up at him as she put the beautiful pen in her little dorothy bag.

'Come on, let's do this dance!'

The music had changed to the new ragtime from America.

Alice was reluctant.

'I can't do that, Charlie – I really can't!'

He was masterful in a lighthearted way. The smile which mirrored the warmth of his personality was irresistible.

'I'll teach you!'

Soon they were dancing the wild, silly, energetic Turkey Trot.

About half an hour later Alice had to return to the theatre.

'Thank you so much, I've had a lovely time!'

'Would you like to come out to supper with me again after the show?'

'I'd love to! 'Til then!'

She disappeared through the stage door.

A distant church clock struck two as Charlie opened the taxi door.

'Alice, it's been wonderful for me too. Look, it would be really topping if you could write to me sometimes. Will you? Do say you will.'

'Of course I will, with your lovely pen.'

Charlie had made their second evening together really special, reserving a discreet table near a potted palm, from behind which they could see other diners, some well-dressed and prosperous, most of the men in uniform. They had surprised Mr Asche and a large party of the principals, who arrived just after they had ordered. His deep, rich voice greeted her in his big-hearted, jovial way as they made their way to their table.

Charlie had ordered champagne, and while they waited for the dessert the tips of their fingers touched across the small table, and for a while they rested their elbows on the table with their hands supporting their chins, and just gazed at each other. His proud and happy expression had said a lot to her.

She knew that for the moment the cares of the battlefields were far from his mind. They toasted themselves and the end of the war.

'You will keep that promise, won't you? To write, I mean? Oh yes, and send me a photograph of yourself – in one of those saucy costumes, please!'

'I'll see what I can do!' she replied cheekily.

He took her hands and for a while they stood looking at each other.

He said, 'Til the next time, Alice?'

'Yes please, Charlie!'

They kissed longer and more passionately than on the previous evening, 'Goodbye, Alice!'

'Goodbye, Charlie – but 'til when?'

''Til the spring – in six months' time. Or when the war's over, if that's before then!'

'It's an awfully long time, but I will write.'

'So will I, dear.'

They parted.

He called me dear . . . he called me dear. Oh heavens, I think, I *think* we're in love!

Chapter 8

'It's no good, Alice, we've got to get back to work. Real work!'

'What do you mean? Surely we're doing enough.'

'But, wee lassie, neither you nor I have done a proper class since rehearsals started. That's bad. So now we're into the routine of the shows we must not neglect our technique any longer.'

'But we do our barre before curtain up, and Mr Espinosa keeps us on our toes with the lively changes he puts into the choreography from time to time.'

'Keeping us on our toes – or *you*, I should say, on *your* toes – is exactly what I'm getting at! Tell me, miss, when did you last put on your pointe shoes?'

'Well, er.'

'Precisely, so from Monday it's back to class.'

'But Mrs Stedman . . .'

'I don't care for Mrs Stedman. She's a good teacher, but you need a superlative one!' He rolled his 'r' as he spoke. Alice looked quizzical.

'We must go to the Pheasantry!'

'The *Pheasantry*! But I couldn't – I'm nowhere near good enough.'

Alice had heard of the famous studio and its even more famous Russian teacher mentioned in hushed revered tones at Stedman's. It was her classes that the most famous ballerinas and male dancers attended.

'You are, you can, and you will! We'll go along together. I'll introduce you to Madame, she's lovely, I know you'll like her. Then we can talk afterwards.'

The following Monday morning they walked west along the King's Road to the unusual building which housed artists and craftsmen in its upper stories and provided a huge studio on the ground floor.

Madame Astafieva was a Russian Princess who had been a member of the Ballet in St Petersburg, married into the Russian Royal family, and eventually settled in London. A tall, elegant woman who always wore black, flowing dresses and scarves and white tights which matched her soft, satin ballet shoes, she gave an active but lyrical class which Alice found fairly difficult but enjoyed more than she expected to.

After it was over the great teacher called her and Alex over.

'Alex, my darlink, so you have a little protegée? Well, she is beautiful, very elegant. I like blonde ballerinas – they look so much more graceful than dark-haired beauties!'

Turning to Alice she went on, 'My dear, you move beautifully and have obviously been taught very well. I know Mrs Stedman – she is excellent. The line of your extended arabesque already is perfect, but you know your *pirouettes* are very weak, and those *entrechat* need a lot of help. However, with dedication . . . and I'm sure you have that . . .'

'Yes, Madame.'

'So you two are partners in the famous *Chu Chin Chow*! My darlinks, I happen to know Oscar Asche, he is a splendid man . . . very colourful, like his productions – and indeed like Sergei, who also speaks well of him.'

Alice's eyes opened wide. She realised that the Sergei Madame mentioned was the great impresario, Serge Diaghilev. She was actually in the company of someone who knew *him*!

'I think we should build up your partnership. Alice, you are quite tall and I can see why Mr Espinosa put you two together. Tomorrow after class, we will do some work on a classical *pas de deux* – yes?'

'Oh, Madame, thank you – that would be wonderful!'

Alice was transported.

'But from now on, no more missing class for weeks on end – either of you. It must be work, work, work! And, Alex my darlink, can I rely on you to do my shopping as you used to when you were out of work?'

'Of course, Madame. I'll do it before class.'

After they had changed, walking back to Tryon Street Alice said, 'She's not at all formidable. I expected her to be – being royal, and with her background – but she's a dear. Have you always helped her?'

'Yes, she's been marvellous to me. I always used to do her shopping for her, and any little bits of re-decoration that needed to be done to the studio – painting, plastering, things like that – and she used not to take money from me for the classes. But while we're earning we must pay up, of course.'

'Of course, that's only fair.'

So morning class became an important part of their schedule, and on days when they had no matinées, they stayed on afterwards. It was these hours that enthralled Alice. She and Alex were getting together a considerable repertoire. They could perform with confidence the Black Swan *pas de deux*, excerpts from *Giselle* and *Les Sylphides*, and a wonderfully showy, exhilarating sequence from *Don Quixote* – something that Madame assured them had not as yet been seen in the West. Very often a tired, rather wan pianist stayed to play for them. Alice noticed just how downtrodden she seemed, and so from time to time took her some chocolates or a bunch of flowers.

Weeks turned into months. Alice was maturing fast. Not only was she working with older and more sophisticated young women, but living with Alex brought her into contact with a different group of people – mostly lively, artistic young men who made her laugh, who did all kinds of things she never thought men would do. Alex was brilliant at sewing – something she loathed, in spite of all the hours at school in Emma's embroidery and dress-making classes. He and most of his friends cooked very well – all kinds of different exotic dishes – and on Sundays in particular she often ate food she had only read about in travel books. She quickly appreciated the spicy flavours of Indian curries and Italian pastas. The wok, and what could be cooked in it, was revealed to her by a young sailor friend of Alex's who had visited Shanghai.

The other dancers she met casually at the Pheasantry were usually amusing. Some of the young women were a little off-hand at times when they realised she and Alex were getting extra tuition from Madame after class, but Alice managed not to allow this to upset her. There were some very weird types too. On one occasion she noticed Madame talking very seriously to Alex as she was changing into her pointe shoes. It appeared that one of the young men had been working in South America and when he came back to class was found to have become a woman. Madame was conferring with Alex, as she was not at all sure which changing room he should now use. As a result of tales such as this and many others, Alice became worldly wise.

Philip kept her informed of her father's progress. His sight was poor and he would never totally recover, but as he had told her, he had taken up a post at the War Office.

Christmas 1916 was both cheerful and miserable for Alice. She was with dear friends, and they ate as well as wartime conditions allowed, but she missed her family and Eustace and Emma's children, Stephen and Rose, and wondered how they were going on. There was no word from her parents. She and Philip met secretly in St James' Park and they exchanged gifts. He told her that from time to time their father spoke supportively of her, but always his remarks were received with silence or some caustic comment from their mother.

Alice was delighted to hear from Charlie that he had forty-eight hours' leave and, they managed to spend an idyllic Sunday together. It was just after Easter, spring flowers were everywhere. Their tender, blossoming romance was a joy to both of them and, like many young couples of their generation they realised that every second in each other's company was to be treasured, savoured and remembered. For them, an outing to Kew Gardens and tea in a nearby hotel, followed by evensong in Westminster Abbey was special. They lingered together as long as possible, but he had to depart for France on the midnight train. She joined him at the station after he had spent the evening with his mother, younger brother, and sister, Tabitha. He had told the family he would rather they did not come to the station. There, he and Alice parted sorrowfully, and she – along with dozens of other young wives and sweethearts – was left sobbing on the platform as Dover train steamed out of Waterloo.

1918

Chapter 9

Monday, November 11, 1918

In Hammersmith, Mrs Katy Cook was just about to tell her young assistant to go off to tea when she heard shouting and cheering outside her greengrocer and florists' shops in Blythe Road. Rushing into the street she saw that other residents and shop owners were dashing from door to door. Excitement was increasing by the second, and almost immediately she realised what had happened.

Grabbing the first person she bumped into, she cried, 'Is it true?'

'Yes, yes, it's over – the Armistice was signed at eleven o'clock!'

'Thank God, thank God!'

She fell into the arms of a neighbour, old Hannah, and together they sobbed, tears of joy pouring down their cheeks.

The residents and business people of Blythe Road were turning out all kinds of bunting, pennants and Union Jacks to decorate the street and the fronts of their buildings.

Katy Cook was wild with excitement and, being amongst the most prosperous of the business community, she was already suggesting to other business men and women that they might organise a party for the children and an evening dance on the following day in St Matthews' Church rooms, just up the road.

'If we all do our bit we can have a grand time – remember the Coronation and the old Queen's Diamond Jubilee, Hannah? We can do even better this time, in spite of the shortages and the rationing. I suppose all that'll end soon now.'

Old Hannah agreed. As they were speaking a long line of young people who had formed a human chain, led by a man in a clown's costume, was skipping along the street to the cheers of the crowd who had collected on the pavement. Six children from a very poor family who lived in a tenement block in a nearby back alley appeared, banging dustbin covers, three of them with saucepan lids for cymbals. Some Salvation Army lasses and lads mingled, playing their tambourines and trumpets, but their hymn tunes could hardly be heard above the general racket.

Katy's friends and neighbours were all talking, laughing and joking as they made plans for the celebrations.

'And your Jim'll be home any day now, I'll warrant,' said a neighbouring butcher, who had just promised to break the rationing and make some meat pies for the next day. 'Missed him, eh? You two, proper old sweethearts – that's what you are, Katy me darlin'.'

'Yes, Mr Flanagan!'

She blushed as if she were still a bride.

'Look down there, Katy, there's the telegraph boy. He's got news for someone.'

The boy rode up to them, got off his red bicycle, and looked up at the sign over the shop.

'Mrs Cook, please?'

'Yes, that's me.'

He opened his smart leather purse and produced a telegram. Giving it to her, he stood waiting to see if there was a reply.

'Oh, good! I expect it's from Jim telling when he'll be home. That was quick, why we've only known that the war's been over for an hour or two!'

She looked again at the envelope.

'Doesn't seem to be from Dover, looks a bit more official. Oh, I say everybody, it's from the War Office. It must be news from Charlie-boy – so *he'll* be home soon too! I can't believe it! How wonderful, for us all to be together again, after all this time!'

Even more deliriously happy, she tore at the yellow envelope, her eyes glinting with expectation at the good news she expected. As she started to read her sunny expression changed within a few seconds to puzzled bewilderment and she started to shake her head. She automatically gave the slip of paper to Mr Flanagan as she broke away from her group of friends screaming hysterically, 'No! No! No! It's not true. It can't be true. No, not our Charlie-boy . . . no, not him, dear God . . . and the war's supposed to be over?'

'Go after her, Hannah, she needs you,' said Mr Flanagan.

As he spoke, the woman rushed over to comfort Katy, who was in shock and crazy with disbelief.

Mr Flanagan dismissed the boy. 'No reply, son.'

He sighed, suppressing a tear as the rest of the group looked on in stunned silence. He looked at the crumpled form on which the hand-written message said:

'O.H.M.S. War Office, London. Deeply regret to inform you that Captain Charles Cook, of the Royal Fusiliers was killed in action 9th of November. Lord Kitchener expresses his sympathy. Secretary, War Office.'

Sybil, Emma's personal maid, confused and near to panic when a few minutes before she had been deliriously happy, rushed across Kensington Gore to Hyde Park in an attempt to find Tabitha Cook, Charlie's sister who was helper and nanny to the Beaumonts' children. She knew the girl was celebrating with everyone else.

The boys from Creswell and the Rosamund girls, along with Eustace and Emma Beaumont, Lizzie and the rest of the teachers had heard the happy news very quickly by telephone from Robert at his War Office headquarters. They were all in the Park. The grass was wet and soggy with fallen autumn leaves but no-one seemed to care that their boots were thick with mud and their clothes getting splashed and dirty. The sense of relief and freedom, felt by the very young as well as the grown-ups was unbelievable.

Sybil pushed ahead of a throng of people on the path which skirted the Albert Memorial and saw, on the grass in the distance, the splash of colour which were the caps of a large cluster of Creswell boys. She hastily made her way towards them. They were running around at top speed, playing a somewhat disorganised game of tag. Near a group of large trees she spied Emma and Lizzie, who were watching about twenty Rosamund girls forming a circle and playing a ring game.

The distraught Sybil rushed up to Emma and Lizzie.

'Whatever's the matter, Sybil? What's wrong?'

'Oh, Madam, bad news, I'm afraid. I've just had a telephone call from a Mr Flanagan, a neighbour of Mrs Cook. She was too upset . . .'

She stopped to take breath.

'Go on, Sybil! What's happened? Tell us!'

'Well, just now they had a telegram . . . Madam . . . it's young Mr Cook . . .'

Emma looked at Lizzie.

'He's alright, surely?'

'No, Madam. He was killed on Saturday. I'm to find Tabitha – she's to go home at once!'

'Oh, poor Katy, how dreadful to get the news now just as the war's over. Look, there's Tabitha, with Stephen. I'll come with you.'

The two of them left Lizzie, dazed and in a state of grief that the lovely young man, who had made such an impression as Head Boy, had so tragically been killed at the very end of hostilities.

Philip happened to glance over from his game to his mother and saw her wiping her eyes. At first the young lad thought she was weeping tears of joy like so many of the women, but then he somehow realised that she might be upset.

'Mummy, what's wrong? Please don't cry – it's such a happy day!'

'It's Charlie Cook, Philip!'

'Why, what's happened?'

'My dear, Charlie was killed on Saturday. Mrs Cook has just heard. Aunt Emma and Sybil are telling Tabitha, she's to go home at once.'

'Gosh, that's dreadful, poor Charlie, I liked him, he was kind when he was Head Boy.'

'Yes, he was wonderful.'

75

Philip at once thought of Alice. He knew about their romance and how they had spent as much time together as possible on Charlie's leaves from the front. He knew he had to tell her, but how could he? How could he give her the bad news? Was it up to him to do so?

He ran off, telling his mother that he was going to find Stephen and little Rose and play with them. But instead he ran out of sight of the crowd from the schools, and found an empty seat which was too wet for people to sit on. He slumped down on it. This was the most difficult problem he had encountered in all his eleven years. Should he rush off and try to get a bus to Chelsea where Alice might still be at home? Should he go to the theatre? But it was Monday lunch-time, and he knew there were no matineés on Mondays. Should he do nothing and allow Alice to find out in her own time? Or should he take his father into his confidence? But did his father know that, in his own terms, Alice and Charlie were 'lovey dovey'? Philip started to cry, he did not know what to do for the best and he knew he must be quick otherwise his mother would become worried at his absence.

Crowds were now everywhere. Everyone was cheering and shouting, and it was difficult to move quickly.

'Come on, Phil, we must go back and get something to eat – there'll be more time to celebrate later.' His mother, seeing him sitting alone, called to him from across a wide path.

Now Philip knew he could do nothing.

'I don't think there's anything more to do here, Stuart. Go to your mess and celebrate with the rest of your bunch.'

'Thank you, sir. Just one more thing, sir, for your information, here's the casualty list – I suppose it'll be one of the last, thankfully.'

'Yes, Stuart, I hope so. Thank you!'

The Subaltern put the typed list on Robert's desk, saluted and left. Robert started to ease himself up from his chair to go to where the high-ranking officers were having a celebration, when he glanced down at the paper. It consisted of some forty or more names, listed in order of rank. At the top, in capital letters he saw

'CAPTAINS'

Cook, Charles A.J. Royal Fusiliers. 9.11.1918. At Corbie.

There was one other name before the next lower rank.

In shock, he sat down once more, deeply grieved. After a while he got up, and left the office.

'Come on, old man, we're having a celebration lunch, then it's home!'

'Er, no – don't feel in the mood for it. Sorry, just had bad news.'

'Christ! Not now, surely?'

'Yes, a young chap I taught and knew well. Bloody well killed on Saturday, can't believe it. His mother must have just been told. What a disaster! Must be by myself for a bit, you understand.'

'Of course. Take care, it's crowded out there.'

Robert knew he should have called for a duty car to take him back to Edwardes Square, but could not do so. He wandered out of the building, ignoring the milling throng. After a few minutes of slow walking, relying more than usual on the stick he still used, his eyes reacting quite well to the dim November light, he found himself in St James' Park.

He took a path which would lead him to the Mall. Above the cheering and shouting, more than once being hugged by complete strangers, he heard some singing above the cheering. He saw that it was a group of young dancers who were entertaining a large company of enthralled spectators

'Surely 'tis so, you ought to know,
Any time's kissing time!'

The crowd roared their applause, delighted to have been given a free scene from the famous show.

'Encore, Encore!'

Alice and her friends looked at each other in glee.

'Shall we give them another chorus, Alex? Elsie?'

'Yes, right, follow me!' It was Dot's turn to take the lead.

Robert looked at the young people and, recognising his daughter, was happy to see her laughing with her friends and giving so much pleasure to the crowd which was adoring every second.

After the first line, Alice let out a little cry, broke away from the impromptu performance and, almost pushing over one elderly man, rushed towards her father.

'Daddy! Oh, Daddy, it's so good to see you! How wonderful – but why are you here? Why aren't you back at the schools with Mummy and the others?'

Robert said nothing but smiled at his daughter who fell into his arms and they hugged each other with a passion that neither of them could control.

Breaking away, and looking up at him with tears of joy in her eyes she cried, 'Daddy, this is simply marvellous. It is so good to see you and on this wonderful day!'

'Yes, my darling, of course it is, and you look wonderful.' He held her at arms' distance. Her friends glanced at them in a quizzical way as they continued their singing and dancing, so as not to disappoint the crowd.

Alice looked seriously at her father, sensing that something might be wrong, and at once assuming that it was to do with their problem.

'Daddy, I know . . . But you know it's not only me . . .'

He nodded.

'Yes, Alice, but I do wish . . .'

'So do I, Daddy, and perhaps now that the war's over . . . do you think you could . . .?'

77

'I'll try, Alice, I'll try. But for the moment I'm a bit upset about something else.'

'What's wrong, Daddy? Surely you and Mummy haven't quarrelled, or Phil? Oh, don't say there's anything the matter with Phil!'

'No, he's fine. But remember Charlie Cook, the Head Boy who went to Sandhurst?'

'Why yes, what? Daddy, tell me, what about him?'

Robert could see anxiety in her eyes.

'You remember him well?'

'Why, yes – very much so, in fact . . . Oh, Daddy, he means a lot to me! We love each other. I hope you'll not be cross about it – of course you don't know.'

Robert could see the love in her eyes as she spoke, and felt the grief that he knew he would all too soon have to share with her. It had been bad enough for him to get the news at such a poignant moment, but hearing that his Alice and the young man were in love was another, even worse, shock for him. He knew that he would have to shatter her happiness.

'Alice, my dear, it's bad news, I'm afraid. I've just learned in the office that Charlie was killed on Saturday.'

Alice froze motionless in disbelief.

'It can't be true, it can't be. The war's over. Daddy, it must be a mistake, it must be – surely.'

'No, darling, I'm afraid not, the War Office doesn't get things like that wrong.'

The song ended for the second time, but as soon as the applause broke out, Elsie and Alex, not bothering to acknowledge it, rushed over to father and daughter. As they approached, Alice cried, 'No, no! Charlie – oh, no, not Charlie!'

'You're Mr Townsend. I'm Alex, her friend. What's happened, please?'

Elsie rushed forward to support Alice's fainting figure, with Alex at her other side.

'I'm afraid I've brought Alice bad news. I didn't know that Charlie meant so much to her.'

'Oh, Alice, darling, how awful, how awful – he was . . . well.'

The tearful, weak young woman was only able to stand because of their support, while Robert attempted to soothe her. They moved to a seat and, after a silent minute or so, Alice looked at her father and between her sobs, holding his hand, bravely said, 'Look Daddy, you better go home to Mummy and Phil. Elsie and Alex will look after me. They always do. I'll be alright.'

'God! I hate to leave you like this.'

'Please, you must. You weren't to know we were going to meet. Go to Mummy, and – oh yes, she doesn't know about me and Char . . .' She broke down again as she started to mention his name. Then taking a deep breath, she went on, 'Do give my love to Mrs Cook, and Tabitha, too. Tell them I'm very, very sad.'

'Of course, darling. Get in touch if you need me.'

Her friends moved away as father and daughter stood up and locked in a long, sad embrace.

Robert, who suddenly seemed to have aged, turned away and went back to the War Office, feeling he could not face pushing through the crowd to find a taxi.

When the others had finished their number, Elsie re-joined them and told them what had happened. It was decided that Alex must somehow get Alice back to Tryon Street so that she could rest before having to go to the theatre for the evening performance. With difficulty, through the excited crowds and the totally blocked traffic, they eventually arrived. He made Alice a warm drink and laced it with brandy, and for about an hour she slept deeply.

It was almost four-thirty when she awoke, putting on her dressing-gown, she staggered into the living room. Alex was reading the latest edition of the *Evening News*.

'I'll make us a cup of tea, then we must go. It's not going to be easy to get to the theatre. Let's hope the tubes are running normally.'

'Alex, I don't think I can face the show tonight. I really don't.'

'Look, you're as professional as they come. You can and you must – especially tonight, of all nights. The house'll be packed and you must do your bit – that's what your Charlie would have wanted, you know. You must put all your personal sadness on one side, go out on the stage, and give your very best.'

Alex knew he must encourage Alice to get on with her life, and do so right away.

'To think he did all that fighting, and now this – just as the war's over. Alice, we're all so very sorry, girl. Is there anything we can do?'

Alice, who was struggling to get some mascara on her wet lashes, shook her head.

Madge was especially sympathetic.

'Poor love! Mine was taken too, so I know what you're going through – but it's even worse for you, hearing today.'

'Well, we've all got to help our Alice through the show tonight, as much as we possibly can.'

Elsie was mustering the support of the rest of them. As she spoke the wardrobe mistress appeared.

'Here you are, ladies, here's your share. You're to wear them over your costumes. It'll be a riot tonight – you should hear 'em all. The house is full already, and it's twenty-five minutes to go.'

She put a big pile of bunting down on Elsie's chair. It turned out to consist of the flags of all nations.

'What larks! Who wants to be who? I'll be Great Britain. Here's France! Alice you have that.'

But Elsie realised she had been tactless.

'Oh my gawd! Oh, I'm sorry, Alice – no, you have Canada!'

'Elsie, I'd really like to wear France. I think Charlie would like that too.' At this all the girls who had been cheerful yet sad for Alice, were moved to tears, and quietly sobbed to themselves for a while.

The noise of cheering and shouting in the auditorium eventually subsided as the orchestra struck up the familiar overture, and until the final curtain call the performance went much as usual. During it, Alice realised that the word had got round about her tragedy, for the principals and several members of the mens' chorus were very kind and supportive as they briefly met her during 'waits', or in the corridors and wings. Their kindness gave her strength to continue, especially as everyone seemed to be remarking what a professional trooper she was. Alex made a point of being with her during the 'waits' that they shared, and he made certain that he held her extra firmly when they danced together, since he knew she was in shock and that as a result, her sense of balance and usually very precise movements might be less good than usual.

The delighted audience made the cast take curtain call after curtain call. Just when everyone was expecting to leave the theatre, the dancers and mannequins appeared draped with the flags over their costumes. Then, as one of the principals started to sing 'Rule, Britannia', she released a white dove which flew right around the auditorium, and landed on Alice's head as she took centre stage to the orchestra playing the *Marseillaise*. She stood proud and smiling, but thinking all the time of her Charlie and the land where he had so recently fallen. She managed to control her feelings until the curtain finally came down, but once back in the dressing-room, she gave way.

The girls took off their make-up, and got ready for a big celebration party, organised by Mr Asche. But Alice was in no mood for it.

'Sure you'll be alright, Alice?'

'Yes, Elsie, thanks. I'll just be quiet here for a little while. I've asked Alex to bring me along in about half an hour – he'll call back for me. See you later.'

She smiled weakly, blinking tears.

Gradually the theatre became quieter and quieter as the cast and back-stage workers left for the party. Alice sat isolated in the long, stuffy dressing-room. Automatically, she picked up the framed photograph of Charlie that she kept on her dressing table and kissed it. She went to her handbag and took out the fountain pen he had given her. It was still among her most treasured possessions. It always would be, to remind her of what might have been and was never to be.

She looked at herself in her mirror. The lights surrounding it hurt her sore eyes. Behind her reflection, the dressing-room seemed unusually dark. After a while she saw Charlie's happy, fresh-complexioned face smiling at her.

'Dance for me, Alice, always dance for me. I'll be watching you.'

He blew her a kiss. The vision faded.

1921

Chapter 10

Summer, 1921

CALL NOTICE

Mr Asche requests all cast members and stage staff on Stage at one o'clock sharp, on Wednesday 17th August.

As they suspected, Mr Asche was due to announce the closure of the longest-running show on the London stage. It would finally close on Saturday the 27th.

'However, because of the great success, I want you all to know that immediately after we close we will be auditioning for my new show. Needless to say, while we will want to encourage fresh faces and talent, you my faithful crew, *old* that you all are by now' (groans from the cast), 'will be given exceptional priority!'

With everyone talking at the same time, the cast made their way up the long flight of stairs to prepare for what would be their penultimate Wednesday matinée.

'Well, I'm going to retire and get married, at last!' Madge had found herself a new man. Elsie and the others decided to re-audition.

That night after the show, Alice and Alex talked it over. They decided not to re-audition.

'Look, Alice, I think it's worth taking a risk. We've both saved up quite a lot of money, and I'm ready to do something quite different. Let's see what Madame has to say, and take her advice.'

Two days before the announcement Alice had come of age. Her twenty-first birthday had been marked by a large Sunday party on a Thames river boat with friends from the show. Since the end of the war she had thrown herself into her work more than ever. Charlie's death had matured her. She realised that she had some very powerful emotional resources, which at first were expressed through grieving. The sense of loss, the deep hurt, took over a year to heal – if it would ever completely heal. But Alice, like most young women, came to terms with her feelings as she gradually realised that if she did not she would become a depressive, self-pitying woman obsessed with regret for a life which might, and indeed should, have been very different.

There had been times during the course of the exceptionally long run of 'Chu Chin Chow' when she and Alex had considered leaving the show, but because of a number of cast changes they had been given more and interesting work, and a year ago Alice had taken over the important non-speaking rôle of a slave trader, when the original cast member left to have a baby. This had meant more money in addition to the pay increases that all the cast enjoyed as they went from success to success.

'Now, my darlinks, what next?'

Astafieva's Russian accent, thick as ever, caused her to speak slowly, savouring every word as if it were caviar.

'At last your show is ending, and you are deciding what is best for you – yes? Well, I have some news for you.'

She went on to tell them that Serge Diaghilev was shortly to attend one of her classes. He was looking for new dancers for an important ballet he was to mount in London, at the Alhambra Theatre: a full-length production of *The Sleeping Beauty* – re-named *The Sleeping Princess*, so that the public would not confuse it with a pantomime.

'Do you think either of us stands a chance of being selected?'

'But of course – if after class you perform for him the Black Swan even 'alf as well as you usually dance it!'

They walked home in the August sunshine.

'Oh, Alex, if only . . . If only we could work together with Diaghilev – that would be what I'd like, more than anything else in the world!'

Alex grinned.

'Marvellous, eh?'

And so, later that month, prepared with their best practice clothes and Alice having made sure that her pointe shoes were at just the right stage of wear for what they hoped they would be asked to perform, they went to class as usual.

Diaghilev sat beside Madame, not missing a movement that any of the dancers made, his bright eyes darting from one to the other, penetrating into their very souls, and intuitively knowing what was motivating them. After class, Madame beckoned Alice and Alex over and introduced them. She spoke for the great man as his English was not very good – the two expatriots normally conversed in their native tongue.

'Darlinks, I've spoken to Mr Diaghilev about you and your work for Mr Asche . . .'

Looking up at Alice and Alex in turn, the white streak in his black, brilliantined hair shining in a beam of sunlight, Diaghilev smiled and said, 'Oscar Asche – good man, very, very, er . . . talent. Good to work for, yes? You happy with him? You would be happy with my company?'

The dancers exchanged surprised glances, amazed at his response to their ordinary class work.

'But, sir, don't you want to see us perform a *pas de deux*?'

Madame translated. The big man laughed and muttered something in reply.

'He says it's not necessary – he really wants to use you both.'

More than delighted they expressed their thanks.

They were employed for the run of performances, which was expected to last for six months. Alice was engaged as a *coryphée*, which meant that she would dance with the taller girls of the company and it was written into her contract that she might be called upon to learn solos and leading roles with a view to future work, while Alex was taken on as a member of the male chorus, with the same proviso.

Madame told them, after he had left, that Diaghilev knew about their excellent work together, and that it very much looked as if they would be allowed to perform a *pas de deux* in due course.

Alice was third in line to dance the part of the Fairy of the Golden Vine, and Alex was to be her '*cavalier*'. So, in addition to learning their *ensemble* dances, they had to work hard with the soloists.

The production was lavish, with the most beautiful costumes, thick with real embroidery in gold threads, often trimmed with ostrich feathers, while the classical tutus were set off with trimmings representing the various characters. Alice was fitted for her fairy costume – shared with the two more senior soloists – and delighted in the golden and russet colours of the vine leaves and bunches of grapes that adorned the sleek, well-shaped skirt and velvet bodice.

Rehearsals were often stormy, with the dancers, repetiteurs and pianists speaking a polyglot of languages. Tempers became frayed as the opening night drew near, and the cast soon became aware that the extravagance of the lavish production had put the company well over budget before they opened.

About a week before the opening, during a very brief lunch break, Alice was called into Mr Diaghilev's office. A handsome young man was sitting beside him, helping him with his English. It was the young man who first spoke.

'Miss Townsend, it is company policy for our dancers to have Russian, Polish or French names, and like all the English dancers you will have to change yours, I'm afraid. As you know Sokolova was a Miss Munnings and Miss Moreton is to become Mortonova. We think that you should become Alicia Tonsova. We hope this does not trouble you; but it is our rule.'

Alice smiled to herself. She felt as if she were some exotic snake, shedding a skin to reveal a new a different one.

'No, it doesn't upset me. It will seem very strange, but I really don't mind changing my name for professional reasons – though I'm beginning to be well-known under my own name.'

Serge Diaghilev joined in.

'Not mind, no? Your work – not bad. Astafieva is good teacher, yes?'

'Wonderful, sir, she's taught me a great deal.'

Conferring with Alex later that afternoon she learned that after discussions of a similar nature, he was now Sasha Mekinski.

The final days of rehearsal were even more frenetic. They were often not in bed until two or three in the morning; but this production was so special and so different from anything the West End had seen, that the excitement in the cast was electrifying.

And so, at eight-thirty on the night of November the second, the curtain went up on the production. Its sets, as well as the costumes, designed by the famous Baskt, made the audience gasp – not so differently Alice thought, from the way they had done at the opening scene of '*Chu Chin Chow*'.

The audience was in raptures over the production, but the immediate press reaction was mixed, some of the critics saying that London simply was not ready for a full-length ballet spread over four acts – up to that time the company had always presented three short, very contrasting ballets during an evening. However, for Alice and Alex and several of their friends who had managed to get tickets, the performance was a triumph.

A week later they were told that due to cast changes the two soloists and their partners who were sharing the role of the Fairy of the Golden Vine had to cover for illness and injury, so, unexpectedly, Alice had to dance her attractive variation, and was supported by Alex in the final act – 'Aurora's Wedding'.

As she was getting ready, her dresser responded to a knock on her dressing-room door. It was a messenger with an envelope containing a mixed pile of photographs and programmes for her to autograph. Her make-up done, head-dress in place, tights and ballet shoes comfortable, she only had to be helped into her tutu, and there was time to spare before she needed to go down to the wings for her special entrance in the Christening Scene.

She took the package from the dresser, and put it down on her table. She went to her handbag to get her fountain pen, and as she turned to open the big brown envelope she noticed that the office had typed the date on it. It was the 9th of November, the third anniversary of Charlie's death. She caressed the pen in her right hand before opening it to write. Its familiar smooth, sleek, black form brought back the memory of his ghostly message. Tonight of all nights, she thought, yes, of course I will. I will dance for you. I know you're here with me.

By the end of the evening, she knew that her performance was the best she had ever given.

'My dear, you were quite wonderful, you could *just* have held your final reverence to the audience a little longer – after all they were cheering you. Do not be modest. You British dancers – too modest, that is your failing. It does not pay in our profession.'

'Madame, we didn't know you were there. We didn't think . . .'

'No, Alex, you didn't think even Sergei knew. But he knows everything! It was he who telephoned me. So I come to theatre. I have decided that I teach you the Bluebirds. And who knows, I catch Sergei in a . . . a . . .'

'Good mood?' queried Alice.

'Ah, yes a good mood . . . one day . . . Well, we'll see.'

Over a period of several weeks they worked hard, and as often as possible on the extremely complex *pas de deux* and its dazzlingly brilliant variations.

Now the drabness of the war years was passing, and at last life was more colourful. Fashion was, once again, headline news in the weekly periodicals, and the Russian ballet, which had given several London seasons since the end of the war, had produced the exotic *Scheherazade*, with its rich fabrics and dramatic use of colour, and this had done much to influence the fashions of the immediate post-war scene. It had been said that no female member of the grand audiences would have been out of place had she stepped onto the stage.

The company benefited from this kind of publicity, and the women members were, from time to time, invited to choose clothes by the designers of the day, so as to be seen wearing them to and from the theatre or at any social function they happened to attend.

Alice was able to choose a rich purple velvet coat trimmed with silver fox, and a dress in matching pure silk satin. A large purple turban trimmed with black ribbon and a slim spray of osprey feathers completed her outfit.

Having come to terms with Charlie's death, and resigned to the fact that she would never restore her relationship with her mother, she could, once again, sparkle with enthusiasm and gaiety. However, she did keep in touch with Philip, who was able to phone her at Tryon Street – Alex and she having pooled their resources for the luxury of a telephone. She made friends easily, although she and Alex were as close as ever, they had their separate friends within the company. Like Alex she spoke no Russian, but French was commonly used at rehearsals – it had always been the language of the ballet – and her schoolgirl knowledge of it was more than useful.

During the last three years she had distanced herself from anything like an emotional relationship, and for the present, because there were now opportunities of the kind she desired so much opening up for her, she and Alex concentrated on their ever-developing stage partnership. With their interpretation of Bluebirds improving, Madame had made sure that Diaghilev knew of the work they were putting into it. One day they were called to rehearse it with other couples from the company. He was present, but when the rehearsal was over he just got up and left without a word.

'Well, at least he's seen what we can do,' remarked Alex philosophically.

However, one evening in the middle of January Alice found a note on her dressing-table: 'Mlle Tonsova to dance Bluebirds at the following performances: Monday, February 6, Wednesday, February 8 and Saturday (matinée) February 11.' Scribbled in handwriting beneath the notice, a copy of which

87

would be put up on the cast notice board, Alice read, 'Please go to wardrobe at once for a costume fitting.'

At once she rushed over to Alex's dressing room. Sasha Mekinski was to partner her!

That night, after the performance, the triumphant pair of dancers gave a party to celebrate. Theirs was, after all, the most spectacular *pas de deux* in classical ballet. Yes, they would be nervous; but they knew that they had been well schooled and were thrilled at the possibility of becoming well known as a result of all their hard work. Madame was as excited as they themselves.

But a few days later they arrived at the theatre to find several of the cast crowding around the notice board. To their horror the notice, in Russian, French and English, said that the run of *The Sleeping Princess* must terminate on Saturday the 4th of February.

The whole company were devastated, but the two friends more so. Now they would not have the opportunity to dance the Bluebirds. Seeing her Bluebird tutu hanging ready for the performance that was not to be, Alice burst into tears.

'Well, we'll just have to start going to every audition advertised. I'm sure we'll find something – even if it's only a provincial pantomime! You'll make a wonderful Good Fairy, and I, well, I . . .'

'You can be Demon King.'

They sighed, knowing that a future something like they had just jokingly described faced them. But one stroke of luck came Alice's way. Between the matinée and evening performance on the closing day the wardrobe mistress came to her dressing-room to collect some costumes she had finished with.

'Oh, your poor Bluebird tutu. You won't be wearing it now, will you?'

'No, it's very sad.'

'Look, dear, I made it out of materials and trimmings in the store. I didn't have to buy a thing. All the costumes are only going to be stored under the Coliseum theatre – do keep it – and the head-dress too.'

This cheered Alice enormously, she was very grateful. Then a bright idea struck her.

'Did you also make Mr Mekinski's costume from stock?'

'Why yes! Would he like his?'

'I know he would!'

'He shall have it, then!'

And so they did the last performance, and faced an uncertain future.

Chapter 11

'Please may I speak to Mam'zelle Tonsova?'

Alice hesitated.

'Who is speaking, please?'

'Frederick Bulstrode. She won't know me.'

Puzzled, she replied, 'Alicia Tonsova speaking.'

'Oh, Mam'zelle Tonsova, my name's Bulstrode – at last I've found you, it's been so difficult.'

'Yes, Mr Bulstrode. What can I do for you?'

'I expect you know that the cabaret is becoming more and more popular – perhaps you have been to one?'

Alice had, and had enjoyed the food, dancing and entertainment.

The stranger went on, 'I manage the Queen's Hall Cabaret. We have opened a large ballroom at the top of the concert hall, and are engaging some very varied acts. We do two shows a night, and the customers come to eat and dance to Jack Hylton's band, and watch the cabaret. Now, you are a beautiful young woman, and I've heard all about your dancing with the Russian ballet. Let's face it, mam'zelle, you and I know that the company has gone broke, so you might as well forget it. Why not come and dance for us? Do you think you could find a partner? I would want you to do one of your pretty little toe-dancing numbers, but I would also need something more dramatic – for your second appearance – something, shall we say more adult, more intimate . . . modern.'

As he searched for words to describe what he had in mind, Alice could hear overtones of East End cockney in his accent. She was interested in his suggestion and, putting her hand over the mouthpiece, in a stage whisper called to Alex who was doing some washing in the kitchen. They listened to the stranger together.

'Well, Mr, er, Bulstrode, I don't know . . .'

She hesitated, but turning to Alex he rubbed finger and thumb together – she got the message.

'How much do you pay your acts, and for how long would you want me and my partner?'

'We could say fifteen pounds a week each, with something towards the purchase of costumes, if you need any. And you would have to change your act every month.'

The money was excellent.

'I will talk to my partner, Mr Mekinski. We could well be interested. About our second number: would an exhibition torch dance be suitable?'

'The very thing, the very thing – just what I 'ad in mind.'

Alice looked at Alex who was nodding.

'Well, what do you say? Do you want to think it over, or can I have a decision right away?'

'Well, Mr Bulstrode, I think we would enjoy the work – thank you. When and where can we meet to discuss the details?'

'Why don't both of you come to my office at the Queen's Hall, on – let's see – Thursday afternoon, and we'll draw up contracts. Goodbye, Mam'zelle, 'til then!'

Alice hung up the telephone.

'What larks!' Alex exclaimed excitedly. 'I think we're going to enjoy this – and of course the money's excellent!'

'Yes, Alex! And we can do Bluebirds – that'll make that cabaret audience sit up and take notice!'

'Call me Freddie.'

The huge, overweight man swung back in his revolving leather chair, holding a long unlit cigar between his teeth.

A secretary brought in the two neatly typed contracts. He handed one to each of the dancers, who read them carefully.

'Now if the contracts seem fair to you, sign, and I'll get you on the bill from Tuesday week. Ten days to arrange your music – the pianist'll play for your toe dancing, and the band for yer big second number. Okay by you?'

They agreed. They planned to have final rehearsals in the ballroom on the following Tuesday week, and with the band in the early evening in the ballroom before the cabaret opened. Shaking hands on the deal, they left his office.

'Weren't you the clever lassie to ask the wardrobe mistress if I could have my Bluebird costume!' They were walking down Regent Street towards Oxford Circus. 'I'll go to Nathan's for a Spanish suit for the torch number.'

'What shall we dance to?'

'"Jealousy" would be ideal. Look, let's call in here and get a copy – and we'll speak to old Miss Smithers and see if we can rehearse it after class, she'll play for us if we slip her ten bob. I'm sure Madame won't mind. Then one or two run-throughs of Bluebirds, and we'll be set fair.'

They went into a convenient music shop to purchase the music.

'Now, about your frock for the torch number?'

'Shall we buy one?'

'Och, of course not. No, my wee one, we'll go to Selfridges, look at the evening gowns, and then pay a visit to the fabric hall.'

They continued their walk in the damp, ever-darkening February afternoon to Oxford Street and the huge department store. Going first to evening gowns, they examined a red georgette dress with fashionable dropped waistline and mid-calf-length skirt, and decided something like it would be right. Alex cast an expert eye over it before a salesgirl approached.

'Right, now for the fabric hall!'

They bought five yards of red georgette, and matching taffeta for lining. Then, in haberdashery, cotton, hooks and eyes, a great many packets of red, black and silver sequins and a long length of red ostrich feather for a boa.

'Don't you want a pattern, Alex?'

'Of course not, I can do that on my Lizzie!'

'Your *what?*'

On hearing her mother's name Alice's stomach lurched.

'Oh, sorry dear, that's the name I've given to my dressmaker's dummy – old Joan upstairs lets me keep it in the loft, as I don't use it very often!'

Alex was brilliant at costume design. All weekend he worked on a mockup of the gown from an old sheet and, having fitted Alice, cut out the two fabrics and machined the dress itself. Meanwhile, she was kept extremely busy sewing sequins and making a plain red hair-band decorated with a single osprey feather which would be placed at the side of her head. Alex hired his suit from Nathan's, and over the next ten days they worked on their numbers. By the following Tuesday week they were ready for the rehearsal with the band pianist for Bluebirds, and with the band for 'Jealousy', their spectacular and slightly shocking torch dance (which could not have been more different from the purely classical *pas de deux*). Basically an elaborate tango, it became very acrobatic when, having spun her around several times, Alex flung Alice across the floor, then went on to pick her up and hold her tightly against himself in a very close embrace. They ended the number in a striking pose, holding a long, passionate, stage kiss.

The ballroom was large and beautiful, lit by tall upturned bronze lamps. The diners sat at small tables where supper was served. The programme listed the acts: the show was opened by four tall, elegant showgirls in brief but elaborate costumes of net and feathers, and then the two Trix Sisters rendered songs at the piano. After these 'scenes' the programme announced the 'dancing floor', which meant that everyone who wished could take the floor and dance to Jack Hylton's Band. Alice and Alex ended the first half, and appeared to cheers, though Alice overheard a coarse comment from one member of the audience, which she hoped Alex missed.

Surprisingly soon they found themselves into their sixth week of performances, and their second programme – in which they enacted a scene influenced by the Arabian Nights, wearing exotic Eastern costumes. This was again designed and created by Alex, who this time was influenced by *Chu*

Chin Chow; their second number was a Mexican scenario in which they wore bright green. A great deal of their spare time was spent in making the costumes, but the cabaret was closed on Sundays and Mondays, which allowed them extra precious hours in which to relax and catch up with seeing friends, who were highly amused at the turn in their careers.

One morning at around two-thirty, after they had finished both performances, Alice was just about to pick up her bag and get a taxi back to Tryon Street alone – Alex was meeting a new admirer – when there was a knock on her dressing-room door. It was Freddie.

'Want to have a chat with you, Alice.'

She gestured him to sit down.

'Now look, don't get me wrong, I'm delighted with your act – I say *your* act – but, well, I'm getting a few funny comments about Alex. Some of the men don't like nancy-boys, and have told me so in no uncertain terms. In fact two members have resigned. Now, Alice, darlin', I'm going to have to sack him, but I want you to stay. I'll double your wages in two weeks time. You can dance solo.'

'But I can't dance without a partner! How can I? It's preposterous! Those members aren't worth having, if that's how they feel. Nancy-boy, indeed – I'd like to see them lift me like he does! He's so strong . . . besides what's his private life got to do with them anyway?'

'Quite agree, quite agree, but it's the *law*. It's all so illegal, and one word to the police . . .'

'Well, I don't care about that. Sack him, and I'll go too, so there!'

She got up and started towards the door.

'Now, now, don't be like that, listen to what I'm going to say.'

He took her by the wrist and led her, reluctantly, back to her chair.

'Think of that thirty quid a week. This is what I want you to do. I want you to work out a nice fan-dance. Oh, nothing immoral – you'll wear a body stocking if you must – but I want a fan dancer. That'll pull the punters in! Good-looking girl like you – you're wasted on all that toe-dancing stuff. You could do it, I know you could – you've really got "It" in your torch dances. It takes talent to do that, and nerve – and you've got it.'

She stood up, furious.

'How *dare* you ask me to do that! Get one of the show girls – Margery, for instance, she's talented – but I'm a ballerina. Forget it!'

He liked to see her so angry. He looked at her with his huge, red-rimmed, fish-like eyes.

'Please, Alice, do this for me. I'll give you more money if you'd like it. Forty?'

He stood up and took her hands, gripping them as he spoke. She turned her head away from him.

'Fifty. Come on, now – fifty quid a week. Not bad for a youngster like you.'

'Get out of my way. I want to go home, it's late.'

He laughed.

'Quite the little snob, eh? Well, we'll soon cure that.'

And with that he thrust her arms to her sides, and nimbly throwing his fat arms around her, forced his wet sloppy mouth down on hers and attempted to give her a deep kiss. She smelt the stale cigar smoke on his clothes. His flabby body and its unpleasant, excited nearness repulsed her. She somehow managed to wriggle free. In doing so she pushed him, he over-balanced and fell heavily against the chair he had occupied earlier, which tumbled over with a loud crash, taking him with it. She grabbed her bag and rushed out of the door, leaving him on the floor, struggling to stand up.

Badly shaken, she rushed out down the many stairs to the street where, fortunately just across the road outside a big hotel, there was an empty taxi. Furious, she got into it and was driven home.

The next morning she told Alex what had happened.

'That was very brave of you, Alice.'

'It was dreadful, Alex – I hated him! And what an insult!'

'The beast! But don't let me stand in your way – after all, fifty quid a week . . .!'

'*Never!* No, no, no! Beside's he's deeply insulted you and our partnership. No, Alex.'

'Well, I'm sure we can pick up another cabaret or musical show soon – we're not exactly short of money, are we?'

'No; we can afford to be choosy – for the time anyway.'

The following evening they each received letters saying that their engagement would be terminated in two weeks time, when their current programme was due to be changed. Their contracts would not be renewed.

1922–1923

Chapter 12

Summer, 1922

Since the termination of their cabaret contract, life for Alice and Alex had been far more difficult than either of them had expected. They had earned some money by giving the occasional solo performance at charity functions – always to the delight of their audiences; but performing in ballrooms was not the same as working in a theatre.

Alice got a job in a revue, and danced a lavish waltz number *en pointe*, wearing a beautiful flowing gown, and for two months enjoyed the work. Meanwhile Alex had a part in a different show, in which he had to perform a pastiche of a classical ballet solo with an over-sized comedienne. The work for him was depressing. For ten weeks they were out in a number one tour of a revival of *The Merry Widow*, and very much enjoyed it, as they got to know several big provincial cities. Tantalisingly, from time to time they had news about the reformed Diaghilev ballet, which had been touring America and performed very successful seasons in Monte Carlo, but had received no call from the management. They felt quite envious, and not a little bitter, when postcards arrived from friends in the company with pictures of the beautiful little Monte Carlo Opera House where the Company had a permanent home when not touring.

There was a whole new repertoire of ballets in which they had no part. But, as ever, Madame Astafieva continued to encourage them. They religiously went to class every day, and joined in a variety of experiments with dancers who were coming under the influence of the 'free dance' of Isadora Duncan and her followers. Alex, who had acting experience from his early days in Edinburgh, suggested to Alice that she might attend acting and singing classes. These new skills, they felt, might be important to further her career if all else failed.

But the months dragged by, and in spite of what they had so far achieved neither of them felt really satisfied. They lived in hopes of re-joining the company, but these diminished. They became depressed and their relatively healthy bank balances became increasingly less so, so that as summer faded they were having to economise, seriously, and in September Alex became a dresser to the mens' chorus at Covent Garden Opera House.

*

'Here you are. Fish and chips tonight!'

Alex rushed into the living room and put the parcel of hot food on the table. Alice took out plates and knives and forks and separated the portions.

'How did it go?'

'*Rhinegold* – that's why I'm early. No male chorus. But they kept me busy all the same and . . .'

He became distracted.

'Well what? Tell me.'

'Alice look at this, look at this!'

On the greasy newspaper, they could just read DO YOU WANT TO BE A HOLLYWOOD STAR?

It was a preliminary announcement in the *Daily Sketch*: the famous Hollywood screen actress Norma Talmadge was looking for a typical English girl to appear with her in her next feature film. While there were many 'film-star competitions', this one was to be very special and on a huge scale. All young British women were free to enter. More details would be announced in the very near future.

Alex gripped Alice's arm.

'You must go in for it – you really *must*!'

'But, Alex – how can I? I'm a professional dancer. Besides I'm not sure that I want to go to Hollywood, not that I'm likely to win. No, I can't consider it. In any case, I'm too well-known already.'

'Well, *I* think it would be exciting just to try. Yes, you are quite well-known, but don't forget your public know you as Alicia Tonsova. And it was a year ago that you left *Chu Chin Chow*, where you were on the programme as Alice Townsend. Why not revert to your real name? No one will know, unless you tell them.'

'But my drama and singing classes . . .'

'Please, Alice – try! It would be a marvellous experience and think, when you've won you can show off your talents – in Hollywood!'

'Alex, it's unlike you to be impractical. Thousands of girls from all over the country will be simply crazy to enter. Honestly, the chances of my even being short-listed are tiny. Still, I'll think about it.'

'Well, I'm going to buy the *Daily Sketch* every day, so that we won't miss any announcements.'

'I'll think about it,' she repeated.

'Well, I think it's exciting. It'd be a terrific experience for you – and if you don't win, I'm sure there'll still be time for you to audition for pantomime.'

'It's true I *am* getting rather fed up with all this . . . this nothingness. I know I'm filling my days, but I'm twenty-two now, and I do so want things to happen.'

Two days later Alice was studying another announcement in the *Daily Sketch*. The Film Editor had published a letter from Norma Talmadge herself, who asked for the help of '. . . the splendid *Daily Sketch* to find me a young girl in England, Scotland or Ireland – a true British girl – who would like to become a really great heroine of the films.' The letter went on to say that Miss Talmadge did not want the search to be among professional actresses, but to find her in the home of her parents, working in her office or shop. She wanted the girl to be very ambitious and to be able to work extremely hard in front of the cameras.

Reading this, Alice was a little concerned about the exclusion of professional actresses. But after all, there was no mention of dancers, and she hadn't *acted* professionally, even though her part in *Chu Chin Chow* had called upon a certain amount of acting talent.

The letter ended by saying that when the final selection had been made Miss Talmadge would, at her expense, take the lucky winner to her own studios in Hollywood, where she would stay at her palatial house in Los Angeles and be paid a handsome 'Hollywood salary'. Later, the beauty would be cast in an important part in Miss Talmadge's next photoplay. All that was asked at this stage was for girls to send a photograph of themselves (a studio portrait, if possible, rather than a snapshot) to the Film Editor, and to write a couple of lines about themselves.

Alice looked through a pile of very attractive photographs that had been taken at the expense of the Russian Ballet, some of which were not in costume, and decided that one portrait showed her off to her best advantage. It was a full-face close up, her chin resting on her right hand with a long rope of pearls entwined around her third and little fingers. Her fashionably bright lipstick showed clearly, and she had a narrow beaded band low on her forehead, below her smooth, sleek, ballerina centre parting. At first she thought that she looked a little too much like a dancer, but then decided that as the Russian Ballet had such a powerful influence on fashion it did not matter.

She knew that she must give considerable thought what she wrote about herself. She could not say too much about her real dreams, or of what she had done so far . . . After scribbling for ages, she complained to Alex, who looked at the problem from a different angle.

'Think about how you are at this particular moment – don't mention your drama and singing classes.'

'But what about my dancing?'

'Tell them you learned when you were little.'

Together they came up with – 'My name is Alice Townsend. I am twenty-two years old. I enjoyed going to dancing classes when I was a little girl. I love going to see photoplays and I am *very* keen to become a screen actress.'

She went right out and posted the package.

Practically every day there was some new announcement or piece of news in the *Sketch*, **TALENT BEFORE LOOKS: I ask my protegée only that she be worthy of England.**

Readers were advised that they should not miss seeing Miss Norma

Talmadge in her latest photoplay, *Smilin' Through*. The paper printed a full-page photograph of the star in a huge crinoline gown and listed the main cinemas all over the country where the film was showing. The Pavilion, Marble Arch was its London venue.

By September the twenty-third, Miss Talmadge had announced that her pupil would be playing the part of a girl named Aggie in the thrilling drama, *Within the Law*. Very soon local committees would be sitting all over the country to start the arduous task of short-listing the girls, from whom a hundred would eventually be chosen to meet Miss Talmadge, who would make the final selection. Her equally famous sister Constance Talmadge would accompany her, as would her husband Mr Joseph Schenck, their manager, director and wealthy backer.

Every day the photographs of several candidates were published, from different regions. There were girls from Wales, from Manchester, from the South West, Scotland, Ireland. Some had fashionably bobbed hair and wore heavy make-up on lips and eyes. Others were more angelic, still clinging to girlish long ringlets. Some were extremely suave, and wore large hats pulled down on low on their foreheads. Now even rival papers began to be interested.

Alex rushed in to Alice's bedroom one morning before she was up.

'Look, you're in!'

She took the paper and read, 'Our selection of candidates today all live in London, Central West, and will go before their district committee. From left to right: Mary Laverson, Paddington; Lucille Anderson, Hammersmith, Alice Townsend, Chelsea, and Margaret Leahy, Marble Arch. If selected, they will have to compete before the Grand Committee on an equal footing with girls from all other parts of the country.'

'Your picture's by far the best – you look absolutely stunning, Alice!'

'Thanks, Alex! Look at *her* – that hat does simply nothing for her . . . but *she's* nice . . . and she's terrific!'

'Yes, she is pretty – but not a patch on you!'

'Please attend the London West Central selection committee at the Marble Arch Pavilion at 9.30 am on Thursday morning. Arrive in good time, and show this card to the commissionaire in attendance at the main entrance to the ground floor foyer.'

To Alice, it was another audition. She was amused rather than nervous, but carefully spent extra time on her make-up. She had decided to wear her special purple outfit, and her hair, which was easy to manage, was shining and set off by a matching turban-style hat. Before she left, Alex gave her some sound advice.

'As this is really a competition for amateurs and you are a thorough professional, the committee could just become suspicious. Not that there's any real reason why you shouldn't enter, but control that flamboyant streak a little, and try to be a bit modest!'

'I will!'

'Break a leg, wee one!'

She was ushered up to the circle foyer, where rows of ballroom chairs were gradually filling up with young women of all types, shapes and sizes. One or two looked extremely common; others were obviously débutantes, and spoke in high-pitched, affected voices while smoking black Russian cigarettes in long black holders. Some sat alone, perched nervously on the edge of their chairs. Their clothes ranged from the most expensive and fashionable to poor, worn, dreary winter coats and hats that looked as if they had been through the battle of the Somme.

What all the young women shared was good looks. Some were coquettish, some handsome, some already looked like the screen vamp of all time, Theda Bara. Others were simply beautiful and charming – pure English roses.

Each girl was called in turn and went through a door marked 'Manager'. The interview seemed only to last a very few minutes. Some came out smiling and obviously feeling pleased with themselves, others were downcast, with forlorn expressions.

At about ten o'clock Alice's name was called. As she got up and passed in front of other girls in her row, she heard one whisper to the other, 'Look at her – wish I had a coat and hat like that!'

'It isn't for the likes of you and me, but we'll show em, won't we?'

It was obvious that friendships were being struck as they waited.

She entered a room and found herself facing a row of three men and a woman. They all smiled very kindly.

'Please don't be nervous, Miss Townsend, we just want to have a little chat. Do sit down.'

Alice quietly thanked the friendly woman and did as she was bid.

After she had been greeted by the rest of the committee, one man, looking at his notes said, 'Tell me, Miss Townsend, what do you do?'

She had thought that that question might be asked. She told them that she was a specialist in bead embroidery on theatrical costumes. A friend she lived with designed them. They seemed impressed.

Another said, 'So you danced when you were little. Do you still like to dance? At ballrooms or cabarets?'

'Well, I have been, once or twice – but no, not really. I'm not very good at ballroom dancing, I'm afraid.'

As she spoke, she folded her hands in her lap and momentarily looked down at them, knowing full well that as she did so she would show off her long eyelashes.

'I am admiring your outfit, Miss Townsend. Is it French?'

'Yes, it was a twenty-first birthday present from my parents, who took me to the Ritz for lunch. It's nice to, er . . . have another opportunity to wear it!'

A member of the committee who up to this moment had been silent, enquired, 'How would you feel if you won the contest?'

'Oh, I'd be very, very happy, sir – there's nothing I would like to do more than be a film star!'

She gave him a really dashing smile.

The committee members nodded approvingly at each other.

The man who Alice supposed was the chairman thanked her for coming. She stood up, surprising them by shaking their hands all in turn, and elegantly moved towards the door to leave.

The next girl was waiting to go in.

'What are they like, are they awful?' she asked Alice.

'Don't worry a bit. They're really very nice – but don't forget to smile.'

A rule she had learned ages ago.

As she was about to leave the cinema, someone pressed a leaflet into her hand. It invited her to a special performance, the following Monday, October 16th, of Norma Talmadge in *Smilin' Through*. As the competition had aroused such nationwide interest, the event was to be filmed by Topical Budget, a news film company, in order to keep the general public up to date with its progress. The organisers wanted as many candidates as possible to be present.

As Alice approached the Shaftesbury Avenue Pavilion, traffic was brought to a halt by people spilling from the pavements onto the road. The dense crowd was one seething mass of humanity. All the London candidates, many hopefuls who still had time to apply, some having made a journey to London from the provinces, were there in full force. They came not only to see the film, but also to attempt to get themselves into the newsreel and actually be seen on the screen. Eventually, somewhat dishevelled, Alice pushed her way to the cinema entrance.

She heard someone shouting, and realised they were trying to attract her attention. Looking up she saw a man with a huge motion picture camera on a sturdy tripod, standing on the roof of a taxi.

'I say, you – yes, you, there – get over there!'

She saw that some policemen had cleared a space where several girls were standing in a row. Alice joined them.

'Right, girls, now start talking to each other, then as I call you – you'll be number one,' he said pointing to a flaming red-head standing at the far end of the row, 'each of you turn towards the camera and give me a big smile. Don't wave – if you want to be film stars just smile. Pretend you've unexpectedly seen your boyfriend! Right, when I say action . . .!'

'*Action!*'

The girls thrilled to the word. Were they beginning their film careers already?

They struck up a buzz of inconsequential conversation.

'Where are you from?'

'What a pretty hat!'

'I got lost! I've come up from Brighton – isn't it exciting?'

After a few minutes the cameraman – or was he a director? – thanked them and went on filming the crowd, many of whom waved and made faces at the camera. Some young women put on smouldering expressions in the hope of attracting attention.

It was a beautiful, sad, romantic but exciting film. Alice, like the whole audience, was enthralled. About half-way through the screening, Wyndham Standing, the leading man, who had welcomed the girls before it started, made his way along the aisles, and picked out some of the members of the audience.

Gently he leant over the girl on the end of Alice's row, and tapped Alice on the shoulder. She jumped at the distraction. He beckoned her to leave her seat.

'Please come this way. I'd like the newsreel men to take some shots of you and a few others.'

In whispers she explained that she had already been filmed.

'That doesn't matter. I want some more film of you.'

His voice was far more high-pitched than she would have expected, and he smiled engagingly at her. Even in the darkness of the cinema auditorium, she could see that he was staggeringly handsome. They went out into the foyer where the camera was set up. As he interviewed her, the camera caught her lively expression in close-up. He went through the same routine with about six other girls, and explained that each of them would be featured in the news-reel, with a caption edited into the film telling the audience who they were, where they lived and what they had said. Before they returned to their seats a secretary took their details.

Madame Astafieva glared angrily at Alice.

'So . . . you have entered the big Hollywood competition. Tell me, Alicia, is that a good thing? Is it right that you, a ballerina, should stoop to put yourself in a level with servants, street girls and stupid, empty-headed débutantes? I think that you are demeaning your art.'

'Madame, in many ways you are right, but, you know, life has been very depressing for Alex and me recently, and I don't suppose for one moment I'll get anywhere near Hollywood. I thought it would simply be an interesting experience.'

Madame Astafieva sat down on the stool near the huge mirror in her studio, sighed, and picked up the copy of the *Sketch*, its page turned back to show Alice's photograph. Looking at it somewhat quizzically she remarked, 'Well, it is a charming picture. But, Alicia, my darlink, do be careful. I will be most upset if you win. Come now, I am going to keep those feet of yours in your pointe shoes for just a bit longer today, so that you won't forget where you really belong.'

Announcement followed announcement in the *Daily Sketch*. By late October the Grand Committee had met to choose the final hundred from among the girls recommended by the host of regional committees. The press constantly stressed the fact that every British girl had an equal opportunity. They published frequent letters from Miss Talmadge herself, who repeated her gratitude for all the generous help and time the paper was giving her (they were of course delighted with the additional sales the competition was bringing them). They published a photograph of the Grand Jury which would choose the winners – it included personalities from the stage, the screen, business and sport. There was also a foreign princess, and the stunningly beautiful Lady Diana Cooper, who had herself recently achieved considerable fame in photoplays.

On Thursday, November the second, Alice received confirmation that she had reached the final hundred in the competition, and was requested to send another photograph of herself for publication. She found one which was suitable, and it appeared in the paper two days later.

Soon the 'Lovely Hundred' as the paper called them, started to arrive in London from all over the country. They were chaperoned and put up in one of the best hotels. Miss Talmadge and her entourage, including her husband and Constance, duly arrived from New York and moved into the royal suite at the Savoy. All the girls were to be presented to the great lady at a special dinner to be held there.

Alice had one special evening dress, which she had bought while in *Chu Chin Chow*. It was pale blue satin, and she wore it with a very glamorous silver lamé cape, matching accessories and a silver head-band. Her star quality shone, and as they arrived at the Savoy she put a great many of the other girls arriving at the hotel in the shade. She was determined, whether she won or not, to have a good time and enjoy every minute of the contest. She felt very tongue-in-cheek about the whole thing, and being honest with herself, really didn't think she was what they would be looking for.

Each girl was announced, shook hands with and was greeted by Miss Talmadge, her sister and the important Mr Schenck. They were then shown to their places at large circular tables where the meal was to be served. Alice was put with a group of girls from a variety of regions, among whom was a truly beautiful young woman called Marion, from Bournemouth, and a Pat Seins who lived in Hammersmith. The young women talked freely. One girl, who had obviously never been to a formal function before, spilled soup all over her gown, and two or three others at their table, uncertain which knife or fork to use, hesitated as each course arrived, and only ate very little – nervousness and shaky hands preventing the enjoyment of a very good meal.

While coffee was served there were several short speeches of welcome from the organisers, who were nicely light-hearted and made the girls feel relaxed and comfortable. Miss Talmadge was charm itself.

She was not as tall as Alice had expected – five-feet-two at most. Her bobbed dark brown hair was perfectly styled in beautiful deep waves which swept gently back from a centre parting. Her speaking voice was a joy to listen to – warm and rich – and with every word she said she inspired the girls to do their best in the days ahead, reassuring them that she would always be on hand to help and advise. She wanted them to enjoy what was in store, and whether they reached the final selection or not, hoped that the experience would be one they would always treasure.

Then they were taken by a fleet of charabancs to the Albert Hall, where they had been invited to a ball held annually to benefit the nursing profession. Miss Talmadge had booked a whole tier of boxes for the occasion. The girls had been told that although the theme of the ball was eighteenth-century France they had special permission to appear in their own fashionable gowns – because the star thought they would be able to relax and enjoy themselves more if they were wearing their own clothes.

As they stepped down from the coaches, the flash bulbs of many cameras went off, and they had to turn and smile to press photographers and newsreel cameras. Crowds of onlookers, in the hope of getting a glimpse of the 'Lovely Hundred *Daily Sketch* Girls', were cordoned off by the police at the front entrance of the Hall, its foyer a blaze of lights. As they entered, most of the girls gasped at the size of the majestic place, and were greeted by colourful decorations, unusually dressed dancers in powdered wigs and often comic interpretations of the dress of the court of King Louis. Alice and her Hammersmith acquaintance were especially amused at a group of young women, obviously débutantes in crinolines cut well above the knee.

They had plenty of partners with whom to dance, and during the course of the evening Miss Talmadge visited in each box in turn to meet all the girls individually, who by now adored her because she was so kind and charming.

'And, my dear, where do you come from?'

Her warm American accent would calm any nervous girl.

'From Chelsea – it's very near here, Miss Talmadge.'

'So I don't have to ask you if your hotel room is to your liking.'

'No, Miss Talmadge. Welcome to London. I hope you will have some time to enjoy your stay.'

'Every minute. I love it here more and more, my dear. Will I be seeing you at the studios tomorrow or the day after?'

'I'm called for tomorrow.'

'Well, don't be too late home, even if you do live nearby. We have a lot of work to do, and it will be a tiring day for all of us.'

The Stoll film studios in Cricklewood, North London, housed the biggest film studio floor in the capital. Alice joined the other forty-nine of the Lovely Hundred who were due to be screen-tested that day. In spite of the cameramen, the secretaries, the make-up artists, who were all very kind and friendly, most of the girls were plagued by nervousness. They were in a large green room waiting their turn to be called to make-up, when a tall willowy girl decided to stand up and start parading up and down. The rest looked at her with some surprise.

Her hair was black and bobbed. Her dress was very short, clinging, and obviously pure silk. It had a low cut neckline and no 'modesty', which gave the impression that she was wealthy, but a tart.

'Just practising my walk, darlings, and . . . move over, can't you,' she barked at a very nervous-looking girl who was sucking her finger. 'I'm going to sit down . . . like this'

She sat in a chair exactly opposite Alice.

'I say, you over there! Can you see my suspenders?' she requested in a haughty, high-pitched voice.

Alice could.

'Yes, and if you take that pose you'll look dreadfully vulgar.'

'Oh, I say, girls, she's a spoilsport. Whatever you think, I've simply got oodles of "IT". You haven't. Are you still a virgin, darling?'

'That's absolutely nothing to do with you, *darling*,' Alice retorted, and turned away from the other would-be film star in disgust.

A secretary came in and read out the names of four girls who were due to go to make-up. Alice was one of them.

As Alice sat down in the chair and the make-up artist draped her in a large cotton cape, she said, 'You obviously know a lot about make-up. How come you do it so well? Do you work in a beauty salon?'

Alice, momentarily dumbfounded, had to think quickly.

'No, but I've a friend who works in one in Bond Street and she gave me some lessons not long ago.'

'Well, film make-up has to be a great deal stronger – for the cameras and lights, you see.'

Alice thought it might be. The girl proceeded to cover her face in an astonishing shade of yellow ochre. She outlined her eyes in strong purple and plastered on black eye-shadow and mascara – far thicker than Alice had worn in the ballet. Then she powdered her down with a smooth puff, finishing her off with a large, light brush.

'There you are. If you sneeze or have to wipe your nose before you go on camera, come right back to me and I'll repair you.'

'Ah, it's Alice Townsend, isn't it?'

Miss Talmadge greeted her as if she was the only girl she had to test that day. As she spoke, she led her to where the specially constructed set was placed, carefully pointing out the dozens of heavy cables which cluttered the studio floor as they went.

'Now, dear, this is a baronial hall. When I call action, I want you to appear in the doorway. Look up and around at the astonishing place, then turn to your left and sit down in that armchair. You are entering the house of Lord Tonbridge for the first time. You are impressed, but you know that he will like you and you are determined that, in due course, you will be his wife. Is that clear?'

'Yes, Miss Talmadge.'

Alice stood behind the set. Miss Talmadge herself called, 'Action!' Alice appeared, seeing in her mind's eye a beautiful room hung with huge paintings, sporting trophies, a fireplace with a coat of arms . . . in reality she could see little because of the glaring lights, but she was quite used to that. She took her time but was careful not to linger too long. Noticing the chair she calmly sat down in it, taking an elegant, but modest pose.

'Cut!'

Miss Talmadge came up to her.

'Thank you, my dear, that was lovely. We don't need another take – but now I want you to work with Mr Standing. He will come up and greet you – he's the baronet, of course, in the photoplay. You will shake hands, and he will ask you a few questions while the cameraman takes some close-ups of you.'

It was amusing to meet Mr Standing again, and they talked of their previous encounter while the cameras were rolling. As he pointed out, they could say what they liked to each other, since no sound would issue from their lips on screen.

As she left the set she encountered the girl who had sucked her finger. She was doing it still.

'Look, you'll be fine. It's ever so easy – but you won't stand a chance if you go on with that in your mouth.'

She took the girl's hand and lowered it to her side.

'Can't help it, really, I can't! It always happens when I'm nervous.'

'Take a deep breath and pretend to grow several inches. You won't feel nervous, then. It's such *fun*, really it is!'

She gave the poor, pretty little creature a friendly hug, and felt the girl relax as she did so.

She went back to have her make-up removed. She really could not face a taxi driver with that awful heavy mask on her face.

And so, for Alice, that was it. She had done her bit. All she had to do now was to wait to see if she was to get through to the next stage.

Meanwhile, the press, with most newspapers participating, kept up the public interest – in spite of the fact that the government had fallen and Britain was facing a general election.

Chapter 13

During the days that followed, Alice fell into a kind of limbo. Disciplined, she made herself stick to her usual routine, but over the ensuing weekend she became unsettled, restless and not at all happy.

The weather reflected her increasingly pessimistic mood as it turned from clear, sunny autumn to cold, foggy November. On Sunday morning she and Alex went to matins in Westminster Abbey, as they did occasionally. She heard nothing of the lessons or sermons, but being in the rarefied atmosphere of the large building helped, in a strange way, to calm her. She began to think constructively. It could be very exciting and worthwhile to go to Hollywood.

'*If* I win . . . If I *win*.' The words chased round her mind as the congregation stood up for the final hymn. After all, she thought, if I don't dance for a year or so there's no harm done, provided I make time to go to class regularly – there are bound to be good ballet classes in Hollywood . . .

But then a new worry struck her. If she did win she was certain that Miss Talmadge would want to discover a great deal more about her background. If it was revealed that she was a professional dancer who had worked with the great Diaghilev and had appeared in virtually every performance of *Chu Chin Chow* – not to mention her other performances in cabaret and shows – would she automatically be disqualified because she wasn't just a 'home girl'? She couldn't bear the thought of that; the near-cheating she had indulged in might result in a nightmarish situation and, at its worst, disgrace her professionally because she had such an advantage over the 'ordinary' girl.

She talked things over with Alex as they made their way home after the service. He told her to put the negative thoughts on one side and asked her outright whether, in fact, she actually *wanted* to win. Yes, she realised she wanted to win, a very great deal. It would be an exciting experience to be out in the world, and perhaps, too, to become famous, probably more famous than she could possibly become as a true ballerina. Much as the dance was her first love and would always be, the sacrifice, if things went well, of a year, or even two years of balletic fame for greater fame on the screen would be

108

very worthwhile – especially as her chances of getting back into the Russian company seemed, at that particular moment, virtually non-existent.

'Don't doubt it for a moment – you'll dae very well, I'm quite certain!' In his enthusiasm, his Edinburgh accent emerged strongly. 'You've sae much style, Alice, and that'll take you a long way over in California – mark my words!' Suddenly he looked sad. 'But if you do win I'll miss you sae much, you're the sister I never had.'

She smiled at him and took his hand.

When they arrived home from class the following day there was a telegram waiting for her on the doormat.

She tore open the envelope.

'Congratulations. The Grand Jury and myself have chosen you as one of our five semi-finalists. Please telephone me at the Savoy immediately. Norma Talmadge.'

A moment or so later there was a knock at the door. It was a photographer who asked her to change into her favourite evening dress, and proceeded to take pictures, one of which would be reproduced in the paper next day, along with those of the other four semi-finalists.

'Now, my dear,' Norma Talmadge explained on the telephone, 'this is what Constance and I are going to do. We'll examine your screen tests and your still photographs once more, and from the five of you we shall first select three, then from those three, the outright winner.'

'Have I to do anything else at this stage, Miss Talmadge?'

'No, Alice – you have worked hard enough already! If you are a finalist I will ask you to come to my suite, where my sister and I will talk with you and the two others, and decide on the winner after that. My dear, it has been so difficult all the way through. You English roses are all so beautiful, you all have such pretty skin – it's something to do with your awful climate – the one good thing about it is that it's wonderful for the complexion! You don't get burned up as we Californians do. And what's so important, you all keep your young fresh looks – essential for the cruel cameras!'

Alice was taking in everything the movie star said with the greatest of interest.

'Now, my dear, I will let you know as soon as we have decided – either way, of course.'

Alice was delighted. Hollywood had its very special attraction; and now, as the excitement mounted, she wanted more and more to actually *win*. Her ambitious streak was emerging in a new and very much unexpected direction. The challenge was like a taper to a gas jet.

As requested, Alice presented herself on Monday, the thirteenth of November at Miss Talmadge's suite and was greeted by an immaculately-uniformed lift attendant.

'Straight ahead, Miss, and take the door on the right – that's Miss Norma's entrance, Miss Constance's is on the left.'

Alice took a deep breath and politely, but not timidly, knocked on the door he indicated. A maid in a pretty pink afternoon uniform opened it.

'I'm Alice Townsend, to see Miss Norma Talmadge.'

She need not have bothered – the grand and lovely lady, wearing a flowing gown of delicate chiffon velvet with a pointed hemline and draped sleeves, came into the hall and greeted Alice.

'My dear, so nice to have you here. Let's go in and sit down.'

She led Alice into a beautiful boudoir decorated in shades of the palest blue, with a marvellous view of the Thames, misty with weak sunshine, the picture framed by satin drapes surrounding long french windows.

'How pretty this is!' Alice could not help remarking.

'Everyone is so kind! Do you know, the hotel made some structural alterations so that Constance and I could have our own entrances to the suite. Now wasn't that just dandy? – and so very British. You people have such charm! Now, let's talk a little before the other two arrive, and when I've seen them we'll make our decision.

'My dear, I'm a good judge of potential and character. I think you have something special – I could see that at once from your tests. You seem so at ease in front of the camera. So much so that I thought perhaps you have done film work already.'

Alice could answer quite truthfully that she hadn't. However, she did say that she was used to being photographed.

'You said that you danced a little when you were a child. Well, I pride myself on my insight, and I think – of course I may be wrong – that you are under-estimating yourself.'

Alice who had been confident up to that moment, felt herself blush, and was inwardly furious that she reacted so childishly.

She decided to come clean. She explained that she was a dancer and told Miss Talmadge about her career. Had she ruined her chances? She didn't know. Miss Talmadge listened intently and was obviously very impressed.

'You see, Miss Talmadge, my friend – who dances with me on stage and in cabaret – saw the piece in the paper about the competition. I'm not an actress, and though I'm a professional in my own field, there was nothing in the rules to say that a dancer shouldn't enter. At first I didn't think I stood a chance – I just thought it would be an interesting experience. I never *ever* thought I'd get this far, especially as there were fifty thousand candidates. Oh, please forgive me, if I've done the wrong thing, and do put another finalist in my place, I shall quite understand.'

Norma Talmadge was silent for a moment, then Alice saw her lovely face break into a smile.

'Well, you know, don't you, that the competition was meant for ordinary girls – but I think your friend was quite right to encourage you to enter. You are definitely *not* ordinary, in the sense that because of your natural poise and charm you have what we call "star quality". But that has nothing to do with your ballet dancing or all the hard work you have put into it. I assure you your acting ability is quite, quite natural. No, Alice, between ourselves I'm sure I'd have done the same if I'd been in your position. Rest assured, my dear, what you have told me – and I'm glad that you did – will have no bearing whatsoever on the final result. Now go into the sitting-room. I just have to talk to Margaret Leahy and Jean Jay – your two rivals. Your chance is just as good as theirs.'

Relieved and relaxed, Alice went into the next room, where the two other girls were waiting.

Miss Talmadge, following her, turned to one of them.

'It's Jean, isn't it?'

The brunette nodded nervously, and they disappeared into the boudoir.

'Hello, I'm Alice Townsend. You must be Margaret Leahy. I think we're from the same district.'

'West Central? Yes. I live at Marble Arch, and you're in Chelsea, aren't you? Isn't it exciting? I wonder who she'll choose!'

'Only one thing to say – may the best girl win!'

'I'd drink to that, if I had a glass of champagne!'

The two rivals, trying not to eye each other too obviously, smiled and laughed nervously.

Jean reappeared, and Margaret went in for her interview.

After what seemed like an age, during which Alice made light conversation with Jean, Margaret returned. There was an anxious pause. They recognised Constance Talmadge go into the boudoir. They could just hear the voices of the two sisters in earnest discussion in the next room, but not what they were saying. The wait was awful, but they tried to look composed, and managed to do so, in spite of their turbulent feelings.

Eventually, they were asked to join Miss Talmadge and her sister.

'My dears, I know you are terribly anxious to know our decision. It has been dreadfully – no, impossibly – difficult for us, hasn't it, Constance?'

Constance agreed. Her sister continued, 'And so I'll keep you in suspense no longer.'

'We really feel we should take all three of you, because we are sure that you could all do extremely well. But the rules are made to be kept, I'm afraid. Now, Jean . . .'

The anxious young girl sat even further forward on the edge of her seat.

'Jean, dear, you have the most beautiful eyes we have ever seen, and we know they look just marvellous on screen. It is your eyes that have gotten you this far – they are a great asset.'

Jean looked somewhat deflated as Miss Talmadge turned to Alice.

'Alice, all of us have been quite overcome by the simply gorgeous way you move. You have great elegance, right down to your finger tips.'

Alice tried to smile her approval. The film goddess turned to Margaret.

'Margaret, you have all the qualities we are looking for, and while your

111

eyes are not quite as dynamic as Jean's, and you move very slightly less well than Alice, as the all-round British girl who will, I know work hard when we get to Hollywood, we agree that you are the winner.'

Margaret Leahy turned pale and let out a cry.

'I don't know what to say! I can't believe it. Oh! Thank you, thank you so very, very much – I really will work hard.'

Alice and Jean congratulated the outright winner, and bade farewell to the sisters. While they knew that their pictures had enhanced the *Sketch* that day as finalists, tomorrow and the future belonged to Margaret Leahy, who would tour Great Britain and be given a huge collection of superb clothes to send her on her way to Hollywood and stardom.

Jean and Alice, dejected, walked down the stairs to the riverside entrance of the hotel.

Trying to smile they said goodbye and went their separate ways.

It was five-thirty, and dark. The gentle mists of earlier in the day had turned to a steady, beating rain. Alice had no umbrella.

Her mind a black, disappointment and depression overpowering her, Alice started to walk aimlessly, not caring about the rain or the cold.

I'm a failure, she thought miserably to herself. I'm nothing but a failure. I'm obviously not much of a dancer, otherwise I'd have heard from Sergei . . . And now this, after getting so far. Goodbye, Hollywood. Goodbye, fame. I don't want to do anything any more, because I can't do anything well enough.

The rain streaming down her face smudged her make-up and mingled with blackened tears from her mascara. Alice turned north into a side street and then started to walk along the Strand, not caring where she was going or what she was doing.

Chapter 14

Alex looked at his watch. It was ten-thirty. He shrugged his shoulders. Alice was probably out with her new friends. But she had promised to telephone him as soon as she knew the result.

He tried to be rational. Perhaps she was unable to get to the phone, or had been detained by a crowd of photographers, which he knew would surround the winner.

Then a thought struck him. He went to the telephone and dialled 'O' for the operator, asking whether there had been any faults on the line. She assured him that this was not the case, but to be certain called him back. The telephone rang just as it should.

Where was Alice? Every few minutes he went up into the street. There was no sign of her anywhere. He telephoned hospitals in central and west London – again to no avail. He felt he could not go out of the house in case she came home – it would have been dreadful if he were not there to welcome her.

At last he decided to contact Miss Talmadge herself. He looked up the number and rang the Savoy, and was greeted very suspiciously by the receptionist who asked him a lot of questions – it was obvious that the hotel was doing its utmost to protect their famous guests. Eventually, however, he was put through to the Talmadges' suite.

Norma had just rushed in. She picked up a fur and was about to dash out again when the telephone rang. Somewhat annoyed at the delay, she picked up the receiver.

Alex had to be careful. He pretended to be Alice's brother and asked if she was still with her.

'Why no, Mr Townsend, Alice left us here around five-thirty. We've not seen her since then – I'm so sorry. And now if you'll excuse me, I have to go to a reception.'

'Tell me one thing, Miss Talmadge – did Alice win?'

'That I cannot say, I'm afraid – the news is being held until the first edition of the paper comes out. All I can tell you is that Alice did very well. You should be proud of your sister.'

Puzzled and confused, he put the phone down. Once more he went up into the dark, wet, foggy November night. In the distance he saw a lone figure staggering from side to side of the road, not caring where she was going. Automatically he rushed towards her thinking that a car might come round the corner any moment and knock her over. At first he thought she was drunk.

'My God . . . *Alice*! What on earth . . .'

'Alex! Oh, Alex . . .'

She was a pitiful sight, tear-stained and very red-eyed.

'I'm no good! I'm a failure! Nothing's going right for me. I'm just a hopeless mess!'

'For goodness' sake come in and dry off, and tell your Uncle Alexander all about it!'

As he spoke he put his arm round her, and felt her very wet coat. He led her down the steps, although she knew them so well he felt she might stagger or even fall. He helped her off with her coat and hat, its little cluster of felt flowers very much the worse for the heavy soaking they had received. He guided her towards the large, crumpled old armchair, and wheeled it on its squeaky casters nearer the fire.

'I didn't win. Oh, they were awfully sweet, but Alex, what can I do? The truth is I'm just mediocre. I'm really good at nothing. This proves it. Sergei doesn't want me – that's evident, and now all this . . .'

She burst into tears.

'Dear little love, of course you're disappointed at not winning, specially as you got so near, but do try to accept the fact that it was a good experience and it's all water under the bridge. Did you tell Miss Talmadge about yourself – your dancing?'

Between her sobs she stammered a yes, and explained that Miss Talmadge had said it made no difference.

'Did you believe her?'

'Oh yes, Alex, I really did – she's such a true professional. But it's not only that I didn't win. I've just been working so hard for a long time, and now this is . . .'

'The last straw?'

'Yes, the last straw.'

'Oh, come on now! Look, you're twenty-two, you've loads and loads of time ahead of you to make a success.'

'No, no, I simply can't bear it. I can't go on. I can't face another class, another audition. And I still miss Charlie so much. Oh, Alex . . .'

More floods of sobs and tears.

'Look, I'm going to get you a glass of brandy. I'll go up to old Joan – she always keeps some, and never goes to bed until two – I won't be long.'

'Thank you, Alex. I'm so sorry.'

'Why don't you go wash – I'll go and get the brandy. Come on, now, don't be silly. You've got the whole thing totally out of proportion.'

He spoke firmly but kindly, hoping that she would try to see things in a different light.

'Some brandy would be nice. Thanks.'

He took her by the arm and guided her towards the bathroom. She was decidedly weak. He went to fetch his neighbour's brandy bottle.

She went to the bathroom, locked the door and relieved herself. Realising she had a severe headache she filled a glass with water and took three aspirins from the bottle they always kept on the shelf. Her despair and her thumping headache overwhelmed her. She looked at the bottle. It was about a quarter full. Hurriedly, she started swallowing more and more of the tablets.

'All I want is peace. Lots of peace, away from it all. I just want to sleep and forget all about it. I'm fed up. I'm no good, so let's have a nice long peaceful sleep. Alex can wake me in the morning.'

She left the bathroom and went back to her warm, comfy chair. Alex reappeared with the brandy, poured some with a little water, and gave it to her. She was calm. She snuggled down in the chair.

'I'll rest here for a while – I'm simply too tired even to undress and go to bed.'

As she spoke she drank the brandy.

'Och, y' puir wee lassie.'

And Alice went to sleep.

Alex was getting desperate.

He looked at his sleeping friend, and then at the clock. It was almost three.

He decided he would have to wake her.

'Come on, sleeping princess. Time to wake up, and we'll get you to bed properly – you'll get a bad back again if you stay there all night, just like you did when . . .'

He lifted her hand, as he spoke, expecting her to stir, but it slipped through his fingers to return to her lap. Gently he took her by the shoulder.

'Alice dear, time to wake up. Uncle Alexander's going to pop you into your nice comfy bed. Come on now!'

Alice still did not respond. He lifted her in his arms. She was a dead weight. He carried her into her room and laid her on top of the bedclothes, and tried gently slapping her hands. There was still no response. He was beginning to think the worst. But how? It wasn't possible. He rushed over to her dressing table and fumbled for a make-up mirror. He held it to her nose, and heaved a sigh of relief when he saw it mist over. But she still didn't stir.

He panicked. He tried once more to wake her – yet again without success.

He rushed out and ran four doors down the street where he knew there was a young doctor. Banging on the door he eventually saw a light come on in a first floor window. The window opened.

'I say, shut up, will you? God knows, I don't get much rest, and you're disturbing it!'

'Jamie, I need help!'

'Oh, it's you, Alex. What's wrong?'

After the briefest of explanations Jamie came down, raincoat thrown on over his pyjamas, his medical bag in hand, and together they rushed back to Alice.

'It's alright, old chap – she does have a pulse, but it's weak. What did you give her? It's certainly knocked her out.'

'Just brandy and water, here's the remains.'

Alex handed him the near empty glass. He smelt it and dipping his finger in the small remaining quantity, tasted it.

'That's fine, just the right strength, I would think. This couldn't have knocked her out like that. She must have taken something else. Let's go through her handbag, she must have something there.'

There wasn't.

'Are there any sleeping pills here? Or in the bathroom?'

'No, only aspirins.'

'Go and check the bottle. Are they in a cupboard, or just on a shelf?'

'We keep them on the shelf.'

'Quickly! See if they're still there.'

Alex went into the bathroom and found the empty bottle on the floor.

'Dear God in heaven . . .' he cried as he picked it up.

In shock, he handed it to his neighbour.

'Alex, think carefully. How many tablets were left in the bottle? It holds a hundred. Was it full – or nearly full?'

'About a quarter full, even less, perhaps. That's good, isn't it?'

'Can't say. Some people can get seriously ill if they take only ten. We'll have to take her to the hospital immediately and get her stomach pumped. Bring her up to the hall. I'll find a taxi. It'll be quicker than trying to call an ambulance!'

Folding her in her coat Alex carried the totally comatose Alice up the creaky stairs. By the time he got her out of the house Jamie had found a taxi, and they were soon speeding their way through the deserted night streets towards the centre of town and the Charing Cross Hospital where Jamie was a houseman.

Everything was black. As black as the darkest, most starless night. Suddenly the blackness started to swirl round her, slowly at first, then with ever in-creasing speed. While she could see nothing, Alice felt the blackness touch-ing her, gently, all over, with what seemed like long strips of silk. The swirling became more intense, more distinctively circular in its motion. As it did so, Alice was aware of being in a tunnel – a long dark tunnel, menacing yet intriguing. It was straight and seemingly endless. She was alone. There were no animals or plants or even buildings. There was no sound either, just the swirling darkness along which she was compelled to walk then to run, at ever-increasing speed. In the far distance, although she could not precisely see it, she knew the tunnel turned to the right, and eventually, as she approached the corner, she saw a glow of light. It was a mere pinprick at first, but with each step it became bigger, rounder, warmer and yes, she decided, welcoming.

She further increased her pace, and as she did so she realised that from the blackness were slowly emerging colours reminiscent of the sun – shades of pink, pale yellow, then a darker, richer yellow which gradually merged into a deep glowing orange red. The light that had been a mere distant dot was brightest of all, and it had increased in size so that it was wider in circumference than she was tall. She knew she had to reach it, and continued, with a renewed sense of urgency, to hurl herself towards it. As she did so, she became aware of a shape, the figure of a man with his arms open wide, his body forming a cross. He was in uniform. An army captain's uniform.

'*Charlie*, darling, darling Charlie – I love you, I love you!'

As she spoke, in spite of the glaring light behind him, she saw him smile. Stretching out her arms, she rushed to embrace him. Their eyes met, but as they did so he gestured her to stop and she saw that although he smiled, he was shaking his head.

'Alice, dearest, go back – you must go back. Don't come any further. You have much to do. And I am watching over you.'

She hesitated and fought against his power, her love for him overwhelming her. His expression became firmer.

'You must return – you must return. Go, Alice, go – here is not for you. Here is not for you.'

The brightness of the orange red faded to strong yellow, to pale yellow, to pink, and as it did so, her beloved Charlie merged into it. She felt the blackness and the swirling sensation return, then the void, and the emptiness . . .

She stirred.

'Alex . . . where am I?'

'You're alright, thank goodness.' He took her hand.

Sleepily glancing up she saw a nurse, but before she could say anything he reassuringly repeated, 'You're alright. You're in hospital. I wondered if you would ever make it. You've been a wee bit silly, you know.'

'Have I?'

'Oh, yes. You've had us all worried. But don't concern yourself now. I'm just pleased to see you awake again.'

Remembering everything that had happened she started to cry.

'I just wanted to get away from it all. Oh, Alex, I'm so miserable. I'm no good. No-one wants me or my work!'

'Don't be silly, of course they do, and of course you'll get a lovely dancing job again soon . . .'

The nurse intervened.

'Sir, Alice will have to stay here until tomorrow, just to make sure she's

117

completely recovered. We'll keep her quiet and relaxed, then perhaps you can come back for her in the morning and take her home.'

'Why, of course.'

'Look, Alice, I've to go now. You just rest. I'll come in again in the morning.'

'What time is it now?'

'It's about half-past-four.'

'In the morning?'

'No, Alice, in the afternoon. Tuesday afternoon. You've been asleep for a long time!'

Chapter 15

Basil Cavanagh looked out of the window of his Queen Anne terrace house in Henderson Place on the Upper East side of New York City, and saw it was raining. He sighed, knowing that the worst of the winter was yet to come. To divert himself from the misery of the season he turned to his collection of photographs, and escaped into a host of memories he had been collecting in Europe over a period of years. A group of informal pictures of male members of the Russian Ballet caught his eye. One in particular made him smile nostalgically. It showed himself and four dancers sitting with Sergei Diaghilev at a table in a fashionable London restaurant. He couldn't remember which – and there was no note on the back to refresh his memory – but looking at the picture again he remembered the evening very clearly. It had been one of many he had spent with that particular group of friends whilst in London especially to see the spectacular production of *The Sleeping Princess*. He had loved the ballet and extended his stay for a further two weeks to enjoy more performances and to get to know Sergei and other members of the cast better.

There was Patreek . . . Errol . . . Mikolaichik – each handsome and exceedingly good company. He cast his eyes further along the group. On the end, smiling a big broad happy smile, his shock of brown hair about to fall over his forehead, was Alexander. Yes, Alexander – the best looking of the lot of them! After that supper they had returned to his suite at the Ritz and had given each other a great deal of pleasure.

He had an urge to contact his London lover, to discover where he was performing at present – if it was a big show he would plan another trip and perhaps spend Christmas with him in London.

Alex folded the long, bulky letter and put it back in the envelope.

'He's made a suggestion which is tempting.'

'What does he say?'

'Oh, Alice, I just can't consider it.'

'Don't be silly! What is it?'

'He suggests I join him in New York for a while – that is if I'm not

119

working or have anything lined up. If I'm in a show he says he'll come over here. I know he has a lot of theatre contacts, and he says he's certain he could get me a good job on Broadway.'

'On *Broadway!* Alex that's marvellous – you must go!'

'But leave you here – out of work and alone?'

'Oh, don't worry about that. I've got friends at Madame's, and I'll spend a bit more time with Elsie – I've always been fond of her since *Chu,* and we don't see nearly enough of each other. I'll be fine. I'm sure to pick up a pantomime in a week or two. When does he suggest you come?'

'As soon as possible. But I can't, I really can't.'

'Alex, you like him, and he's obviously wealthy. You could get really to love him maybe, so don't spoil your chances. Please, you must go. I'll be fine, I really will.'

'Dear wee thing, you're too kind. I must admit I would *like* to go'.

'Then write and tell him you'll come.'

In just over a week Alex had a telephone call from Cunard at Southampton: 'Mr Basil Cavanagh has booked a first class suite on R.M.S *Mauritania* for Mr Alexander McIntyre. She sails at noon on Monday the fourth of December.'

'I'll only be away for a couple of months, three at most! Unless any show I get work in is a spectacular success it shouldn't run much longer than that. Look, if Basil's got a big house – and it does look big, he showed me pictures of it – I don't see why you shouldn't join us. It isn't as if he hates women, especially beautiful ballerinas . . .'

Alice was putting a brave face on things. Inside she was already feeling a great emptiness. Alex's suggestion cheered her. However, the last thing she wanted was to intrude on his love life – just as, if the occasion had arisen, he would not intrude on any romantic relationship of hers. That was their unwritten agreement.

Alex paid the rent for their flat for two quarters in advance. By then, they calculated, he would be back. Until the end of the following June she had no worries about where she should live.

They were very much relieved when, a few days before his departure, Alice succeeded in getting a job as Fairy in the Wimbledon Theatre pantomime. Rehearsals would start on the day he sailed.

Steam gushed from beneath the carriages.

'Alex, this is it, isn't it? I think you'd better get in, don't you?'

'Yes, m'dear. Take care of yourself, and don't forget to have lots of photos taken in your Fairy Starlight tutu. I'll want copies immediately. I'll write, of course, and send you a cable when I arrive.'

Alex was wearing a smart well-cut suit and a quality cashmere camel overcoat, both of which he had picked up at a bargain price from a shop that sold off clothes which had been previously hired out.

'You look terrific. Have fun on the trip. I wonder if Bunny'll be looking after you?'

'Poor Bunny! But I know, like you, he'd want me to take the opportunity. Anyway, he works on the *Aquitania*.'

They gave each other a long hug as the guard's whistle screeched above the general noise. Alex closed the door and, leaning out of the window, grabbed Alice's hand.

'Now go, wee sweet thing – you mustn't be late for rehearsal.'

'No, of course. I've time to get back to the flat and pick up my things. Goodbye, Alex – dear Alex.'

She tried hard to smile as the train moved off and walked along the platform holding his hand for as long as possible. They waved to each other until the train gradually gathered speed and disappeared out of sight.

She felt the warmth of his hand as she turned. Tears trickled down her cheeks. Momentarily her thoughts flashed back to the War, when with her mother and Philip they had seen her father off to France. But that occasion had been far more distressing: she was filled with hope for Alex. He deserved a breakthrough – both in his love-life and career.

Who knows, she decided, perhaps Basil can provide both.

It had been a very cold morning – calm and icy. In places shaded from the winter sun, which had broken through to give a bright clear winter's day, there were still patches of ice.

She returned to the flat and opened the little gate which led down to the basement. Alex had warned her that the steps were slippery when they left and she had walked up very carefully. But now, as she returned, her thoughts were elsewhere. Yes, she had time for an early sandwich lunch and coffee. Yes, she had several pairs of pointe shoes in her bag along with her practice tunic and tights and washing things. She made herself concentrate on these practical matters to keep her mind off the great emptiness now that Alex had left.

As she set foot on the second step she slipped on a patch of ice. The steps were narrow – she tried to grab the handrail as she fell, but was unsuccessful. She half-fell, half-tottered to the bottom of the steps, twisting one ankle, bruising her knee and damaging her back.

She was stunned and cried for help. An elderly woman happened to be passing, and saw Alice in a painful position at the bottom of the stairs.

'Oh Lor', luvvie, you've had a right walloping. Can you get up?'

'No, I don't think so.'

She moved a few inches, but her back was agonizing. In her painful stupor she could see that the passer-by was far too large to get down the steps to help her – besides, she might even fall on top of her.

'Look, could you go to the front door and ring the bell, please? Joan'll answer.'

'Of course, ducks.'

The woman waddled to the door. Soon Joan appeared and, with warnings about the ice, cautiously made her way down to the injured girl. The passer-by went on her way.

Joan carefully lifted Alice to her feet.

'Can you put any weight on that ankle?'

Alice definitely could not.

Although Joan was well into her seventies she was strong, and having taken Alice's door key unlocked the entrance to the flat and eased her into it, and into the old armchair. Alice was deathly white, and about to faint with pain.

'Lean forward if you can, dear – that'll help.'

Alice tried, but the pain in her back prevented her head reaching her knees.

'Look, I'll see if Doctor Jamie is in, he just might be.'

Fortunately, he was.

'Oh, Alice – you're in the wars again!'

Joan left doctor and patient, saying that she would call down again in an hour.

'Oh, Jamie, I think I'm bruised all over.'

He looked at her ankle, and told Alice to take off her tattered stocking.

'Cold water and a crepe bandage on that, and I see your knee is bleeding. I can just bathe that – it's not too bad. A dressing and some healing ointment will do the trick. Anywhere else, Alice?'

She tried to move in the chair.

'I'm afraid it's my back. It's very stiff.'

'Let's get you on your bed, and I'll examine it.'

He helped Alice stagger to her bedroom and she tried to undress. This proved impossible and rather shyly she had to ask Jamie to assist her. The young doctor was totally professional – he could have been Molly undressing her when she was a few years old.

He helped her to lie on her stomach. After testing reactions, prodding, and massaging her spine he turned her over as he came to his conclusions.

'Well, you'll have to rest entirely for three weeks at least. And from then on we'll just have to see how you progress. No going to class – that's doctor's orders. So Alex will have his hands full looking after you!'

'You don't know, then?'

'Know what?'

'Alex left this morning to spend a few months in New York. I've just been to see him off on the boat train. He has connections there with people who'll get him work on Broadway.'

Jamie looked very surprised.

'No, I didn't know!'

'It all happened very quickly, and I suppose he hadn't run into you in the pub.'

'No, I've not seen him for over two weeks. I've been as busy as ever.'

122

He sighed. 'So you'll have to look after yourself. That's not going to be easy. Do you have other friends who will help?'

'Yes, but, Jamie, the thing is I'm due at the Wimbledon Theatre in two hours. I've been given the part of Fairy in their pantomime. This is the first day of rehearsals. The contract's all signed. Will I be able to go? Surely you can give me some strong pain-killers? I really can't afford not to take this job.'

'My dear, if I do that, you will never dance again. Putting strain on that back when you are doped will make the condition worse, whereas if you rest it completely for about three weeks or so, it will get better, and then, perhaps from early in the new year, you'll be able to go back to ballet class again – you go to the Pheasantry, don't you?'

'Yes, but what about the show – you really mean I'm not to do it?'

'I really mean that you simply *cannot* do it.'

Alice started to cry and Jamie did his best to comfort her.

'I'll give you a sedative, you're in shock and the shock has followed a stressful morning for you anyway – it may be because of Alex's departure that you were less cautious than usual. I know dancers are always very careful about their backs and ankles.'

'But what can I do about Wimbledon – can I join the company later?'

'Yes, but only if the run extends well into February – would you like me to telephone the producer?'

'Oh heavens, it looks as if you'll have to.'

Alice gave him the name and number. She could just hear him talking in confidence to the producer from the telephone in the passage. Then she heard him hang up the earpiece.

'He was very understanding but disappointed – you were to have had a high billing, "of the Russian ballet", he said. But, Alice, I'm afraid it's bad news. He says the run might go on until the end of February, but that as you could at best only join the company for the last two weeks, it would not be worthwhile to have a cast change at that late date. He says he'll get onto his office and cancel your contract. I'm so sorry. I'll come in every day and see how you are. Can Joan get this prescription?' As he was talking he wrote it for her.

'Why yes, and I think I can contact another friend who will help.'

'Well now, it's vital to remember that the less you do the quicker you'll get better. *Don't* do anything silly. For these first few days, you'll even need help to go to the bathroom. But now I must get to the hospital right away. I'm on the same shift tomorrow, so I'll come in at about this time.'

He took both of Alice's hands. She was extremely grateful for his help and knew she had to take his advice.

Not long after he had left, Joan returned. She helped Alice to the bathroom and settled her back in bed. She went around to the chemist in the King's Road and had the prescription made up and bought a tube of 'Germoline' for Alice's grazed knee, then came back and brought her down some soup for her lunch.

Alice was very grateful for the help her old neighbour was giving her. But she was extremely worried. She knew now that without her pantomime she had no money coming in. She was not penniless – yet – and was extremely thankful that she would have no rent to pay, – but to get into debt to old Joan would be unthinkable, as apart from the minute old age pension, her entire income came from the rent they gave her.

She looked at the clock. It was one-thirty. By now she knew that Alex would be having a grand lunch in the first-class dining room. The ship would have already steamed out of Southampton water and be making her way towards the Channel. With every minute her friend was going further and further away from her – at a time when she needed him most. With those unhappy thoughts in mind she fell asleep. The sedative worked.

When she awoke it was almost six o'clock. Joan returned with some tea and cake, and said she would come again before she went to bed. Alice tried to settle down to read, but this was difficult. She had far too much on her mind. She reached to a shelf near her bed and grabbed her writing case. Taking her pen from her handbag she started a letter to Alex. But then she had second thoughts. She realised that if she told him about her accident, she would also have to tell him that she was not able to be in the pantomime. She realised that if she did he would more than likely get the next boat back, and that simply was not fair on him – why should her problem spoil his chances? She had to think again, and decided for the time being anyway, not to write. In any case, sitting propped up was not that comfortable, even with the extra pillows from Alex's bed, since it put strain on her back. Slowly the evening drifted by. From time to time she dozed, until around ten-thirty when Joan paid her final visit of the day.

'You're too good to me, I can't thank you enough.'

The old lady smiled, and said, 'Well I'm very fond of you two – you're right proper people, you and Alex – that I know. I wouldn't tolerate a young man and a young woman living together like you do, but somehow I knows you're good Christians and that you don't do nuffin' wrong – if you gets my meaning.'

Alice smiled.

She took a glass from Joan who was also handing her a sleeping pill that came with Jamie's prescription, Alice swallowed it and Joan said she would come down again in the morning.

The next day, while still suffering considerable discomfort in her ankle and back, she decided she would drop a postcard to Elsie, knowing that Joan would post it for her. She felt it simply was not fair on the old lady to have to look after her all the time. She had hopes that Elsie could, perhaps, come round occasionally and maybe cook her a few cakes or a pie and do some shopping so that she might eat independently of Joan.

'So you have got problems, darlin', haven't you? But I'm so glad you wrote – it's lovely to see you again, nevertheless.'

Elsie had been in the run of *Cairo*, Mr Asche's latest show. This she had enjoyed but it had now closed and she was taking a break, the first one she had taken since 1916.

'I'm getting too old for all this, you know.'

'What are you going to do next?'

'Not sure really . . . well, I thought I'd try for a job in Selfridges, I dunno . . . perhaps I'll do one more show next year. But more to the point what are you going to do?'

'Start going to auditions again, as soon as possible.'

'Well, remember Doctor's orders – be patient and you'll get better much quicker.'

Days passed and Alice fell into a dreary routine. Elsie's visits were the light of her life, and Madame sometimes dropped by to see her. She supported what the doctor had said, and promised that when Alice was able to get out of bed she would give her special help to get her back into practice again.

Meanwhile, Alice had the promised cable from Alex, who had enjoyed his voyage and had arrived safely. A week later she had the first of many long letters.

New York was cold but very exciting. Alex was being thoroughly spoiled, meeting a lot of people, and had a wonderful suite of rooms in Basil's sumptuous house. They had been to several Broadway shows and he was always taken backstage afterwards and, as had happened in London, Basil would pay for expensive suppers with cast members, producers and choreographers at restaurants in the theatre districts – the famous Sardi's was their favourite.

Alice knew she had to reply to his letter – and soon. Again she faced her problem. She simply had to make up stories about the pantomime, but tried to keep her white lies to a minimum. She said that the show was opening on Boxing Day (which was true) and that it was going very well. Thankfully, she had not to dance with a partner – much preferring to do solos rather than having to put up with some young dancer who might not be of their standard. Then she remembered how she had faithfully promised she would send him photographs so had to make up a plausible excuse why there were none. She fabricated a story which inferred that the photographer had ruined all his film and so there was a delay. That, she knew, was only a very temporary excuse, she would have to improve on it in her next letter.

Elsie and her family were kindness itself. At their expense on Christmas Day, Elsie arrived with Sandy and a taxi. They carried Alice up the basement steps and into the car and took her to Tennyson Street where she was very much guest of honour with the family who, although she could see signs of some increased prosperity, were not well off. They gave her a marvellously friendly family Christmas Day, and brought her back later that evening when she and Joan shared a Christmas drink.

However, when the old lady had left Alice felt very much alone. She had been so grateful for the attention and love she had been given that day; but after all, Christmas was Christmas, and she had not shared it with her family of whom she had been thinking about rather a lot lately and picturing them all at the Beaumonts . . . celebrating in grand style . . . of her brother, with whom she had not been in touch for some months, now. Though he did know of her just missing out on the film contest – it was in all the papers and he told her he collected as many cuttings as he could which was sweet of him. How she hoped that he would be able to . . . But that was out of the question. She knew that her mother now was even more adamant because from her point of view Alice was living in sin . . . And now today of all days there was no Alex with whom to laugh and joke, to have fun, to go out with . . . Sighing, she settled down for the night.

1923

Chapter 16

Daisy Lloyd rushed into her dressing-room eager to get ready for the opening performance. On her dressing table she could not help but notice a huge bouquet.

'Oh, how lovely – how positively *sweet* of him!' Fascinated, she looked for the card. On the outside it simply said, 'For Fairy Starlight.' Opening the tiny envelope she read, 'Break a leg, dear wee lassie – your ever admiring Alex.'

She was puzzled. She knew no-one of that name – her boyfriend was called Ronnie. And certainly no-one had ever called her a 'dear wee lassie'!

She realised the flowers were not for her and asking around, she tried to find out who they were for. She would have loved to have kept them, but in all honesty she felt she could not deprive anyone of the glorious and obviously very expensive bouquet. She had an understudy, a young dancer from the chorus, who was reasonably good on pointe, and decided that they were meant for her. 'Break a leg' could only mean that the sender was in the profession. The bouquet must be meant for little Annie Wakeham.

She rushed up to the chorus girls' crowded dressing-room and asked for her – but the girl said she knew no-one called Alex. Daisy had to get ready, and for the time thought she would let the matter rest until the break between matinée and evening performance. As she was getting into her white and silver tutu the producer popped his head round the door with the same phrase: 'break a leg'. Thanking him, she drew his attention to the mystery.

'Oh, I expect they're meant for Alicia Tonsova – you know she was injured, so you got the part, my little sweetie.'

Daisy – a kind-hearted girl – was upset, although thrilled that she had a role which would show off her talent.

'Give me her address, and I'll take them to her tomorrow morning.'

'Well, that's really nice of you. Alicia'll appreciate it. She must be feeling pretty miserable.'

That night Daisy put the flowers in a bucket of water in the outside lavatory, and next morning made the journey to Tryon Street.

*

Alice, who had just said goodbye to Joan, heard a knock on the front door.

'Who is it?'

'You won't know me, but I'm Daisy Lloyd. I've got something for you.'

'Come in, the door's not locked.'

The stranger timidly opened the front door.

'I've brought you these. They were put in my dressing room. I'm Fairy Starlight – I knew someone else had been cast, and that she was injured. Yesterday the show opened, and I saw at once these were not for me so I asked the producer, who told me all about you, and well, here I am. Do have them, I hope they've not suffered too much!'

Alice's face lit up as she took the huge bouquet. Smiling, she read the very characteristic message on the card. She had wondered why she had only had a pretty Christmas card from Alex, and no letter for well over a week, now.

'That is so kind of you.'

She pulled back the beautiful silver paper lace container for the bouquet. 'But look, as you've come so far you really should have some for yourself.' She gathered together several roses, carnations and a spray of pale pink chrysanthemums.

The young girl – who could not have been much over seventeen – blushed and thanked her.

'It's my first show, and these are the first flowers I've ever had!'

'I expect there'll be a lot more for you in due course.'

They talked for a long time. She too was keen to become a real ballerina, and Alice suggested that after the pantomime season she should audition for Madame, if she was really serious about her work.

'I'm so sad you have this awful injury – I do hope it'll be better soon, then you can get back to class. I must go now – we're having matinées every day for three weeks.'

'Yes, I know. But my loss is your gain – so make the most of it! And, Daisy, when you get applause make the most of that too. Don't be in any hurry as you make your reverence – we British dancers are far too modest!'

'Thank you – oh, thank you!'

To her, Alice seemed very experienced and very confident, although she was feeling anything but confident. They kissed goodbye.

The days between Christmas and New Year passed slowly for Alice, who was working very hard at doing as little as possible, and fighting boredom. Every day she grew increasingly restless, and depressed. Life was being very hard on her, she felt; while she had experienced some good and exciting times, there had been too many lows. Missing the English Rose contest so narrowly. Missing performing Bluebirds with Alex in *The Sleeping Princess*. Not being able to continue the lucrative cabaret performances. It seemed that the fates were against her. She thought, too, of Charlie: even he had been taken from her.

130

These were dark days, when she felt as if she were in a void. She fought her feelings and tried to keep her spirits up, but it was not at all easy. However, she did as she was told and very slowly strength returned to her ankle. She could not wait to put on her pointe shoes again, and one afternoon in about the second week of January she tried – but unsuccessfully. Her ankle was still more swollen than she realised. This depressed her further, but in attempting to put on the shoe she noticed that at least her back was less stiff.

Her one escape was that she read a great deal. Madame had made it her duty to collect and exchange books from the nearby Chelsea library for her, and Alice wallowed in the latest novels, biographies and the history of dance – something that had always fascinated her. The books certainly assuaged her boredom.

Alice was anxious for Alex's news.

'It really is great here, Alice, although it is very cold, much colder than London . . . Basil is a dear and he is more than willing to welcome you . . . The house has central heating, and is so cosy, and there are four servants including a housekeeper and an English butler. Basil has some lovely paintings too. Now look, sweet one, I know I'm going to get work very soon – I think I made that clear in my last letter. When your pantomime is through, why don't you come over? It is exciting here, and from the discussions I've had with theatre people, it really looks as if we could dance together – if not in one show, there's always another on the horizon! Do write and tell me you'll come . . . *soon* Alice – *soon*! I'm going to class regularly too – no problem with that. There are one or two Russians teaching here who like Madame escaped from the revolution.

'Come, Alice, please come. Just let me know when . . .'

She smiled to herself as she finished reading the letter. As soon as she was well enough she would book her passage and go. Why not? It would be the experience of a lifetime, and very prestigious to have worked on Broadway – a good contrast to her appearances in *The Sleeping Princess*.

But she knew she would have to be entirely well again before she left. Later that day she asked Jamie when he thought she could start working again. He said that it would probably be in about two weeks, provided she was extremely careful. This was good news indeed, and she told Madame to expect her back to class in due course.

As far as Alex was concerned, he thought that she was in the pantomime and that the run would continue until the end of February. She sighed contentedly. She did not want him to discover that she was injured, so decided not to tell him for a few weeks that she had definitely made up her mind to join him and Basil.

She had written to him immediately after Christmas telling him of Elsie and her family's kindness to her and saying how much she had been delighted by his wonderful bouquet – most of which had adorned their flat – that she had made new friends with people in the cast and that her tutu was quite lovely (Daisy had described it to her in detail). Now, some two weeks later, she wrote again saying that she would think about coming over, but as she was enjoying the lively atmosphere of the pantomime she did not want to come to any definite decision yet about her next move. She would let him know one way or the other in a few weeks' time.

'Now, Alice, come here, face the barre, hold it with both hands.'
Alice did as she was told.
'I will support your stomach and your back as you do a *demi-plié*.'
It was not painful, but Alice felt very stiff and heavy.
'My darlink, you cannot do a full class today but I'll take you through the barre – that will be enough. Only lift your leg to forty-five degrees and stop if you feel any pain at all. You will be quite alright in a couple of weeks, providing you do not overdo things.'
Madame proved correct. Every day Alice made progress, and towards the end of February she felt strong enough to do a full class. She became her usual enthusiastic and lively self. She was getting increasingly excited about the prospect of Broadway, and on the last Saturday of February – which was the day she knew the pantomime closed – she wrote to Alex telling him she was coming, and that very soon she would cable him to let him know when she was arriving, and on what ship, so that he could meet her at the docks.

'Yes, madam, can I help you?'
'Can you tell me, please, when there are sailings to New York within the next two weeks, and the prices of the cabins?'
'First or second class, madam?'
All the while she had been nursing her injury Alice had been drawing on her reserves of cash, and knew she had to economise, so replied.
'Third, I'm afraid.'
'Well, madam, that will be ... The *Aquitania* sails on Wednesday the seventh, and the *Mauritania* on Wednesday the fourteenth.'
'Thank you. That will suit me very well. Please book me on the *Aquitania* on the seventh.'
'Certainly, madam.'
He ran his finger down a passenger list.
'Yes, we have a third class cabin for that sailing – though not a single cabin. You would share with one other young lady. Will that suit you?'
He had a somewhat supercilious expression, and Alice smiled in a successful attempt to disarm.
'Why, of course. Thank you. You will send me the tickets?'
'They will be in the post within three days, and you will be given a full

132

itinerary. The price of the ticket includes the third class boat train fare from . . .'

'Yes, I know, from Waterloo to Southampton.'

'Precisely, madam.'

Alice wrote out a cheque for the total amount – twenty-two pounds four shillings and sixpence. Delighted at having finalised her arrangements, she made her way back to Tryon Street. After class that day she decided she would start to sort out her wardrobe.

Picking up the expected letter, she was puzzled to see that it had the name of her bank printed on it. Puzzled, she tore open the envelope, to discover a formal and rather terse letter to which her cheque and a statement were attached.

'Dear Miss Townsend,

'We must regretfully inform you that there are insufficient funds in your account to honour the enclosed cheque. We suggest that you increase the level of your account and re-present the cheque. Please find enclosed a statement made up to three-thirty today.

'Yours faithfully . . .

Alice could not believe what she was reading. Hurriedly, she scanned her statement. The credit stood at eighteen pounds, five shillings and fourpence, some three pounds, nineteen shillings and two pence short of the price of her ticket.

She was devastated.

'I can't go! I can't go!'

She had already planned to meet Elsie that afternoon, to tell her of her plans and to say goodbye. It was too late to put off their arrangement. Over a cup of tea and biscuits in a Lyon's tea shop in Piccadilly, Alice tried to put a brave face on things.

'That's rotten luck, Alice. But even if you did have just enough money to go, you couldn't cross the Atlantic totally penniless. I'd lend you something if . . .'

'No, certainly not – I wouldn't hear of it. I'm just glad I've not yet cabled Alex to tell him when I was going to arrive. I was waiting to know the time of day from the itinerary . . . and now this.'

She started to cry, knowing that her financial situation was desperate. If she did not pass an audition soon she would have to try for a shop job.

Elsie stretched over the little table and put her hand on her friend's shoulder to comfort her. She was quiet for a moment, then said, 'Surely there must be ways to cross the Atlantic other than paying lots of money to do so?'

'Why – what do you mean? I can't swim across!'

'Why don't you see if you can get a job working on a liner? I don't know, cleaner, waitress, stewardess? Something like that? It might be possible. I bet there's an agency, somewhere.'

Alice wiped the tears from her eyes, which started to brighten at the suggestion.

That evening she found the address of Cunard's employment office in the telephone directory. She knew she must take action immediately. If there was no chance of getting some sort of a job on a liner to cross the Atlantic she was in deep trouble. Her money would only last out for another three weeks or so, and even if she passed an audition right away there would be several weeks of rehearsal which would more than likely be unpaid. She could not understand where so much money had gone, and she would have a telephone bill to pay before she left, not to mention gas and electricity. She knew she would have to put cash aside for all those.

Alice stepped through a heavy mahogany door. A middle-aged man looked up and smiled at her. Why did she want to work on liners? She said she had always wanted to travel, and that she had decided to change her career – she wouldn't mind becoming a trainee waitress, though she had some experience in hotel work, not true, but the lie was necessary.

He asked her what her present career was.

'I'm a dancer.'

'Oh, how interesting.'

He was quiet for a moment then said, 'Show me your legs.'

Alice was more than a little shocked, and asked him why that was necessary. Was she encountering Cunard's Freddie Bulstrode?

'I beg your pardon, young lady, but I have a job in mind that could appeal to you rather more than that of a waitress. During the evenings we have young ladies like yourself selling cigarettes and cigars from trays in the bars and ballrooms. They wear attractive, short dresses – rather like pretty stage costumes. I was wondering . . .'

'You were wondering if my legs were good enough to be shown to advantage in a very short dress?'

'Precisely.'

Alice stood up, moved back a couple of paces and lifted her skirt to below her suspenders.

'Now just turn around for me, please.'

Alice obeyed.

'Right, come and sit down. Yes, you will make an excellent cigarette girl – that's if you would care for it.'

'Yes, I would like that very much.'

'We will sign you up for a two year contract.'

This surprised Alice. She had other plans, but smiling she looked at the paper he put in front of her, and said, 'That will suit me very well. Thank you, I'm sure to enjoy the work. Where do I sign?'

'Just there.'

Alice went to her bag, and took out her pen. As she dotted the 'I' over her name it made a large blot.

'Oh dear, I'm so sorry!'

The man handed her a piece of blotting paper. As she screwed the top back onto her pen, she felt an ominous shiver run down her spine.

Chapter 17

'Right, Miss Townsend. Go along that corridor and down the stairs to E deck. There'll be a steward on duty, and he'll show you to staff cabin sixty-seven. You're sharing with the other cigarette girl.'

The purser smiled kindly at her. The crew were boarding for the sailing due at noon the following day.

Alice had tidied up her affairs in London and said goodbye to Madame and Joan, who wept. She had just managed to pay all her bills, and with four pounds, thirteen shillings and eightpence in her handbag she had travelled to Southampton to join the *Mauritania*.

She cast her eye along the deck. She imagined Alex in his smart clothes being shown to his first-class suite. She had to descend to the bowels of the liner to find what turned out to be a very cramped cabin, with no porthole. She had arrived before her colleague, and decided to take the top bunk. There was a small wardrobe and a high shelf where she assumed suitcases could be stored. The steward had told her that the women's bathroom was at the end of the corridor. Putting her heavy case down on the bunk she was about to open it when the narrow door opened.

'Hello, I'm Eileen.'

Alice returned the greeting, introduced herself, and asked Eileen how long she had been working as a cigarette girl.

'Several months now. It's not so bad. Sometimes the men passengers give tips, so smile, girl, smile – it'll do you no harm!'

'Well, I need the money.'

'Don't we all?' replied her room-mate, tossing and shaking her head so that her bobbed black, heavily permed hair bounced over her forehead.

Eileen asked Alice about herself. She just said that she had been a dancer, but that because of injury she had to give up and this was the nearest thing to show business she could aim for. Then she asked, 'What about our frocks?'

'The chief laundress'll bring them along before we sail. I should think that Amy's'll fit you – what are you, "small womens" or "womens"?'

'"Womens" – but they usually have to be taken in a bit because I'm slim.'

'Lucky you!' Eileen heaved her heavy bosom up and down. 'With my shape I'll never be fashionable, whereas you ... well, these new long-line fashions'll look lovely on you – and your beads will always hang straight.'

Her long string of mock amber beads insisted on falling inside the line of her breasts, which did look rather odd. Try as she might, they would not hang gracefully.

'Don't worry,' she went on, 'that laundress is a dab hand with her needle – she'll make it fit okay.'

Alice asked Eileen if she minded having the lower bunk. No, she said she preferred it as she had no head for heights. They settled in and went to the staff canteen for six o'clock supper.

Their dresses appeared and Alice's needed some small adjustments. When they had been made she looked at herself in the long mirror which was fixed to the back of the tiny cabin's door. Yes, it was short – well, above her knees. It was black cotton satin, and she had a very frilly white lace apron and matching cap, which was worn prettily low on her forehead. There was a stiff taffeta sash that sat on the dropped waistline of the dress. Eileen tied the sash for her, making a large bow at the back. They were provided with long black 'opera hose' – ordinary length stockings might have revealed white flesh and suspenders, unsuitable for Cunard. That sort of thing belonged to cabarets in Berlin and Paris, Eileen said.

At noon the next day, passengers aboard, the tug turned the huge liner to port, moving her slowly towards the River Test then down the narrow channel. From the portholes of the staff canteen, Alice watched as the dock gradually slipped into the distance. Soon she could see the dockside no longer; she really was on her way to join Alex and his new friends.

'Now we have to do the stock.'

Eileen took her to a small room behind the purser's office. He unlocked it, and they sorted out a variety of packets of cigarettes and singly packed cigars, which they placed in large trays with wide webbing straps to hang around their necks. When they had finished, the purser locked the stock away again. They would return at nine o'clock that evening, when they would be given a float in both English and American currency.

'If you take my advice, you'll rest now. Every night is long and hard on our feet. We're not allowed to leave the bars or the ballrooms until all the passengers have gone to bed. We do the rounds of the first-class ballroom, the cocktail bars, then the second-class, and finally the third-class pub and dance hall. Then we start all over again. We'll be among the last to go to bed. Only the barmen work later – they've more clearing up to do. And look – do you understand dollars?'

'No, actually, one dollar's worth four shillings, isn't it?'

'Yes, but before we start I'll show you the coins and how to distinguish the difference between a one dollar and a five- or even ten-dollar note. You have to be careful – they don't look that different.'

'Thanks a lot, Eileen. And I will come and rest, but as this is my first trip I'd really like to go on deck and watch the coast for a while.'

'Well, don't go into the first-class part of the ship – that's not allowed when we're off duty. There're two areas where we can go – one in the open and the other with glass. Go and get to know some of the rest of the crew. They're a nice lot, on the whole.'

It was cold in the open, and no-one else was braving the very fresh almost gale force March wind. Alice was quite alone.

She watched the distant coastline as the liner swept down the channel, and then passed outside the Eddystone lighthouse – inland was Plymouth, the Hoe, and her grandparents' house, where she used to spend summer days with them and her parents when she was a little girl and Philip was tiny. Her thoughts turned to her mother and father. By now they would have read her short letter telling them that she was going to spend some time in New York and giving them Basil's address. In spite of everything she felt that they should know she had left the country.

After supper – the food was good but rather heavy, and she had to wait while Eileen had a third helping of apple pie and cream – they changed into their uniforms and collected the stock, then Eileen said, 'We'll work together tonight, so you know exactly what to do. I'll lead the way.'

Eileen made her entrance into the first-class ballroom as bold as brass, as if she were a prima donna. Seductively swinging her hips, she walked around the edge of the dance area, smiling down on the passengers who were sitting drinking and listening to the band. Alice followed her, carefully dodging the few dancing couples.

'Miss – I say, Miss – a packet of Rothman's, please! Golly, not seen you before!'

A bespectacled young man with large bulging eyes gazed up at her from his seat.

'Er . . . no, this is my first trip.'

'Jolly good, jolly good – it's my ninth! I'm Reggie, don't y'know. What's your name?'

She told him, and handed him the twenty Rothman's. An elderly gent called her over, and she sold him a cigar. Glancing across the ballroom to Eileen she saw that she was cutting off the end of a cigar for a man whose size caused him to spill over the edge of his chair. She watched him pay and when Eileen handed him his change he gave it back to her. He beckoned her down to his level and said something in her ear. She laughed and nodded.

The band was playing a selection from *Lilac Time*, a recent West End show, then to please the American passengers quite suddenly the music changed to the latest selection of Al Jolson numbers. This brought a great many more couples onto the floor. The two cigarette girls moved off to 'do' the cocktail bar and lounges, then descended to the second and eventually the third class. Later they returned to the ballroom.

*

138

It was almost three o'clock when they retired for the night.

Alice was weary, and the weight of her tray for so long had caused pain to flare up in her back. All she wanted was a good long sleep.

'Look, I'm not ready for bed yet, Alice – I'm going to see some friends. I won't disturb you when I come in.'

'I don't think that'll be possible! See you in the morning.'

Alice undressed, hung up her uniform, went to the communal bathroom and returning to her bunk fell into a deep sleep.

With no porthole to let in the daylight, the cabin was dark, and it was impossible to decide what the time was when she awoke, so she put on a low powered light over her bunk, and getting down looked at the clock. It was ten-thirty. She was amazed that she had slept so long. To her surprise she discovered that Eileen's bunk had not been slept in. So Eileen either had a boyfriend on board, or . . . then she remembered how she had seen her whispering to the fat man. She wondered, but put the thoughts out of her mind.

Because they worked such late hours, the cigarette girls were under no obligation to be up at a certain time. But the staff breakfasts had long since finished, and Alice knew she would get no food until the first luncheon service at noon – the restaurant staff had their lunch earlier, but it was forbidden for anyone else to enter the canteen while the waiters and kitchen staff were eating.

She pulled on her wrap to go to the bathroom. The men's bathroom was at the other end of the corridor. As she opened her door a gentle sway of the ship caught her slightly off balance and she fell against a young man who was obviously returning from making his ablutions.

Alice apologised.

'Oh, that's alright.'

She noticed his delightful smile, deeply waving pale brown hair and dark brown eyes.

'You must be another night owl!'

'Why, yes, I suppose you could say that.' She pulled her wrap around herself more tightly as she spoke. Still rather sleepy and not looking her best, she was quite unprepared for such an encounter.

'You're the new cigarette girl, aren't you?'

'Why, yes,' she repeated.

His face seemed vaguely familiar, then she remembered. 'And you are the saxophone player in the dance band, aren't you?'

'Right first time! That's very observant of you.'

'But you're observant too – to recognise me – my uniform . . .'

'Your uniform is very pretty; and you see, the bandstand is a perfect place from which to study people. After all, the music's not that difficult to cope with, and there are always rests while the other chaps do their solos! So one learns a lot. I watched you selling your cigarettes and cigars last night – you work with such style!'

139

Alice was totally charmed by the delightful chap. By now the ship had started to roll quite noticeably. She staggered slightly, and grabbed a rail which ran the length of the passage.

'Look, I say, are you alright? You don't look like the type to lose your balance that easily.'

'There's many a true word spoken in jest,' she replied tantalisingly. 'But excuse me, I must go and have a bath.'

'Of course, but then why don't you come to the band room? We make our own tea and coffee, as none of us is ever up in time for staff breakfast. And there may be something to eat – our lot usually get hold of some pastries and doughnuts made for the passengers.'

Alice thanked him. He told her where the band room was, and then said, 'By the way I don't know your name!'

She introduced herself and asked his.

'Ben Waterman – at your service, madam!'

This made her laugh. They parted and met up again half an hour later in the untidy band room with its piles of music, old upright piano, tables with over-full ashtrays, armchairs that had obviously once been the pride and joy of some previous first-class lounge, and a trolley laden with pots of tea, coffee, milk, juice and pastries. In the far corner the pianist and a trumpet player were working on a new arrangement, otherwise the room was deserted apart from Alice's new friend, who greeted her warmly.

'I feel much more civilised now, I'm sorry you caught me looking such a mess.'

'You looked lovely, Alice – er, may I call you Alice?'

She smiled and replied, 'Yes, if you don't mind my calling you Ben.'

He poured her some coffee and brought her a pastry.

'Now tell me all. How come you're working for Cunard?'

She briefly told him her story. She mentioned nothing about Alex or the break with her family, but told him about *Chu Chin Chow* and the other major events in her life, ending with how she had had to sacrifice her pantomime contract and give up dancing because of her injury.

'You will have to be careful carrying that heavy tray.'

'Yes, I know. I must say I felt a bit of pain last night.'

'And you're sharing with Eileen. How are you getting on with her?'

'She's very friendly . . .'

'But?'

'Oh, I think she has a good . . . social life.'

Alice did not want to start any scandal.

'You can say that again! High spirited, to say the least! But coming back to you, I knew there was something about you that was . . . different. It doesn't surprise me in the least that you are a ballerina and an actress. It's the way you move, and the way you sell those cigarettes – you do it beautifully! How sad that you've had to give up. You must have worked for years to achieve so much.'

'Yes, I did, but I've just to resign myself to this – for a while at least – though I must admit I did rather enjoy my first night. It was very amusing to come into contact with so many different types of people, and in a way which is totally new to me! I've signed a two-year contact – I believe that's usual. But what about you?'

'As you know, I'm a member of the ship's band. It's fun. This is my second year. But I'll not be staying for much more than another year or so. I want to have my own dance band in due course.'

He went on to say that he was also a classical woodwind player, having studied oboe and clarinet at the Royal Academy of Music in London – and he 'tinkered' on the piano a bit, jazz mostly.

Alice hadn't enjoyed herself so much for a long time. The pastries – she had two – were delicious. It appeared there was a Danish chef on board whose job was solely to make them. By the time they had finished, she knew quite a lot about Ben Waterman. As he was free until a band call at noon, they took a walk along the staff's protected walkway. She glanced up at him. His tall, slim figure, warm, friendly smile and delightful sense of humour were appealing. He felt her looking at him, and from his six feet looked down at her. They silently smiled at each other.

All too soon they had to part. Ben said he would look out for her that evening. She left him, and went to the large staff room to read. It was lunch time, but having been greedy with the pastries she was not hungry. En route she called in at the cabin, to find Eileen reclining on her bunk.

'Hello!'

'Oh, Hello – I'm exhausted.'

'That doesn't surprise me. Did you have fun?'

'No, it was awful, but . . . Why not? He's a stinking rich American – and I need the money.'

'Yes, well, *I* need money too, but . . .'

'Yes, but not as much as me!'

'How do you know?'

'Look, Alice, love, can I trust you?'

'Of course – I'm not one to blab, honestly.'

'Well, you see, I've got a kid back in Southampton – my Ma's bringing him up. Soon he'll start school, and I want him to go to a proper one, so I'm saving up . . .'

Alice had come across this situation before, so she was surprised but not shocked. But the girl she had known in the chorus of *Chu Chin Chow* had not indulged in prostitution.

'Eileen,' she said sympathetically, 'I'm so sorry – and I do understand. But do take care of yourself, and don't take risks. I don't suppose you want to get pregnant again – or pick up some nasty infection.'

'No, I don't. I've had good professional advice, not that you'd want to know about that. I did love my little Davey's father. You're really nice, Alice. I thought you might be a bit of a snob at first. Look, don't tell a soul about any of this, will you? I have to be very careful how I work, and if I were found out I'd be dismissed at once – I'd never get another job on a liner.'

Alice was careful not to mention that Eileen already had quite a reputation; anyway, obviously no-one suspected the real explanation.

Alice settled down to the regular routine of the voyage. Late up every morning, and extremely late to bed every night.

One evening there was to be a recital by a well-known opera singer, travelling as a guest of Cunard and about to make her debut at the Metropolitan Opera House in New York. The band had a longer break than usual and Alice, who had told Eileen about her new association with Ben and felt she could ask a favour of her, asked if she could allow her an hour or so while the concert was on, so that she could meet him with a little more time to talk. Alice had been snatching as many moments with Ben as possible during the day, when neither of them were working, but his time was at more of a premium than hers because he had quite a number of band calls. Eileen said that as most of the first-class passengers would be at the concert, she could easily cover for the other parts of the ship.

They met in the area partitioned off for staff at the stern. It was a starry night and a bright crescent moon was shining. The sea was calm, but it was far too cold to be on an outside deck. They approached the part of the walkway protected from the elements by glass.

'Mid-Atlantic is never very warm at night, and decidedly cold in early March,' Ben said.

But then his tone became gentler, quieter, and taking on the glow of a summer sunset.

'Alice, I've never met anyone quite like you. It's such a pity that you can't dance any more – but perhaps later on you'll have the chance to become a famous actress.'

'Yes, that's what I'm hoping. I can probably live inexpensively mostly on board for the coming two years, then I hope to have saved up enough money to go to drama school.'

She hated telling him such an untruth, but was unable to say anything else.

'I think that's a good idea. Yes, you must do just that. But you're beautiful ... so beautiful ... different, and yes, original ...'

As he spoke he turned Alice towards him and, putting his arms gently around her waist, tenderly kissed her forehead.

She relaxed into the warm, affectionate gesture, and enjoyed the sensation of his lips, which she didn't want to end; but after a meaningful silence, she said light-heartedly, 'I expect you have at least one girlfriend in Southampton, and maybe another in London or New York ...'

'No, don't say that. Put it out of your mind. It's simply not true. Some of the blokes do – and some, I admit, flatter and cheer up rich old lady passengers. But that's not for me, it really isn't. You're different ... Haven't I said that before?'

'Yes, you have.'

They strolled on, hand in hand, until they came to the point with a clear view of the stern of the ship. Through the glass they could see foam stretching from the stern back into the distance. In spite of being wintry, the scene had a romance and magic of its own. As they leant over a protective rail they noticed snow crystals appear and almost immediately melt as they contacted the glass. Two large ones, so big that it was easy to see their beautiful symmetrical pattern, came together as they touched the glass.

'Look at that! Aren't they beautiful – I've never seen such large snowflakes!' exclaimed Alice.

'They're not like you and me, though, Alice – we've come together, but we're not going to melt away into nothingness. I know we're going to be good friends.' Ben paused, and then very nervously suggested, 'Or even more? I'm hoping that perhaps we can melt together in due course.'

It had been a long time since Alice felt the warmth of romance – far too long – and she knew that now she must not allow it take over, though she knew that under different circumstances there could have been a bond between them. Reluctantly she replied, 'Yes, friends, or perhaps . . .'

'Even more?' he suggested again.

She silently nodded.

He took her in his arms and they kissed long, hard and passionately.

She wanted to cry out, 'Ben, this is awful. It's beautiful but awful!' But she knew that she must keep quiet. Fate was playing a powerful part in their lives and that which was near to love at first sight must be curtailed.

She sighed.

'For a long time I've put romance right out of my life. I've just worked hard and been friendly with men and women.'

'Dear, dear Alice, I had a broken engagement before I got this job. That's why I took it in the first place. Since then, nothing but work – just like you. But now we can spend so much time together. Oh, this coming summer's going to be such fun! We'll have days off in New York, maybe go to a show or to photoplays – if you'd like that. And when my contract ends, who knows . . .'

Setting her real feelings aside, she put on a cheerful tone, and taking him by the arm as if he were Alex, she added,

'And now, Benjamin Waterman, Esquire, will you kindly escort me to my front door, please? I have to change back into my uniform, I expect the singer will soon be finishing. And you'll have to be back on the bandstand.'

'I'll wink at you!'

'Don't you dare make me laugh, especially when I'm selling to those rich passengers!'

They walked smartly and in step, in an almost childish, friendly manner to the door of her cabin.

In spite of the fact it was only ten-thirty and they both had hours of work ahead of them, the temptation of a lingering goodnight kiss was considerable. He attempted merely to give her a light kiss on the cheek. But the electrifying touch proved too much for either of them. Their lips met, and resistance crumbled.

For the first time in her life Alice desperately wanted more – a lot more. She longed to ask him in. But she knew that she must not allow herself to be overwhelmed by her feelings, and anyway time was against them – Eileen might well be in there putting on yet another coat of mascara to add to her usual several layers.

Thursday morning was the last full day at sea. Eileen was for once sound asleep in her bunk and Alice climbed down, careful not to disturb her. She went along to bath, then did her face and, as she had done on every morning of the voyage, joined Ben in the band room for coffee and pastries.

Smiling and warm-hearted as ever, he greeted her. 'Look, I've quite a lot to do today. There's that wretched tea-dance this afternoon, and tonight the informal dance will keep us working hard. But I'm sure we can have some fun, too.'

'Well, let's not waste a moment – let's take a turn on the staff deck. I could do with some fresh air. How everyone smokes!'

'And whose fault is that, I ask myself!'

She gave him a little good-natured push. After their coffee and pastries they went to the deck. Alice was doing her utmost to keep the atmosphere as light and unemotional as possible. How was she going to tell him that they would not be sharing future Atlantic crossings? That there was no hope for their budding romance, which she wanted as much as she knew he did? The situation was becoming intolerable – worse with every passing hour. Tomorrow, by midday, they would be in New York, and have to go their separate ways. But he was blithely happy and unaware of what was tearing her apart. Taking her hand he said, 'Look, I always get a day pass from the Purser. Staff can, you know. Why don't we go ashore as soon as possible? I'll take you somewhere smart for lunch – I can afford it!'

Would that make things easier or harder, she wondered. It might be just a little easier to talk in some pleasant restaurant over lunch. Or should she simply give him the slip? She knew about the passes, and in any case had planned to get one. But now she must reply to Ben's suggestion.

'Well, what about it? Alice, wake up, dear – you're day dreaming!'

'Oh, I'm so sorry. Yes, I was miles away . . . That really would be lovely – I can't wait to see something of New York.'

'We'll get to know it quite well in due course.'

They went for their walk, and talked about his music, and her shows, all the time realising their attraction was increasing in leaps and bounds. The lunch hour came and went. They were only aware of each other. For long periods of time they were just silent, simply looking at each other. They held hands. At three that afternoon they had to part.

Now Alice had to tackle the problem of getting her case ashore. Several times during the voyage she had been greeted kindly by, and had a few short conversations with, an elderly American woman who was travelling alone. She looked rather frail. In the course of conversation, Alice had asked her how she liked her suite, and where it was. The woman had said that it was quite lovely – on B deck, number three on the port side. This was Alice's salvation. She went to the Purser's office and asked for luggage labels, saying that the old lady had lost hers, and that she would take them to her. The Purser's assistant was only too pleased not to be bothered with any extra tasks, and gave her the directions to the suite. Alice retired to her cabin, and put the woman's details on the labels. She knew that cases must be outside the suites by six o'clock that evening, to be picked up by the porters ready to be unloaded early the following morning.

The corridor was quiet as she staggered to a lift – one she was not supposed to use. She rang for it, and smilingly told the attendant she had special permission from the Purser to use the lift, as she was doing some work for a first-class passenger. She left the case outside the correct suite, where three others were already in position.

She could only exchange smiles with Ben during the tea dance, and saw him very briefly between then and the time when they were both on duty again for the last evening at sea. Half-way through the evening, when Alice returned to the first class ballroom for the second time, he winked at her, nodded to the band leader and they struck up 'You Made Me Love You' – a very popular song. Her first reaction was to smile happily, but she had to turn away because she felt her eyes fill with tears, knowing the situation she must face the next day. How to tell him was becoming an increasing problem for her. Nevertheless, as the piece ended she managed to wave to the band and mouth a big thank-you to the leader and the rest of the boys, who responded with winks and nudges to Ben. She beat a fast and tearful retreat to second class.

The evening ended much earlier than usual. Everyone was keen to get back to their staterooms and have an early night before going ashore the following morning.

Alice had arranged with Ben to have some light food in the canteen when they were both free. She went back to the cabin to change into the pretty suit she had decided to wear the following morning – all her other clothes, apart from her night things, were in her case. She knew that the blouse she had kept out of her luggage would be suitable for the grand lunch she had been promised, and now for their last hours on board she wanted to look good and feel good.

Eileen was in their cabin, fiercely brushing her frizzy hair.

'Look, love, I'll be working tonight – and he's taking me out tomorrow in the Big Apple, so I've got a pass, too. I think he's quite smitten. I've got him to promise to buy me a new outfit in Macy's. So you'll have this place to yourself tonight.'

She dug Alice in the ribs as she spoke and breezed out leaving a trail of expensive perfume in her wake.

After they had eaten, Alice and Ben took their usual walk around C deck to look at the sea and the growing moon, and after about half an hour of delightful closeness they came back to her little cabin door.

He stepped near to kiss her goodnight. As he did so she was overcome with a burning passion for him. She knew that their time together was running out fast, but that they still had several hours. She also knew that if they did not make love that night she would regret it always.

After a longer deeper and more passionate kiss she had ever experienced she said, 'Ben, I love you . . . I want you so very, very much, please . . .'

'Alice, darling . . .'

They went into the cabin together, and he closed the door behind them.

Chapter 18

When Alice awoke the following morning Ben had already left her. She smiled happily to herself. In the hours they had spent together she had achieved a great deal of sexual satisfaction, and the night was something she would never forget. Knowing that it was not to be repeated was heartrending, but she had to follow her ambition.

Ben had said that they must go on deck to watch the New York skyline appear out of the morning mist, and to see the Statue of Liberty. She terribly wanted to spend the day with him, but knew that Alex and his friend would be waiting for her at the terminal, and that she would probably have to say goodbye to Ben there and then, without having that special lunch he had planned. But over coffee in the staff canteen, he said, 'We leave the ship this morning by a staff gangway on C deck – it's there that they hand out the day passes. We show them to the customs men and simply walk through – we don't have to go near the hoards of passengers fighting over their luggage.

Alice was very relieved. She knew that after her eventual farewell from Ben she could take a taxi to where Basil lived, and say, quite honestly, that she had simply missed him and Alex at the terminal.

'Get your coat – we're going on deck. Look – there she is, welcoming my Alice for the first time!'

Ben stood Alice in front of him, putting his hands on her shoulders and protecting her from the strong wind.

'She's lovely, heaps bigger than I expected.'

He produced a little Vest Pocket Kodak camera.

'I want to take a picture of you, to remind us of this special moment on a very special crossing.'

Ben moved back, and after one or two people had pushed by them he lined up Alice in the view-finder with the Statue of Liberty in the background. She posed, trying hard to smile. After the shutter clicked she moved.

'No, stay there, I'll take a couple more. We'll get them developed in Southampton on the next turnaround.'

It was extremely difficult to keep smiling, but Alice's acting ability was helping her. The ship made her way up the Hudson River, giving Alice a good opportunity to see several important landmarks. Ben pointed out the Woolworth Building – the tallest in the world – and she was able to catch glimpses straight down street after street as the ship made its way, now with tugs, to the Cunard terminal.

Eventually *Mauritania* was alongside. Gangways were put in place and they could see the passengers starting to go ashore.

After a while Ben said, 'Come on, let's go – we don't want to waste a moment. We'll have to be back by six.'

He led the way. Soon Alice had set foot on American soil. As she did so she thought, if only we'd not met and fallen in love. Why, oh why? The timing couldn't have been worse! If it hadn't happened I would have been so thrilled to have arrived here after such difficulties – far, far worse difficulties than ever Alex could imagine.

'Welcome to New York!'

Ben, bursting with enthusiasm and happiness, took Alice's arm as they walked into a shed where their passes were examined. The customs man was friendly to Ben, who introduced Alice.

'My, oh my, you're sure a right pretty English rose!' was the gruff New Yorker's cheery greeting.

'We'll take a taxi. I've got it all worked out!'

'You're being very masterful today, Mr Waterman!'

'Oh, Alice, darling, – after last night all I want to do is to love and take care of you – and for us to enjoy life as much as possible.'

She looked up at him and smiled warmly. Feeling tears welling up in her eyes she reached for her hanky and pretended she was stopping a sneeze.

'Look, there's a taxi!'

He hailed the yellow cab and told the driver where he wanted to go.

In spite of her emotional turmoil, Alice was excited to be in New York, and eagerly looked out of the window to see everything possible.

Leaving the terminal the driver turned the car to the left, then they crossed some five streets and turned right.

'We're now on Forty-fourth Street, West. I'm taking you to a restaurant which is becoming more and more popular since it opened almost two years ago. It's called Sardi's – it's where all the movie people and Broadway stage folk eat – I think you'll like it.'

'It sounds marvellous!'

'Only the best is good enough for you, darling.'

He put his arm around her and kissed her lightly on the mouth.

'Here you are, sir.'

The restaurant was full of lunchtime diners. The chatter was noisy, and had a distinctly different sound than Alice was used to. It was rather dark inside, with mahogany panelling and a shining wood floor which set off the immaculate white table linen and fine cutlery and glassware. Ben asked if there was a table.

A plump, jovial head waiter grinned and looking at Alice, smiled even more broadly.

'Well, you two. English, eh? In that case we must fit you in somewhere. Follow me, please.'

They settled at their table, enjoying the incisively cruel caricatures of famous Broadway stars that decorated the walls.

They ordered steaks – 'broiled' rather than 'grilled' – and a green salad, accompanied by deliciously refreshing lemonade. Ben reminded her that she was now in the land of prohibition, and that it was illegal to sell or be seen taking any intoxicating liquor.

'That's why everyone went to bed early last night. We were in American territorial waters, and the alcohol had to be sealed until we're on the return trip.'

Alice knew about all that, but had forgotten – other more pressing problems were on her mind. They decided on some chocolate icecream for dessert.

Ben ordered coffee. Smiling he took her hand on the table.

'Enjoy that?'

'What do you think? It was delicious. Thank you so much, Ben.' She paused. 'In fact, thank you for everything. I'll never forget last night and . . . well, all this.'

'But, Alice, this is only the beginning. We've so much to look forward to! This is just what we could call a . . . a kick-start!'

He looked at her as he was speaking. She turned her head, and at once he noticed a tear running down her cheek.

'What's all this? Why are you crying? Tears of happiness? Silly girl! But then, why not, Alice dearest? That's so sweet, bless you!'

She looked at him across the table and gripping his hand, shook her head.

'No, *not* tears of happiness? Alice, what's wrong? Oh no! I say, you're not married, or anything like that, are you?'

Now audibly sobbing, she shook her head again.

'Then whatever's wrong?'

'This is dreadful, dreadful. Here we are, just having fallen in love and I . . . I . . .'

His expression was agonizing to see.

'Go on, my darling, please tell me.'

'I . . . can't go on loving you. I'm not coming back on the ship tonight. I'm staying here, in New York . . .'

'But why, for heaven's sake? You've just got this job . . . Tell me everything. Perhaps I can help, maybe you'll be able to come back with me.'

'No, Ben, I can't.'

After yet more tears, and taking quite a while to compose herself, the broken-hearted Alice told her story.

'. . . and so, you see, because I had so little money the only way I could get

149

here was to take a job then jump ship. Ben, I didn't know we were going to . . .'

'No, of course you didn't. And you say that Alex and Basil will have come to meet you?'

'Yes, I'm sure they will – I'm just going to say that we missed each other. I'll be alright as soon as I get to Basil's house.'

'Oh, yes, you'll be alright then . . . God, Alice . . .'

Ben was both upset and angry, but managed to compose himself.

'I'm sorry, Alice. As you say, it's not your fault. But I can't take it in. You really mean it's goodbye?'

'Yes, very soon, when you have to go back to the ship. Ben, much as I know I love you, I must make my career work – for me and for Alex. Can you understand that?'

'Of course I can.'

He spoke bravely, but Alice saw he was biting his lip, and that his eyes were filling with tears.

'Thank you. And I really am sorry that I lied to you about having to give up dancing because of my injuries. Yes, I was injured, that's absolutely true, but well . . . you know what's happened.'

'Let's get out of here. We'll take a taxi to Central Park and walk for a while, then I'll have to get back . . .'

'Oh, Ben, *don't* – it's going to be awful.'

The walk in the park cleared their minds. They clung to each other, often walking for several minutes in complete silence. Then they would both speak at once, realising that they had to bow to the fate which had dealt them this cruel blow.

Eventually, the practical aspects of the situation had to be sorted.

'We – er, *I* – have to be back on board by six. Where shall we say goodbye?'

'Oh, Ben darling! But yes, we do have to face up to that . . . Well, my case will be in the passengers' arrival hall, and I must collect it. That is, if the old lady whose ticket is on it has actually noticed it's not hers, and left it behind. If she hasn't, I'm in trouble . . .' She smiled wryly. 'Anyway, I have to go back there.'

By now it was getting much colder. The day had been fine, with the merest hint of early spring in the air. The sun had poured a little warmth on them as they walked, but now it had disappeared behind some thick clouds. It was just after five. The evening traffic was getting thicker.

'Darling Alice, I don't think we can stay here very much longer.'

He led her to a seat, and for a while they sat locked in each other's arms, kissing deeply and passionately, their tears mingling on each other's cheeks.

Wiping their faces, they walked out onto Fifth Avenue and took a cab back to the terminal.

The place was cold and bleak, the grey cement floor and dreary woodwork unwelcoming, though the passengers' arrival hall was far more comfortable, rich in mahogany, with leather seating.

They went up to the counter, where Alice asked for her first-class passenger friend's suitcase. Her elderly companion had mistakenly forgotten to claim it earlier that day, she smiled to the clerk. He disappeared and soon returned with it. As she turned he pulled down a blind. Hers was the last case to be collected from this particular crossing, and the gesture signalled to Alice the end of the voyage and the end of her brief but wonderful relationship with Ben. Now they had to face up to their farewell.

He had told the taxi to wait. Taking the case from Alice, he put it in the cab. They returned to the arrival hall and sat on a leather settee.

'Darling, this is it, isn't it?'

'Yes, I'm afraid so.'

She could hardly speak for sobbing.

'It would be lovely to keep in touch, but . . .'

'No, you're right,' he replied, 'let's stick to what we said earlier. Our lives are going to be so different. Alice, I know that you'll be famous – whether as a dancer or an actress I don't know, but I'm sure you're destined for great things and, darling, I've been thinking, I want to remember you smiling, laughing and having fun. Then, when you're famous and I'm very old, my grandchildren will ask me what was the happiest moment of my life; and I'll say, "Well, you know, once upon a time there was a beautiful young English dancer and actress. I fell instantly, madly in love with her when we were crossing the Atlantic in March, nineteen-twenty-three. She had to leave me to become rich and famous, and at the end of the voyage she went out of my life. I know she loved me too, but that love was not to be. I've never forgotten her." That's what I'll tell my grandchildren, Alice. Remember me too, won't you?'

'Of course I will, dearest, dearest Ben.'

They stood up and locked in each other's arms, exchanged one long last parting kiss. Then they walked to the taxi.

'Don't look out of the back window, Alice – I couldn't bear that.'

'I won't, I promise.'

Standing by the side of the car he kissed her on the forehead. She got in. Heartbroken, he turned and walked towards the terminal and the ship.

The driver turned on the engine.

'Where to, ma'am?'

Alice did not hear him. He repeated the question.

'Oh, I'm sorry – East Eighty-sixth Street – number twenty-one Henderson Place, please.'

The taxi pulled up abruptly, causing Alice to lurch forward in her seat and awaken her from her distressing thoughts. The driver put her case on the pavement. Alice paid him, and looked up at the large red brick house. She could see a light on in one of the rooms below street level.

She pulled on the bell chain, causing a censorious sounding bell to clang inside the front door. She waited for about a minute, becoming somewhat more lighthearted, knowing that soon she would be re-united with Alex.

Eventually the heavy front door creaked open. A cadaverous man in formal clothes greeted her.

'Yes, young lady, what can I do for you?'

'I'm Alice Townsend, Mr McIntyre's friend from London. He and Mr Cavanagh are expecting me. I'm sorry – I think I probably missed them earlier today at the terminal.'

The man was silent for a moment.

'Miss Townsend, there must surely be some mistake. Mr Cavanagh and Mr McIntyre left for Monte Carlo just ten days ago. They gave me no instructions to expect you.'

Chapter 19

'But I . . . I . . . don't understand. Believe me, I am expected.'

The man, who Alice in all her confusion realised was the butler, looked sympathetically at her.

'Well, they said nothing, I assure you. I would of course have prepared rooms had I been given the necessary instructions. But as it is . . .'

'I wrote to Alex – I mean Mr McIntyre – that I would come, and then, when I had been able to book my passage, I sent a cable. I sent it just before I sailed. It should have arrived about five days ago.'

'Come into the hall a moment, Miss Townsend.'

Alice was grateful to step out of the dark and now very wet evening.

The butler turned to a silver salver which stood on an antique chest in the large open hall. There were numerous letters piled on it.

She did not want to appear too obviously inquisitive, but was extremely anxious. From her position a few feet away she saw the cable.

'Look, that's it.'

He looked down at her over his half-spectacles.

'I know it's the one I sent.'

He picked it up, examined it, and hesitantly said, 'I suppose it could be.'

'My letter to Mr McIntyre's probably on the tray as well.'

Again she recognised the envelope before he did.

'Yes, that's my writing, and see – the envelope has a British stamp. Oh dear, I don't know what to do. I just can't believe . . .'

'I fully sympathize, Miss Townsend, but I do not see how I can help you. I do remember hearing Mr Cavanagh and Mr McIntyre making their plans. It seems that the Russian Ballet is appearing in Monte Carlo for several months. Mr Cavanagh dislikes the winter, and although it will soon be over, he was keen to get away. They will have been in the Mediterranean for two days by now.'

Alice knew she faced immeasurable difficulties.

'I've nowhere to go,' she said, more calmly than she felt. 'Perhaps you could advise me.'

He was silent for a moment. He could not allow her to stay at his master's residence without instructions. He glanced down at her worn suitcase. It was obvious that he could not recommend the Waldorf Astoria.

'Without Mr Cavanagh's permission I cannot allow you to stay here, that's for sure. But there is an hotel not far away. Shall I call you a taxi?'

'No, I'll walk, if it's not too far.'

'Turn right when you leave the house. At the end of this street you will find yourself in First Avenue. Turn left, and you'll find the Marco Polo hotel on the corner of Eighty-fourth Street. I think they'll find you a room for the night. It's a simple place, but quite clean and safe. A young lady like you must be careful in New York.'

She thanked him. He opened the door, and picking up her case she walked out into the wet, squally night, the streetlamps and lights from the huge, beautiful houses making bright reflected patches on the black pavements.

Carrying her case, which seemed to become heavier as she trudged with dejected steps in the direction the butler had suggested, she realised she was more alone, more unhappy and more worried than she had ever been in her life. It was unbearable that Alex, who had so encouraged her to cross the Atlantic, had left before her letter arrived. How *could* he do something like that after encouraging her to come? She felt angry, then, as she recalled the butler mentioning the Russian ballet, she wondered if perhaps Basil was hoping to influence Sergei to employ Alex. Yes, that was probably what they had in mind. Knowing how much Alex wanted to dance with the company again, she could only forgive him. But uncharacteristic jealousy crept up on her. Why, oh why, had Alex not suggested that they wait until they had heard from her? After all, he knew how much she wanted to re-join the company, too. But then, Basil and Alex were lovers. And Basil was fed up with the winter. He would always favour Alex, and though he might tolerate women, she was obviously not going to be allowed to intrude on their relationship or any plans that Basil cared to make.

She found the hotel easily. A small illuminated sign over a discreet entrance informed her that the Marco Polo hotel charged THREE DOLLARS A NITE SINGLE ROOM – RUNNING WATER AND STEAM HEAT.

Well, she must sleep somewhere that night, even if she had very little money, so she cautiously walked up three steps to the tiny reception area.

'Yes, Ma'am – what can I do for you?'

Looking up from his comic, the man behind the desk smiled cheerfully at the dejected Alice.

'Have you a room, for tonight, please?'

'Are you alone, or do you have some man waiting to join you?'

Alice was indignant.

'No, I don't have any man. I am quite alone.'

The man eyed her up and down.

'Any booze on you?'

'No, certainly not. I don't want to break the law.' Pulling herself up to her fullest height she added, 'I'm British.'

154

'Oh yeah? I could tell you didn' come from round these parts.'

He had a back room on the fourth floor – nice and quiet – and called in a fog-horn of a voice, 'Matty, come here, right now.'

Almost at once a fat youngish woman appeared. The man instructed her to take Alice's case to the elevator and show her to room four-two-one. Alice turned to go, but he called her back.

'Pay now, if you please, Ma'am.'

Alice went to her bag and took out the necessary dollars, making sure she only gave him singles, and not one of her two, precious ten-dollar notes.

They stepped out of the tiny elevator and along a corridor. Matty unlocked and opened a door which led into a small room with a welcoming bed and wash-basin in the corner.

'Thanks a lot.'

The woman did not turn to leave. Alice realised she wanted a tip. Reluctantly, she gave her ten cents.

Alone, she slumped down on the bed. The misery of her situation caught up with her even more. She could be back on board ship, enjoying the love that she and Ben had shared during the last two or three days. Should she return to the ship? It was not due to sail until the morning.

At that moment it seemed the best option. While she would be sacrificing her ambitions, she would have love – the love of an adoring man. It was tempting. And after all, the small experience she had of being a cigarette girl had not been unpleasant, even if had been a hundred miles from dancing solos with the Russian Ballet, or performing in elaborate successful musical comedies.

But in the end, her sheer determination to succeed on Broadway overruled the easy and delightfully romantic option, despite the fact that she had next to no money and certainly no immediate prospects, and for some time would probably have to combat total loneliness. All the while she was thinking, tears rolled down her cheeks – but Alice would not allow herself to wallow for long in miserable self-pity. The tears did her good, in fact, and while she felt drained she also felt ready to come to some definite conclusions.

She got up and unpacked her sponge bag. Going to the sink, she realised there was no lack of hot water. As she washed her face and took off the remains of her make-up, she made plans for action the following morning. If necessary, she could afford to stay at the Marco Polo for another two nights. That would give her at least three days to sort out her life, find a job of some kind, and hopefully somewhere to live.

Next morning she went down to breakfast, which would cost her fifty cents. Matty, now the waitress, put a plate of waffles, maple syrup and buttermilk in front of her. She enjoyed the rich, fattening food although the weak coffee was a less happy experience – but the combination helped her to face up to the challenges of the day. She returned to her room, collected her coat and hat and, knowing that *Variety*, the American equivalent of the British theatrical newspaper *The Stage*, should be on sale, she enquired where there was a newsagent. She was told that there was a stand two blocks away.

The paper proved a good investment. There was a large advertisement of an audition for dancers and show girls for the '*Music Box Revue of Nineteen-Twenty-Three*', to be held at The Music Box Theatre on Thursday, March the twenty-second. She decided she would go – but then realised that the twenty-second was twelve days away. She could certainly not wait that long. Besides, even if she did audition, there was no guarantee that she would be accepted.

She turned the pages. If she was to find work, she had a great deal to do that day. It was Saturday, and the likelihood of being able to find work on a Sunday seemed remote.

She noticed an advertisement for the John Tiller School. She knew of the famous school of that name in London, and how successful their girls were – they formed large troupes and travelled all over the world performing strict routines with amazing precision. She had not realised there was a branch in New York. The advertisement gave the address as two-hundred-and-twenty-six, West Seventy-second Street. Perhaps as there was a London connection the Principal, who the paper informed her was a Miss Mary Read, might be sympathetic to an English girl. She decided to go to the school at once. Classes would probably be going on at this moment, and maybe at least she could get some good advice. She went back to the hotel, gathered up her practice clothes in case she had to do an audition or join a class, and asked the porter for a street map of the city around which she now had to start to find her way.

Examining the map she soon realised that the avenues ran roughly north-south, and the streets east-west. In theory it seemed, it would be an easy city to find one's way around. The hotel was on East Eighty-fourth Street, and she had to get over to West Seventy-second. She could take the subway, but decided she would enjoy a walk – after all, it was still quite early. With a little help from a passer-by she found her way to Central Park, and was soon walking right across the park itself. It was beginning to feel familiar to her – was it only yesterday that she and Ben had spent their precious last hours together there? She blinked back tears as she walked. It was quite a long way, but the exercise was good for her.

Leaving the park she turned south, and walked for several blocks down Eighth Avenue, which skirted the park on the west side. After some distance she was at West Seventy-two, feeling quite relieved and pleased with herself that with a minimum of bother she had found the New York branch of the John Tiller School.

As she suspected, a class was in full swing.

'Right girls! Hitch kicks, please . . . No, Lesley! Kick with the right, dear! Surely you know that by now!'

Alice crept in. The teacher smiled, and while her students were busily engaged came up to her.

'I'm a dancer from London. Please, may I watch, and speak to you after class?'

'Of course, my dear – have you your things? But no, it's a bit too late for you to join in today. I'll surely talk to you later.'

The girls lined up – some twenty of them.

'Right, girls, left arm under, right arm over, and we'll do the full routine – from the top.'

The long line linked arms. The pianist vibrated a chord and struck up an old war song, 'Goodbye, Dolly, I Must Leave You.' Reminded to point the left foot and kick with the right, the girls sprang into action.

The routine ended.

'That's all, girls. Audition here on Monday at ten for the tour, if anyone wants to come.'

The girls shuffled out and into the changing-room down the corridor.

The teacher smiled kindly at Alice and they introduced themselves. The woman was in fact the principal, Mary Read.

'Nice to meet you. How can we help you?'

Alice explained her situation as briefly as possible.

'So would you like to audition on Monday? From what you tell me you are experienced in a wide range of dancing.'

'Yes, I would like to, very much.'

'Well, my dear, come back just before ten and bring your practice things. I'm sure you'll be fine – you're a lovely height. We're setting up a team to tour a new revue to most of the principal cities – we start in Chicago in the second week in April, then go to Cleveland, Detroit, and possibly over to San Francisco later on. If all goes well we'll bring it to Broadway in August – does this sound something you would like to do? It's going to be great fun.'

Alice was delighted. Having seen some of the work that was going on in the class she felt certain that whatever the opposition at the audition she would pass – all her experience and her varied techniques would, she knew, stand her in excellent stead. She decided she had made excellent progress during her first lonely hours in the city. If she missed out on the Tiller troupe there was the *Band Box Revue* later on and she would definitely try for that.

She left the large and airy studio, which had impressed her, and walked back to the park, now more aware of the sunlight, the crocuses and the hints of spring. These soothed her aching heart, her disappointment over Alex and the turmoil of the last twenty-four hours.

But though she might have improved prospects, she still had nowhere to live. She bought an early edition of an evening paper, but it had little to offer and this worried her. Nevertheless, her mood was still buoyant – she made friends easily and once she had successfully landed her job, she felt certain that all would be well. Surely one of twenty or more girls would know someone, somewhere with whom she could live? Her mind flicked back to the uncomfortable nights she had spent in the old chair during *Chu Chin*

Chow and she shuddered at the thought . . . Passing a park bench she glimpsed a tramp curled up in newspapers and sound asleep. The sight really frightened her, making her realise, in spite of her prospects, just how vulnerable she was. She thought once more about her precious limited supply of dollars. It now stood at just over twenty-eight. Two more nights at the Marco Polo and she would have only twenty-two left. She also had to eat.

If only Alex . . . if only she knew a few more people . . .

She sat on a seat at a distance from the tramp, and once again looked at *Variety* and scanned the accommodation list carefully. Lodgings were certainly less expensive than the hotel – several were quoted at around ten dollars a week. If she moved into a theatrical rooming house she would be on the scene and hear about what was happening – or, more importantly, what was about to happen.

One advertisement caught her eye. The address was fifty-three, West Forty-fourth Street, 'GIRLS AND WOMEN ONLY. PRICES FROM $10 A WEEK, SHARING'.

She decided to make her way there at once.

Consulting her map, she left the park and began to walk down Fifth Avenue. In spite of her problems she felt a twinge of elation. She was actually walking down Fifth Avenue! How – oh, *how* – she wished that Alex, Philip or even Elsie were with her. Her feet were getting tired. Glancing up, at the next street corner, she saw she had got as far as Fifty-ninth Street. She still had a long way to go, but as she left the park behind her, she realised that she was coming into the most exciting part of Fifth Avenue, with Tiffany's and the fabulous shops for which the Avenue was famous.

Her emotions were fighting for domination – one moment she was feeling lonely and forlorn, the next exhilarated, hopeful and excited. It was a strange and confusing state to be in, with worry and fear versus ambition and the acceptance of challenge swirling around in her mind.

The cheerfulness of the people crowding the pavements in a Saturday morning mood fuelled her own loneliness – but she knew what she must do, and was determined to get on with it.

Eventually she turned right into West Forty-fourth Street. Within a minute or two she was outside an impressive hotel. She noticed it was number fifty-nine. She was about to go into the foyer and ask where number fifty-three was, when having walked a little further along the street she found a narrow door with that number on it. Above it in worn lettering there was a sign: MARIA'S ROOMING HOUSE FOR LADIES OF THE THEATRICAL PROFESSION. The paintwork was drab and dusty. She could see that the door was slightly open. Cautiously, she started to push it, but as she did so heard several high-pitched, very American-sounding female voices giggling on the other side.

'Come on, come on – we'll be late, Denise!'

More giggling, and three girls flung the door open and rushed out past her into the street.

'Oh, excuse me, please . . .' But they were wrapped up in their own gossip, and were well on their way, not hearing Alice's plea.

She went inside. There seemed to be no-one around. She saw a narrow reception desk in the equally narrow passage. Behind it was a row of pigeon holes, and on the desk-top, a bell. She pressed it. No-one came. She pressed it again, then after another pause, once more.

'Okay, Okay, I'm comin.'

An enormous, dark-haired woman appeared from a door which obviously lead to the basement.

'Yes? You wanna room?'

'Well, yes, please – or at least to see what you've got.'

'Well – you come, I show. You don' mind sharin'?' she asked in a very Italian-flavoured accent.

'Depends who with.'

The woman, who introduced herself as Maria, smiled warmly, and led Alice up a flight of stairs to a long narrow passage with numerous doors on either side. At the third door she fumbled for a large bunch of keys and unlocked it.

'Nice girl in here, you like her I know. She out now. She don' mind sharing. Your bed 'ere. You like, yes?'

The iron bedstead was around the corner of the L-shaped room.

'See, cupboard for things. Wardrobe 'ere. Bathroom at end. Pay extra for baths. What you think, eh?'

The room badly needed painting, and the filthy window looked out onto a small triangular area in which there were only other windows, a few feet away; but at least it was warm. Alice looked as carefully as possible at the other girl's things. She could see that she was fairly tidy. She also noticed, thankfully, that there was no smell of cigarette smoke – something she hated, in spite of her recent job.

'Yes, I think so.'

'Come down, we fix details. Where you find out about us, eh?'

'In *Variety*.'

'Good. Now, ten dollars a week, twenty cents for bath. Kitchen in basement for cooking, washing, eating. All young ladies go there make food after shows. When you move in? Tomorrow?'

'Yes, if I may.'

'Okay. You pay two weeks' rent in advance. Twenty dollars.'

Alice gasped. That would leave her with only two dollars and a few cents.

'Er, would ten dollars be alright?'

'No, sorry, twenty – two weeks' rent. That's the rule. You no pay twenty – you no get room!'

Maria's thick Italian accent became thicker as she realised Alice's impecunious financial situation.

'You in work – in show?'

'No, but I have an audition on Monday, I'm sure to get it.'

159

'Oh si, si, I know . . . sure, sure, sure – I 'eard that one before! When you got work, you bring me contract. I see what I can do then. You get contract – I get rent. See you Monday, eh? Sorry.'

'But surely . . .'

'*No!* You 'ave no work. I must 'ave two weeks' rent.'

Alice, feeling very uncomfortable, knew she had to leave. She also knew she had to pass that audition.

She walked rather unsteadily out into the street. When she passed her audition – and she knew she would – she could go back with her contract and she would have a roof over her head and a few dollars to see her through the rehearsal period, if she was allowed to pay only one week in advance. With all this going on in her mind, she suddenly realised that she had turned right instead of left when she left the rooming house, and instead of continuing down Fifth Avenue came to a wide and very busy avenue, and realised she was on Broadway. Although it was early afternoon, bright lights lit signs advertising shows and stars' names over the entrances to theatres and cinemas with names that meant nothing to her, then a cinema which was showing *Blood and Sand*, Rudolph Valentino's latest photoplay. That brought back unhappy memories of her lost hopes of a career in the cinema.

Alice stood on the corner of Forty-fourth and Broadway, and looking down to her left she recognised, from photographs, Times Square. She knew she *must* make her life work out as she wanted.

She walked a little to the south, surrounded by people and traffic, fast becoming used to the fact that no-one noticed her. But then she realised she was hungry – very hungry. She had eaten nothing since her early morning waffles. There were several restaurants and little cafés, but she dared not spend very much. From Times Square, she turned into Forty-second Street, and in the distance saw, on the other side of the road, a baker's shop. She went in and bought a huge, fresh loaf for five cents. Returning to Times Square, she sat on a wooden box that someone had left on the wide sidewalk, and without the least inhibition broke off large pieces of the bread and heartily scoffed them. Never had she tasted anything so delicious.

Feeling better, she put the remaining piece of bread back into its paper bag. It would do for dinner that evening. Referring to her map, she discovered that if she walked back along Forty-second Street she would get to Grand Central Station, where she could take the subway north to a station not very far from her hotel.

It had been a long morning and afternoon. She had walked several miles. She gave way to the temptation, and spent a few cents on the fare, making her way back to the hotel, where she fell on her bed and went to sleep.

She woke up, and looking at her little travelling clock saw that it was eight-thirty. She ate the remaining bread, but was thirsty. She longed for a drink of some kind. She went downstairs. People were leaving the dining room. She asked Matty if she could have a pot of coffee, explaining that she had

160

already eaten with a friend. She sat at a table alone in a corner, and the young woman brought her the coffee – free at all times to every resident.

She decided she would not go out again, and picking up a few elderly magazines from a pile in the reception area, took them up to her room and after about an hour of light-hearted gossipy reading about New York society, went to bed.

Sunday was a free day for her. She learned that for her fifty cents she could have breakfast of ham and eggs, juice and toast as well as the waffles, and although heavy eating in the morning did nothing for her digestion, it was good insurance for the rest of the day, which she decided she would spend going to the park again, and to the Metropolitan Museum of Art, where she saw many wonderful paintings that she had only previously seen in reproduction, some historic costumes, and sculpture. The rarefied atmosphere and the beauty of the works of art lifted her spirits – as did the early spring sunshine.

After her long outing she returned to the hotel for her last night there. She sorted out her case, washed some knickers and stockings with toilet soap in the wash basin, and put them on the radiator to dry overnight.

The next morning, after her hearty breakfast, she would check out and go to her audition.

Chapter 20

'Right, girls, high heels first, please – let's see your kicks. Everyone line up from the corner and come to the centre in turn. Then when you've finished or we stop you, go and change into your toe shoes – Mr Ackerman here wants strong toe dancing, so show him just how good you all are at everything we've taught you!'

Mary Read's lively comments eased the tension that the thirty or so girls were feeling, as she sat at a table with an elderly man and a youngish woman.

'Give me eight waist kicks and eight high kicks. Right, on the music!'

The pianist struck up. The first girl took the centre of the studio and performed her sixteen kicks. Mr Ackerman and his assistant made notes.

'Next!'

Soon it was Alice's turn. She realised that her high kicks were considerably higher than any she had seen so far, so much so that the pianist – who was a true professional – at once slowed down a little to allow her to execute the steps in time with the music. She noticed that surprised glances were exchanged as she walked back to change her shoes.

Everyone was tested, though several girls fell out because they were not able to dance on pointe.

Mary Read shouted out more instructions, '*Posé* turns, *bourrée* across the studio and finish as you like.'

When it came to Alice's turn she heard gasps of amazement from the other girls as she completed her little *enchainment*.

After everyone had performed – some very well, others dreadfully badly – Mr Ackerman stood up.

'Now, girls, we're getting on very well. We need twenty of you, and I don't think there will be much difficulty, but to be quite sure, so that we can make our final selection, I want to see what you can do in your tap shoes, so everyone back and change again, please, and Arlette will give you a step.'

Alice was dumbfounded. She had never as much as put on a pair of tap shoes in the whole of her dancing life. She knew nothing about it.

She went up to the three of them.

'I'm sorry, but I've never learned tap dancing. I can't do it at all. We were strongly advised in my ballet school not to take it up, as it needs loose ankles and ours had to be strong and firm for pointe work.'

'So, my dear, you have been classically trained – hasn't she, Arlette?'

'Why, she sure has, Mr Akerman!'

Alice blushed and quietly said that she had danced with the Russian ballet.

'Well, I'm afraid that if you can't do any tap we can't use you. I'm sorry, but the tap number is our first half close-down, and we need everyone in it. Your kicks are excellent and your toe dancing is really beautiful – but sorry, dear, no.'

Mary Read could see that Alice was distraught. Putting her arm around her she said, 'If you want to get into a Broadway show or work for us, you're going to have to do something about tap – we have classes nearly every day – I suggest you sign up for some, and the sooner the better.'

Alice thanked her. She made her way back to the changing room. Fighting tears, she took off her pointe shoes as she heard Arlette setting a step, followed by the noisy clatter of the tap dancing.

The news had been a terrific shock. She tried to collect her thoughts as she changed back into her street clothes and packed her high heels and blocked ballet shoes. Slowly she picked up her bag and walked out into the street.

She had to clear out of her hotel room by twelve, and had packed all her things before she left for the audition, arranging with the hotel that she would pick up her case later that day – she had expected to be able to afford a taxi down to Forty-fourth Street.

She walked for a while, hardly noticing the tenement blocks in the area or the side alleys leading to courtyards where lines of washing filled every available space. She now had yet more decisions to make. She could certainly not commit herself to any tap classes: no matter how much or how little they cost she couldn't pay for them. Besides, she would have to buy a pair of tap shoes – that was out of the question. Her situation was very grim, the importance of tap dancing had never occurred to her. She knew it was popular, but didn't think it was essential – Alex had made no mention of it. It dawned on her that she would simply have to get an ordinary job – as a waitress, perhaps, or in a department store if she was lucky. If she aimed too high employers would be very reluctant to allow her time off to go to auditions.

She felt an affinity with Forty-fourth Street, and decided to go back there to plead again with Maria. Perhaps after all she would allow her to stay and pay just a week's rent in advance, or know someone who could give her a job. She returned to the Seventy-second Street subway station. Once through the creaking turnstile she suddenly felt very cold. She saw a large old-fashioned stove just outside the entrance to the downtown track. She went up to it hoping to warm herself against it, but it was unlit. She walked through some glass doors onto the platform. The train rattled her down to Forty-second Street, the nearest station to Maria's.

*

'Ah, so you're back. You got job – eh? I see your contract, then okay, one week's rent will do.'

'Maria, I'm so sorry – I didn't get job.'

'Oh pity, pity . . . pretty girl like you.' Maria shook her head. 'But I can't help, sorry.'

'Please, Maria, I'm desperate. I just wondered if . . .'

'No – I say *no*.'

'Please let me finish.'

'Okay, okay, but I'm busy. Not much time.'

'Do you know anyone who might want a shop assistant or a waitress?'

'Ah – waitress – you be careful, girl. But shop . . .' She paused.

'You take walk over other side of Broadway. Lots of shops there. Sometimes cards in window saying staff wanted. You could pick up something. Friendly people – good people, work hard!'

'And if I find something?'

'You come see me again, but this place not for shops girls, you know.'

'No – I understand. Thank you, Maria.'

As she left the woman smiled sadly to herself and shook her head.

Alice trudged around the neighbouring streets for over two hours, but saw no cards in any of the shop windows. As she walked back along Forty-third Street for the second time, quite late in the evening, she saw a shop that seemed only to sell cheese and salami. It was situated very near to the junction of Eighth Avenue, on the corner of a narrow alley that led up into Forty-fourth Street – about five minutes' walk at most from Maria's and several well-known theatres. It had a rather tired-looking card in the window saying STAFF WANTED.

She stood looking in the window at the huge variety of cheeses. As she did so, she noticed an elderly man looking out at her. He smiled and waved. Nervously she waved back and, deciding that he looked very friendly, she went in.

'Now, Miss, what can I do for you? A nice piece of *dolce latta*? Or something stronger – some gorgonzola for your boyfriend?'

He stood up straight and putting his hands on his hips fell into a peal of happy laughter.

'Eh? What you say?'

She at once recognised another Italian accent, and by the look of him deduced that he had enjoyed many a good meal of pasta and rich red chianti.

'You have a beautiful selection, but well . . .' she hesitated.

'Si?'

He looked quizzically at her.

'I see you need help in your lovely shop? Er, I'm looking for a job and I noticed your card in the window.'

He opened his large round eyes wide.

'A beautiful young lady like you, looking for a job?'

164

'Yes. You see I'm going to be in a show, later on, but now I have no work.'

'Lots of young ladies like you around here, you know. But you, well . . .'

He was quiet for a moment.

'*Si*, I do need someone. The last young lady who worked here, well, she got into her show so it was lucky for her, but not so lucky for me. I try to work here with my wife helping when we are really busy, but you know, her legs are bad . . .'

Smiling at him, she assured him hers were strong.

'Work can be heavy. You will have a lot to do. Where do you live?'

Alice blushed. She hated saying she had nowhere to live.

'Ah, that's sad – very sad. I speak to my wife.'

He disappeared through a bead curtain. Alice could just hear some excited high-pitched Italian going on in the room behind the shop.

He returned.

'*Mia sposa* Dominica, she says she like to meet you. I say you nice young lady. Come this way, please.'

Alice went behind the counter and followed him into the room. An elderly woman in black was sitting peeling onions at a kitchen table. She looked at Alice, then beamed and spoke to her husband. All Alice could understand was '*Si, si, si.*' It was obvious that the wife spoke little or no English.

He turned to Alice and said, 'My wife, she likes you. She says that if we can arrange the money, you can use the attic to sleep in, so you get up early and open up the shop.'

Alice smiled nervously, knowing she would have to accept, whatever the pay and conditions.

'How much can you manage to pay me, please?'

'We paid our last young lady twelve dollars a week.'

'That's very generous of you.'

'But we have to take five dollars a week out of that, if you are going to live here and eat with us.'

She did a conversion. Twelve dollars – that would be two pounds eight shillings. Five dollars – that was a pound. She would have one pound eight shillings to do what she wanted with. It was very little, but she would have a roof over her head and perhaps she would have enough time off to learn to tap.

'Thank you very much. I'd like to accept your offer.'

'You have things?'

'Yes, they are up-town, in a hotel on Eighty-third.'

'Go fetch them. Domenica will make up your bed.'

Arriving on the doorstep of B. MANDARO, LATTICINI FRESCHI – which she later learned meant 'fresh dairy produce' – Alice put her suitcase on the pavement and looked up at the shop. Lights were on inside. She went in, and her employer called to his wife, who took her up three flights of narrow dark stairs. Opening a creaking door she gestured to Alice to go in. Alice smiled and thanked her in Italian. At this Dominica smiled, clapped and cried, '*Bravo!*' as she left Alice to settle in.

Alice looked around the room. It had a sizeable window, but she could hardly see through the glass, which was thick with New York grime. The walls were covered in wallpaper with a huge floral design, which appeared to have been put up at the turn of the century. It was very faded – apart from two rectangles each side of the window. Obviously a previous occupant had hung pictures there for many years. The bed was narrow but very clean, with an Italian-style feather-bed cover instead of blankets. A crucifix hung above the bed, and on a shelf protecting a rusty radiator there was a sealed bottle which had printed on its label 'Holy water from Lourdes'. The floor was bare apart from a dark red rug. A wardrobe with a broken door and a washstand with a jug, a basin and a po and a tiny dressing-table of uncertain origin completed the furnishings.

Taking in the scene, Alice's sense of relief and gratitude was mixed with a sinking feeling. The room depressed her beyond belief. She had never experienced such run-down living conditions. Though there was far more space than at Elsie's, the room was in a dreadful condition. But she had to be thankful. She would at least have regular money and food. She knew she would have to work hard for it. Just how hard she had yet to discover.

She decided to unpack her things, found a couple of very bent wire hangers in the wardrobe, and knew at once that she would have to buy some more if her dresses were not to suffer. Opening the drawers in the wobbly dressing table was a difficult feat. The top one stuttered, and then as she pulled it, it suddenly gave way and fell right out. She saw her own surprised expression in the damaged mirror, and laughed.

She had almost finished unpacking when she heard Mr Mandaro call from the bottom of the long flights of stairs.

'Dinner time – you come, *si*?'

'Why yes, thank you.'

She went downstairs to the room behind the shop.

'Ah, good. Now we eat. You not have spaghetti before, eh?'

Alice smiled.

'Often – I love it!'

Dominica produced a huge bowl and, placing it on the table, ladled a large portion onto her husband's plate. He virtually fell into the pasta. Alice was given a plateful. It smelt wonderful. The couple looked at her, expecting her not to be able to eat it. She had been given a spoon as well as a fork beside her plate, but knew she would not need the spoon and picked up the fork, and with dexterity that came from eating platefuls of pasta in London, twisted it around her fork, eating it as quickly and a great deal more neatly than the Italians.

She was facing an old kitchen range, over which hung a large framed photograph of four young men. Gesturing towards the picture, she asked Mr Mandaro who they were.

Before he could answer Dominica had got up, picked up the photograph and pointed to each in turn, slowly reciting 'Mario, Marcello, Franco, Angello . . . Nappa Valley.'

'Our sons, they have fruit farm, California – in Nappa Valley – will be successful one day.'

Mr Mandaro made a wry face and shrugged his heavy shoulders.

Before the family went to bed Alice was told what she had to do next day. It seemed she had a heavy schedule, so she decided to retire well before ten o'clock.

She switched on the bare electric light in the dreary room. Dazzled by its cruel brightness, she decided she must buy a cheap lampshade to make the place a little more tolerable. She had been given a large jug of hot water, and washed all over – wondering when, or if, she would ever have the chance of a proper bath again.

Looking around the awful room depressed her beyond measure. Overcome by the sheer bad luck of the recent turn of events she felt trapped. She knew she would have to learn tap – but could only do so if the Mandaros would allow her time off for classes. Life was certainly cruel at present and her prospects were grim. An inescapable trap seemed to be closing around her. It was all she could do to keep even a tiny spark of hope glowing.

She undressed and got into bed. At least that was as warm as it had felt comfortable when she first sat on it earlier that eventful day. She was just drifting off to sleep when she heard some heavy uneven thumping footsteps coming up the stairs, followed by dragging steps across the short passage to a door which creaked open then slammed shut. Frightened, she wondered who it was. Her pulse-rate increased as she listened to footsteps in what was obviously another attic bedroom nearby. Eventually they stopped, and she assumed that whoever it was had gone to bed. But she felt uneasy, and decided to lock her door. She found the lock with a key in it, but both were rusty, and the key would not turn. She had to get back to bed and hope that she would not be intruded upon.

A little later she was further disturbed by what sounded like rumblings from Hades itself. These continued in heavy waves for some minutes, ruining her increasing sleepiness. After a while she heard a woman's voice cry out what sounded something like *'Cazzo! Smettila di Tussare!'*

This was followed by three heavy, squeaky bangs which shook the wall behind her head. The thundering noise continued. The cry was repeated followed by yet more squeaking bangs.

Sitting up in bed, Alice wondered whatever was going on. Hearing the noise for a third time she realised that it was Signor and Signora Mandaro going though what was obviously a nightly ritual. The wife was trying desperately to stop her husband snoring by thrusting her heavy body up and down on the very worn springs of their bed, in the room immediately below Alice. The growling noise changed key and rhythm.

'*Ma Vaffancula!*' came the protest from the equally furious husband whose sleep had been disturbed.

'Dear God in heaven, please help me to survive this!'

On the point of tears of frustration, Alice's sense of humour got the better of her, and she ached with laughter. Adding ear plugs to her mental shopping list, she eventually drifted off into a deep dreamless sleep.

She had to be first up, and at six-thirty she put on her oldest jumper and skirt, a heavy starched white overall which was far too big for her, and a three-cornered headscarf to cover her hair. She went downstairs to open the shop, ready for a churn of milk to be delivered. She rolled yesterday's empty churn out onto the pavement, and when it was replaced rolled the full, fresh one into the space allotted to it inside the shop. Having washed pint and half pint aluminium ladles, she weighed up a half a pound of gorgonzola cheese and took it to the baker's shop next door where, in return, the baker gave the Mandaros their supply of bread for the day. She realised that this was the shop where she had purchased her loaf, before the weekend. The baker was friendly and gave her little sponge cake to eat mid-morning.

Her next task was to wash the tiled floor of the shop, its doorstep, and the pavement outside, using a heavy mop and a galvanized bucket containing steaming water heated on a hulking gas stove which complemented the range in the Mandaro's kitchen.

As she mopped the pavement, she saw the street come alive. The traffic increased by the minute. People of all ages and ethnic types hurried to work. A Jew dressed in black, with red hair and plaits, hustled his two boys along the street, obviously on their way to school. Dogs of various shapes and sizes nosed for scraps along the pavement. A cat came face to face with one, hissed and backed off.

Soon Alice was serving her first customer.

'Thank you, madam. Will that be all?'

'Oh, sure. But no – I'll have that bit of gorgonzola.'

Alice noticed the woman's small son plunge his grubby hand into a vat of large green olives.

'Excuse me, madam – your little boy . . .'

'Yeah?'

The mother turned to see what the child was doing.

'Ben, no! Don't do that! Come here at once!'

Ben stamped his feet in temper. The woman hastily paid for her purchases and, taking the recalcitrant Ben by the scruff of the neck, led him out of the shop as he stuffed handfuls of olives into his coat pockets.

Alice shook with repressed anger at the child's behaviour, but his name rang in her ears. Ben . . . Ben . . .

She pictured her Ben looking at her, and wondered if perhaps she had made a dreadful mistake.

Sighing, she began cleaning the wide pane of glass inside which was displayed an enormous variety of cheeses from all over the world, and staggered out of the shop with a bulky notice that she could hardly lift, which advertised, RICOTTA TUTTA CREMA – 30c 1b and RICOTTA FINA – 25c 1b.

By this time her arms were aching, and she saw from the old ticking clock inside the shop that it was eight-thirty. She had been so involved that she had not noticed any activity in the kitchen – no-one had been there when she heated the water. But now she smelt welcoming coffee.

'*Prima colazione*, Alice.'

Dominica's voice came from the back kitchen, at the same pitch as through the floorboards on the previous night.

Alice was offered croissant, a little bread roll, and two sticky dishes, one of marmalade, the other of peach conserve, and a huge mug of coffee which was the best she had yet encountered in New York.

After a while, letting out a loud yawn as he trod heavily downstairs, Mr Mandaro joined them – but not before he had been into the shop to see if Alice had done what was expected of her. He came in grinning.

'You work well.'

'I'm pleased that you're pleased.'

They ate their breakfast without conversation, but with a great deal of noise. Just as they were finishing Alice recognised uneven footsteps on the stairs.

A young man of about twenty lumbered in, he had a pronounced hump and one shoulder was higher than the other. By his cheerful but empty expression she realised that he was not very bright.

'Ah, Riccardo – meet Alice.'

'Alllice, Papa?'

'Yes, Riccardo, Alice.'

'Helllooo, Alllice.' He grinned at her and picked up his mug of coffee, slurping down the hot liquid.

'He's a good lad. No 'arm to no-one. He does some work for us, but well – you can see. Now I show you how to slice salami. We have best salami in New York – straight from Italy.'

Alice and her employer went into the shop. Soon there were customers wanting pounds or half-pounds of butter (Alice had to make pats of it from a large lump); she learned how to cut cheese with a knife that was as long as her arm and to weigh it and slice the various kinds of salami that the Mandaros also sold in great quantities. She smiled at the customers, many of whom spoke little or no English. Those that did – young and old alike – were kind and made friendly jokes. There were elderly Greek women, Italians, several Irish and one or two blacks. Alice realised just how true it was that America was the melting pot of the nations.

After lunch when the shop closed for an hour, Mr Mandaro told Riccardo

– who had not been seen all morning – to go on an errand. But the young man was surly. He gripped the edge of the table, shouting 'No, no, no!'

'Ah, Riccardo . . .' sighed his mother.

'Alice, I don't know why, but Riccardo here will not go. So you deliver cheese, yes?'

'Of course, Mr Mandaro. Tell me where I've to go.'

'Not far. Walk up the alley and you'll be on Forty-fourth. Turn right and cross the road and you go to number fifty-three.'

'Number fifty-three – that's Maria's?'

'You know already, *si*?'

'I know already, *si*!'

Dominica handed Alice a large parcel wrapped in grease-proof paper, and signalled to Alice that she must get a signature for it. Alice assumed that Maria had an account with the Mandaros.

'Excuse me, I'm delivering this for Maria – it's from Mr Mandaro.'

The young woman at the reception desk gazed at Alice, her eyes wide open.

'Say, I sure like your accent – it's real cute. Where do you come from? Australia or somewhere?'

Alice was taken aback. She had never been accused of being Australian.

'Well, no, actually I'm English.'

'Yeah? Well, we all speak English, but not like you, sister. So where's home, and what are you doin' working for Mandaro?'

'It's a long story . . .'

'I got the time.'

She leaned on her elbow preparing herself for some nice juicy gossip.

'But I don't think I have.'

'Well, tell me some of it. You're sure different!'

The young woman smiled, and Alice although still surprised at the effect she had had on her, liked her cheerful, forthright manner and was not put off by her inquisitiveness.

'I'm Alice Townsend – from London.'

'Gee, *London* . . . I've never met anyone from London before. I'm Trixie Lamont. Sure pleased to meet you.'

They shook hands. As briefly as possible Alice told her new acquaintance about herself, omitting a lot of the detail, but explaining why she was working for Mandaro. Then it was her turn to ask a question.

'You must be a dancer or an actress, otherwise you wouldn't be living here.'

'Yeah, I'm a dancer. Done one or two shows. But, sister, you'll have to learn tap – it's getting more and more popular.'

'Yes, I'm going to ask Mr Mandaro if I can have time to go to classes up at the Tiller School.'

'You'll be lucky.'

'Why, what do you mean?'

'I mean that *he's* mean. Mean as shit. He won't allow you time off for that – I know several girls who've worked for him. And they got trapped. They needed his money – and the food's good,' she added grudgingly.

'I'd noticed that . . . but you don't think?'

Trixie smiled.

'No, I don't. But if you can come round here after work I'll help you. Got some tap shoes yet?'

'Well, no – but I will after I've been paid on Saturday.'

'Get yer shoes, come round, say, at nine next Monday night – the shop closes at eight.'

Alice was amused that Trixie knew so much about Mandaro's.

'Oh, and, Alice, watch out for that Riccardo. He won't hurt you – too shy for that – but, well, he sure belongs to the W.H.S.!'

'What's that?'

'The Wandering Hands Society!'

She picked up the packet to go down to the kitchen, her short dark curly hair bouncing as she took every springing step.

'*Ciao*, Alice. Nice to know you!'

'*Ciao*, Trixie!'

'You late, you take too long – quick, put overall on, get back to work!'

Mr Mandaro was not best pleased. Alice realised that there was obviously truth in what Trixie had said. Without complaint she got back to work, and at the end of the day went to bed with a vision of pats of butter, salami, milk and cheese dancing in front of her eyes as she tried to relax into sleep.

Chapter 21

'Now come on, Alice, tap-step-ball-change. Tap-step-ball-change!'

'Heavens! It feels so strange.'

'Try to relax your ankles.'

'That's the problem. They're tight – which is the way I need them for pointe work.'

'Well you'll just have to loosen 'em up for this.'

The new tap shoes felt heavy and clumsy, but Alice was doing her best. She soon learned the simple step. Trixie encouraged her to travel as far as possible with each step, and to add swinging relaxed arm movements to it. Alice had no difficulty in doing that as they danced around the large, scrubbed kitchen table.

It had been a hard few days. Alice's job was heavy; she was working more than twelve hours a day, apart from meals. Fortunately she was strong, and on one level the very different experience and the fact that she was so busy, helped keep her mind off her situation, her brief but meaningful love affair on the ship, and from too many thoughts of Alex, who she was sure was doing precisely what he wanted. She was envious of any other ballerina he was partnering.

As she got into the swing of the step, however, the misery of her situation caught up with her. Here she was, learning wretched tap-dancing in a New York basement, and employed as a sales girl in a dairy produce shop. There was no glamour in her life – just hard, tiring physical work. Even so, it was very kind and friendly of Trixie to offer to teach her when she could do so little in return. But then an idea struck her.

'Trixie, you're helping me with all this, can I help you with ballet?'

The bouncy young woman clapped with glee and, jumping up and down, replied, 'Could you really do that, Alice?'

'Of course.'

'I've done some, and a bit of toe-dancing when I was little. Look, let me go buy some toe shoes and if you could get me up on 'em, that'd really help.'

Alice agreed.

With that they heard singing coming from upstairs.

'You made me love you,
I didn' wanna do it,
I didn' wanna do it . . .'

'That's the rest of the girls! We usually have a singsong this time of night –
those of us who are out of work.'

The song tugged at Alice's heart strings, and for a moment she felt slightly
dizzy.

'Say, are you okay?'

'Oh yes, it's just that song . . .'

'Memories eh?'

'Well, yes, actually.'

'Don' worry, Alice, we all have 'em!'

Alice was introduced to another five or six girls, all residents of Maria's,
all of whom, she learned, had had to pay their two weeks' rent in advance.
Some were more experienced than others, but all had great hopes of getting
into a show. They were planning to go to the *Music Box* auditions on Thursday morning at ten. Alice also wanted to go and try, but knew that she could
not risk her job, and said so.

'Well, knowing him, he *would* sack you, and at the moment you do need
him and his miserable job. I know, I worked there when I first came to the
Big Apple.'

It was Denise who was speaking. They decided that Alice should practise
her tap for a while, because, as Mary Read had said, she would not get a
Broadway job without it. But they reassured her that she would not take
long to learn enough to get by.

As she walked home she felt more light-hearted. She had some lively
and encouraging friends, and their optimistic chatter had been very
cheering.

She had been given a key to the shop to let herself in – the Mandaros
would have gone to bed. She reached the shop, and stooping down to release
one of two locks which was near the ground she felt someone pinch her
bottom.

'Ah, Alice, lovely little Alice . . .'

The gesture made her jump, and she let out a sharp little cry. Turning
abruptly, she realised that it was Riccardo, also arriving home after an evening out. He came face to face with her, panting. She caught the smell of
drink on his breath. Quickly unlocking the top lock before he could repeat
the unwelcome gesture, she flew indoors and raced up the stairs far quicker
than he could manage, but she heard his insane giggling as she went, and
realised that he must have been visiting some speakeasy. Scared, and well
aware of Trixie's warning, she slammed her bedroom door and pushed the
rickety dressing table in front of it. The last thing she wanted was an intrusion from a half-drunk simpleton.

*

173

Alice made regular visits to Maria's and with Trixie's help began to get the hang of tap dancing. She managed time steps, but was always having difficulty with winging. She was nervous of the step, and hated it. Meanwhile, Trixie was not the easiest of students to get on to pointe. Her movements were sexy, rather spiky, and not at all elegant. Between them the two girls had everything that was needed – if they had been one, there was no doubt they would have passed any audition they attended.

After a few weeks Trixie decided that Alice was ready to audition. Scanning *Variety* they discovered that a new show was to open at the end of May, and that auditions were to be held at the Ambassador's theatre, Broadway and Forty-ninth, on a Friday morning in mid-April.

Having worked solidly for the Mandaros every day since they had employed her – even on Sundays, when the shop was open and she was often alone, as the family attended Mass with great regularity – Alice felt quite justified asking for time off.

'No! Dominica is so unwell at present – she cannot move easy. You see that. She can't stand in shop. Too much for me to do alone.'

'But I've worked all these weeks – I've not complained. You do feed me well, and I'm grateful, but I'm a dancer, not a shop assistant, and I must get into a show.'

'You go to audition, I give you sack.'

Alice was frustrated and furious. She had saved some money – apart from her tap shoes, she had bought only toiletries and some new stockings. She was far more independent than she had been, but she had to decide whether the time was right for her to risk her security.

A week later, after one of her lively evenings with Trixie and friends, Alice arrived back at Mandaro's just after midnight. As she made her way up the stairs she heard the front door open again and assumed, quite rightly, that Riccardo was home from yet another of his evenings out. Ahead of him on the stairs she felt secure enough to turn round and quietly, so as not to disturb his parents, say goodnight.

She noticed he was carrying a large cardboard box. In the half-light she saw it had HOMINY GRITS BREAKFAST FOOD printed on the side. It was obviously heavy, and she smiled to herself as he staggered up the stairs with it. She had her wash and went to bed.

Almost asleep, she heard a police siren – nothing new in that, they hurtled by most nights. But instead of getting fainter, it became louder then suddenly stopped. At the same moment she heard the sound of breaking glass from the yard behind the shop, and several crashes followed by loud knocking on the door. After a pause Mr Mandaro shouted, '*Si, si*. Okay, I come!'

With difficulty, Alice opened her window and looked into the yard. At the window next to hers, Riccardo, in his pyjamas, was throwing bottles down into the yard. Immediately realising she could do herself a bit of good, she slammed the window shut, and rushed into his room.

'Riccardo, stop, stop – do as I say!'

174

She snatched a bottle from him and threw it very quickly out of the window, glanced at the box, which fortunately was now empty. She flung the window shut, grabbed the box in one hand, and pulled the young man by his pyjama jacket towards the door of his room. She stopped for a moment, as she heard two policemen talking to Mr Mandaro on the ground floor.

'Quick, quick – come in here!'

Just as she managed to get the slow-moving Riccardo into her room, she heard the police and Mr Mandaro coming up the stairs.

'Get into bed!'

She pushed Riccardo onto the bed and tore off his jacket, pulled back the quilt, threw the box under the bed then got in beside him. Holding her breath she heard the police go into his room. They were obviously searching it. Eventually one said to the other, 'Nothin' here – right, let's move on.'

She put her hand over Riccardo's mouth.

'Keep quiet – don't say a word.'

He nodded anxiously. Within seconds the police knocked on her door.

'Come in,' she called, in a sleepy, embarrassed voice.

'Excuse me, ma'am, but I must ask you – have you seen or heard anyone come into this house in the last few minutes?'

Sitting up in bed and acting herself silly, she pulled the quilt around her chest, making sure that the police saw Riccardo's head.

'Why no, officer, my boyfriend and I have been here for several hours. We haven't heard or seen anyone – except each other. Isn't that right, darling?'

'Oh, *si, si, bellisima Alicia*!'

'You must excuse him, officer, – he speaks very little English.'

The officer was suspicious.

'I can see . . . but, ma'am, excuse me, is that the truth?'

'Officer, the truth, the whole truth and nothing but the truth. I am British – we do *not* tell lies to the police, I assure you. This is very embarrassing, but I will swear on oath that Riccardo and I have been together all evening, and I can prove it.' She had visions of hurried messages being exchanged between her and her friends at Maria's.

'Is that all you can tell us?'

'Well actually, officer, Riccardo and I were somewhat disturbed a while ago by a noise as if someone was throwing glass out of a window into the back yard – so you might investigate the other apartments. It was frightful! Riccardo here, who is a rather nervous young man, was frightened by it.'

'Well, I guess that'll be all, ma'am. Thank you for your help. Thank you, sir.'

Riccardo smiled and said a quiet *grazie*. The police left.

All the while, Mr Mandaro had been standing silently by. He followed the police out of the room. Immediately they were downstairs and out of the front door, Alice pushed Riccardo out of bed.

'Thank you, thank you, Alicia. You very kind.'

'Well don't expect to come into my bed *ever again*, will you? And, Riccardo, I *really* mean that!'

As she spoke she put on her dressing gown. Mr Mandaro, joined by Dominica returned to the room. Dominica hugged her. They could not thank her enough. Alice said it was the least she could do, but as she had done them such a favour perhaps they could give her a little more help in future. She suggested they talk about it in the morning, as now it was well past one o'clock.

'So you will allow me time to go to my weekly tap dancing class, and to attend auditions. One half day off a week would also be most welcome.'

'*Si* – you have saved us from dreadful scandal, and poor Riccardo from being sent to jail.'

'Well, Mr Mandaro, I will certainly stay with you and Dominica if you keep your side of the bargain, and I think you must also explain to Riccardo, that what I did was to keep him out of trouble, and I am definitely not his girlfriend and never will be – is that understood?'

'Why yes, of course, Alice!'

Dominica toddled up to Alice and gave her a smacking kiss and hug, obviously relieved that she had saved them from a very unpleasant situation.

Later that day, Alice heard Mr Mandaro pouring the wrath of God on his stupid son, who confessed everything to his father. The young man, head hanging low, went out.

'Alice, Riccardo has been in bad company. He has been working as a messenger for a Forty-second Street speakeasy. He took the hootch from there and was paid to deliver it to their clients. He has confessed to me, now he's going to the priest.'

The matter was closed, and from then on Alice had things the way she wanted them.

'Oh, Alice, it was awful! I really didn't manage those funny turns – I nearly fell over!'

'You mean *posé* turns? No, you don't have the hang of them yet – not on pointe, anyway. And I got thoroughly lost in the wretched second time-step.'

The two friends were commiserating over their failing an audition on which they had both pinned such big hopes.

'Well, we'll just have to put in a lot more practice. Look, you should go to proper ballet classes, and I must go to Tiller's for tap. I can afford it, now, and Mr Mandaro has come to his senses and daren't refuse me the time off.'

Spring turned to summer. The weather became hotter by the day, and as it did so Alice became more and more aware of the smell of the cheeses and the clumsiness of her hygienic overalls, which with the increasing heat felt heavier every hour. She now went to tap class once a week, and on her half days occasionally visited a cinema. When Norma or Constance Talmadge appeared she felt sad at what she had so narrowly missed. She wondered how Margaret Leahy was getting on – the photoplay in which she was due to star would surely be premiéred soon. She decided that she would not be able to face seeing it.

She saw in a magazine that the Russian Ballet was still based in Monte Carlo. How she envied Alex. How she wished, too, that she could manage to go to a proper ballet class every day, as she had done in London. At times she all but decided to go back home, but Broadway still held a glamorous thrill for her, and the hope of making a name for herself over-ruled the easier option of returning to London. She wondered whether she should write to Alex, care of the ballet, but pride prevented her. She did not want anyone for whom she really cared to know that she was working in a cheese shop in downtown New York, not that she would have to tell Alex that – but he would have become suspicious that something was wrong unless she told him a whole pack of lies, and that would have been equally difficult for her. It would also have been worse than dreadful if in some roundabout way her parents discovered what she was doing. So, depressing though it was, she must battle on with as much optimism as she could muster.

The other girls Alice had originally met at Maria's strode well ahead of Trixie and Alice, and either went on tour or found smarter addresses, so it was not long before the rooming-house was full of a new set of hopefuls. The two friends became extremely depressed when they failed yet another audition – this time the great Florenz Ziegfeld, whose spectacular shows were the talk of Broadway, and who employed the cream of the showgirls and dancers on the New York Theatre scene.

It seemed as if all Alice's flair, talent and charisma had deserted her, and the more she failed the less confident she felt. She was on a vicious spiral, and knew it. Perhaps the lack of going to class every day was one reason for her failure? There was little she could do except constantly tell herself to keep trying, and to convince herself that in the end she must succeed.

Sometimes she would practice in her bedroom, but it was dangerous, as the floor was extremely weak and the boards cracked. Any heavy movement might cause a collapse. So her tap class, and continued practice until the next class started, plus the bits she did with Trixie in Maria's kitchen, were about all that she could manage. Time and circumstances were against her.

Chapter 22

'Of course, you know what this means!'

'I sure do, Alice – it means simply *everything*!'

'Now I can say goodbye to the Mandaros, and never, ever touch another piece of cheese!'

'And you can move into my room at Maria's. It's going to be such *fun*! Go back right away and tell them. You won't have to give notice – he didn't say anything about that, did he?'

'No. I'll leave as soon as I can pack.'

It had been a thrilling morning. At last Trixie had got away with her weak ballet and Alice had managed the surprisingly simple tap. Then, when the choreographer had made his choice of forty girls he had asked who did pointe work. This delighted Alice – it showed that he took ballet seriously, since everyone who merely tolerated it called it 'toe-dancing'.

Alice had put her hand up, and with four other girls was re-auditioned for the role of principal dancer – who was to become the leading lady in a spectacular dream sequence, while the lead herself slept on what was promised to be a massive curtained bed. Alice was by far the best of the four, in spite of being more out of practice than she cared to admit – she felt twinges of pain with every movement.

Rehearsals were due to begin immediately, and they were going to be paid for them, something that Alice had hardly experienced in the past. Her situation had changed completely. All she had to do was to make her departure from the Mandaros, accepting the fact that they had served their purpose and that she had given them more than good value for their money.

Italian emotion gushed as she came downstairs for the last time. Dominica was crying, Mr Mandaro said he would bring his family to her first night on Broadway, and hugged her. Sighing, he added that they would never find another assistant like her saying, 'English, reliable – you work hard.'

Riccardo looked sad, and just as she was at last breaking away from their expressions and gestures of affection he limped up to her and hesitantly said, 'Goodbye, *bellisima Alicia*!'

She could see tears in his eyes and feeling sorry for him, kissed him on both cheeks. He blushed. The family waved to her as she went out of the shop, along the alley and into Forty-fourth Street, thence to Maria's, where she felt most at home in this bustling, dirty but vibrant city.

Her welcome there was as enthusiastic as her farewell at Mandaro's had been emotional. For the first time in many months she felt happy. And that night Maria brought a bottle of illicit liquor into the girls' common room as a welcoming celebration for Trixie and Alice's success.

Alice was part of the dance ensemble, but as ballerina and principal dancer was also to be given a credit on the programme, and to receive a hundred dollars a week as opposed to seventy-five. Trixie was delighted for her friend, and they decided that the rest of the troupe were a friendly lot, though the three who had missed out on being principal dancer looked at Alice with envious eyes, realising that her dancing was in a totally different class to theirs. Alice could not have cared less. That was their problem. She was particularly delighted that her work involved some classical ballet, and felt on the way to achieving her ambition.

At the first rehearsal the producer told the excited cast about the production. *Prunella's Progress* was a musical comedy with an original score, and needed the resources of a large theatre. After four weeks' rehearsal in New York, it would open at the Fox Theater in Philadelphia, where it would run for four weeks, going on to Boston for a further four before coming onto Broadway. The production would be colourful, exciting and spicy. There would be dazzling sets and costumes, a good story line, lovely songs – now being completed – and everything was set for one of the biggest successes on Broadway that autumn. The show was expected to run for many months and – smiling at Alice – would no doubt make the names of many new stars, while the well-established leads would add to their past successes.

'Right, boys and girls, we'll make a start on the opening chorus. The scene is Paris at the turn of the century. Young Prunella has just arrived from finishing school in Switzerland. You are artists, models and *modistes*.'

Back at Maria's that night, they were too excited to go to bed. They stayed up quite late then, knowing that the next day would be demanding, made themselves turn in.

Alice's bed was not quite as comfortable as the one she had been sleeping in recently, but she knew she would not miss heavy footsteps on the stairs and Italian cursing and snoring. She drifted off and dreamed delicious dreams about Ben, who gave her a fountain pen.

The weeks of rehearsal flew by. Working hours were long and exhausting in the summer heat. The sessions were interspersed with fittings for an ever growing number of costumes, each more bizarre than the last. In one scene they wore mackintoshes and danced with large umbrellas. In a number showing Prunella in London, they had to make quite certain where they stood in relation to the girl next to them, as during the scene the stage was all but

179

blotted out by fog! In another scene, where the heroine was in an opulent hotel room, the dancers became animated furniture, and four of them had to carry and dance with a vast eiderdown, while two male dancers were bathroom taps and another was fitted for a hat in the shape of a shower head. Alice was a bright yellow lampshade, with a huge, circular wired skirt and wide fringe, and Trixie was even more unusually dressed – as a hotel Gideon Bible. Several of the troupe became pillows, another group a dressing table. But it was at the end of this scene when all the furniture and fittings had drifted off stage, that Alice had her big moment. She had to rush into the wings, get out of her bulky lampshade costume, and put on a flowing nightgown identical to Prunella's – who, by now, was asleep and starting to dream. Alice's music, a pretty waltz, was a joy for her to dance to, and during the work she did with the choreographer she made a lot of suggestions about the steps and *port de bras* which he readily accepted, knowing that what she suggested was far more lyrical than he could have devised.

There was a lot of singing for the leading lady who met, lost, then found her man, and the show was laced with romance, humour and comedy, with a second lead couple as Prunella's maid and the leading man's valet.

At the end of the four week rehearsal period, the train call notice went up in the dingy basement rehearsal rooms; LEAVE PENN STATION TWO-THIRTY WEDNESDAY AUGUST 8.

Bulky personal luggage could be sent with the costumes and scenery and on arrival they would be given a list of boarding houses and inexpensive hotels in Philadelphia. Alice and Trixie bought a theatrical skip – a large, square basket – for the clothes they would need for the four weeks in Philadephia and Boston. There was to be a week of on-stage rehearsals at the Fox Theater in Philly, and the show was due to open on Wednesday the fifteenth – Alice's twenty-third birthday.

Early on the evening of the eighth Trixie and Alice, along with the chorus and some of the principals, arrived in Philadelphia. Coaches were waiting to take them to the Fox Theater.

The theatre, which had only been open a few months, was situated on Market Street and Sixteenth, in the heart of Philadelphia's thriving theatre district. They entered from the front of house, through a spacious Moorish foyer (with, they noticed, an opulent lounge set aside for male patrons), and once in the auditorium itself gasped at the wealth of pink marble and the matching brocade drapes decorating the side niches of the circle. The rich effect was completed by the large crystal chandelier in the centre of the domed roof. The proscenium opening was wide, and the depth of the stage would do justice to what they had been assured was some of the most exciting and adventurous scenery yet to be designed for the American musical theatre.

Already sets were being assembled, and the company sat in the stalls seats,

180

covered by dust sheets. The producer addressed them, saying that he hoped they were as delighted with the beautiful theatre as he was, and made announcements about the coming week's rehearsals. The promised sheets of accommodation addresses with prices were handed out, and the company was called for stage rehearsals at ten the following morning.

Alice, Trixie and some of the other dancers decided on an inexpensive hotel in Market Street, two blocks away from the theatre.

The dancers already knew the routines and ensemble work, and most of the rehearsal time was spent in refining the technical side of the production. A particularly difficult transformation scene from the fog of London to a giant representation of Anne Hathaway's cottage at Stratford-on-Avon was very time consuming: the roof of the cottage seemed always to stick as it was lowered into position. The spectacular first half closedown was set on a storm-beleaguered liner in the mid-Atlantic, in which the heroine was being gallantly protected by her lover. This set also suffered from certain growing pains, but eventually the special effects worked well.

The cast had dressing-rooms large enough to accommodate themselves and their numerous costumes – there was no overcrowding. Alice, as principal dancer, was given one to herself, but invited Trixie to share with her. Looking along the rail of costumes and head-dresses she found them rather over-elaborate, and the weight of Trixie's bible costume was unbearable, stiffened at the shoulders as it was, and worn like a large placard, with the words 'Gideon Bible' printed right across it. The lampshade resembled a Spanish dress but, like everything about the show, was exaggerated, and altogether Alice felt the production appeared a mite vulgar, though she said nothing. Having had experience of marvellously elaborate costumes in the past, she was well aware of the borderline; but she assumed that as this was America the defining line between good taste and vulgarity was rather differently drawn. And at least she was, like the rest of the dancers, happy with the numbers. Everyone expected the Charleston number – set in a Hollywood night club – to be a show stopper, since this was the very latest and as yet almost unknown outside the most fashionable New York clubs.

The dress rehearsal went without a hitch, and the cast was out of the theatre by eight o'clock on the Monday before the Wednesday opening. Tuesday had been put aside for adjustments and 'notes'. The call for the chorus and Alice that day only lasted an hour, so during the afternoon Alice and Trixie went sightseeing, visiting the Betsy Ross House, the Independence Hall and the Liberty Bell. That night they found a traditional Pennsylvania eating house and had a happy time with four other girls and three of the boys from the chorus. Around midnight, knowing that the next day would be so busy, they wished Alice a happy birthday, and toasted her in lemonade. In the liveliest of moods they returned to their hotel deciding to lie in bed after a room service breakfast and look forward to their first night.

*

Singing Chorus:	'You're free, you're free,
	At last you're free . . .'
Prunella:	'Yes, yes I'm free, no more school for me,
	At last I can be *me, me, me!*'

The curtain was up on the opening scene, set in front of the Eiffel Tower. The high-spirited leading lady and chorus were revelling in the fact that she was now away from the restrictions of finishing school, and starting to live the exciting life of a pretty and extremely rich young lady.

> 'At Maxim's tonight
> I'll be in the spotlight . . .'

A bright pink spotlight poured down on the diminutive star.

Alice glanced across at Trixie who was working nearby. They felt a certain restlessness in the audience. Other dancers also noticed it, and their natural reaction was to smile and dance even more enthusiastically.

As the leading lady went off (to change for Maxim's) there was further shuffling, which stopped as the leading man made his entrance. The audience was quiet while he said a few lines, and seemed to enjoy his solo number – he had a good voice and was handsome – but they soon became restless again.

At the end of the first scene the cast, most of whom had a quick change, rushed to their dressing-rooms.

Trixie said to Alice, 'Listen, it's okay, they're applauding.'

The audience was applauding, but all too soon they realised it was a slow handclap.

'Oh, my God – they don't like it – they don't like it!'

The producer came round the dressing-rooms in turn.

'It's alright, girls – they'll love it from now on. It'll be just fine, especially when we get to the London and Stratford-on-Avon scenes.'

They changed into their shiny mackintoshes and picked up their black umbrellas ready for fog and rain. That scene did go rather better, and there was a modicum of applause as they rushed to the wings for the quick change into Elizabethan farthingales. While they were changing, the transformation to Anne Hathaway's cottage took place. Alice was fastening Trixie's dress and another girl was fastening hers.

'Heave ho!' came a cry from the audience.

They went on, on cue, and saw that the thatched roof was hanging at a precarious angle half way down, with a huge slanting gap at the top of the walls of the cottage. The audience rocked with laughter while the cast battled on.

After the scene on the liner came the interval, followed by more slow clapping; and there were a great number of empty pink plush seats to be seen as the curtain went up on the hotel bedroom scene.

As the dancers entered, clad in their bizarre costumes, cries and hoots of laughter from the audience reached a peak. Trixie had to come down centre stage and execute a few rather solemn priest-like movements in her Gideon's Bible costume, and one man in the stalls stood up and shouted, 'Why don't you read us a lesson, honey?' and cries of, 'Blasphemy, blasphemy!' were shouted down from the gallery.

The poor girl was terrified. Similar remarks were called out from all parts of the house at the human dressing-table and the quilt. The reaction to Alice's lampshade was, 'Why don't you light up this goddam show for us!'

In tears, she rushed off to change into the nightgown for her solo, and took up her position at the end of the enormous draped bed. Fortunately, anger and determination soon overcame her upset emotional state. The conductor started her little waltz and she began her dance.

Thoroughly caught up in the angry mood of the audience, a man stood up and yelled at her, 'We don't want that old fashioned stuff – get off!'

The man next to him punched him on the nose and responded equally loudly, 'Give the girl a chance, give the girl a chance!'

Alice could just see this, and could not fail to hear it, but she danced on. When the solo ended she got a round of applause. But the show went from bad to worse. People started to leave even during the lively Charleston number – the only man to stand and applaud was the one who had objected to Alice. At the end, a mere third of the audience remained.

The well-rehearsed curtain calls were not needed. The cast took one bow – among boos and jeering.

Speechless, with many of the cast in tears and the leading lady hysterical – she had been particularly badly received – they returned to their dressing-rooms. All celebrations had been cancelled. The show was a total disaster, the morning papers scathing. Alice completely forgot that it was her birthday.

They were called for noon the following day.

'We've been having discussions all night with the backers and the managements in Boston and Broadway. We tried to devise drastic changes to the production, but the show would have to be re-written, the score radically changed and most of the sets and costumes redesigned and made. So the backers have come to the sad decision to close the show and cut their losses.'

A wave of shock and cries of, 'Oh, no!' ran through the stunned cast. The producer continued, 'You will all be paid for this week, and my secretary will give you your return train tickets to New York. We know that the failure of the show is nothing to do with you; we sincerely trust that you will soon find new jobs when you return to Broadway. Sadly, this is goodbye – and thank you.'

Alice and Trixie were back at their hotel packing the skip.

'I can't believe it, I really can't! Here we were, set for an honest bit of success at last, and now this. What are we going to do, Alice?'

'Well, I don't think we should make any rash decisions yet. We're too much in shock.'

'I heard some of the girls talking about cabaret. Four of them are going to form a sister act – what about that?'

The idea had no appeal for Alice, who remembered her unfortunate experiences in that branch of the business. It was not at all in line with her main objectives – to express her dancing and acting skills and to make a real name for herself. But how to do that, now her promising role was no more? She was thwarted and her outlook depressing. They attempted to keep their minds on the practical issues of checking out of their hotel, collecting pay and rail tickets and taking the train, all too soon, back to New York and Maria's. They also had to make arrangements for their large skip to be delivered.

The girls and Maria had read of the disaster in *Variety* that morning, and were very upset. To cheer Alice and Trixie the motherly Maria produced brandy and served it in teacups, but they were in a very unhappy and confused state when they went up to their room that night. The situation was so unexpected. Hopes which had been so high had been dashed within minutes of the show opening. It was totally damned both by the trade papers and the critics, though one writer managed a kind phrase about Alice, having earlier referred to the caterwauling of the leading lady, the ghastly dancing bedroom furniture and the unruly scenery.

'One bright moment in the fiasco,' he wrote, 'was the lyrical dancing of Alice Townsend, though her sickly sweet music was excruciating . . . This show is a disgrace – and a very expensive disgrace – both to the American musical comedy theatre and its backers. The producer should have realised early in rehearsal that the plot was unbelievably stupid, the sets and costumes tasteless and the score and performances of the principals banal and amateurish.'

'Well, honey,' Trixie said when she'd read it, 'you seem to have been the only good thing in the whole production, so *you* shouldn't find it too difficult to get another job, though everyone else'll have to keep very quiet about it.'

'But, Trix, we're back to square one.'

Alice was sitting on the edge of her bed looking down at her feet. The girls were exhausted, but felt unable to settle down and sleep after the dreary train journey back, during which no-one had spoken, everyone was immersed in their own thoughts as they tried to come to terms with the huge disappointment.

'Let's try to get some sleep. Sleep on it, that's what my mom always says. We'll feel different in the morning.'

They went to bed, but sleep would not come. For well over an hour they kept tossing and turning until, at last, Alice sat up in bed, realising that Trixie was as awake as she was.

'I can't sleep, can you?'

'No, I'm wide awake.'

'Let's go down to the kitchen and make some cocoa.'

They put on their dressing-gowns and made their way noiselessly down to the basement kitchen. Sitting at the large table they sipped the hot cocoa silently.

'Any ideas?'

'Well no, but I've come to one conclusion – that I'm not going to go back to selling cheese, and I'll only leave this place for reasons of work, not because I'm no longer in the profession.'

'Good thought. But where do we go from here?'

'Well, we'll first have to work out exactly how much money we've got, decide how long we can last without paid work, and discover what auditions are coming up. Money's the most important. I've got the hundred dollars I was paid today, and you had seventy-five. How much have you saved during rehearsals?'

They had been on half pay for rehearsals. Alice had had fifty dollars a week and Trixie thirty-four. Out of that each had paid ten a week to Maria for lodging, but Alice had paid two weeks' rent out of her money from Mr Mandaro. They had bought some new summer frocks and an evening dress apiece, and had spent a certain amount on food, cinema visits, and the occasional taxi.

Having done their sums they found that Alice had three hundred and twenty-six dollars, while Trixie, who had been in a revue until fairly recently, had two hundred and sixty. She was less careful than Alice, but Alice had had to spend quite a lot on her tap classes and dancing shoes.

They were not too badly off – but the money they had might have to last for quite a number of weeks. They could survive for quite a long time, if they were careful and didn't become a soft touch for any friend wanting a loan, or allow themselves to be seduced by glamorous gowns in expensive New York department stores.

'Now do you want to stick it out here?'

'Why? Where else is there?' Alice looked puzzled at her friend's remark.

'Only I was thinking coming back in the train – you know while everyone else was sad and quiet –'

'Go on.'

'Well, you know I've got a friend – Annabelle – from Texas, nice dancer, got fed up with waiting around here, and . . .' Trixie paused to take her last mouthful of cocoa '. . . went over to Hollywood. I had a letter from her just a few weeks ago. She's doing alright. Lots of extra work in films, and she's getting noticed by important film directors. She's actually been tested for a small part. What d'you think? After all, you nearly made it – you know the camera likes you. I was wondering – why don't we go while we've got some money?'

Alice had put all thoughts of a film career out of her mind; but as Trixie had said, they did have the money – enough to set themselves up at least for the time.

'I'm not sure – it's very risky. It's such a long way. What if it doesn't work out?'

'But it might. And we can always come back East if doesn't work. I just don't want to be in another turkey.'

'No, neither do I.'

'Look, you'll be just fine, you're such a good actress too. You've got so much talent. It'll only need you to get one job and they'll recognise it! And me – well, we'll just see.'

'I must say it's not a bad idea.'

The plan fired Alice's imagination and her determination to succeed. She also found it exciting as an antidote to the crashing disappointment she had felt last year, when she so nearly won the competition. She thought, but what if I run into Margaret Leahy, and she's a big star and I'm a mere extra? That would be dreadfully humiliating and severely damage her sense of pride. But it was a situation she could surely deal with should it arise. Then, what if she met Norma or Constance? But by now they would have forgotten all about her, having seen so many faces in England. Did she really like New York and the Broadway scene? Yes, people had been kind to her – even if she had had to rise above her disastrous arrival, and work so dreadfully hard at Mandaro's.

Then, what about Alex? He was probably now well-established with the Russian Ballet, and no doubt dancing with other partners – all more famous than ever she could hope to be. She missed him so much – his good advice, his warm, brotherly affection and his sense of humour. She wondered what he would have suggested. Probably something like, 'Go, sweet lassie – go!'

So why not move on? She had experienced several months of Broadway and had just one disaster to show for it. She was not getting any younger, and, as Trixie had said, there was no reason why they shouldn't return if things went against them.

Trixie could put up with Alice's silence no longer.

'Well – what do you think? Shall we sleep on it, or decide now? I know what *I* want to do. *I* want to go, and the sooner the better!'

'Right, let's go!'

Chapter 23

Alex, sitting at an outdoor café a few yards from the Monte Carlo Opera House, opened his letter from Basil. His lover told him how much he had missed him since his return to New York, gave news of mutual friends and forthcoming Broadway productions, and said that his business commitments were very satisfactory. Alex was slightly bored with this gossip until his eyes fixed on the next paragraph –

'Jameson tells me that a few days after we left a young woman turned up here claiming to be your friend Alice Townsend. Quite rightly, he did not allow her to stay ... It appears her cable and letter arrived after we left ...'

A small newspaper cutting fell out of the hand-written pages.

'From curtain up at the Fox Theater, *Prunella's Progress* was a disaster, relieved only by a fragment of pretty ballet dancing – albeit to a banal and sickly waltz – by English dancer Alice Townsend ...'

Basil had scribbled in the margin, 'Presumably this is your friend!'

Alex sat motionless as he read this unexpected news. This was why he had received no letters from Alice. He had written regularly since suggesting she join him in New York. There had been some news about her pantomime, but nothing since and, what had hurt him, there was no word of encouragement or congratulation when he had hurriedly and excitedly told her that he was now an established member of the Russian Ballet.

So was she still somewhere in New York, or did that disastrous flop send her scurrying back to London? He was overcome by the irony of the situation. If only her letter had arrived a day or so earlier he was certain that Basil would have allowed her to stay on in his house after they had left, and equally sure that a few words in the right direction from his friend would have given Alice the golden opportunity really to show off her talents where they would have been readily accepted. But this flop had only happened just over two weeks ago. What had happened to her during the intervening months?

Alex was puzzled and unhappy. Then in his despair his thoughts turned in another direction. Perhaps Alice could have been here with him – working together again in the ballet – if Basil would have agreed to allow Alice to travel to Monte Carlo with them. But sighing, he thought that would have been unlikely. Basil might well have felt that Alice posed a threat to their relationship, though Alex, knowing Alice so well, knew that simply would not have been the case.

But what could he do now? He desperately wanted to know where Alice was, and what she was doing. Due to his commitments with the ballet company he could not go over to London to see if she was in the flat, neither could he return to New York and start a search for her there. He decided he would telegraph Joan. If Alice had arrived back, she would know immediately – yes, that was a much better idea than sending a wire directly to Alice at that address. Joan would immediately pass it on to her if she *was* there, and perhaps he would get news of his favourite girl very soon, to end the months of his nagging anxiety over her whereabouts.

Finishing his coffee and croissant and blinking in the strong sun, he picked up his bag of shoes and practice clothes and crossed over the wide road to the Opera House for the first rehearsal of the company's latest ballet, *Les Noces*.

Two days later there was a cable in his post box at the Opera House. Tearing it open he read, 'ALICE LEFT IN MARCH STOP NO NEWS STOP LETTER FOLLOWS STOP LOVE JOAN.'

The cable had been handed in at Chelsea Post Office.

Until Joan's letter arrived, he knew he could do nothing.

'Thank you ma'am. Two single tickets to Los Angeles. That'll be thirty-six dollars and twelve cents each. Change terminals at Chicago.'

'And is that difficult?'

'No, ma'am – there's a regular service between the terminals. Nope, no problems. Next, please.'

Alice handed Trixie her ticket.

During the last few days they had each packed a case, and arranged with Maria to have their skip sent on once they had an address in Hollywood, where Annabelle was to meet them. She said that by the time they arrived she would have found accommodation for them. Their seats and sleeping accommodation were booked for the following evening.

Alice had no qualms about moving on. Her adventurous spirit had been ignited by Trixie's suggestion and she was buoyed up by the encouragement she had received not only from Trixie but from other girls at Maria's, when they heard just how well she had done in the film star competition.

The famous 'Twentieth Century' train was extremely luxurious for first-class passengers, but even their accommodation was good. Sleeping bunks lined each side of a long compartment, arranged on two levels, one above the other, with little curtains to pull over for privacy once the passenger was settled down for the night.

The train left at eight sharp from the magnificent Grand Central Terminal, and the two girls debated whether or not they should afford dinner, or simply have some food at the station before they boarded. With difficulty Alice persuaded Trixie that the latter was the most sensible thing to do.

They found their bunks, and settled down to the journey as the train increased speed and, scurrying through the night, headed west on its journey to Chicago.

The following morning they went to the dining car for breakfast, which they enjoyed in considerable luxury and decided that as they were smartly dressed they could risk sitting in the observation car set aside for first-class passengers. The girls spent the morning looking out of the window and reading bulky American fashion magazines with advertisements for smart Hollywood boutiques and for the great stores – Bloomingdale's and Bonwitt Teller's in New York and Marshall Field in Chicago. Gloating over the pages, Trixie sighed, 'Do you think we'll ever just be able to breeze into any of these and not bother to ask the price of an outfit?'

'If I know you – and I think I do – and if I know *me*, yes, of course!'

They smiled and giggled. Enthusiasm, ambition and huge optimism kept them in the happiest and most positive of moods.

Leaving the train at Chicago with other passengers, Trixie grabbed Alice's arm.

'Look at *them*!'

They saw four extremely menacing-looking men in vicuna overcoats and dark sunglasses emerging from the next carriage. They knocked over an elderly woman as they rushed to the exit, not caring who they pushed out of the way to get there.

'Don't like the look of them do you, Trix?'

'No, not a bit! We must be careful – there's loads of crime here. It's worse than New York.'

'Well, we'll not be here long – and the sooner we get to the West Railroad terminal the better.'

The coach stop for the bus to take them to the terminal for the Atchinson Topeka and Santa Fe train for the long journey was nearby. It would take them another three days and two nights to get to Los Angeles.

They were the last to board the third coach, staggering on just as the driver started to move away. The coach made its way along a wide impressive boulevard then abruptly turned right. After crossing several blocks police whistles caused an emergency stop which threw the passengers forward in their seats.

'Look at that, Alice.'

Trixie was sitting by the window.

Down a side street they saw the bodies of two men on the pavement surrounded by pools of blood, and armed police scurrying around, guns in hand. One tackled a heavy man who was attempting to run away, and assisted by a colleague led him towards a wall where he was searched ('frisked', Trixie said) and forced into the back of a police car. Further gunshots were heard, but from where they were sitting they could not see what else was going on.

'Why does this always happen to us? We only want to get to L.A. This damn Chicago!' sighed an impatient man in the seat in front as the more nervous passengers crouched down under the protection of their seats, to make sure they were out of the line of firing.

After a delay of about ten minutes, during which an ambulance picked up the two bodies, the coach was waved on its way to the terminal, where relieved, but in rather a state of shock, the young women and the other passengers boarded the famous train. Alice felt that England and home were a very long way away indeed.

Their accommodation on the train was similar to that on the 'Twentieth Century', but the observation coaches seemed wider and broader, affording plenty of space in which to sit, stretch out and enjoy the passing landscape. There was no lack of bars and restaurant cars, and they decided that on the second night of the trip they would have a really good dinner. If they were clever and put on their most fashionable outfits, they just might find some interesting company.

The journey was memorable for the changing landscape of the huge country as Iowa and Nebraska gave way to Wyoming, and eventually the plains of the Nevada desert opened up. At last the train entered the state of California to stop at San Francisco before turning due south towards Los Angeles. As they made their way to their bunks late on the second night of the trip, Trixie said,

'Well, we did alright there, didn't we? Pity they had to get off at San Fo!'

They had had a long and enjoyable dinner at which they had been joined by two middle-aged men who were delighted to have the company of two beautiful young women. The men told them they were in insurance, (though Alice rather felt that 'insurance' probably meant 'protection'). The meal had been chatty, flirtatious and good fun, but they declined an invitation to join the men in their compartment for champagne – the suggestion having been whispered to them in discreet undertones.

'Yes, they were delighted to learn about London, and your knowledge of horses really impressed them! And when we said we'd been in a big show you should have seen Dirk's eyes!'

They giggled at the memory.

'And of course our show was a *huge* success, wasn't it?'

Now in hysterics, they reminded themselves that they had not mentioned that it had flopped after one performance!

'And what's more . . .'

190

Alice was about to continue but Trixie spoke for her, 'They picked up our check! Pity we didn't meet them sooner.'

'*That* could have caused a lot of complications. After all they weren't exactly handsome, were they?'

'Might have been rich, though,' said Trixie, thoughtfully.

Later that day the train at last pulled into the Los Angeles Terminal, and the girls stepped out into the blazing sunshine of the high Californian summer afternoon.

'Annabelle said she would be at the end of the platform . . . Look, there she is!'

Alice saw where Trixie was pointing to a tiny curvaceous girl with a mass of short, very blonde curls poking out from under a pink frilly organza sun hat.

The old friends hugged each other and Trixie introduced Alice.

'Why, hi! Great to meet you. I've got Ivan outside. He'll take us all to your apartment. I've found you a place in a block where I used to live until I moved in with Ivan. You'll like him – he's Russian – came here after the revolution with his parents. He's rich!'

'So are you getting lots of work in films, like you said?'

'Well, er, no, Trixie – actually, Ivan . . .'

'Is looking after you?'

'He sure is. Look here he is, and there's his car!'

Annabelle pointed to a long red open tourer. On seeing her and her friends, a youngish, fair haired man got out and made a little bow to the two of them, saying, 'Welcome'.

'You'll have to excuse him. He can't speak too much English.'

Turning to her man and tending to shout, 'Now, Ivan, you know where.'

'Yes, I know where.'

He put the two cases in the trunk of the car, and very politely opened the back door for Alice and Trixie to get in.

They drove off.

'The apartment isn't very smart, but you said you needed somewhere inexpensive to start – like I did.' Chewing furiously on her gum, Annabelle went on, 'You'll soon be able to find something better. You must get over to Central Casting tomorrow and sign on.'

'Yes, that's what we plan to do. How much do they pay?'

'Depends on what you do. Five dollars a day, usually – but if you have to wear your own clothes or get a closeup, then luck's in. Not that that happens very often, unless a director takes a fancy to you. The more you can do the better, because they'll put it all on your cards.'

'How do we get to Central Casting?'

Annabelle turned back to Ivan and thumping him on the shoulder, said, 'Spare street map, gimme.'

'Yes, okay. Look in pocket.'

It was not where he suggested. She got annoyed. How stupid Russians were.

'Don't be unkind, Annabelle – he seems so nice.'

'Oh, sure, he has his uses.' Then she smiled at him and stroked Ivan's arm, knowing that he did not understand what she had said.

'We're going to drive you round for a while to show you some of the sights.'

Alice appreciated the idea, but disliked the girl. It was kind of her to have sorted out things at this end, but she hoped they would not have very much to do with her. The wealthy Russian boy seemed far too nice for her.

By now Annabelle had found the map, and marked the Central Casting offices on it. They drove on.

'Look, there's Grauman's Egyptian Theater – that's where all the big photoplay premiers are held. Up there to the north is Universal Studios.'

Alice felt a pang: Norma and Constance had mentioned Universal during the competition. After driving through Beverley Hills they left the film stars' beautiful houses and grounds far behind them, returning towards West Hollywood. Eventually, Ivan turned into a wide but unmade, dusty road where small single storey houses and low apartment blocks stood cheek by jowl.

'Okay, Ivan, remember? It's the second block on the left. Stop anywhere along here.'

The car drew to a halt.

Alice looked up at the rather squat building, with an outside flight of steps up to a front door, which was swinging in the breeze.

'Well, here we are – like it?' Annabelle's cheery voice rang out above the noise of two babies crying and a very loud gramophone scratching discordant jazz.

It was awful, but Alice smiled weakly.

'Yes, it's fine. Thanks – and thanks for all your help – and Ivan's too.'

'Well, he has his uses!' she repeated and made certain that Alice saw the large solitaire diamond glistening on the third finger of her left hand.

'Yes, we are grateful, Annabelle – we really are!' added Trixie.

'Anything for an old hoofer.'

By now Ivan had meekly carried the two cases up the long flight of steps, taken them into the apartment, and was returning.

'I had to pay a month's rent in advance for you. Fifty dollars.'

Alice and Trixie gave her twenty-five each. Mentioning that there were plenty of food stores nearby, and a market where they could buy fresh fruit, Annabelle got back in the car and Ivan drove off, raising a vast cloud of dust.

'We'd better go up.'

They tried to shut the front door, but the lock was broken. It took a while for their eyes to get accustomed to the dark interior, but when they did they could hardly believe what they saw.

The sun glinted through a cracked window, lighting up so many dust particles that it looked as though there was a smoking chimney in the long, narrow room. At the far end was a faded cotton curtain hung on a droopy wire, and when they pulled it back they saw the bedroom, furnished only with a large iron bedstead, some not very clean sheets and pillowcases folded on top of several blankets and striped ticking-covered pillows.

The girls looked at each other.

'It's . . .'

Trixie paused. 'It's, well . . .'

'Awful? And dirty?' said Alice.

'Filthy!'

Trixie scraped her foot along the thin, worn lino. It made a gritty sound, as though the dust from the street had been blowing in for weeks and no-one had taken the trouble to sweep the floor.

'Where's the bathroom and kitchen?'

'Look, there are two doors.'

A foul smell greeted them from behind the first. The lavatory was cracked, and the shower area heavily discoloured. Water dripped from the bent shower head.

'Yuck – how *can* anyone . . .' sighed Alice.

'Quick, shut the door! I can't bear the smell!'

The second door revealed an equally squalid, tiny kitchen, with a gas stove that looked as if it might be coaxed into action if given a good clean. A row of battered saucepans was ranged above it, hung on nails, and in two drawers by the sink was a collection of tarnished cutlery. A few mugs and plates were scattered untidily on a shelf.

They returned to the living room and sat on a battered sofa, falling against each other as its broken springs gave way under them. They fell silent for a moment.

'Have you ever seen *anywhere* so dreadful?'

'Quite honestly, Trixie, no, never. Well, we're stuck with it for a while. At least it'll give us the incentive to work hard and get out!'

'Like Annabelle did?'

'Well, perhaps not exactly like she did. But after seeing this, who's to blame her.'

Heaving a sigh, Alice went on, 'But look, let's be practical. I'm not going to take a thing out of my case until we've cleaned the place right through. Did you see any mops or buckets?'

'No, but here's the rent book Annabelle gave me, and there's the name and address of the landlord. Perhaps he's nearby, and we can borrow some – and complain about the state of the apartment!'

Referring to it and the map they discovered that the landlord lived miles away.

'We'll have to find the shops and buy some cleaning things.'

'Yes, and some kind of a lock for the front door. Can we fix it ourselves, do you think?'

'Well,' said Alice, 'I think I could, but we'll need a screwdriver. Let's see if we can find an ironmonger's. The shops seem to be just down the road.'

Apprehensively leaving their cases hidden under the bed amid what looked like years of fluff, they ventured into the road, and found a row of tiny but very practical shops. They bought a bucket, floor mop, dusters and cleaning cloths, washing soap and soap powder, some very strong disinfectant, household bleach, two pairs of rubber gloves and a trash can. At an ironmonger's they made enquiries about a lock. The young man there was helpful; he enjoyed meeting two such attractive young women. He asked where they were living, and said he would come and fix the lock for them after six o'clock when he closed his shop.

Returning to the dump (as they immediately called their apartment) they stripped off their summer frocks and in their underclothes started their 'spring cleaning'. Exhausted, by half-past five they were satisfied that the place looked very different, but they still had to tackle the cooker and the shower. Next day they would buy scouring powder and steel wool.

The young ironmonger was as good as his word and by the time it was getting dark they had the security of a front door that not only closed, but locked as well.

'Well, we can't cook ourselves anything. We'll just have to go out, whether we can afford it or not,' said Trixie, and Alice had to agree.

They felt filthy, but rather than attempt to use the shower in its present state they filled the bucket and gave themselves all over washes. Around half past seven they went down the road again to a tiny café, and had a good broiled steak and some French fries.

Returning to the dump, they realised that the bed linen was just discoloured rather than dirty. It smelt as if it had been dried in the open air, so they made up the bed and turned in, deciding that next day they would continue their cleaning, and scrub a large clothes closet before unpacking. Getting to Central Casting would have to be delayed until the afternoon, by which time they hoped they would be settled in, with a relatively clean kitchen stocked with food, and a bathroom appearing well-worn rather than filthy (the disinfectant and bleach had already worked well on the lavatory).

The bed creaked and groaned every time either friend turned over, but fortunately, because of its size, there was plenty of room, and surprisingly they failed to roll towards each other and collide, as is often the case with old beds.

Alice woke first and, getting out of bed, pulled back the faded window curtain to be dazzled by the brightness of the light. The dusty street was deserted except for a farmer's truck lumbering towards the shops delivering, she supposed, fruit and vegetables.

Trixie stirred.

'Hi! Did you sleep well?'

'Better than I expected.'

As Alice replied, she automatically scratched her arm.

'Oh, I've been bitten! It must have been a fly, when we were out at the shops yesterday. How odd that I didn't notice it before!'

Sitting up in bed, Trixie cried, 'My God – I've got three on my leg! Look! Oh no, it can't be!'

'What, Trix? Fleas?'

'No, Alice, worse. Bed bugs. I'm sure it's bed bugs. They live in the furniture and floorboards by day, and come out at night. They like human warmth. They must have got into the mattress!'

Alice was horrified. She'd heard of such things – but as for actually having them crawling all over her . . .

'How awful!' she said with a shudder. 'What are we going to do?!'

Trixie took control of the situation.

'I've seen this before – in my first show, when we were in a slum district of Baltimore.'

'I don't care about Baltimore! What are we going to do?'

'First, calamine lotion. I've got some in my case. That'll cool the itching.'

As they applied it, Alice anxiously asked, 'But what about the *bugs*?'

'Don't touch the bed. Get that big cake of kitchen soap. I'll see if I can catch at least one or two.'

'One or two? Will there be a lot?'

'Scores, I expect – they breed like rabbits!'

Alice mystified, and shivering at the horror of the invasion, got the soap, and gave it to Trixie.

Holding the soap in one hand, Trixie stealthily crept up to the bed, and very quickly threw back the blankets and sheets. As she did so she slammed the soap down onto the under-sheet three times.

Then turning it to look at the side that had been in contact with the sheet she smiled with satisfaction.

'There you are! That's three of the little devils.'

Alice, almost faint with disgust, not wanting to see but knowing she would have to look, cautiously leant nearer.

'Ugh! They're not that little, are they?'

'Nope! We'll have to spray the whole place with insecticide, so it's back to the ironmonger's to buy some, and I suppose a spray gun, if he's got one. And we'll have to get rid of that mattress and buy a new one.'

They put on their oldest clothes and heaved the thing towards the door, rolling it down the flight of steps to the back yard and an area obviously set aside for rubbish. They managed to find an inexpensive mattress which was delivered right away. They kept the receipt for it, hoping against hope that the landlord would reimburse them.

Those wretched but necessary tasks, and the spraying of the insecticide, took up their morning; and during the afternoon they attacked the shower and the cooker. It wasn't until four o'clock that they felt they could go and buy food, hoping that the insecticide would kill the bugs and satisfied that the shower and cooker were as clean as they could possibly be.

It was the end of the second day before they could unpack, and think seriously about what they had really come to do. They made a list of complaints for whoever would come and collect the rent.

'This is hardly glamorous Hollywood, is it?' said Alice, as they settled down for their second night.

'No, but the bed's more comfortable, and at least we won't get bitten again. Tomorrow we'll put on our best and go visit Central Casting – they won't know what's hit them!'

'Next, please.'

Alice and Trixie exchanged glances.

'Well, come on – I've not got all day!'

Trixie got up from the end of the row where she was sitting and went to the desk. Meanwhile, Alice took in everything that was going on around them.

They were waiting to register with about twenty other young men and women. Earlier that morning, having examined their map, they discovered that they were living more centrally than they had realised. The dump was just off a busy street that led up to the Santa Monica Boulevard, and from there it took them only about twenty minutes to reach the corner of Vine Street and Sunset Boulevard and the twelve-storey Taft Building which housed Central Casting, where everyone set on a career in movies must register.

They had found their way to the registrar's office down a long corridor lined with dozens of hopefuls waiting to see if there would be work for them – every studio referred to this agency for their needs.

After about ten minutes Trixie returned, but before she could say anything, the rather surly shout of, 'Next, please' sent Alice towards the desk.

Having asked her name and age, the registrar muttered,

'Right – Anglo-Saxon type. Do you have a good wardrobe?'

'Why, yes – quite good, really.'

'You Irish?'

'No, English, actually.'

'Well, what can you do? Ride a horse, anything like that?'

'No, but I'm a dancer – all types, classical ballet, musical, tap, torch numbers – I've done the lot!'

'Oh, you have, have you?' The man sounded as if he did not believe her, and when Alice, to enhance her position, added that she had danced with the Russian Ballet he replied with, 'So what? Can you act?'

'Of course. I've trained in London – and I came second in Miss Talmadge's competition for the English Rose Hollywood star.'

'Oh yeah? All you English girls say that!'

Alice was appalled at his negative, bored reaction. She was tempted to suggest that he check with Norma, but decided that it would do no good to put his back up.

'Well, I daresay we can use you from time to time. Your number's seven-hundred-and-eighty-six. Report here every day, and we'll do the rest. Okay, next, please.'

They left the large office block realising that they had done everything they could. They would just have to report again tomorrow, and the day after, and the day after that, until . . .

'At last, our first day's work!'

After a week which had seemed like an eternity, a clerk gave them a card which had their individual numbers printed on, and with instructions for the following day. They were to meet outside the Taft Building at six on the following morning, where they would be picked up and taken to a location. No particular dress was necessary, but it was suggested that they wear sun hats, as that would suit the crowd scenes to be shot at an out of town location.

Excited at the prospect, they arrived on time. Several charabancs were lined up to take some fifty extras of varying ages and types to an open space which was obviously being prepared for building. The crowd had to rush at a young man who was attempting to escape from the police. There were numerous takes, but eventually the director was satisfied. At the end of the day the extras lined up and were given envelopes with their pay – all of five dollars – and the transport arrived to take them back to the corner of Sunset and Vine.

'Well, that was alright, wasn't it? But not exactly thrilling.'

'No, but it's a start, Alice, and someone important might have seen us. After all, we were put right in front of the crowd, so who knows . . .'

Trixie's eyes started to shine in anticipation of stardom yet to come.

'Well, let's hope for some more work soon.'

During the next few weeks they had several more days like the first. Sometimes they had to wear old crinolines, sometimes they formed part of the crowd in huge historical epics – the most rewarding, was *The Hunchback of Notre Dame*, starring Lon Chaney. In this they wore rough, ragged medieval costumes. If the photoplay happened to be set in Roman times they were given very brief costumes, but they had no real opportunity to show off their skills. However, the dollars came in handy, and they soon realised that they were hardly drawing on their meagre reserves of cash at all.

One day there was a knock on the door. It was the rent man asking for the fifty dollars for the coming month. They told him about the mattress, but he said that it was not his fault that it was full of bugs, and would not allow them anything for it.

Life fell into a pattern. On working days they would go in the evenings to their little local restaurant for a steak, and on others buy good fresh vegetables and fruit, bread and meat, and make salads and simple dishes and eat at the dump. They passed the time of day with neighbours when hanging out washing, and the shopkeepers were friendly. Life was endurable, but really rather dull. They wanted more out of life in Hollywood than they were getting, but at present it seemed that they would have to be content with things as they were.

Chapter 24

'I'd like to welcome you to our production. It's going to be a lavish photo-play about a small girl who dreams of becoming a Hollywood star, dancing on the silver screen. My name is Sheldon Leroy, and I'm the director. I expect the agency told you we'll be wanting you for several days.'

Alice and Trixie looked at each other. They had been in Hollywood for three months, and this was the best work they had been given so far. The pay was good – twelve dollars a day – and they knew they would be dancing, along with eighteen other girls of roughly the same size and height.

'You're very fortunate – this is a good opportunity for you. I plan to pan across your beautiful faces, so you'll all be getting a BCU.'

He noticed one or two girls look rather blankly at each other.

'Oh, I can see some of you are new to the movies! BCU means Big Close Up. So keep smiling! Now, for the next few hours you'll be working with our dance director, and be fitted for the first of your costumes. We'll go for the takes tomorrow, when the star of our photoplay, little Miss Baby Bettykins, will be on set with you.'

The steps they learned were extremely easy, though some of the girls, while very pretty, had some difficulty, hardly knowing their left foot from their right. By the time transport arrived to take them home from United Artists, they had learned three simple routines and the partially made costumes had been fitted. With seamstresses working through the night they would be ready for the take the following day.

As they were leaving the lot, Sheldon Leroy called, 'Goodnight, Alice! See you tomorrow!'

'Goodnight, Mr Leroy.'

'Call me Sheldon – and that goes for you too, Trixie.'

His black hair shone in a bright studio light and his slick, narrow moustache emphasised a dazzling smile.

'Goodnight, er, Sheldon!' called Trixie, nudging Alice in the ribs.

'Right, Magnolia Dell, I take it Bettykins knows her routine.'

'Of course she does, Sheldon.'

The woman who was obviously Bettykins' mother was wearing a dress completely covered in pale blue tulle frills. Her bleached blonde hair fell over her shoulders in a plethora of ringlets, crowned by a large matching bow.

'Right, get her from make-up and we'll go for a take.'

Magnolia Dell teetered off the set, and returned a few minutes later with a little girl of about six years. To Alice and Trixie's surprise, they were dressed identically.

'Now, darling, you stand there, then when Uncle Sheldon shouts action . . .'

The child lisped, 'Yeth, I know, Mommy – I thtart my number.'

To Alice's horror, the little girl was wearing pointe shoes. She was far too young to dance *en pointe*. But worse was to follow.

On cue, the band struck up and the child jumped up onto her toes and started to tap dance on them. Alice and Trixie, who were working next to each other, hardly dared glance at each other for fear of laughing and making a mistake in their own steps. The routine had been going for almost a minute, the child putting a massive amount of cute energy into her hideous routine, when suddenly she cried out, 'Mommy, Mommy – I can't go on, I can't go on!'

'*Cut*!'

Sheldon Leroy glared angrily at mother and daughter.

'Magnolia Dell, come *on* now – we'll be behind schedule and over budget.'

The child, stamping her feet and rubbing her eyes, started to bawl loudly enough to make everyone jump, as well as sighing with boredom at the delay.

'Mommy, Mommy – a tooth's come out.'

'For Christ's sake . . .!'

Furious, Sheldon walked up to mother and daughter. The child grinned toothlessly.

The three of them conferred, then Sheldon made an announcement.

'Well, everyone, that's it for today. We'll have to break while Bettykins goes to the dentist to have a false tooth made. This will be done immediately, and you'll be called as usual tomorrow morning. The delay won't effect your pay, you'll be glad to hear.'

With the wretched child still throwing the most awful tantrum and yelling that she would *not* go to the dentist, they all trooped out of the studio and changed into their street clothes.

As they did so another dancer, Babs, said to Alice and Trixie, 'This is the third photoplay I've been in with that brat and her equally awful mother. There's always some sort of a fuss to delay shooting – but least that way we get extra money!'

'Tell me, will she really have a false tooth?' asked Alice.

'Oh, sure – they often do that with child stars. She's really seven, and it won't be the first she's had! Her mother tells everyone she's only four to keep her in work that much longer. But they'll have to stop using her soon.'

*

199

'Right, girls. I've just heard that Bettykins won't be available today. The false tooth and plate are proving a problem. So we'll shoot part of your third number, where she is out of shot. I'll be making that long pan, so get ready for your close-ups.'

All the girls were wearing identical white wigs with knee-length flowing satin gowns, and carrying long georgette scarves which they wove into flowing patterns. At one point they stood in a line, their heads slightly tilted back towards the girl next to them.

'Right, that's beautiful,'

The camera rolled. Each girl smiled in turn . . .

When Trixie and Alice got back home that evening, Trixie said, 'You know, I think we should be more adventurous. We should go out and make sure we're seen. We must go where the stars go, and look as if we've just landed a huge contract.'

Alice agreed.

'We should have been doing that for weeks and if we've not been able to afford it, now we're getting on a bit we ought to make the effort. Besides, it'll be fun.'

'I was talking to Babs earlier today,' said Trixie, 'and she said the best place to go is Henry's – it's a restaurant up on Sunset. You can sit there all evening with wonderful coffee and cakes, and their turkey sandwiches are real good. Charlie Chaplin's got money in the place. Who knows who we might see there?'

They put on their best frocks, made sure their nails were varnished bright red – to match their immaculate lipstick – and made their way to the restaurant, which was crowded with lively, chatting, laughing diners, the air heavy with cigarette smoke. After waiting for a few minutes they were shown to one of the many little box-like compartments which surrounded the walls of the wooden structure, and ordered the famous turkey sandwiches and coffee. Making the food last, they spent a couple of hours looking out for personalities. They spotted Lillian and Dorothy Gish – who smiled charmingly at them – and Adolphe Menjou passed by with Ramon Navarro. This was what being in Hollywood was all about! Their confidence grew: they were, after all, just that little bit more successful than mere crowd extras.

That evening, Sheldon Leroy was watching the rushes. He ran the film through three times. The girl second from the end in the BCU line-up was stunningly beautiful. He could do a lot with her. Smiling and rubbing his hands, he went back to his office and prepared the shots he wanted to get in the can for the next day, when, he expected and hoped, Baby Bettykins' false tooth would be in place and she and her mother in a better mood.

The day's shooting had gone well. As Alice was returning to the dressing-room Sheldon called to her, 'Alice, will you get changed and come to my office, please?'

'Why, yes, Sheldon.'

Trixie nudged her in the ribs.

'Well, how about that honey? Do your stuff!'

Alice changed, took off her heavy film make-up and went up to Sheldon's office. He greeted her and gestured her to sit down.

'Look, Alice, I've been watching you. I'm planning my next photoplay, and we need a gypsy dancer. You're very versatile – I see from your card you've had a lot of stage experience – so I would like you to work out something.'

'Is Baby Bettykins appearing in it?'

Sheldon laughed, charmed by Alice's cautious reaction.

'No, not at all. But I think you could go far. In two weeks' time, when we've finished shooting this, let me see what you can do with the idea for a gypsy number, and if I like it, and if you approve of my ideas, there's no reason why you shouldn't have the part. What do you say? Like the idea?'

'Sheldon, it's a wonderful idea! Yes, of course I can work out a gypsy dance – I've done several in the past. Will I have to show it to Bert?'

'No, we don't need a dance director. You'll be the only dancer on the screen. If you want any help I'm sure I could get him in for a session with you, but I don't think that'll be necessary.' He smiled warmly as he spoke. 'Of course, we'll work out a proper contract for you – and you'll be earning a great deal more than twelve dollars a day! It's not sudden stardom, or anything like that, you understand, but it will get you noticed, and who knows what might happen after that?'

Alice had put her cardigan on the back of her chair. The interview seemed to be over and, getting up, she profusely thanked Sheldon. He also stood, and stepping around to her side of the desk, took the cardigan and placed it gently over her shoulders, allowing his hands momentarily to rest there as he did so.

''Til tomorrow then, Alice – I'm so pleased you like my idea.'

Alice, smiling more happily than she had done for months, thanked him again.

Trixie was waiting for her in the foyer, eager for her friend's news.

'That's swell, Alice – you've made a hit, you really have. I'm sure pleased for you! Come on, I feel like eating at the Chop Suey Restaurant next door to Henry's.'

Alice was delighted. She decided that once she had shown her dance to Sheldon, if he approved of it, she would write to Alex; with success coming her way she would have something exciting to tell him.

Jubilant, they went home and changed, then celebrated well into the small hours, with Alice paying the bill.

Little Dot's Daydream was due to be premiéred the week before Christmas – it would hopefully be a popular entertainment over the Christmas and New Year holiday period. Trixie and Alice were given privileged cut-price tickets for the big night, which was to take place at Grauman's Egyptian Theatre. They knew that for one fleeting moment their faces would be seen as the camera glided past them. Dressing up in their best evening clothes they took a taxi to the theatre, and while the newspaper men made no attempt to interview or photograph them they were thrilled with the atmosphere of their first such occasion.

Just after they had arrived, an adoring cheer went up from the waiting crowd outside the theatre. Baby Bettykins and her mother – dressed in identical pink frilly frocks with flowers in their hair – made their entrance. Mother pushed herself in front of everyone else in the foyer, and lifted Baby Bettykins onto a convenient plinth, crossing the child's legs for her and arranging her skirt, making sure that she would also be in the pictures before telling the photographers that they were ready. The cameras clicked and flashed.

Laughing to each other, the two friends made their way to their reserved seats in the elaborate auditorium, with its copies of the huge Karnak Temple columns and the ceiling encrusted with hieroglyphics.

The photoplay was well received, and the two girls gripped each others hands as they saw themselves for a few brief seconds, their faces filling the big screen; Alice cringed with embarrassment at the child's awful dancing.

There were speeches, Sheldon thanked everyone – from the young star to the clapper boy – and eventually the audience got up to leave.

As the crowd crossed the foyer Alice felt a tap on her shoulder.

'Alice, tomorrow at six, at the studio. I take it you've worked out your dance?'

'Why yes, Sheldon, of course.'

'Bring it and your music. We can go for dinner after I've seen your work.'

'Thank you, Sheldon. I'd be delighted.'

He disappeared with a group of celebrities who were making their way towards some impressive limousines.

'Well, honey, short of his asking you to join him this minute, I'd say you're not doing too badly. And it's nearly Christmas!' There was innuendo in the tone of Trixie's voice.

'Oh, shut up! But it is a bit exciting, isn't it?'

'Yes. Next time it'll be you, and maybe me too, being photographed and with our names in lights.'

She pointed to the huge sign which advertised the photoplay.

'Alice, that's exactly what I want – it's just beautiful! No, you don't need any help from Bert. I don't want you to alter a thing.'

Sheldon thanked and dismissed the pianist. Taking Alice by the arm, to protect her from tripping over a group of studio cables, he said, 'Go and change, I've booked a table at The Montmartre Cafe – I think you'll like it there.'

Soon Alice and her escort were walking towards his car – a Buick Tourer –

and they speeded their way to Hollywood Boulevard and the fashionable cafe.

Once settled at their table he looked across at her and said, 'You know you really are a very clever young lady to be able to work out a dance like that. I'm most impressed.'

'It's not that difficult, Sheldon.' She lowered her eyes as she replied.

'Typical English girl, that's you – modest, far too modest. But does your modesty also tell me that you're shy?'

Alice laughed, throwing her head back and revealing a very different side of her personality as she replied, 'Why no, of course I'm not shy! It's just that I know what I'm doing, I'm a well-trained dancer – er, though I shouldn't say that . . .'

'There you go – that English modesty again!'

But inwardly Alice was fast realising that his reference to her possible shyness was nothing to do with her attitude to her work.

After their grapefruit cocktail starter he asked her about her past achievements, which were considerably more than he expected. He had just about heard of the Russian Ballet but bluffed and got away with a few comments which were obvious, and actually showed his lack of real knowledge. But Alice purposely made nothing of these, since she was keen to keep up his interest in her – he was powerful enough to progress her career in precisely the right direction. The chance to dance a solo on screen was something well worth following up, and so far she had made excellent progress – he liked what she had produced and now she was enjoying his company and getting to know him better.

They had roast turkey because it was in season, and the meal ended with some delicious cream and fruit-filled patisserie.

'You know you are very beautiful, and the camera is kind to you, I want to be able to see much more of you on the screen after *The Gypsy's Revenge*.' He paused, then taking her hand sighed a little and looking right at her said, 'Well, we'll have to see, won't we?'

Not taking her hand away and looking straight at him she replied, 'Yes, Sheldon, we will have to see, won't we?'

Smiling, she momentarily gripped his hand; but they were interrupted by the arrival of the coffee. After which they left the restaurant and returned to his car.

'Now, where do you live?'

She was reluctant to allow him to see her awful apartment so said, 'If you drive me down to Santa Monica Boulevard and drop me off on the corner of Hudson Avenue that'll be just fine.'

'Your's to command, m'lady!' He attempted an upper-class English accent which made her laugh, especially as she had noticed that she had slightly slipped into American phraseology with her last remark.

'Are you sure this is near enough? I'd hate to think of you walking miles by yourself.'

'Yes, it's there,' she said, pointing to an imposing looking block of four smart apartments.

He parked the car in the shade of the building, out of sight of direct street lighting.

'Alice, we're going to be good friends as well as colleagues, aren't we?'

'Why of course, Sheldon.'

As she spoke he leant across to her and, taking her in his arms, passionately kissed her. She responded and although he was extremely handsome, the kiss did not thrill her. Nevertheless, the thought rushed through her mind that it was the least she could do because he was being very good to her.

On breaking away, she smiled at him and said, 'Goodnight, Sheldon.'

With all the charm of every screen hero, his dark eyes gazing at her, smiling he said, 'Good night, Alice, but . . . before you go, I always give a party on Christmas Eve, and I would like you to come – please say you will. My friends are all well known, and you'll find them friendly and helpful.'

'It's frightfully kind of you to ask me, and I'd like to very much, but I don't want to leave Trixie on her own over Christmas – we are such good friends, you know.'

'Bring her along too, that will add to our pleasure. I'll send a car for the both of you at nine – er from here?'

Alice had to bluff. 'Yes, look, Trixie and I will be waiting over there.'

She pointed to the ornate Spanish-influenced porch of the smart little apartment block.

He kissed her again. She waved to him as he drove off, then she turned down Hudson Avenue, into the unmade road and up her flight of steps.

Alice wore a pale blue evening dress with her velvet coat over it, while Trixie was in red, her dark hair decorated with a matching bandeau. The Buick pulled up on the dot of nine, driven by Sheldon's driver from the studio – he explained that Sheldon was already receiving his guests – and whisked them off to a Spanish style house in Beverly Hills.

It was a huge party, maids and a butler were in attendance taking wraps and, to the girls' surprise waiters offered glasses of champagne, which everyone elegantly accepted as if there was no question that they were breaking the law.

They were shown into a wide hall, drawing room, and a large patio which, protected from the slightly chilly evening air by huge glass panels, was filling up with more guests.

Alice and Trixie felt confident as they knew they looked as fashionable as the other women, though many were laden with several ropes of pearls and a few wore diadems. Most smoked turkish cigarettes held in long black holders. The girls' eyes were darting around, and while they saw a few recognisable faces there were no top-ranking stars. This disappointed Alice – she was hoping to see Norma and Constance as that would have been a marvellous opportunity for her to renew her friendship with them, but it was not to be.

It turned out that a great many people were technicians with their wives and girlfriends. Some of the young women were make-up artists, and secretaries. They made new acquaintances as the evening wore on and felt that their presence was no bad thing, as most of the people they talked to were connected with famous names and told Alice and Trixie that they would see what they could do for them.

The excellent buffet supper was being served in the dining room and Alice had just taken portions of fresh cold salmon and some interesting salads when Sheldon came up to her and asked her if she was enjoying herself.

'Why yes, it's a wonderful party – such interesting people who seem to be so well connected.'

'I thought you might make some good contacts. But where's Trixie?'

'Just now she was talking to a stills photographer who was, I think, arranging a photo session with her.'

'And you – you're not lacking good company?'

'Why no, I've chatted to lots of people; that young dress designer over there, she's a dear, and then there was a girl called Dolores – she's in make-up, I met her briefly when we were shooting *Dot's Daydream* . . .'

'But have you made no new gentlemen friends?'

Smiling coquettishly, she replied, 'The night is young, Sheldon!'

They were sitting on a comfortable sofa and she was steadying her plate of food in one hand, her fork in the other, nevertheless he put his hand on her lower arm and looking right at her said, 'I hope it's not that young, I'll be quite jealous if I see you flirting with any handsome man.'

'So I'm not to enjoy myself?'

'Umm, within reason. Look, I simply must circulate – not that I want to – but I'll be back to wish you a happy Christmas later, for now I'll send you a nice young man who I know I can trust as he's . . . well . . .'

'Not too keen on the ladies?'

Sheldon blinked, surprised at her pert response.

'How do you know about things like that?'

'Never mind, but I'll enjoy meeting any friend of yours, Sheldon.'

The young man Sheldon sent over to Alice turned out to be a crashing bore – she would have much rather gone back to gossip with Dolores who was a hive of information about the stars she had been making-up for the last few years, than go on listening to his boring criticism of most women in the room saying things like, how awful *she* looks, and look at her – what does she think she's wearing, wallpaper? Such comments made Alice giggle a little at first but they became tedious, so she excused herself saying she had to find the bathroom. When she got back the bore had moved on and was flirting outrageously with a young blond German.

At midnight the lights were switched off and a tall Christmas tree was lit. Alice felt an arm round her waist and Sheldon nuzzling her ear.

'I've got a present for you – here it is.'

He pressed a small box into her hand. When the lights came up again she expressed her surprised delight and opened it. It was a tiny silver brooch in the shape of a rose.

'Oh, Sheldon, it's really beautiful, thank you so much.'

In the middle of the crowded room while a great many other guests were exchanging gifts, they kissed.

'Look, my English rose, I've to visit my family in San Francisco from tomorrow until just before New Year, but I would like us to spend New Year's Eve together – so that we can see in nineteen-twenty-four.'

'That would be lovely, thank you again, Sheldon – and we'll be starting shooting soon after?'

'Yes, on the Monday the seventh. So between New Year's Eve and that day we can have some fun – and I'll get your costume designed.'

'Thanks again, Sheldon. I must find Trixie, as I think it's time we went home – can I 'phone for a taxi?'

'No, I'd take you but I can't leave the rest of my guests. So I'll get George.'

Alice looked everywhere for Trixie but could not find her. Giving up, she asked the maid who was looking after the cloaks if she had seen her leave. The maid said she had, with a young man the maid knew was a photographer.

So, she thought to herself, Trixie's got herself a new boyfriend, well so have I. Sighing, her thoughts drifted back to Ben – she decided that Sheldon was not a patch on him – but then Ben was . . . where? And Sheldon was around, or promised to be again, very soon, *and* he was useful. She smiled gleefully to herself.

George, who had brought them, drove her back, and dropped her off where he had picked them up much earlier that evening. Alice thanked him and waited until he had turned the large car and started his trip back to Sheldon's house.

Alice hurried along the dusty road to their apartment, unlocked the front door and put on the light. She noticed a small envelope on the mat. It was a Western Union telegram. She was aware that no-one knew where she was living, nevertheless her pulse rate increased. She turned the envelope over and saw it was addressed to Miss Trixie Lamont. It was stamped Columbus Ohio.

Chapter 25

Alice sat on the bed holding the telegram. It was obviously extremely urgent: whoever had sent it had paid an extra fee for delivery late on Christmas Eve. She realised that Trixie may not be home for hours. Looking at her clock she saw it was almost three a.m. How she wished Trixie had come home with her and not gone off with the photographer! She also wished that they had a telephone, because Sheldon would know who the photographer was and where he lived. She tried to think of any neighbour who might have a 'phone, but that was unlikely. She was extremely agitated, and became more so as the minutes ticked away.

She wondered if she should open the envelope, so that she could break any bad news gently to Trixie when she eventually came in, but decided against it. After all, all mail was private, and only for the person to whom it was addressed.

It was now almost four, and Alice felt cold and shivery. She made a cup of drinking chocolate. It was comforting. She felt she could not go to bed, so changed from her evening dress into a warm jumper and skirt, and lay on the bed fully dressed.

She must have dozed off, because the next thing she knew as she turned over she saw a hint of daylight peeking through the curtain. She hurriedly sat up, annoyed that she had slept, but feeling better for it.

She got up and looked out of the window. It was obviously fairly cold outside, as there was some condensation on the glass. There was no movement or sign of life in the street. It was half-past-six.

She was making herself some coffee when she heard a car pull up. Rushing to the door she saw Trixie stagger out of it. Looking up at Alice, she called out in a slurred voice, 'Pay the cab, pay the cab!'

She stumbled towards the foot of the steps, grabbed the handrail and stood there swaying.

Alice saw at once that Trixie was extremely drunk.

'Oh my God, Trix, for heaven's sake . . .'

'Come on, lady – I want to get home to my kids. It's Christmas Day, if you didn't know!'

The taxi driver was irate.

Alice went back inside and grabbed her purse. She ran down the steps and glanced anxiously inside the cab, in case Trixie had vomited in it. Fortunately she had not. She paid the driver and gave him a bigger tip than she could actually afford. Grunting, he drove off, leaving her to all but carry Trixie up the steps and into the bedroom.

'I've had a wonderful time . . . a wooonderfulll time. He's b-b-beautiful and he's going to take . . .'

'Yes, well, never mind that.'

Alice took a cup and filled it with black coffee.

'Here – drink this.'

'Don' wannit – Trixie wanna go to bed.'

'You can't, you can't. You must drink this.'

Alice offered the cup to her friend's lips and managed to persuade her to swallow some.

'Sit there. No, don't lie back.'

Alice filled a bowl with cold water and grabbing a face cloth and towel took them over to the bed where the highly inebriated Trixie was miles away in a world of her own.

'Had a wonderful time . . . had a . . .'

Without sympathy Alice splashed Trixie's face.

'Shurrup – I'm not dirty.'

'No, but you must sober up, do you hear me?'

She splashed her face with more water, then firmly holding her by the shoulders shook her.

'Oh God, I've got a headache!'

'I'm not surprised.'

Alice remembered they had some Alka Seltzer in the bathroom. She got a glass and put two in water.

'Here you are – drink this.'

Trixie did as she was told. Alice knew that she could not give her the telegram immediately, and that she would have to allow her to sleep for an hour or two.

'Alright, go to sleep – but not for long.'

Trixie flopped back onto the pillows and crashed out.

The two hours that followed were two of the most nerve-wracking that Alice had experienced in a long time. She did her best to keep calm, and tried to work out the best way to tell Trixie that something important had happened. What, she did not know, of course, but in her mind she went through all the possible disasters – that someone had died, that her family had lost their money, that a family member had run away . . . fire . . . flood . . . what? She knew that when Trixie woke up two things would surely happen: she would be suffering with a far worse headache than the one she went to sleep with, and that the news – whatever it was – would surely jolt her back into sobriety.

It was a Christmas Day the like of which Alice had never experienced before, and sincerely hoped she would not experience again. They had planned to go to Henry's for Christmas dinner and had decided to take a walk around Hollywood and just watch what ever was going on. There were to be carol services in several of the nearby churches, and they expected they would attend one of them, but the day was free, apart from their planned Christmas dinner and special celebrations, to which they had been looking forward.

Now Alice had to expect the unexpected, and was more than anxious that Trixie would be in a fit state to open and read her urgent message as soon as possible.

She had coffee ready on the stove for when Trixie came to, and more Alka Seltzers and aspirin. All she could do was to wait and try to be patient.

It was just gone half-past-eight when she saw Trixie stirring. She went over to the bed. Trixie opened her red eyes and looked up at Alice.

She went to raise her head, but immediately sank back onto the pillows.

'Head aching?'

'Yes, like hell.'

'I'll get you some aspirins – I think they'll help.'

'Oh, I feel awful, awful! My head! I feel sick!'

'It's as well you got a taxi home. You could have been picked up by the cops – what did you drink?'

'Can't remember – I think it was rum . . . Taxi? Don't remember getting a taxi. I feel awful.'

She rushed to the bathroom and Alice heard her vomiting.

She staggered back and fell into bed looking extremely pale. But Alice knew she could wait no longer.

Trixie was mumbling on about the photographer, who had promised to feature her in a movie magazine as a new face. Alice simply nodded, but all the while was trying to soothe her and telling her just to be quiet.

She put a cold cloth over her forehead, then when Trixie looked more relaxed and a mite of colour had returned to her grey face she said, 'I got home at just after half past two – and yes, I did have a nice time too. But Trixie, dear, when I opened the front door this telegram was on the mat. It's addressed to you.'

'Telegram . . . Why? What does it say?'

'I don't know. It's not up to me to open your mail – even if it is an urgent telegram. It was sent from Columbus.'

'That's where my Mom and Pop live, and my brothers and sisters. Oh, you open it . . . and read it . . . see if I care!'

Alice tore open the envelope.

'What does it say? Who is it from?'

Alice read, ' "MOM HAD BAD HEART ATTACK STOP COME AT ONCE POP". It was sent at seven o'clock yesterday.'

Suddenly Trixie was coherent.

'Oh no, no – it can't be true! She's always so well! It's Pop who's not very strong!'

'Trix, I'm so sorry, I really am. Of course you'll have to go to look after the little ones. But I doubt if you'll get train connections today. What a journey!'

'Yes – I'll have to go, until Mom's well again, that is.'

'Look, get up and pack some things, and we'll go to the terminal and see when you can go. I daresay there'll be trains tomorrow. Where will you have to change?'

'I'm not sure. Probably Chicago. Oh gee, it'll take days. I hope, I hope . . .'

Trixie was doing her best to think straight and to forget about her splitting headache and aching stomach.

'Don't, Trixie. I'm sure your mom'll be alright. Hospitals are so good these days.'

'But my brothers and sisters . . .'

'They'll be delighted to see you.'

They learned that Trixie would have to journey back through Chicago, and that she could leave on the following day. So most of Christmas Day was taken up with sorting her things. She would take just one case, as she expected to be back within a few weeks at most. She asked Alice to contact her new photographer friend and tell him that she had to go away for the time, but would be in touch in later.

They went out for their Christmas dinner, but were in no mood for celebration, knowing that they would be parting the following morning. They talked about the last five months, which had been so eventful. They had shared a great many high hopes and deep disappointments, and now, just as their luck was changing, this news had come to spoil everything.

'But it need not. Your mother's not old – there's every chance she'll make a good recovery, and I'm sure you'll be back again in a few weeks.'

'That's what I hope. I so want to be successful, Alice. We've both got new opportunities – you've just been noticed, and I could be put on the map by this big magazine article, so we're on our way.'

'Don't worry, this'll only hold you up for a little while. Cheer up, Trix! It's not like you to be pessimistic!'

'No, you're right, I guess. Let's not drink to Christmas but to nineteen-twenty-four, which is going to be our year!'

Smiling through their tears and provided with heavy china mugs of illicit champagne by Henry (though Trixie had earlier sworn she would never touch alcohol again, legally or otherwise) they did just that.

Alice came back from the rail terminal. She opened the door to the apartment and looked around. It was a great deal more cheerful now than when they had first set foot in it. Over the months they had made minor improvements which had made a great deal of difference. They had borrowed a neighbour's sewing machine and run up some bright chintzy curtains, made cushion covers and bought some cheap and colourful china and potted plants. But as she looked, she felt lonely and sad. She was going to miss Trixie's cheerful friendship a very great deal. The place seemed hollow. There was an empty space on the battered dressing-table. She went to the closet to hang her coat. While a lot of Trixie's clothes were still there, there was a long gap on the rail. The next few days, before Sheldon's return, would be a dull time for her.

She realised that with the possibility of some much better paid work she could afford to stay on in the apartment without having to find another girl to share with her. That was cheering. She decided, too, to contact a famous dance teacher who she knew had an excellent ballet school in Hollywood. Once she had some more money she would be able to afford to go to class again. She had wanted to earlier, knowing that she was dreadfully out of practice, but even with the additional cash from her previous dancing role she had decided that she could not commit to an outgoing of several dollars a week. In the New Year she would be able to have a different and more rewarding routine.

For the present, however, time would lay heavy on her hands. She decided to write a long letter to Alex. She had good news to tell him. She was not certain whether the ballet was still in Monte Carlo, but intuitively felt that it was; and if the company was on tour the letter would either await its return, or some secretary would send it on to where ever the company happened to be.

She got her writing case, took out several sheets of paper, and her pen. When she put it to paper, however, it was empty. She had to fetch ink and re-fill it. She started again – and made a big blot. A chill ran through her. She ignored it. Eventually the pen responded. She poured her heart out to Alex, and wondered if ever their paths would cross again.

Cars were dropping off revellers outside the newly opened Plaza hotel. Its main entrance had recently added an impressive splendour to the corner of Hollywood and Vine – directly opposite the Taft building, which housed Central Casting. Sheldon pulled on the hand-brake and at once a smart doorman opened the car door, allowing Alice to step out. He signalled to a young man in hotel uniform to come and park the car for Sheldon.

Lightly taking Alice's arm, Sheldon led her into the glittering foyer.

'I'll leave my coat. Where's the ladies' cloakroom, Sheldon?'

'Oh, don't bother.'

'But I won't want it with me in the restaurant.'

Smiling beguilingly at her he replied, 'We're not going to the restaurant. I've booked a private suite!'

'Good evening, Mr Leroy – your usual suite is ready for you.'

'Thank you, Eric.'

They made their way to the elevator and a boy of about fourteen took them to the penthouse.

Sheldon explained that the building was L-shaped and that from certain rooms there was a particularly magnificent view. As he spoke the elevator boy led the way along a corridor and unlocked a door. This revealed a charming suite of rooms beautifully decorated in the colours of spring flowers. Sheldon tipped the boy and turned to Alice.

Smiling he asked, 'Like it? I thought it would be much nicer for us to dine here than with that noisy mob downstairs. Come over here and look.'

Alice was thrilled. This was much more what she had expected of Hollywood.

'Sheldon, it's beautiful! Thank you for being so thoughtful.'

He stood close behind her. She could feel his breath on the back of her neck.

'This is the highest building in Hollywood, and we're on the twelfth floor. Look, isn't this a glorious view? Down there's the little garden, and you can just see the fountain and the tops of the palm trees. Right across there is Culver City.'

The lights twinkled, and the view thrilled Alice. She was delighted and kept thinking to herself, 'at last – at last I'm arriving'.

They moved to a large settee. Nearby was a coffee table with an ice bucket, a bottle of champagne standing in it.

'Let's drink.'

'But . . .'

'Laws – like rules – are made to be broken, and we'll be breaking a few before nineteen-twenty-three is quite over!'

He smiled dazzlingly at her. But something in his expression made her feel slightly uneasy. She smiled back, rather nervously, but a few mouthfuls of champagne relaxed her, and once again she was enjoying the lovely suite. She felt a little flushed, and asked Sheldon where the bathroom was. He pointed to a door which led to a luxurious bedroom, with a huge double bed and lavish draped pale lemon satin covers. The bathroom matched the bedroom in both colour scheme and lush fittings. Alice made use of the excellent facilities, powdered her face and checked her hair and lipstick.

By the time she returned, a waiter had wheeled in a large trolley which he extended so that it became a dining table. The meal promised to be delicious and not too heavy: three kinds of melon, chicken with corn, pineapple and salad, accompanied by another bottle of champagne.

Their conversation over the meal centred on Hollywood, and the stars Sheldon knew. He reeled off a list of names each more famous than the last, ending with Dougie and Mary – or the Fairbanks, he added in case she did not realise to whom he was referring.

'I'll introduce you to them later on. I'm sure they'll like you.'

'Sheldon, I would like to meet Norma and Constance again. They were so kind to me in England.'

'Well, I'll see what I can arrange. It won't be difficult.'

By now they had finished their main course and, with a polite knock on the door, the waiter arrived to take away the used dishes and to bring a selection of ices for their dessert. As he opened the door to leave, they heard the muffled sound of a big party which was going on in a much larger private suite along the corridor.

'They seem to be enjoying themselves,' remarked Alice.

Looking directly at her, Sheldon replied, 'Yes, and we are too. But there's better to come.'

'Oh, yes – when it's midnight, and we can drink to nineteen-twenty-four!'

He didn't reply.

The ices were delicious, and in due course coffee came. The waiter served it on the coffee table, and they moved to the settee. As he was about to leave, although they still had quite a lot of champagne left in the second bottle Sheldon ordered a third, which was brought within a couple of minutes.

'We don't want him to disturb us again.'

'No, I suppose not.'

In silence they drank their coffee, sitting together on the settee. She got up to look at the view again.

'It really is lovely, Sheldon. I can hardly take it all in. So many lights stretching away into the distance . . .'

He got up.

'You know, you sparkle like those lights, and I'm going to make certain that everyone sees your shining beauty. There's so much I can do for you . . .'

He took her in his arms and kissed her passionately. As on their previous meeting she responded, but again felt nothing more than that it was just fun. And after all, he was giving her a delightful evening.

He took her back to the settee and re-filled her glass. Not long after, although the door to their suite was shut, they heard cheering coming from the large gathering down the corridor.

Sheldon looked at his watch.

'Alice, I make it almost midnight.'

She had her glass in her hand. He lifted her arm and passed his own through it. They drank their New Year's toast with arms linked.

'Now, come on, we don't want to stay out here any longer.'

As he spoke he suddenly picked her up. At first she thought he was simply joking. Laughing, she cried, 'Sheldon, put me down, please put me down!'

'Oh no, not yet – not for a long time, Miss Townsend!'

He carried her through to the bedroom, roughly dropped her onto bed, and lay down beside her. His hands gripped her shoulders and almost immediately he hastily pushed down her narrow shoulder straps, so that they cut uncomfortably into her arms.

'No, Sheldon, I don't want to go that far – it's not fair of you to do this to me.'

'Oh, but it *is*, Alice! Come on, you're a girl of the world, it's the least you can do for me. After all, think of what I'm doing for you – and going to do.'

He roughly pulled at the top of her dress, plunged his hands under her chemise and aggressively ripped it, exposing her breasts. His usually warm expression had changed to a determined glare.

'No, Sheldon! I hardly know you. Please, I don't want . . .'

'That's got very little to do with it – it's what *I* want that matters.'

He thrust his mouth on hers so that she could not answer him. His hold on her body was painful. She was frightened. He pulled up her skirt and pushed his other hand up between her legs. He was very strong, but she was no fool. Her initial fear turned to cunning.

Somehow, she managed to break away from his deep heavy kiss and strangle-like hold on her body and said, 'Alright, Sheldon . . .'

Then assuming a steamy, very sexy voice, she leant over close to his ear, 'There's no need to rush things like this . . . no need at all.' She gave a little passionate sigh directly in his ear and allowed the tip of her tongue to come into contact with its lobe. He was delighted at the change in her attitude and eased off.

'Wait,' she purred, and quietly re-arranged the bodice of her dress, so that she was covered. She noticed that her shoes were just by her side of the bed.

'You'd much rather I was nice to you, wouldn't you, Sheldon? Besides I want to enjoy our love-making too, you know. After all, you're so handsome and how can a girl like me resist you? We'll have a lot of fun and games, 'cos it's only *just* nineteen-twenty-four.' She smiled and caressed his face. He nibbled her fingers. He was flattered.

'Lie back and let me do nice things to you, darling. After all, as you say, you're doing nice things for me, it's only fair, isn't it?'

'Yes please, Alice, my lovely English Alice. I thought for a moment you weren't going to be nice to your Sheldon.'

'Why of *course* I am, as if I wouldn't be nice to *you* of all men. But a little fight is all part of the fun, isn't it? I was only teasing you, you naughty boy!'

She knew she had him in her power. He was lying on the bed and she got up and kneeling over him started to undress him. First she took off his partially untied bow tie and the stiff collar of his evening dress shirt. These she threw as far as she could from the opposite side of the bed. She then went on to relieve him of his shirt and vest. The garments landed in the most distant corner of the room. She caressed his chest and nipples so that he squirmed with delight at her touch. Then with help from him, she removed his trousers and underpants, and although a little apprehensive, she delicately stroked him. Now all he had on was his shoes and socks. Smiling inwardly to herself and very provocatively to him, she said, 'Now I'll strip for you – stay there.'

'Don't keep me waiting too long, Alice.'

'I won't, but it'll be worth waiting for! Don't forget, I'm your dancer.'

She arranged the pillows and made a great fuss of making quite sure he was comfortable in his aroused state. She slipped away from the bed, slinkily swaying her hips with every step and, without him seeing, somehow managed to kick her shoes to a more advantageous position. She stepped back near the door and started to dance, she lifted her skirt, sexily thrust her hands through her hair and then put her arms to her back to undo the fastening of her dress. He was in a dream of delight – living a glorious sexual fantasy. She watched him looking at her with rapturously half closed eyes. She blew him kisses. Then, at what she assessed was precisely the right moment, she grabbed her shoes, rushed out of the bedroom and through the lounge, where she slipped into her shoes, snatched up her coat and handbag which were near the settee, and ran into the corridor.

Fortunately, several people were beginning to leave the big party. She mingled with them as the elevator arrived. As the doors opened they heard a man shouting from the entrance to a suite not far away. They looked surprised. Alice shrugged her shoulders, reacting like the other party goers, and as she entered the elevator she just caught a glimpse of a bare leg with sock and shoe emerge from the door of the suite.

'That guy must be drunk or something,' said an annoyed man.

'Such goings on in a place like this. We should call the police, don't you think, my dear?' remarked a dowager-like woman.

'Why certainly complain to the management,' said another. 'It's simply frightful . . .'

Alice hurried through the foyer without anyone noticing her slightly untidy appearance – after all, it was New Year's Eve. She asked the doorman to get her a taxi. One drove up immediately and took her the short journey back to her apartment.

As she mounted the steps she realised what she had done. Yes, she had prevented herself from being virtually raped, and knew she had done the right thing.

'Well, Sheldon certainly won't be employing me any more,' she thought.

And it was New Year's Day.

1924–1925

Chapter 26

Alice knocked on the door of Sheldon's suite. From the outer office his secretary, without looking up from her typing, told Alice to come in, and to sit down and wait. She sat by another young woman and, smiling at her, wished her a happy new year.

'Thanks, and the same to you – but don't I recognise you?'

As she spoke Alice also recognised her as Patsy Ruth Miller, the leading lady in *Hunchback of the Notre Dame*.

'Why you were the lead in *Hunchback* – how nice to meet you properly.'

'Sure, and you – I remember your face, because I saw you reacting so beautifully in the crowd scenes. You should do well, my dear!'

'Thank you. I hope so.'

Miss Miller was a very chatty and pleasant young woman, Alice liked her.

'Do you know Sheldon?' she asked.

'Yes – quite well,' replied Alice.

'You know, I'm *so* pleased,' she leant towards Alice and speaking in a confidential tone went on, 'he telephoned me yesterday. He wants me for a small but interesting part in his next photoplay – a gypsy girl. And I have to dance. You know, I love the ballet. In fact, I am a ballerina, so I know I'll make a good job of it, even although it's no way as important as *Hunchback*. Isn't that wonderful?'

Alice's heart sank, but she managed to reply, 'Why yes, it'll be lovely for you.'

She knew immediately what had happened. She also knew that she had to get out of that office as quickly as possible. As she was trying to make up some kind of an excuse, the secretary's intercom buzzed. She picked it up, and murmured into it.

Looking up at Patsy Ruth she said, 'Miss Miller, Mr Leroy is so sorry to have kept you waiting – but he'll see you right away. Please go in.'

Patsy Ruth smiled and said goodbye to Alice who did her best to smile. As she went through the door the secretary turned to Alice, about to say something she did not want to hear. But before she could utter, Alice got up and rushed out of the office into the corridor.

Once outside the building she made her way across the car park, through the entrance gate and into the road. Staggering slightly, she burst into tears.

It was quite cold and raining hard by the time she had completed the long walk back to the apartment. She went in, flung herself on the settee and cried long and hard into one of the colourful cushions. She felt dreadfully lonely – and angry. Angry with Sheldon who, she now realised, was just like so many other producers and directors she had heard about in his attitude towards aspiring actresses. She really had thought that he actually liked her. Perhaps he did. After all, he had spent quite a lot on her, and certainly hadn't attempted to force her into sex in his office, as sometimes happened. But then, if he had *really* liked her he would shown her a little more respect and not have treated her so roughly. He would have allowed their relationship to develop.

But would she have wanted it to develop? Did she feel ready for another commitment? Even now, after several months, her thoughts – and very longing thoughts they were – often drifted back to Ben and their shipboard romance. As she sat sobbing she remembered him – his gentle, tender loving approach, and how she had given herself to him so willingly . . . But he was not with her – could not be and would not be . . .

She decided that her relationships with men were doomed – right from when, as a mere eighteen year old, she had suffered from Charlie's death. And now here she was alone in a city where no-one cared for her, and with no-one in whom to confide.

She went to her drawer in the rickety dressing-table and took out a clean hanky. She looked out of the bedroom window. Outside the rain continued to pour down on a tall, almost dead palm tree, the drops making slapping sounds as they hit the fronds. She felt as dreary as the tree looked. There had been times when, seeing the tree glinting in the Hollywood sunlight, she felt elated and excited. But now the tree echoed her mood, it seemed to take on the role of a sympathetic friend – the only friend she had.

Almost smiling at the stupid impression, she felt she should have something to eat. All she had in the kitchen was yesterday's bread and some cheese.

In a happier moment she had sworn never to touch the stuff again, but was compelled to. As she cut off a piece her heart sank lower and lower. She compared her progress in life to a graph she had seen on office walls. It zig-zagged up and down but was always sinking lower and lower. At the moment her hopes and progress had yet again slumped. She was not at quite such a low point as when she had just lost the competition, but not far off.

Finishing the rather stale bread and cheese she made some strong black coffee, and felt a little better as she drank it. She came to the conclusion that it would be no good going to plead with Sheldon. Although she had done the 'right' thing, she felt a mite guilty at the way she had tricked him, but justified her actions because of the revolting way he had attempted to force

220

her into having sex with him. She knew that she must have caused him considerable embarrassment, so she must keep well clear of him.

At least she was still on the books at Central Casting. She decided go back there and see what work they had for her. She looked in the mirror. Her eyes were swollen, her face very blotchy. She looked out of the window yet again, it was still raining. She decided to stay in for the rest of the day, give her face a mud pack and her nails a thorough manicure, then, the following morning, go to Central Casting. In the early days of the new year many new productions were starting up in all the busy studios.

Alice sat at the end of the long line of hopefuls in the corridor outside the large office where the clerks interviewed them. In due course, as the actors and actresses were called in, she made her way to the top of the queue, and was seen by a youngish woman, who took out her file and made some phone calls. After keeping her there for some time she looked at Alice and sighed, 'I'm sorry, Miss Townsend, there's nothing for you today. Come back on the seventh – Monday – I expect there'll be some work then. I see they'll probably want dancers over at Culver City from the middle of next week.'

Alice thanked her and left. The rain had cleared. She did not feel like going back to the apartment, and took a walk along Hollywood Boulevard. She walked past Henry's and decided that she might have some lunch in there later – it would be cheering. Her problems still depressed her, but she felt a little more hopeful. It was early January, the ninth day of Christmas, but there was warmth in the sun.

Over the months she had distanced herself almost entirely from her family. But as the thought of London flashed into her mind, her thought drifted back to the Christmases of her childhood, before the war. Of Aunt Emma's elaborate celebrations, of services in Kensington Parish Church, and her having to play the piano to entertain the grown-ups. The thought of the piano, which had so long since been buried in her unconscious, jolted her like the sting of a wasp. It was because of enforced piano playing that her life had changed so drastically. If only her mother had accepted the fact that she had so little talent for it.

Then there was Philip. He was out of her life too. That was sad – she loved him dearly. She smiled to think how he had stood by her and helped her – and she felt a pang of sorrow as she remembered the support her father had given her, pulled between his love of her mother and herself.

The next few days dragged by. Alice made herself do things. She wrote to Trixie, but then tore up the letter because she had told her about her recent experiences, and felt that they would not be exactly cheering. She cooked a large pasta sauce which would last her over the weekend, and each day turned the old settee so that the seat was against the wall, changed into her practice clothes, and did some ballet exercises, using the back of the settee as a barre. She was very stiff, but she liked the slight muscular pain her efforts

221

caused, because it told her that she was exercising again. She put on her pointe shoes, and though she brought up a small blister on one of her toes, the fact that she was moving vigorously lifted her depression. She knew she would be ready for the possible job at Culver City.

On Monday morning she made her way once again to the Taft Building. The offices were busier than ever, but as she was early she did not have to wait very long.

She presented herself to the clerk and gave her number. He took out her file, and she noticed a letter clipped to it. The man looked at her, unclipped the letter and read it. He was silent for what seemed like ages. He looked up at her.

'Miss Townsend, I'm afraid there's nothing for you. I have instructions here from the Director of Central Casting to take you off our books. We can't employ you any more, and of course, no studio will take you unless we send you. I'm sorry, but that's the way it is. Good-day to you.'

'You mean . . .'

'That's exactly what I mean . . . And now, if you'll excuse me . . . Next, please!'

Alice was dumbfounded. As she got up, she saw the clerk tear up her file and ostentatiously throw it into his wastepaper basket.

She left the building in a state of shock, and absent-mindedly crossed the road, without looking, and not hearing the voice which called, 'Alice! Hi, Alice!'

She was oblivious of everything until she felt a tap on her shoulder.

'Hi! Say, you *are* in a world of your own. Must be in love!'

Babs, noticing the tears streaming down Alice's face, gasped in astonishment.

'You're some upset. For heaven's sake, what's happened? I've got the Culver City job – have you?'

'Babs, Oh, Babs – no. And I won't get any more.'

'What?'

Seeing how distressed Alice was, Babs led her into a nearby coffee shop and ordered two coffees.

Alice told her tale.

Babs had been around in Hollywood for a long time.

'This is not the first time it's happened. Sheldon can be quite shitty – *and* he's got a wife and three kids in San Francisco. I've known two other girls he's treated like you. They both suffered the same way – taken off Central Casting. One, he actually raped. He's very dangerous, Alice. God, I wish I'd warned you, but I didn't know he was leading you on like that! I'm real sorry. What'll you do?'

'I don't know.'

'Well, at least you've got Trixie. She'll help you, she's a good friend.'

Alice agreed, but told Babs what had happened to her.

'So you're on your own? Poor honey! But if I were you I'd try to get an ordinary job, unless you've enough cash to go back East. Have you?'

'No, I've just got enough for a couple of weeks more rent and some food. I do need Trixie to come back to help with the rent.'

'Well, you know there are other jobs in Hollywood. You just gotta bounce back.

She smiled broadly.

She managed to make Alice smile, in spite of her desperate situation.

To encourage her further she went on, 'Let me tell you about *my* emergency plan, in case something like this happens to *me* – and it might! I would go home, make myself look as smart as possible, and go out and ask in every shop, restaurant or beauty parlour that takes my fancy, whether they want anyone. I know I'd have to walk miles – and let's face it, girls like us are ten a dime, but I'd try. And that's what you must do, otherwise you'll be on the streets.'

'I had to do something like that in New York and it wasn't a very pleasant experience. Of course you're right; but I do feel so awfully let down – so much has gone wrong in my life.'

'Yes, you're having a really rough ride. But you must always look to tomorrow. *Don't* give up hope, even at this point, Alice, you just mustn't. Besides, you'll get to look old if you cry too much!'

Alice nodded, knowing that Babs' comments made sense.

'Look, I must go. I'm meeting Bill, my boyfriend. He's a cameraman. Here's my card. Don't feel you're totally alone – you're not. Let me know how you get on. And if you *don't* get anything in the next couple of days for heaven's sake tell me, and I'll revise my emergency plan!'

Alice was so grateful. She knew that Babs had come along at precisely the right moment. While her situation was unchanged and she was desperate, she did have a life-line and, as Babs realised, that was essential. Alice thanked her for the coffee and for listening to her miserable story.

The fact that she had talked things over and listened to good advice had a very positive effect on her. She went back to the apartment. There were two letters in her postbox at the bottom of the steps.

One was from Alex, the other from Trixie – the first letters she had received in all the time she had been in America. In her highly emotional state they brought tears to her eyes. She went in, took off her coat and hat, and sat on the settee deciding which to open first.

Because Alex was so important to her and she had longed (oh, how she had longed!) to hear from him, she decided to read Trixie's first, hoping it would be news of her return.

'Dear Alice,

'Just to tell you that Mom died on the 30th of December. We are all heart-broken. I am doing my best to look after Pop and the kids. Needless to say I'll not be returning to Hollywood – all hopes of a career in the movies is just not on any more.

'I must do my duty for the family. I'm sorry to let you down like this, but I hope you'll understand. Please write to me soon and tell me how you are getting on with Sheldon.

'Your friend, Trixie.'

The news could not have come at a worse moment. Now she really *was* alone – not just for a few weeks, as they both had assumed. She felt so sorry for Trixie. She would have to think very carefully how to reply to the sad note.

But for the moment she had the opportunity to take her mind off her problems and read Alex's news. The letter was bulky, which delighted her.

It was addressed from the Opera House Monte Carlo.

'My dearest Wee Thing,
    'I was jubilant to get your letter at long, long last, and to hear all your good and bad news. You are obviously doing so well now, and I'm de-lighted for you . . .'

The letter went on to say how horrified he was that they had just missed her in New York. He had been enjoying minor roles in some new ballets, none of the girls he had been partnering were in any way as talented as she was, and while he hoped they would dance together again some time, he expected that was not to be, as now she was well on her way to stardom in the Great Movie Capital of the World.

If only he knew, if only he knew – she fought tears as she read on. The Russian Ballet was due to be in Monte Carlo for a few more months, then the company would make appearances in Paris, and much later in the year, in London. During the course of the year Alex expected to visit Basil in New York (was there any chance of their meeting up while he was there?) Basil had been so good to him – and, he added, 'by the bye, I wrote to Joan back in June to tell her to store the rest of my things and re-let the flat. Later I heard that a young dancer called Daisy Lloyd had taken it – it appears she said she knew you slightly, having visited you after I left for New York. Do you remember her?'

The letter ended with vows of undying friendship and an urgent appeal for more news from Alice very soon.

Sighing, she tenderly folded the pieces of notepaper and put them back in the envelope. She would only be able barely to acknowledge his lovely letter – she could not tell him of her present predicament. Daisy Lloyd! – well, that was rather nice. She was obviously making progress. Perhaps the Wimbledon pantomime last year got her off to a good start. The pleasant thought momentarily lifted Alice's spirits.

Tremendously resilient, she knew she could not sit around feeling sorry for herself, she did feel just that; thinking over what Babs had said, she knew that whether she wanted to or not she would have to take her advice. By now it was almost five o'clock, too late to go out in search of a job that evening. She forced herself to eat some scrambled eggs on toast and two oranges. She read and re-read Alex's wonderful letter again, and an hour or so later went to bed.

Sleep would not come. She turned over and over, onto her back, her side, her tummy but she could not get comfortable. Her mind was active. Where could she go to look for work? What should she wear when she did? She had the smart outfit that she had been presented with while she was in *Sleeping Princess*. She got out of bed, put on the light, and took it out of the wardrobe. She looked at it critically. There was no doubt about it, it was looking decidedly dated. The latest skirts were much shorter and she did not want to go into beauty salons or shops looking unfashionable. She examined the hem of the coat, and realised that it would be well beyond her limited dressmaking experience to cut and shorten it. But she had a black leather belt. She put the coat on over her nightdress, and by tightening the belt found that she could make the coat appear shorter.

The dress would be easier to shorten. She got out her sewing kit and a good pair of scissors and carefully cut off two inches, making the new hem as neatly as she could. It was past three in the morning when, exhausted emotionally and physically, she went back to bed – and slept solidly until nine o'clock.

Alice prepared herself with as much care as if she were going to be interviewed for a leading role. Her make-up was perfect, she made certain that her long hair was even more neatly arranged than usual in its draped chignon style, and double-checked that the seams in her stockings were straight. She turned into Hudson Avenue and walked up to Santa Monica Boulevard. Although she felt like going into every shop and restaurant, for the moment she decided to be choosy and was attracted to a friendly looking beauty parlour. The manageress talked to her for a while, realising that with all her experience of stage make-up she would be useful; but as she had no hairdressing experience and was too old to become an apprentice, there was no suitable position for her. She then came to a bookshop. They liked the fact that she was a well-educated English girl, but had no vacancies at present – if she had come before Christmas they could have used her. At a florist's her Englishness went against her, because she knew nothing of the sub-tropical flowers that they sold.

She continued her walk, but stopped suddenly outside a music shop as she caught sight of an enlarged photograph standing on an easel in the main window. At once she recognised Ben, and read the notice beside it, 'The British saxophonist Ben Waterman, whose fame is spreading across the continents of Europe and the Americas, recommends Selmer Saxophones – the best in the world.'

Surprised and suddenly shivering, Alice found her memory jolted back to the time when they parted. The thought was a stab through her heart, and at that moment she desperately wished that she had stayed with him and had not taken what had turned out to be such a difficult and unsuccessful direction in life.

She trudged around for the rest of that day, and came to the point where she was asking in cafés and restaurants whether they needed staff, all to no avail. She enquired at fruit and vegetable shops. No vacancies. At some, where the owners spoke Spanish, all she got was a mere shrug of the shopkeepers' shoulders. Her feet were aching. She went back to the apartment extremely dejected.

Next day she again made herself look her best, and though feeling far less optimistic, once more went out on her rounds. But again she met with no success. When she went home that second evening it was raining, and after she had gone to bed she heard water dripping. She hurriedly got up and went into the living room to discover a big puddle on the floor. It was obvious that the roof was leaking. She put a bucket on the floor, and decided that even if it poured all night the bucket was big enough to take the drips. She went back to bed, depressed, miserable and wakeful because of the constant irregular drips of water.

Up to now she had kept reasonably close to home, because she felt that the shorter distance she would have to travel to work the better it would be. On the third day, in spite of feeling tired after her bad night, she decided that she would walk up to Hollywood Boulevard. The shops there were more exclusive, and while it would be considerably further for her to get to work, she might just have a better opportunity of good work. Turned down at The Gainsborough Beauty parlour, she spent an hour or two on the south side of the street, past Grauman's Egyptian Theatre. Should she see if they wanted any usherettes or cigarette girls? But working in the smoke-filled dark for hours on end was something only for a last resort. She would rather wash dishes at Henry's.

She asked in the various shops in the courtyard of Grauman's, to no avail, then, although she felt extremely jaded, she decided to walk further along the famous boulevard. She stopped for a coffee, and looked at the exhausted girl who served her. Glancing down at her shoes she saw that they were cut at the toes for extra comfort. The poor creature's appearance sent shudders through Alice. She realised that if she didn't find work very soon she could all too easily become like her.

From the back of the shop a man's voice yelled unkindly at the girl, who grumbling, shouted back that she was coming.

'What a life!' she muttered to Alice – who in her eyes must have been looking like a million dollars.

Alice found a rather dirty powder room, refreshed her make-up, and because she had been sitting for a while, felt ready to move on. Nearby there was a very smart dress shop – 'Magnin's' – she had seen advertisements for it in glossy magazines. She went in.

Smiling, an elderly woman came up to her and asked her if she cou her. Alice, expressing all her natural charm, asked her if she had a vacancy for an assistant.

The woman's smile dropped immediately, and she looked Alice up and down with eyes that pierced her like dressmakers' pins. Then she invited her into an office which had swatches of fabric, drawings and dress patterns pinned to the walls and a long rail of exclusive looking gowns.

They sat down, and the woman asked what experience she had of selling clothes. Alice had to reply that she had not sold clothes before, but said that she had been living in New York and had sold jewellery in a small exclusive shop just off Fifth Avenue, adding that when she lived in London she had worked with a costume designer and had learned bead embroidery, and had worked in Harrods' millinery department for six months.

This impressed Madame Magnin, who also liked her English accent. She went on to tell Alice that she had recently to dismiss a girl, so there was a vacancy.

'I expect you realise that this is the most famous fashion house in Holly-wood. *All* our clients are stars. You present yourself well and are obviously intelligent. I think I can employ you. Of course, as you will be the most junior member of staff I very much doubt if you will sell to our famous ladies. You see, I take the first client, then we all serve in turn according to seniority. *You* will only speak to a client if the rest of us are serving. It is our very strict rule. You will hold pins for the other sales ladies, and pick them up if they get spilled; you will make tea or coffee for the clients – indeed do anything that is needed. Is that suitable?'

Alice was delighted, and asked how much she would be paid.

'Fifteen dollars a week. If you do make a sale you will have a commission of five per cent. You will be here by eight-thirty to work with Cheri, dusting and tidying, before we open at nine-thirty.'

'What would you like me to wear?'

'As you see, I wear black velvet, and I like my girls in black satin. Do you have a black satin gown?'

'I'm afraid not.'

'Well, no matter. We'll lend you one. Cheri will see to you.'

Arrangements finalised, Madame shook hands with Alice. She would start work on the following morning.

She walked out into the street feeling quite pleased and very relieved.

Chapter 27

The atmosphere between staff members at Magnin's was not always pleasant. There was considerable bickering over which assistant should serve who and when, and while, as far as the clients were concerned, everything appeared calm and relaxed, Alice soon realised that the young women were under constant pressure to sell, and sell hard. Because the clients were famous and wealthy that should not have been too difficult, but it was the rule that always the most expensive garment was produced first with the assistant extolling its virtues, and very often adding a hundred dollars to the price, which was on the label in code so that the client herself would never know the actual price. During three weeks of working there Alice had had no opportunity to sell anything, so would get no commission. However the work had its compensations since she saw a great many stars and now and then showed them to the elaborate changing cubicles and handed gowns to a more senior assistant who was taking care of the lady in question. She also made endless cups of coffee, tea and fruit drinks, and packed gowns which had to be protected against creasing with a great deal of tissue paper and placed in beautiful striped boxes. She handed out pins when a gown needed alteration, though she herself was never allowed to fit anyone.

But Alice's frustration was mounting. She was extremely fed up with herself and her lack of progress. It was depressing to see famous women flouncing in and buying whole new wardrobes, especially as it was a very busy time of year, with gowns for spring and summer from New York and Paris arriving daily, for general stock, as well as individual model creations made to special order for photoplay premiers.

Somehow Alice managed to keep her temper when other members of staff criticised her for not replacing a gown on a display mannequin in exactly the way they had intended, or for standing around in the salon when she ought to have been tidying up the office. Once or twice she had to take a taxi to a star's home to deliver an urgent outfit. That was interesting – not that she ever got to see the star herself as the garment was always taken in by a maid or butler, but the outing as far as Beverly Hills was pleasant. She was sent because she was the 'junior' – and that had nothing to do with age.

She was also on the receiving end of all kinds of gibes from other girls, Cheri in particular. Alice had mistakenly told her that she had been trying to get into photoplays, then in a particularly bitchy moment the girl, having criticised her for placing a vase of flowers at the wrong end of a display unit, very cattily retorted in a loud voice to another colleague, 'Of course *I* know that I'm doing well in *my* career – next year I'll be first sales, and I much rather be that than a miserably failed film actress, with a plushy English accent!'

But Alice, in her Cinderella-like role kept her temper. Her future was uncertain and she knew she had important decisions to make, but was biding her time as she realised that she could do nothing until she had a little more money behind her.

Most of her first week's wages had been spent on employing a builder to repair the roof, but to her surprise the man who collected the rent allowed her for it. She was also getting a useful lift to work every morning. It happened that a friendly farmer who delivered vegetables to the shops down the road from the apartment, had seen her leaving for work each morning, and one day enquired where she had to go. As his route took him right along Hollywood Boulevard he dropped her off in good time.

The weeks dragged by and her boredom increased; from time to time she compared her present situation to when she was working at Mandaro's. At least she did not smell of cheese and while she always had to look very smart and came into contact with the famous – if only at a distance – she missed the lively banter and jokes of the multi-national New Yorkers. She met Babs once or twice and on several occasions went to the cinema with her and her cameraman boyfriend. Once they arranged a blind date for her which was fun, but on the whole life centred around sweeping, dusting, handling and packing other women's gowns, being nagged and feeling extremely down-trodden. She was constantly reminded that in spite of living in what was considered the most exciting and glamorous city in the world, life for her was extremely dull. She was tempted to spend some of her money on going to ballet school after work, but by then she was tired having been on her feet all day (the assistants were on no account allowed to sit down in the salon) and if she did she knew she would not do well. So she would go back to her apartment and after resting, she would do her exercises there without fail before she went to bed. She discovered a large, badly damaged mirror in a junk shop and invested a mere four dollars in it. It cheered her and as the apartment was by no means small she was able to do a certain amount.

In all this time her bank balance was improving. She decided to make herself stick to another month of misery then she would be in a position to travel back to New York and try, once again for a Broadway Show, and maybe appeal to Basil Cavanagh for help. But as yet the time was still not right.

Fairly late one afternoon when Alice had been working at Magnin's for about three months, she came out of the office, where she had been sweeping up, to see three women in the salon. Madame was fussing over them while the other assistants were standing back, not daring to move.

'Why look at that, Norma, isn't it just dandy! I do think John would like me in it, don't you?'

'Jean, it's beautiful – do try it on!'

Alice stopped dead in her tracks.

'Yes, that will suit you, Mrs Montgomery.' Madame smiled at her client.

'Miss Cheri, show Mrs Montgomery into number two cubicle. Miss Alice, go and get some refreshment for our guests. Tea or coffee, Miss Talmadge?'

'Why thank you, tea would be lovely – with lemon please.'

Alice, shaking with excitement, darted behind the scenes. She glanced out and saw both Norma and Constance looking over the latest collection of gowns and talking to Madame.

'Come on, come on!' she said to the kettle, which duly hissed a lively response. She made the tea and set out the best china which was kept for important customers. A fresh bunch of roses had just been delivered for an arrangement in the salon. She hurriedly pulled three out, trimmed them and arranged them decoratively on the neat tray. Taking a deep breath and relaxing for a moment she then walked back into the salon and placed the tray on a low table in front of Norma and Constance who were now looking over a folder of designs.

They were involved in their study but she knew she had to attract their attention, so at the risk of upsetting Madame she said to Norma, 'I do hope that this is the way you like your tea, Miss Talmadge.'

Without looking up, the star thanked her, and continued examining the designs. Out of the corner of her eye Alice saw Constance nudge Norma in the ribs.

'Yes? What?' she asked her sister, who raised her eyebrows and nodded towards Alice.

Norma looked straight at her.

'Why it's Alice, isn't it? I am surprised to see you here . . . how?'

Alice to the envy of the other assistants went over to the sisters who, to their amazement, both kissed her.

'Well really, Miss Alice – I don't think . . .'

'It's perfectly alright, Madame Magnin – we know this young lady from London very well,' Norma assured Alice's employer.

Then turning back to Alice she went on, 'Now, my dear, of course we mustn't interrupt your work here, but let us meet at five-thirty, we'll be in the lounge of the Plaza Hotel where we are meeting Mr Montgomery. Ah, there's Jean . . .'

'Yes, Madame, I'll take this costume it's just what I need . . .'

Alice was introduced to Jean Montgomery. By now Madame was very annoyed.

'Miss Alice, pack the costume for Mrs Montgomery *at once!*'

230

'Of course, Madame.'

'Until five-thirty, Alice – we so want to hear your news – I must admit I'm amazed and mystified. Come, Jean, Constance.'

Smiling broadly at Alice they left the salon. Madame barked at her

'Come on, girl – and don't forget to put tissue paper in the sleeves, you can deliver it tomorrow. No – on second thoughts I think Cheri had better have that honour.'

'I *quite* understand, Madame.'

'But, my dear Alice, why *ever* didn't you get into contact with us? We would have been delighted to help you, and saved you a lot of suffering.'

'Well, Norma, I must admit it's not been easy, but you were so kind to me in London that I simply didn't feel I could bother you, knowing how busy you are.'

'I should say you've had a really horrible time! I do think I'd have given up ages ago, wouldn't you, Connie?'

'Yes, but then Alice is very determined.'

'Thank you, as you know I am keen to get on.'

'We know that, Alice. Norma and Connie have been telling me about you and how you so nearly won the English Rose competition, and I'm quite sure now I've met you, you would have made our lives a great deal easier if they had picked you.' John Montgomery was speaking. His warm smile and fatherly manner complemented his soft greying hair.

The five of them were taking non-alcoholic cocktails in the lounge of the Plaza Hotel. Alice had told her story and had received far more understanding and sympathy from Norma and Constance than she could have ever imagined. It appeared that John Montgomery assisted Joe Schenck, who was Norma's husband, in running the finances of United Artists Studios. The Montgomerys were close friends of Norma and Constance, and Alice's first impression of Jean was that she was one of the kindest and gentlest people she had met in a long time.

Jean looked particularly thoughtful, as she noticed how beautiful Alice was.

'My dear you're being wasted at Magnin's – isn't she, friends?'

They agreed.

She turned to Alice, 'And you say because of this . . . er incident with Sheldon Leroy, Central Casting have taken you off their books? He really is awful, we've heard of that sort of thing before! If he doesn't mend his ways then it'll be him who is driven out of Hollywood – after all he's not the most brilliant director we have in these parts.'

'That's why I'm working at Magnin's – I was pleased to get the job, but I can't say I'm happy there.'

Norma and Constance exchanged glances with John who nodded.

'Well, you won't be for any longer, we'll see that your career takes off from now – right away!'

'You mean you can actually get me back on Central Casting's books? That would be lovely!'

Laughing to each other, Norma clarified her statement,

'I think we can do better than that for you – I take it you still dance?'

'Yes, but I've had to just keep practising at home because I simply could not afford to take classes with a teacher, but I am in practice.'

'Where are you living?' asked Jean.

Alice told her.

She was horrified. 'But, my dear, that's a dreadful slum area. It's not safe for you! You must leave at once, and for the time come and live with us, then . . . well, we'll see.'

'We certainly will! I've got a pretty good idea in my mind already, and I think – I *think* Joe will agree!'

Norma smiled smugly as she spoke. Her sister and friends knew that she would have no difficulty in influencing her husband.

Everything was happening so quickly Alice felt as if she was being whisked up to the clearest of blue skies.

The next day Alice said goodbye to Madame as a member of staff, and was looked on enviously by Cheri and the others. She went back to the apartment, packed her things and wrote to the landlord enclosing the amount of rent that was due, and another letter to Trixie from whom she had heard again recently having sent the rest of her clothes to her in Columbus.

During the week that followed, Alice was thrust into a totally different lifestyle. Staying with the Montgomerys was like heaven. She was given a beautiful guest suite with a bathroom. Breakfast and lunch were taken in a conservatory that looked over a lush, typically Californian garden. Jean was, as Alice had suspected, more kind and friendly than could be imagined.

A few days after she was settled and relaxed, Norma came to see her.

'Connie and I have talked to Joe who is willing to put you under contract because in three weeks time we are putting an important photoplay into production, and we have a role in it for you.'

'As a dancer or actress?'

'A dancer – we hope to use you as an actress later on, but we feel that it will be best for you to make your debut as a dancer. You'll be called to a meeting very soon.'

'This is wonderful news, Norma – I can't thank you enough, and I'll not let you down.' Hesitating, she said, 'I don't want to seem too inquisitive at this stage but have you any idea how much I'll be earning when the contract comes through?'

'Why yes, we're not ungenerous once we've recognised real talent, it will be in the order of seven hundred dollars a week. Then as you become more famous and play more important roles so your salary will increase accordingly.'

That evening she somewhat tentatively asked Jean and John whether she could possibly stay on with them until she became more established.

'My dear, you can stay here as long as you like – we've masses of room now our children are grown up and living back East. Why, it'll be delightful for us.'

Then she turned to her husband and said, 'I won't mind having Alice here for a nice long time, will you, John?'

'No, it'll be great, but there will come a time when we'll be plagued by reporters at the gate, you know I'm certain our Alice is going to become very famous!'

'Our Alice' – those words made Alice choke with emotion. She felt that she had acquired a new family, with Jean and John her adopted parents.

But when she went to bed that night she could not sleep. She smiled to herself thinking of other occasions in the not so distant past when she had been kept awake, and now suddenly, she had very different things on her mind and was wildly excited.

The next day she learned that she was to attend a production meeting at the studios on the following Monday. She was both delighted and apprehensive at the news. However, on trying to work out what to wear she became painfully aware of the fact that, against her new friends she was looking extremely dated and really quite shabby. She decided to take Jean into her confidence and tell her that while she badly needed new clothes she simply did not have enough money to buy them until she was paid.

Jean Montgomery was well aware of the needs of any young rising star. Over the years she had helped a great many to fame and fortune – and through their difficulties. She had already noticed that Alice's wardrobe was sadly dated, and when Alice told her of her predicament she said that John would make her an advance on her contract to tide her over.

'So, my dear, you and I are going shopping and you'll be opening an account with Madame, as you probably need several new outfits – and must have one right away to wear to that meeting!'

The reception that Alice and Jean received from Madame Magnin's that Saturday morning amused Alice greatly. Madame was welcoming but the assistants were very sulky.

Alice decided to try on a pretty mauve afternoon gown and was shown into one of the changing cubicles by Cheri.

She could feel the girl's animosity towards her so she said, 'Look, Cheri, not long ago you remarked how pleased you were with the progress you were making in your career – so I'm sure you must understand how I am feeling now I'm moving on in mine. If you're contented there's no need to look so glum.'

Cheri looked at her blankly for a moment then her face broke into a smile. 'Yes, you're quite right, I did say something like that – and I know I'd be no good in front of the camera.'

'So we're both happy then?'

Cheri nodded and helped Alice into the gown which she purchased, along with a light-weight spring coat and matching hat. She then bought shoes from a shop she had looked in with such admiration not so long ago.

She was ready for the meeting.

The next morning after breakfast she drove with John to the Taft Hotel where the Talmadge sisters had taken a meeting room.

John took the chair and after welcoming everyone, he introduced Alice to the director, a pleasant enthusiastic man in his late thirties called Dayton Holt, a scenic designer, lighting engineer and several other actors and actresses, who were also being introduced for the first time.

'Now, ladies and gentlemen, we are proposing to put into production a photoplay to be directed by Dayton here. It is to be an important production, and will run to thirteen reels. It will be in four sequences, based on the theme of Temptation through the ages. The first will deal with the Garden of Eden and will be a balletic and mime sequence between Adam and Eve and the Serpent. The second will be the temptation of Christ – and here we will of course have to be extremely careful not to offend, or exhibit an iota of bad taste. It will be tricky, but we think we can cope. The third sequence will be set in the time of the French Revolution where a young woman who, smitten with love of Danton pretends to be a peasant, but is, in fact, an aristocrat. Her family are wanted by the Committee, and Danton, thinking she is a family servant, offers her not only money but his heart if she will tell him where they are. So the temptation here is love or family. Only she can decide. The fourth and last sequence is set in modern times, and tells of a poor man who is involved with bootlegging and makes a lot of money – but the gang kills his brother. His temptation is whether he continues to make money from the illicit trade and live comfortably, or go to the police.'

John went on to talk to the technical team and, after a long discussion about the shooting schedules, they adjourned for lunch. Afterwards the meeting divided, with the Talmadge sisters and Dayton taking the proposed cast, John went with three financial backers to work out the costing in greater detail and the technical team made up the third group.

It was arranged that Constance would be the aristocratic servant girl while Norma would play Mary Magdalene. They intended to test male newcomers for the very special role of Jesus.

Then continuing to address the meeting in a very business-like way Dayton said, 'Miss Townsend, we thought you would like to play Eve in the first sequence. We will, in the next week or two be looking for someone – perhaps oriental or Indian – to play the serpent, and we have not yet cast Adam. He will have to move well, and someone with dance experience would, of course, be useful.'

'Mr Holt, will there be a choreographer?' asked the extremely excited Alice.

'Possibly, why do you ask? Do you know someone?'

234

'Well, I may be overstepping the mark, but I have done a certain amount – for the theatre and cabaret in London. If you are not going to start shooting for a week or two, perhaps you would allow me to work out something which I could show you. Obviously, I would get busy right away, so that if you didn't like what I did there would still be time for you to get someone else in?'

The Talmadge sisters and Dayton Holt went into a little huddle, and after an anxious moment when Alice was wondering if she had been too forthcoming he turned to her and said, 'You realise, Alice, we cannot promise you the work, though we know you'll be marvellous in the part. But we are willing to let you try your hand at choreographing the dances and mime. Have a meeting with Norma to decide the details – where you want to rehearse, and what music you'll need.'

Then, addressing the whole meeting, he added, 'We'll be commissioning a full orchestral score, but the composer will, of course, follow the scenes after the filming and editing has been completed.'

He closed the meeting. Afterwards Alice, Connie and Norma ordered coffee in the lounge, while Dayton rushed back to the studios to continue his planning.

'Oh, Norma, I hope I wasn't too pushy!'

'No, my dear, of course not. You were quite right to suggest it – we Americans like that – and I know from what I experienced in London that you English girls, and men too, are far too modest and retiring. No, we'll give you the chance, it's up to you to grab it and show us what you can do.'

This appealed greatly to Alice's ambitious streak. All the while she felt her confidence grow as she began to have ideas for the sequence but she now realised that she was in a position to go back to ballet class. Whilst working with Astafieva she had heard mention of an excellent ballet school in Hollywood called the Kosloff Academy which was run by another émigré Russian. She asked Norma if she had heard of it.

'Why yes, Natacha goes there nearly every day, and I know Alla does too – when she feels so inclined. I'll telephone Natacha when I go home and I'm sure she'll be only too pleased to take you along. Yes, he is a good teacher, you're quite right!'

Alice was amazed. It was well known that Natacha Valentino was a dancer – but that Norma should speak so casually about someone so famous.

To be quite certain she asked, 'Er . . . Natacha Valentino?'

'Yes, of course, you'll like her she is a dear in many ways but we are always warning her not to boss poor Rudy around quite so much. And I expect you know Alla – that's Alla Nazimova, her friend – they spend a lot of time together.'

Two days later in the Montgomerys' second car, driven by their chauffeur, Alice was taken round to Whitley Heights, the Valentino's Hollywood home, to call for Natacha to go to ballet class. The house was attractive with a lovely view. Natacha was ready and came out and met the car on the drive.

They introduced themselves and, as they drove along, Natacha said, 'He is very good teacher, Alice, and Alla said she would come today. I am hoping that in the future we will be able to work together. I'll have to speak to Joe about it. I hear you're going to be in *Temptation* – so good, my dear. I hope they find you a beautiful partner!'

'Yes – so do I, and that Dayton Holt will like my choreography.'

She did well in the class which presented no difficulties, and was complemented on her work by the ballet master. She told him she hoped to come to class as often as possible and explained to him about her role in the photoplay.

After being collected by the chauffeur and taking Natacha home, Alice was about to leave Whitney Heights when there was a deafening roar of a car's engine. Immediately the chauffeur drove onto the grass verge to get out of the way of a very large, open sports car as it surged into the uphill drive scattering dust and gravel.

In the split second during which the vehicle rushed past Alice caught her first glimpse of the great Rudolph Valentino.

Chapter 28

Alice began to think seriously about the *Garden of Eden* dance drama.

John Montgomery hired one of the Kosloff's studios, and a pianist to work with her. Alice had a meeting with the designer to discover what the set would be like – and learned that it was to be a somewhat stylised Garden of Eden with the Tree of Knowledge; having been shown where the pieces of set were to be placed, she could think constructively about the detailed scenario. Natacha was to design the costumes – something that she had a great deal of talent for, and enjoyed doing.

While she could easily choreograph a solo for herself, Alice's priority was to work out moves for the man cast as Adam, who she met at their first rehearsal. Mike Dawson turned out to be a large, blond, rather simple fellow with a generous smile and extremely muscular body. Asked whether he had ever danced, he shook his head and told her he had got the part because of winning a weight-lifting and body-building contest. However, his face was very expressive – he was, Alice decided, a gentle giant.

Their pianist was helpful, and played in exactly the right kind of rhythm and at the correct speed, she and Mike soon began to build up a good working partnership. Alice devised a short sequence where they were wandering happily together, looking at the flowers and plants in the garden. Then she thought she would perform some sensuous and exotic moves, and suggested that he could lift her, cross to another part of the set, put her down, and join her at the foot of the Tree of Knowledge to lift her again. He lifted her beautifully and easily, but she had to be very tactful about the way he moved from one position to another – he had very little natural grace, and simply stomped from position to position, swinging his arms and planting his feet very solidly on the floor like the weight-lifter he was. She would have to give her Adam the very simplest of movements; but at least his physique was stunning, and his expressions were responsive as they portrayed the first pair of lovers.

Later the Serpent turned up – a young Mexican boy of about fourteen. He was very slim and supple and could slither superbly along the floor. Alice planned to have several shots of him up the tree, once the set was built. He reacted marvellously, and she could tell by his delightfully wicked grins that he would perform his part splendidly.

They and the pianist worked for several days perfecting and extending the sequence, which would eventually run for about eleven minutes – the time she had been given by Dayton – and at the end of the second week they felt ready to show the work to him, and to Norma, Constance and John.

Alice was extremely nervous, but she had done her best and knew that the three of them – all such different personalities – had worked up a strong rapport which she thought would come over very well on the screen should her work be accepted.

Smiling at Adam and the Serpent, she gave a nod to the pianist and the little performance began . . .

'Congratulations, my dear – it's really lovely. You were obviously very observant when you worked in the theatre. It's simply fine, isn't it, Dayton?'

Dayton Holt took both Alice's hands. He was delighted with all three of them, and with what Alice had done. The next stage was to work out the camera angles which would make the most of the beautiful positions she had devised, and to give the impression of additional height to the Tree of Knowledge. They would go through it again next day.

Alice and her colleagues were very excited, and looked forward to the final rehearsals and filming – which would begin on the following Monday morning.

As they left the Kosloff studio, the sisters suggested she should join them for afternoon tea at the Plaza Hotel.

'Now, the next thing, Alice, is publicity. After the first few days of actual shooting the studio photographer will take a series of pictures of you, both in costume and day dress. As we proceed with the production these will be released to build up public interest both here and in Great Britain – having an English star will certainly boost our U.K audiences, and already the distribution companies are wanting to make the most of you.'

'When will the premiére be, Norma?'

'We think in October. Now, there's more to the publicity than photographs. A journalist will be interviewing you in depth, and this will form the basis of a hand-out to the press.' Norma paused for a moment, then added, 'I think we had better arrange for you to have a whole day for all that. You can use our bungalow at the studios, which in any case will serve as your dressing-room. We'll be at Culver City for several weeks, and there's no point in keeping it locked up. You might as well be really comfortable. Get John to drop you off there on Monday morning.'

Temptation was to have a large budget and a reasonably generous production time. The 'Garden of Eden' scenes would be shot over a two week period during April. Meanwhile, plans were well in hand for 'Danton and the Servant Girl', and many of its scenes would be in production at the same time, using a different back lot and studio. Dayton had an experienced assistant and cameramen, and while he was shooting one scene others would be set up, rehearsed and lit. The second half of the schedule would be devoted to 'The Temptation of Christ' and 'The Modern Criminal'.

As Norma and Connie promised, Alice was given the use of their bunga-low at the studio, which had been specially built for them. It was one of a short row known as Bungalow Alley, part of the United Studios site.

The little building was delightful – a complete home. It had two steeply pitched roof sections and large glass French windows, even a tiny garden. The living-room was decorated in green and yellow and beautifully fur-nished, complete with deeply cushioned settees; studio portraits of the two sisters in many of their famous roles hung on the walls. There was a large dressing-room with two identical dressing-tables, places to hang costumes, two small bedrooms, and a bathroom. A pretty but practical kitchen, its windows complete with lacy muslin curtains, made up the rest of the one-storey building. John told her that the adjoining bungalow belonged to Mary Pickford and Douglas Fairbanks – it was somewhat bigger. Other stars occupied the rest of the row, which was slowly being expanded as the studios grew in prosperity and put under even more important stars under contract.

Later that day she was joined by Natacha to discuss the costumes.

'So, my dear, you and Adam should really have no costumes at all – I should only provide two fig leaves for you to cover yourselves after you have taken the fruit!'

'As far as the Bible describes them, of course you're right, but somehow I don't think . . .'

'No, I don't think so, either! This is what I have in mind.'

She produced sketches from a folio.

Adam's outfit consisted simply of trunks, his body decorated with painted trails of vine leaves and plants which started on one shoulder and twisted down the opposite leg. The Serpent would be encased in a snake's skin which, Natacha explained, would be made up of satin scales fixed to a stretchable wool fabric to enable him to slide around the set with reasonable ease.

'Now . . . this is yours.'

Alice would look virtually naked, wearing a body stocking with a similar plant decoration to match Adam's, and a very long, blond wig that would reach down to her knees. The stocking would be thoroughly lined, so that no intimate details of Alice's body would be revealed.

'It's great fun, but I hope the wig will stay in place – I have to move a great deal.'

'Yes, I noticed that the other day when I watched the run-through. I'll have it made in threads of rayon, which I think will be lighter than hair. I hope you'll won't feel at all embarrassed in this costume, Alice.'

Alice had worn far less on stage when she was in *Chu Chin Chow*, so was not concerned about it, provided that the wig would not hamper her movements and the body stocking was made of the same knitted pure silk as used for ballet tights. Natacha thought this an excellent idea.

The shooting of the 'Garden of Eden' sequence came out on time. Alice had now completed her first major Hollywood role. There would be time during the coming weeks to enjoy what Hollywood had to offer – which she had not been able to relish during the dark earlier months on the West Coast.

Socially, life was fascinating. Before she had arrived in Hollywood she was under the impression that the stars continually gave wild parties which went on until dawn; but she soon realised that this was not so. Certainly, there were lavish parties and dinner-parties most weekends, especially on Saturday nights; but on Sundays there were usually only lunchtime or early evening affairs, because everyone who was working had to be at the studios very early on Monday mornings. Some stars entertained informally, and there was usually dancing to a gramophone or small group of musicians, while others arranged musical evenings or bridge parties.

As spring turned to summer, Alice spent a great many weekends at Connie and Norma's beach house, really relaxed and enjoying the sea and sun. She decided never to ask questions about the prohibition laws, and was tactful when she was given the best champagne and wines or cocktails with a rum base – rum illegally imported, she gathered, from the Caribbean.

Other opportunities came along, and she performed several solo dances in a number of photoplays. Every day, when not working at one studio or another, she attended Kosloff's ballet class – usually with Natacha. She found the woman fascinating – she was so versatile and creative – and her exotic circle of friends added yet another dimension to Alice's rich and rewarding lifestyle.

The summer months were exciting as well as very busy. Then she was given a leading part in a fairly short film about a ballerina who worked in a circus – a touching little story. As the heroine, she fell in love with a heart-broken clown whose wife had just died, and restored him to happiness. Later in the year she, with Natacha and Nazimova (who was also a talented costume designer), created a classical ballet dream-sequence in a film called *Billions*. Both went well, and her friends assured her that both photoplays, when they were released, would add considerably to her increasing reputation and fame.

Her picture quite regularly appeared in *Picture Show* and *Picturegoer*, and she received an ever-increasing amount of fan mail, increasing from a trickle to almost a flood. Norma told her to enjoy the freedom of not having to sign hundreds of photographs, for once she had appeared as Eve, she would receive a very great deal more.

Sensible if occasionally extravagant, certainly where clothes were concerned, (she made regular visits to Magnin's, and always enjoyed the attention she was given) Alice was steadily becoming financially secure. She had now appeared in five photoplays, and while *Temptation* was still to be released, United Artists increased her salary. In addition, there were rumours that Dayton was preparing another epic which would star Alice – if *Temptation* came up to the studio's expectations.

Because of all this Alice felt that she would very soon be able to buy, or at any rate lease, her own home and furnish it. Houses were always coming on the market, but with the film industry growing so fast they sold extremely quickly. She discussed her idea with John and Jean.

'It's an excellent plan, Alice,' responded John. 'Have you anything specific in mind?'

'I've not, as yet. I would like a pleasant view – but I wouldn't want to be too far away from the studios, so it's not going to be easy.'

'Your first decision is whether you want to have a house designed and built to your own specification, or whether you want to look for a home that already exists.'

Jean added, 'If you have a house built, the architect could include a dance studio, which would be essential for you, wouldn't it? And perhaps you should also think about learning to drive – a sporty little roadster would be useful, and a good thing for publicity. Why, you might even get one free from a manufacturer if you would be willing to promote one of his models!'

'I'd not thought of that. At home, we've had a car for almost as long as I can remember. Daddy always favoured the Wolseley, but I don't suppose they have them here. Yes, I'd like that – do you have any connection with the motor trade, John?'

'No, but Dayton does – so ask him.'

Alice had a poor night. She kept thinking about the house. Was the idea going to be too extravagant? After a couple of sleepless hours she decided that she would start from scratch, and have her own home designed and built to suit herself – and that, yes, she would acquire a car and learn to drive. Turning over she went into a deep sleep, dreaming of opening doors in her parents' home and finding new rooms, all painted white, with mirrors in which she saw her own reflection dancing.

'Are you quite certain you want to have a house designed and built to your own specification?'

The real estate agent looked at Alice over his spectacles from the far side of a huge desk.

'The idea does have its appeal. After all, it would be mine, and exactly to my taste.'

'I'm sure your taste is perfect, Miss Townsend, but the terrain, the climate, the atmosphere here is very different from London, and while you'll have some fine ideas, they mayn't in the long run work out very well for you – even with the most sensible architectural advice.'

Alice felt somewhat deflated. Her expression made the man smile.

'Don't look too dejected. I'm only thinking of your comfort and happiness.

241

Of course, we can provide you with the right people to find a site and design and build a house, if that's what you finally decide. But just for the moment I would like to take you to see one which has just come on the market – it's most desirable, I assure you – with a tennis court as well as a swimming pool.'

'But I hate tennis, even although everyone else seems to love it! The last thing I want is a tennis court.'

'But knowing your work, Miss Townsend, that tennis court could serve a very different purpose. Am I right in assuming that you mostly work at United Artists?'

'Yes.'

'So it's important to be near those studios?'

'Very.'

'Good. The house is situated just around the corner from the studios – on the other side of the gasworks. Yes, I know that's not so nice, but it won't spoil your views, and the smell never drifts west – I promise you. I would like you to see it.'

Alice rather reluctantly agreed.

Miss Tasmania Duval went to the gramophone that stood in the corner of the drawing-room and chose a record of 'Alexander's Ragtime Band'. She wound up the machine and switched it on, then carefully placed the sound-box, with its new steel needle, at the edge of the record. Returning to her feather duster she flicked it around the ornaments and the tops of the pictures in time to the music. She was thoroughly enjoying her light chores. After the record had been playing for about a minute the telephone rang. She went into the entrance hall to answer it.

Listening to the voice on the end of the phone for a moment she said, 'Right, Mr Swartz. Yes, that'll be just fine. So I'll see you in few minutes.'

She hung up the receiver. By now the record had finished and the needle was merely making a scratching sound. Hurriedly she switched off the gramophone and dashed through the kitchen to her small apartment. She quickly changed into a fresh pink spotty afternoon dress, combed through and repinned her heavy black hair, lightly powdered her nose and made sure her lipstick was neatly shaped. Looking at herself in her long mirror she ran her hands down over her large breasts and wide hips and, satisfied with her appearance, rushed out onto the front patio to welcome her visitors.

Alice and the estate agent turned into the drive of a breathtakingly attractive house in the Spanish style with white walls and red tiled roof.

'Oh! It *is* pretty – I do see what you mean.'

They drove up through a sloping garden with three lawns on different levels, rose bushes, hibiscus shrubs and several small palms. At one side was a round wrought-iron pergola. Alice immediately visualised musicians playing for her guests under its copper roof.

'Miss Townsend, may I introduce Miss Tasmania Duval. Miss Duval is employed by the owner of this house.'

'Why! How do you do, Miss Townsend. I'm sure pleased to meet you!'

Alice immediately like the woman's warm smile and kind greeting and they shook hands.

'Miss Duval is staying on here until the house is sold, Miss Townsend.'

'Yes, Miss Townsend. You see, Mr and Mrs Illingworth have had to go back to Philadelphia to live. They sure wanted me to go with them, but I said I didn' want to leave Hollywood, and so I promised . . . well, like Mr Swartz said . . .'

'I see.'

'Miss Duval, perhaps you would make us some fruit drinks while I show Miss Townsend around.'

'Why of course – I'll be delighted.'

Miss Duval left them.

The drawing-room was large, with tall windows with semi-circular tops. A door led to a dining room with the kitchen beyond it, and beyond that a small self-contained apartment for the live-in maid. A curved, marble staircase took them upstairs where there were three main bedroom suites, each with its own bathroom.

The light, feminine charm of the place enchanted Alice. She now could see why the agent had been eager for her to view it. He took her through a side door which opened onto the tennis court.

'Oh, that! It's such a lot of wasted space – honestly it's the only thing that puts me off. I love the house, but I don't see why I have to tolerate a tennis court, just for my friends.'

'And why should you, indeed? But don't you see, Miss Townsend, that we could build your dance studio – right here entirely to your own design.'

Alice's eyes brightened.

They went on to examine a sizeable swimming pool and a garage. She asked the agent if she might walk around by herself for a while.

It was a big decision. The price seemed right and, though buying the house would commit her to Hollywood, she was now happy and increasingly successful. And as John and Jean had said, property is always a good investment – especially somewhere like Hollywood. She looked again at the bedroom suites. They were spacious and beautiful. She went into the master bedroom. Here she would sleep . . . perhaps too, make love – with whom?

Returning to reality she rejoined the agent.

Yes, she would like to buy the property.

They went back to the drawing-room where Miss Duval served the fruit drinks.

'Mr Swartz, may I speak with Miss Townsend, please?'

'Go ahead, please.'

'Miss Townsend, once the house is sold I'll be out of work. Now I love this house, and I'm wondering if you already have a personal maid and someone to look after you and the house?'

'Well no, I haven't . . .'

'Then would you consider employing me? I know the house, and . . . and . . .' she hesitated,

'Go on, Miss Duval,'

'Well, I like the look of you, and I think we could get on real well!'

Alice was amused at her outspokenness. She also liked the huge smile which matched the young woman's generous proportions.

'Do you think you can cope with *me*? I'm British, not American, you know.'

'Why, yes – I noticed that at once from your pretty accent.'

'Miss Duval is very versatile,' said the agent, 'and she has been with Mr and Mrs Illingworth for what is it – ten years?'

'Sure is, Mr Swartz!'

'Miss Duval, you obviously are good at your job, and as you like the house, why not stay with it and join me?'

'Thank you so much, Miss Townsend. Oh there's one thing . . .'

'I'll pay you what ever the Illingworths paid you at first, then when we know each other better – well, we'll see what can be done!'

'Thank you. That'll suit me fine!'

The Montgomerys were the first to hear her news.

'When will you move in?'

'Quite soon, Jean. There are a few repairs, and of course it will take some time for the studio to be planned and built – but that doesn't bother me too much. I so want you to see it, it really is beautiful – and by the way, when I do move in I'll have my very own maid.'

Alice told them about Miss Tasmania Duval.

After an independent surveyor had produced a satisfactory report she returned to the agent the following week.

'Sign here, please, Miss Townsend.'

And Alice took her pen from her handbag and signed. Her writing was steady and confident, and the ink from the pen flowed in a beautifully clear black stream.

'Now don't you worry, I'll unpack all your gowns and press any that's creased. You go sit on the patio and rest, you've had a busy morning. I'll bring you tea and cookies in about half an hour. Soon you'll be nicely settled, you'll see.'

'Thank you, Miss Duval.'

'Now excuse me, Miss Townsend, but please can we get somethin' sorted out right away?'

Alice was puzzled but amused at the maid's remark.

'Why yes, of course!'

'Well, Miss, you see, I'm always called Miss Tassie, and I'll always call you Miss Alice. If you don' mind, that's the way it is!'

Surprised at hearing this unusual request, but at once seeing it was important to her, Alice agreed.

'But your first name's Tasmania, isn't it? It's very unusual to be called after a place!'

'It sure is, you see my Mammy, well she didn't have much money and Pappy left her – went back to Paris to live then we never heard from him again. He was no good – always drunk – always saying to Mammy, "I'll take you to Paris, I'll take you to Paris", but he never did. But we got by. Well, when my Mammy was a little girl she was given a globe, and she liked all the names of those places she would never visit, so she called me Tasmania, then there's my sisters – India and Tunisia. Pappy couldn't have cared less. I'm the youngest, but there's Dixie, well that's not the name of a country, but she thought it sounded nice. And Mammy's called Queenie!'

'Do you have any brothers?'

'Oh I sure do. She was keen for the boys to do well so she called the eldest King, then there's Duke and Earl. Duke trains racehorses, Earl's a chef in New Orleans . . .' Miss Tassie prattled on. Alice learned that they had lived in Talahassie, and the mother was now a housekeeper to a wealthy New York City family.

After all this Alice realised that she had not only a maid with a strong character but one who was interesting and great fun. She soon discovered that Miss Tassie was an excellent cook who was always surprising her with delicious light food. That she was also scrupulous over the housekeeping money that Alice gave her, and the way she kept the house perfect and Alice's clothes immaculate was marvellous.

A few weeks later when they were really settled, Miss Tassie suggested that Alice should employ a part time gardener, and with her usual efficiency Miss Tassie found just the right young man for the job.

Since she had moved into her house Alice had not been totally happy with its name. 'High Hill' was somehow not right for her and it, even if it suited the previous owners. She called to Miss Tassie.

'You know I don't really like this house's name. It doesn't seem quite right to me – what do you think?'

Miss Tassie pursed her lips and rolled her eyes upwards deep in thought.

'I guess you're right, Miss Alice, but what have you in mind?'

'Well I just don't know.'

'Okay then, let's consult the cards.'

'The cards?'

'Why yes, of course, they'll tell us. Just a moment.'

She disappeared and soon returned with a small wooden box. On opening it she unwrapped a pack of cards from a blue silk handkerchief.

'They aren't ordinary playing cards.'

'Why no, of course not, they're Tarot cards. I'm good at reading them.'

Miss Tassie gave them to Alice to shuffle and told her to pick out three. Miss Tassie who turned them over.

'The Empress – that's you, Miss Alice, lovely. And look there's the Sun – that's the house!'

'And what's that?'

Miss Tassie was quiet for a moment.

'That's great too – ten of coins – it represents lots of money. So the cards tell you to call your house "Sunshine"!'

'That's – well, it's nearly right,' said Alice, she paused. 'But I think, yes! "Sunburst" would be better.'

'Yes, "Sunburst" – real nice idea!'

October

The dense crowd pushed even more against the barriers. Searchlights beamed down on the Hollywood celebrities as they left their limousines to cross the forecourt and enter Graumans Egyptian Theatre for the premiere of *Temptation*.

Press photographers battled for positions to get the best shots of the stars as they arrived, and among the last of them, a few minutes before the film was due to commence were Dayton Holt, Alice and the Montgomerys in one huge automobile and the Talmadge sisters with Joe Schenck in another. They waved to their wild cheering fans and were asked to line up for a photograph at the main entrance to the foyer. As the cameras and flash bulbs clicked away, the women in the crowd gasped approval and amazement at the stars' dresses. Norma was in a white satin cloak trimmed with white fox, Constance in a draped pink ensemble and Alice in a matching rich blue silk dress and coat, heavily embroidered with silver thread and beads, with a bead fringe decorating the sleeves of the coat and the skirt of the dress.

The audience stood as the cast and crew of *Temptation* appeared in the auditorium and sat in the front row of the circle.

Alice, who had attended several premieres at Graumans during the intervening months, was quite used to the theatre, but this was different. This was a very important photoplay and she was being 'introduced' to the public in it.

The orchestra struck up. The credits rolled, 'Starring Constance Talmadge as the Servant . . . Norma Talmadge as Mary Magdalene . . . Jesus Christ, Anonymous . . . Mike Dawson as Adam . . .' Then on a separate caption

AND INTRODUCING
ALICE TOWNSEND
AS
EVE

The technical credits followed, after which the audience was taken into the

246

Garden of Eden. A long slow pan took them across the Garden with its stylised trees and plants. The camera turned low and panned up across Eve who stood with her arms raised. She turned and outstretched them towards Adam. There was a decided gasp from the audience at Alice's appearance in what looked like the semi-nude – her body seemingly covered only with a few leaves and petals. It turned to 'Ahhs' of admiration as Adam picked her up in a beautiful lift, and balancing her in the middle of her back on one hand, walked to the base of the Tree of Knowledge, where he released her and sat down to admire her perfectly formed body and her gloriously erotic dance movements.

The next surprise for the audience was the remarkable appearance of the snake-like serpent. Eve succumbed to his temptation, tasted the apple and he wended his way, smiling smugly as he slithered out of shot. Adam picked up two huge fig leaves, he and Eve covered themselves and walked, bent with shame, into the distance, out of the garden.

As the last shot faded some of the audience booed, others cheered. There was a riotous noise, and it took quite a while before they settled down to watch the next episode, 'The Temptation of Christ'.

Dayton had made quite certain that the audience did not see Christ's face, leaving it to Norma to reflect every mood, nuance and sensation. This sequence was also greeted with a mixed outburst, just as powerful as that for 'The Garden of Eden'. All went well during 'Danton and the Servant Girl'. The audience's reaction was one of total sympathy and understanding – they loved it, and became completely involved in the powerful acting. The final episode was also well received.

Cheers and claps battled with boos and cat calls as the final caption appeared on the screen. The photoplay was a sensation. In the foyer, the rest of the audience, still expressing their feelings in no uncertain terms, parted to make way for the stars and crew.

'Now, my dear, you'll certainly be famous after this!' remarked Norma as she smiled and elegantly waved to a group of fans.

By now they were at the doors of the theatre and the crowd was even denser – the word had got round that newcomer Alice Townsend had appeared in the nude . . . The story lost nothing in the repetition.

Alice was ogled and cheered by young men and women. One fashionable middle-aged woman, who had obviously attended the premiere, attempted to spit at her, but Dayton managed to usher Alice into their car just in time.

The reporters were waiting for them at the Plaza hotel where a large party was due to take place. They bombarded Dayton with questions. Keeping remarkably calm he said that his conscience was clear about the portrayal of Christ, which he hoped was sensitive and would not offend. While he was attempting to answer yet more questions, another reporter started interrogating Alice. At the same time his colleague was busy with his large press photographer's camera. The flashes, coming thick and fast, momentarily blinded her.

What would her fellow countrymen think of her outrageous appearance? How did she feel about being notorious? What was it like to be seen nude in such close contact with a man in front of cameramen, and now the general public? Didn't she think she had behaved brazenly? Wouldn't she be a bad influence on the young?

Standing up very straight, looking the reporter directly in the eye, her English accent and imperious expression putting him thoroughly in his place Alice said, 'I am an artist. I have done nothing of which to be ashamed. My costume was perfectly modest and I did not – repeat did *not* – dance with Mr Dawson wearing little or no clothing. If you had watched the photoplay with any attention at all you would have realised that my body was totally covered from my neck to my ballet shoes.'

Tossing her head she made her way into the reception.

The large ballroom was filling up with guests – stars, directors, financiers from other studios, gossip columnists – all of whom started to surround them. Alice had to repeat her statement several times.

But she was also determined to enjoy herself. Looking around she saw Natacha with Rudy talking to Alla Nazimova. As yet she had not met the great man, and decided that this was a good moment to be introduced.

She went up to the little group and after congratulating Alice, Natacha introduced her to her husband who admiringly said, 'You were wonderful, Miss Townsend – and I'm so pleased to meet you at last. Natacha has told me so much about you, and she is quite right, you are a beautiful dancer. You know I am dancer too, and I appreciate your work very much.'

As he spoke he took her hand and kissed it. A photographer's camera clicked and flashed.

'What did you think of Alice's costume, Rudy?' asked the exotic Natacha.

'Beautiful – really beautiful – congratulations, my darling,' Then he turned and kissed his wife lightly on the cheek. Alice wanted to stay with them longer, but Dayton called her away.

'Alice, you've made a sensation! Remember all publicity is good publicity, and you're in for a lot of it. You'll be so much in demand after all this, from all sorts of directors, but I'm going to see to it that none of them steal you – so there!' He winked at her, knowingly.

They joined the Montgomerys. The party had an excited buzz and enlightened opinion was full of praise for the cast and Dayton's brilliant direction. The photoplay would net a very great deal of money at the box offices world-wide because people would go and see it for very different reasons.

248

Chapter 29

'Now, Miss Alice, you put on your fur coat. It's very blustery out there. You can't trust the weather in January, even in sunny California!'

'But the car's picking me up, and I'll be dropped off in reception. I'll not be cold!'

'Now you do as I say. You don't want a red nose that the make-up ladies'll have to disguise when you starts shooting again!'

'No, you're right, as ever! Look, I don't know when I'll be back.'

'Well, I'm gonna make some nice soup so that you can get warm again whatever time you come in.'

Smiling at Miss Tassie's thoughtfulness, Alice was helped into her musquash just as the studio car drove up to the door to take her to the production meeting in the Board Room of United Artists.

Dayton welcomed everyone – especially Alice, who knew she was destined for a starring role in the new picture.

A small group of the principal technicians was sitting round the table. John Montgomery was next to Dayton, and on his left an elderly actress who Alice did not know. She was introduced as Mary Carr.

'Now, ladies and gentlemen, there is only one person here who knows of my plans and he is with me all the way. Needless to say, Mr Schenck has given his approval. So I welcome you. You'll have gathered that this is to tell you about our next venture, and I think you'll be as excited about it as I am. I read through a great many scenarios and scripts before I found one to inspire me and when I did well, quite honestly, I cried "eureka!"'

He had grabbed the attention of his audience.

'The photoplay will be called *Nocturne*, and Alice here will have a demanding time because – I hate to tell you this, Alice, but we know you can cope – you have to play the part of twins.'

'Twins?'

'And Miss Carr here is to be your mother.'

The older woman smiled up at Dayton and over to Alice.

'Yes, my dear – twins it is. One twin, Angela, is training to be a ballerina – so that means you'll have plenty of opportunity to do some dancing – while the other, Maria, is training to be a concert pianist. They are both in love with the same man, Maria's piano teacher.

'At first they argue, and begin to hate each other after having been very close all their lives. However, it turns out that when Angela becomes a ballerina she falls in love with her dancing partner, which ends her love for the piano teacher. Meanwhile Maria becomes successful as a concert pianist, and at her first big recital the teacher realises that after all, it is she he loves. The photoplay will end with the two sisters giving a huge charity concert with Maria playing the piano for Angela to dance to – performing solos and *pas de deux* with her lover on the stage of a big Broadway theatre.'

The assembled company applauded.

Alice was quiet. After the applause had died down Dayton turned to her and said, 'Well, Alice, what do you think? Of course we'll have to get a double and use her when you and your twin appear at the same time – that won't be difficult. Oh, yes, and don't worry, we don't expect you to play the piano – that can easily be faked. We'll just get a piano teacher to give you a few lessons to show you how to move your hands and fingers up and down the keyboard when you are Maria; and when the photoplay is being shown then the cinema's orchestral pianist will play the actual music that Maria is playing!'

Alice's heart was racing, though she tried to be calm. The idea of her dancing was marvellous – and in fact the double role would be exciting to do. But no-one knew she had ever touched a piano. She decided to keep quiet about it.

'Dayton, it's a stunning story, and I'll love the challenge – it is a big one!'

'You'll be just fine, Alice. We all agree, don't we?'

Everyone did.

'And,' Dayton continued, 'don't you think that Alice and Mary will make wonderful mother and daughters?'

Chatter broke out for a while, then Dayton called the meeting to order.

He went on to tell them that he and John had cast Lloyd Hughes as the piano teacher, and another British actor, who had made good in Hollywood in recent years, Reginald Denny, as Alice's partner and lover.

'Dayton, I know Reg is British like me – and that'll be nice – but I heard somewhere that he was originally a boxer, not a dancer. So who will partner me?'

'We thought we would audition the men from Kosloff's, Alice, and find someone who looks reasonably like Reg.'

She nodded, but was sceptical. She regularly worked with Kosloff's male dancers in class, and knew that most of them were pretty pathetic as far strong technique was concerned.

'We'll have to decide that very soon, won't we?' she asked

'Yes. You and I can sort it out between us, if that's alright with you, John?'

John agreed. As was usual, the meeting split up into different groups. Later, Alice and the motherly Mary Carr had a light lunch in the studio commissary and she assured Alice that both Lloyd and Reginald were thoroughly professional actors and very nice men. They decided it would be a happy team.

'Welcome home, Miss Alice – had a good day?'

'Oh yes. It's all very exciting, Miss Tassie. Any messages?'

'Why, sure – Madame Magnin has some new outfits she thinks'll suit you, and there's a fat letter from England for you.'

'From England! Oh, where is it?' Alice was anxious.

Within seconds she was puzzled no longer. With tears of joy she read Philip's long, long letter, and was delighted that he had got in touch. First, her brother congratulated her on her performance in *Temptation*. He had taken Rose to see it – she had enjoyed it – and he had easily found out the Hollywood address of the Studios from their London office. She was saddened to hear that her mother was still antagonistic, but happy that her father seemed to approve. Though this did not surprise her; she knew he had always been far more sympathetic than her mother. Could they please keep in touch from now on?

'Oh, yes, yes *please*, dearest Phil! I'll write right away,' Alice thought aloud.

She spent the evening – after Miss Tassie's soup dinner – writing to her beloved brother. There was so much to tell him – though also a very great deal that she must for the time gloss over. It was wonderful to be in touch with at least one member of her family again.

'Right, next please!'

The aspiring male dancer took Alice around the waist as she jumped up *en pointe* and gracefully drew her leg to the side, then turned so that it was lifted high behind her in an arabesque, and she was ready to lower her arm and body towards the ground. He did not hold her firmly enough, and she almost fell. Sensing that she was insecure, she saved herself. When her would-be partner had rather sheepishly left the room, Alice said angrily, pushing one toe of her blocked ballet shoes into the floor, 'It's absolutely no good, Dayton! These men aren't strong enough or experienced enough to dance with me. He's the ninth we've auditioned and each one is worse than the last.'

'I know, Alice, and I'm sorry – but you must have a partner. Do you think that we could get hold of that Scottish chap you worked with in London?'

'I was hoping you'd ask me that, but it won't be easy. He's with the Russian ballet, and doing very well. I think you would have to make it very worth his while, and perhaps the company's too, if he is to be released.'

'I'll speak to John and Joe about it. Joe has his ways.'

He dismissed the group of mediocre dancers, and Alice told him where they could reach the Russian Ballet and its awesome impresario.

*

251

'So who's this guy Dee Agaleff?'

Joe Schenck, unlit cigar between his teeth, shuffled papers on his huge desk. Dayton explained.

'Alice used to work well with this Alex.'

'What's he look like?'

Dayton produced the photo Alice had given him.

'I guess he's presentable enough. Fine figure of a man, not too nancy looking – even if he is one, but no matter. Will he cost much?'

'He's quite famous, and you'll have to bargain with Diaghilev if you want him.'

'Okay, let's see. Cable the Rusky right away.'

'I think it better come from you – he's as important to the ballet as you are to the studios.'

'Is that so? Never heard of him up to now, but if you say so!'

Three days later, after a flurry of cables and United Artists' agreement to pay a large sum into the fragile coffers of the Russian Ballet, and offer Alex excellent terms, Joe received a final cable from Monte Carlo,

WILL RELEASE SACHA MEKINSKY FOR DURATION OF PRODUCTION OF PHOTOPLAY ONLY STOP OFFICIAL AGREEMENT FOLLOWS STOP SERGE DE DIAGHILEV

Joe was confused, Dayton mystified, Alice delighted and amused. She explained that Diaghilev was using Alexander McIntyre's Russian Ballet name. That evening she went home to Miss Tassie in a very jubilant mood.

Later she learned that Alex would be arriving in just over two weeks.

In the meantime rehearsals began. Alice spent several days working with the cameramen and a young unknown actress who was the same height and had identically long ballerina-styled hair to Alice, and who was to act as her double. She would be filmed from behind when Alice and her twin were supposed to be in shot together. The technicians had coped with this kind of problem several times before, but wanted to be certain that once shooting schedules got under way there would be as little delay as possible.

A few days before Alex was due to arrive, Alice, (by now very excited) was collected from 'Sunburst' as usual by studio car in the early morning, and was taken to Dayton's office rather than to the studio where she and the other members of the cast had been working for the last week or two.

Dayton was there with a young man who had very long black hair.

'Alice, I want you to meet Franz. He's going to show you how to mime at the piano keyboard when you're supposed to be playing.'

The slim, elegant, rather superior young man clicked his heels, kissed Alice's hand, and greeted her with a thick mid-European accent. She was amused but slightly nervous.

'Right, let's go down to one of the orchestra rehearsal rooms and the piano we'll be using on the set,' said Dayton.

They walked down to the ground floor. The young man was silent. Alice noticed he was carrying a bulging music case.

On entering, a group of string players picked up their instruments and left the large, hollow room.

'I'll leave you two to it. There's a telephone – you can get through to my office on it. I'm doing paper work with John today. We'll be there until lunchtime, by which time I expect, Alice, you'll have had enough.'

'I expect so, Dayton! Thank you.'

He left.

Alice and the silent Franz walked across the vast expanse of room towards the black concert grand.

'Please. Sit there. That is piano stool.'

'Yes, I know.'

Alice sat down. The feel of the studded black leather seat instantly brought back horrific memories. The stool was too high. Automatically, Alice felt for the round wooden handles at each side and started to turn them to lower the stool, so that she would be at a comfortable height in relation to the keyboard.

This somewhat surprised Franz but he was keen to get on and said, 'Put hands to keys.'

She lifted the piano lid, but did not attempt to place her hands on the keyboard. There was a pause. She simply sat gazing wide-eyed at the keys . . . Franz was speaking.

'You lift your hands like this . . . you place them . . .'

But he saw at once that she was not taking in a word he was saying, and withdrew his hand before he actually touched her wrist. He thought perhaps she felt faint.

'Miss Townsend, are you alright? Shall I get doctor?'

She blinked several times, her hands resting in her lap. She could feel that the blood had drained from her face.

'No, I think I'll be alright in a moment . . . It's just . . . well, no matter.'

There was a pause, and when he felt she was looking a little better, he said somewhat impatiently, 'So perhaps we get on? I have recital tonight at the Hollywood Hotel – not got all day.'

He was sitting beside her at the keyboard and, as he had attempted to do a moment before, picked up her hand by the wrist, but she hastily released it.

Taking a deep breath she said, 'What music do you have? I assume you've a copy of the Chopin Nocturnes, because that's the name of the photoplay.'

Confused, he said, 'Of course I have, but that won't mean anything to you.'

His tone was thick with sarcasm.

'Let me see it, please.'

Trying to keep his eyes on his pupil while he fumbled in his music case, he produced his copy. Alice took it from him. It was so familiar. A rough grey paper cover with a lovely engraving of Chopin on it. She felt as if the composer was staring at her. The very feel of the music brought back even more memories for her. Then, as she handled it, she unexpectedly felt a wave of wonderfully warm emotion surge through her body. She looked up over the raised music rest and as she put the book down in position, she felt a presence . . . another presence. Someone quite other . . . from another dimension. Momentarily, a young man with a smile as rosy as his rounded cheeks came to her. He nodded, and she knew he was saying, 'Go on, Alice, you can do it!' – then was gone.

Blinking again, she turned to Franz, who was now breathing heavily with impatience.

'I suppose it's Opus thirty-two, number two,' she said in a very matter-of-fact way.

'Why, yes – but how . . .'

She found the opening page and glanced at it. For a moment she remembered the last time she had played it – badly, on purpose, in her music exam. But this was different. Her long-since dead Charlie had given her confidence. She had not touched a piano for . . . she could not remember how long, and did not want to remember. She read the first few bars. The work sprang back into her mind. Smiling broadly at her instructor, she took the book off the music rest and closed it. He was mystified and once more picked up her wrist.

'Now, you put your hands . . .'

'Like this?'

Her hands were over the keys. She glanced at him, and started to play – as she had never played before. In spite of the years during which she had not touched the piano, she could play – and play well. She was totally involved. Franz was speechless. The theme changed; she remembered exactly how to cope. All the previous years of agony and torture, fell away. This was something special and glorious. As she played she knew that there was now a kinship between her artistic expression as a dancer and her newly-discovered expression as a mature pianist.

'But . . . but . . . I must get Dayton.'

Poor Franz rushed to the telephone and within a minute Dayton and John crept into the orchestra room. They were amazed.

Alice let the final chord die away, and coming out of what was almost a trance-like state, smiled up at her colleagues.

'We didn't know! Why didn't you tell us? That was truly beautiful! What do you think, Franz?'

'Remarkable! You obviously won't need me any more.'

'I'm afraid not.'

They thanked him. He turned to Alice and congratulated her.

'Well, Alice, why didn't you tell us?'

'Oh, Dayton, it's a long, long old story. Maybe I'll tell you one day!'

Chapter 30

'It's all quite unbelievable, here I am – little ol' me – having lunch with you in Hollywood!'

They had just been served coffee after an excellent lunch in the famous Montmartre Café. Alex was dazed. His journey had been easy, but he was still in a dream as he tried to take in everything going on around him in the café, the powerful sunlight outside, and the bustle of the street.

'Well, you'll not fail to be happy with the Montgomerys.'

'They're treating me like a son already – and John was telling me he's Scottish.'

'Oh, Alex! That's something that always amuses me with Americans. They're never American! They always say, "You'll like her, she's Swedish, or Spanish, or Irish,' or whatever. In reality, of course, because this is such a young nation, it was their parents or grandparents who came from those countries. In John's case, I think it was his grandfather who trekked across in a wagon train. But they are darlings. I expect he's told you what we have to do.'

'And I've got a copy of the script. It's good we don't have to learn any dialogue.'

'Yes, especially as we've such a lot to get on with, with all the dancing. But I do think in a few years' time we'll have to – learn lines, I mean. Talking on film is already being discussed, though how they'll actually do it, heaven knows!'

'But just to be here, knowing we're going to be working together again! So much has happened to both of us! It's going to take us days to catch up. I was so delighted when I heard from you, but shocked and appalled when I read your letter. Missing you like that in New York was unbelievably awful! However did you get on while you were there?'

'Alex, it was dreadful.'

Alice told him about her life in New York, and her job in the cheese shop. Looking back on it from her now successful and prosperous position, she couldn't help but smile occasionally, though it had been awful at the time.

'So the Mandaros fed you well, at least?'

'Oh, yes! I put on pounds! That part of it was fine. But I had to work so hard for most of the time – and the disappointment when the show flopped was ghastly.'

'Then you came out West?'

'And things got worse. Then Trixie's mother died! Oh, Alex, I have been through the mill.'

'You certainly have, you poor wee lassie!'

Alice warmed to hear him say that, after what had seemed such a long time. She went on to complete her story, and Alex told her how Basil had encouraged Diaghilev to engage him, then how after many happy months together in Monte Carlo Basil had to return to New York. Meanwhile, Alex had been enjoying increasingly major roles with the ballet until he had been summoned by Diaghilev who informed him of the Hollywood offer.

'Of course I knew at once it was your idea. And you know Sergei was so artful, he got a huge dollar cheque out of United Artists for the company, so everyone's happy – not least of all me to be working with you. Alice, it's really terrific – I'm so thrilled.'

'So am I, Alex. It seems such an age since we last met . . . but it's only fifteen months!'

'Far too long for friends like us, Alice!'

'You're so right, honey!'

'"Honey", indeed! You've been living in the U.S.A., alright! But just wait until my Auntie Isobel and Uncle Finlay see me in Edinburgh . . .'

'You'll be the talk of the town!'

During the following two weeks Alice and Alex discussed with Dayton which *pas de deux* they should perform on screen. When they told him how much work they had put in, in the past, on the Bluebirds he agreed to use it, though it might have to be somewhat abridged. They would also film two *pas de deux* from *Giselle*, and the 'Black Swan' from *Swan Lake*. Once this was decided the two dancers had a meeting with Alla Nazimova and Natacha, who were jointly to design their ballet costumes – both friends were involved in another production and would not be free to play dancing or acting roles in *Nocturne*.

Alice and Alex worked daily in Alice's newly completed dance studio. The building was her pride and joy: the floor was well sprung, and the walls covered in mirror, from floor to ceiling. Dayton arranged for the studio to lend a piano, and paid for a pianist to work with them during the period before shooting.

Alice and Alex had also to work on the 'Nocturne' sequence for the final scene of the photoplay. This would be influenced by *Les Sylphides*, but as it was to be a *pas de deux* and not an ensemble, liberties had to be taken. Late in the evening after Alex and the pianist had left Alice would go back to the studio and practise the piano . . .

At a reception one evening just before shooting began, Alice introduced

Alex to the crew and cast. They loved his Scottish accent and, with typical American generosity of spirit, everyone made him feel very much at home.

Alice expected to see both Natacha and Alla, but spied Alla without her close friend, wearing a dark purple sheath which exposed her perfect legs in the front and trailed for about fifteen inches along the floor at the back. She was fighting off three unwanted admirers. She joined Alice and said, looking seductively over to Alex who was across the room happily chatting to a young cameraman, 'My dear, he is so handsome. I could fall for him.'

'Don't, Alla! He's a wonderful friend, and I love him dearly, but . . .'

'I understand! But his body – so slim, wiry and elegant . . . Mmmm, yes!'

Alice changed the subject.

'Where's Natacha? She should be here, and she wasn't at the production meeting.'

Alla took Alice by the elbow and turned her away from the throng of happy, chatting people who were filling the hotel reception room.

'Oh, Alice, she's having such a bad time at present. As you know, she and I are best friends, and I'm covering for her as much as possible. Yes, she should be here this evening, but you see, it's Rudy.'

'What's wrong with him?'

'She says she can't go on living with him much longer. In fact their marriage is breaking up. So sad. They are wonderful together, and their dancing and advertising tours are so very popular – but he is difficult, you know. It's awful. She says she's going to continue to try and patch things up, and I think she'll stay until our shooting is finished. She knows she and I must supervise your costumes. Aren't her designs superb? That Black Swan tutu of yours . . .'

As she spoke she made a dramatic gesture with both arms, her dark crimson fingernails emphasising the beauty of her long, sensitive hands.

'Yes, it's going to be quite beautiful – I'll buy it after shooting's finished.'

Alice was already on good, friendly terms with both Lloyd Hughes and Reginald Denny, and the three of them had lively flirtatious conversations and were photographed during the course of the evening. They decided it was going to be great fun working together.

During the rest of the rehearsal period, as each scene evolved, Alice developed slightly different responses and gestures for Maria and Angela. Discussing their respective characters with Dayton, they decided that Maria should be of a more jealous and passionate disposition, and would express her passion as anger toward her twin but also as artistic fervour when she sat down to play. During the course of the photoplay Alice would be performing several other piano pieces, and now she had experienced this miracle breakthrough she had no problems in working up two Chopin Preludes, a Brahms Waltz and the slow movement of Beethoven's Pathetique Sonata, which had been another of her ill-fated Senior exam pieces.

Costumes were fitted and finished, sets were designed and built, final rehearsals were held with the whole cast, and the shooting of the compli-cated twin sequences was well under way. When these, and all Alice's straight acting scenes in her dual role with her two leading men, were completed, and she had been filmed playing the piano (during which she was totally calm and had to admit to herself she loved the experience), Dayton gave her a few days off to rest before he commenced filming the ballet sequences with Alex.

He was pleased with the progress that was made, they were up to sched-ule and not over budget. Alice and Alex spent a lot of their leisure time together, but Alex was increasingly developing a lively social life of his own. Alice was delighted to see this: she wanted her friend to enjoy both work and leisure during the time he was in Hollywood, knowing that once every shot was 'in the can' he would have to return to the ballet, and to Europe.

Towards the end of shooting, when Alice and Alex had almost finished their scenes together, Alice went to make-up one morning as usual to find a different assistant working with her usual artist. At once she recognised the face.

'Margaret, what a surprise!'

Margaret Leahy looked sadly at Alice, her huge, beautiful dark eyes ready to shed tears.

'Oh, Alice, it's a sad story – but I'm making the best of things. I can't tell you now.'

Alice realised that her past rival wanted to talk – but she had only an hour to make up and get into her costume for a difficult scene that still had to be finally plotted and lined up with the cameras.

'Let's go to the commissary in the lunch break. We can talk there, if you'll be free.'

Margaret looked anxiously at the senior make-up girl, who kindly agreed. The expert got to work on Alice, while Margaret turned to work on some extras for another production.

'Are you alright?'

'I'm better than I was. But I really have had a wretched time. You know that Mr Keaton, through Connie and Norma's other sister Natalie's influ-ence, got me a nice part in a photoplay. Natalie's his wife, you know.'

Alice nodded.

'He was so kind, and they made it as easy for me as possible. But, Alice, it was really awful! I actually hated it. I couldn't do what they asked, and – well, as a result, Norma and Connie suggested that I try my hand in other areas of the film business. At least it's a little reassuring that my one film did well in England, because everyone went to see me on screen simply because I was the winner of the competition. But I can't go home, I feel I've really let everyone down.'

Alice sighed. It was a sad tale. She asked Margaret where she was living.

'Oh, it's not too bad, I've a tiny apartment in a small block not too far away. It's a bit poky, but then you see, I'm not earning that much – not any more – not like you.'

'Margaret, a lot has happened to me since November, nineteen-twenty-two. I may be successful now, but you don't know what I've been through! You can't be living in a worse dump than I was, for ages. So I know what you're feeling. Let's keep in touch, and get to know each other better. I may be able to help you when we've finished filming. Remember, you've a good speaking voice – perhaps your turn is yet to come. Anyway, with an English accent you could do other things, like compéring fashion shows . . . And the make-up training must be good and enjoyable in its own way. Remember, you didn't actually *like* acting in front of the cameras, so maybe you've lost nothing, after all.'

They finished their salads and went back to work.

At the end of the day's shooting Alice, who was using Connie and Norma's bungalow dressing-room, was relaxing with her feet up when she heard something drop through the letter box. She lazily got up and on opening it realised it was a bundle of press cuttings. The first was a boxed item from the front page of a screen magazine. She read, 'which will she choose? – see pp.17–18'.

Alice turned to the more substantial cutting: 'That beautiful English goddess of screen and dance Alice Townsend has been seen in all the right places with her *two* handsome leading men in her next photoplay. Here she is seen at a reception with fellow British actor Reginald Denny on one arm and handsome Lloyd Hughes on the other. Is love in the air for Alice? If so, which will she choose?

'Another constant companion is the electrifying, athletic dancer Alex McIntyre, who hails from Edinburgh, Scotland. All three men, we are told, are madly in love with her. Only time will tell which she will choose to be her partner in real life. We eagerly await the premiére of the latest Dayton Holt epic, *Nocturne*, in which our English Rose stars in a dual role as twin sisters Angela and Maria.'

Alice rolled over onto the huge be-cushioned sofa in fits of laughter. The article was accompanied by two photographs – one of her standing, with arms linked, between her two leading men, and the other of her and Alex in practice clothes rehearsing one of their *pas de deux*.

By the time shooting was completed it was high summer. Dayton had arranged for one of the studio's publicity people to do a deal with a French motor company which was attempting to break through into the American automobile market. As a result, Alice had been presented with a beautiful Hispano Suiza open touring car in a glorious shade of yellow, with disk wheels of the same colour, and chromium alloy trim. It would take one passenger by the driver in the front seat, and for short journeys two slim people, somewhat uncomfortably, in the back.

Alice had a long photo session in the front garden of her house, which was now looking quite superb. She posed in the driving seat, on the bonnet of the car, and giving Lloyd and Reginald a 'lift'. All these pictures and some copy to support them, would be used in magazines to advertise, 'This extremely chic but powerful automobile, with its six cylinder engine, and four wheel brakes – so easy to drive and light to handle, and suitable for the glamorous young woman of the twentieth century.'

She couldn't drive, but Don, the Montgomerys' chauffeur, promised to teach her. Meanwhile the car was parked in the garage at the east end of the house.

As the heavy shooting schedule ended, Alice spent as much time as she could with Margaret. She liked the young woman, partly because of what they had shared, and because she felt sorry for her. They had a great deal in common. Provided Alice could satisfy herself that they were compatible, she decided, in due course to ask Margaret to move into 'Sunburst' with her.

Parties after the completion of a photoplay were always fairly wild, because of the release of tension; but tiredness often struck all concerned far more than they might wish. In a blaze of flashlights from press cameras and cheers from devoted fans, always eager to catch a glimpse of their adored ones, carload after carload of tired, happy actors and technicians rushed through the studio gates, glad to be making their way home.

Alice shared a car with her two leading men and Alex, and she was dropped off first. As their car drove up to 'Sunburst' and she was about to get out, she gave all of them a sisterly kiss on the cheek, and thanked them for what had been a lively hard-working but thoroughly enjoyable and rewarding experience. In their respective ways the three men adored her, but both the actors were under no illusion: Alice was only concerned with the progress of her career, and wanted no emotional relationship at present.

Yawning, she went into the living room and flopped onto the settee.

'You looks real tired, Miss Alice.'

'I am, I am, but happy and contented too. If a little lonesome.'

'Yes, you wants a good man, Miss Alice, that's what you want.'

'No, I don't. At least, I don't *think* I do.'

Her thoughts flew back to the two men she had loved. Darling, dead Charlie ... living, virile Ben ... But he was dead, too, as far as she was concerned. For a while the thought made her feel nostalgic and sad.

But sitting up abruptly she said, 'No, it's my career that's all-important.'

She was quiet for a moment, and Miss Tassie was about to leave to make her a milk drink before she went to bed, but Alice called her back.

'You know Margaret Leahy?'

'Why yes, she's another nice young English lady. Why?'

'How would you feel if she were to move in with us? She's not been very successful, and she's living in an awful place – just like I used to. We've masses of room here, and I like her a lot – what do you think?'

'Why yes. Miss Margaret would be a nice friend for you, but I don't want to have to look after her, and not have enough time for you, Miss Alice. All that extra washing and pressing besides getting the food, and this is a big house to keep looking nice . . .'

'You'll need more help, of course. Now, let's see . . .'

'Miss Alice, if you could employ a cook-housekeeper and perhaps a daily, or a young girl to train for the cleaning . . .'

Alice smiled. She knew Miss Tassie was right. They did need extra staff, and thinking of her own, now doubled, salary she decided to promote her.

'How would you like to be known as my companion in future, and just look after me and attend to Miss Margaret when she needed help? And I'll employ a cook-housekeeper and general maid. Would you like that?'

'That would be real nice, Miss Alice, but . . .'

'Oh, yes, I'll raise your salary, and we'll make it quite clear that you'll be head of my household staff.'

Miss Tassie was jubilant.

By the beginning of June, Margaret moved in and the additional staff were employed, and because Alice was enjoying a lull in filming she was able to concentrate on learning to drive. Soon she was competent enough to breeze around Hollywood in her beautiful car, going from appointment to meeting to interview – and shopping. She also enjoyed a great many light-hearted dates with Reg and Lloyd, who took her to fashionable restaurants and clubs, and as the weather was at its best, once again time was spent on the beach with the Talmadges and the Montgomerys.

The one thing that had saddened her at this lively social time was having to say goodbye to Alex, who was needed again by the ballet. But he promised that he would join Alice for the London premiere of their photoplay – which, the publicity people promised, would be spectacular.

'Now take care of your wee self, and we'll meet up in London.'

'I'll look forward to that, but I just don't know how I'll get on there – you know, all that parent trouble!'

Alex had heard that Alice's mother was still dreadfully antagonistic.

'Well, that brother of yours is bound to help. Meanwhile, don't do anything I wouldn't do!'

'That's a pretty cryptic remark, coming from you!'

They hugged each other and Alex departed. Their friendship was even deeper. Alex was determined to make quite certain that before they both had to retire he would do his utmost to ensure that he and Alice took their balletic partnership further. Just before he left to re-join the ballet, unknown to Alice, he called on Dayton. He had a plan that he knew he would have to keep under wraps – perhaps for quite a long time to come.

Chapter 31

'Miss Alice, Mr Valentino's here to see you. Shall I ask him to come round, or do you want to change and see him in the drawing room?'

Alice, who was relaxing by her pool, was fascinated and, at once said she would see him. Asking Miss Tassie to bring fresh lemonade, she hastily adjusted her beach wrap, ran her fingers through her hair and hoped her lipstick was as it should be. She was extremely flattered that he – arguably the most famous and sought after man in the world – should call on her, and wondered what he wanted. She knew from Alla that he was unhappy – Natacha had finally left him a few weeks previously, and was now living in Paris with her mother. This had upset Alice, too: she and Natacha were good friends but Natacha had departed without a word to Alice.

'Hello, Alice, it's nice to see you.'

She got up as he spoke, and they shook hands rather formally. She could tell by his handshake that he was rather shy and nervous – very different from his screen image. There was a slightly awkward pause, which she broke by asking him if he would like some lemonade. He accepted.

Rather hesitantly he said, 'I hear you have a very beautiful French car.'

'Yes, it's lovely, and I'm enjoying driving it.'

'I don't know if you know, but I also love fast cars.'

That was something she did know.

'Yes, your hobby is well-known. Would you like to see mine?'

'Very much. Would you allow me perhaps to drive it?'

Still flattered, Alice agreed. She changed, and within ten minutes or so they were heading towards Venice beach.

'It's beautiful, it really is. If ever you want to sell it . . .'

Smiling at him with a certain smugness, she quickly replied, 'I don't – and I don't think I shall!'

He put his foot further down on the accelerator. She held on to her sun hat, and watched him in something of a daze. She had met him on several occasions since their first encounter, having dined with him and Natacha at their home, Whitney Heights; and they had attended many premiéres in the same party. But now she was alone with him – she had this paragon of screen idols to herself! Though she had to tell herself that he wasn't interested in her – only her car – the situation was fascinating.

He increased the speed of the car still further. She would never drive this fast! He slowed up along the promenade that skirted Venice beach, and made a turn to the right into a courtyard, part of a tiny, exclusive Italian restaurant, where he gave her lunch. They talked quietly, and she encouraged him to unburden. The fact that Natacha had refused to move into a new and beautiful house that he had had built had made him even more sad. Now he was there, alone – or so he said. Alice was not entirely convinced of this, having heard rumours that another exotic movie star had also moved in.

However, it was very flattering when he told her that he admired her looks, and went on to talk in an extremely knowledgeable way about her dancing. She knew he was a superb dancer in his own *genre*, so they shared some common ground. There was good feeling between them. She greatly admired him, not simply because he was such a handsome man, but because he was astonishingly self-effacing, shy and polite. It was only in the driving seat that he expressed a certain bravado.

With some trepidation she let him drive back to 'Sunburst'. He kissed her hand and departed in his own giant automobile.

She went into the drawing room, its louvred blinds drawn to keep it cool from the hot sun, and sat down on the settee, deep in thought. Was she falling under Rudy's special charms? Or was it that she still hankered after the deeper emotions – the searing passion that surged within her every time she thought of Ben? In her heart, she knew he was a thoroughly lost cause – why he might even be married to someone else by now; and if he were, who was to blame him? But try as she might, she was not finding it any easier to rid herself of her longing for him, in spite of the passing of time and no matter how absorbed she was in her career. Surely the light-hearted flirtation she was now enjoying with the man millions of women craved for must make a difference?

Margaret, who had now been living with Alice for some weeks, usually arrived home around six. That evening Alice confided in her friend.

'Well, all I can say is that you obviously loved your afternoon, so go on and enjoy whatever happens – but if I were you I'd not entirely trust him.'

In her heart Alice knew that Margaret was quite right and, in spite of her unsettled emotions, that night she snuggled down in bed realising that in many ways the world was at her feet. And how good it was to have another young woman of her own age in whom she could confide! She was delighted that things between them were working out so well, and that Margaret and Miss Tassie also hit it off.

Miss Tassie had never been so excited or happy. She looked critically at herself in her long bedroom mirror and smiled with pleasure. The warm, autumn colours of her brocade gown and matching coat were trimmed with gold lamé, and she had plain gold court shoes to match, along with a little

263

beaded evening bag into which she put a new lacy hanky, a phial of perfume, a powder compact, and her lipstick. With a final twirl in the mirror she sighed with satisfaction.

'Miss Tassie, are you ready?'

'I sure am, Miss Alice!'

With swaying steps she sauntered into the drawing room where Alice, resplendent in pink trimmed in silver, was waiting. At the same moment Margaret appeared, wearing a green silk gown.

'You both look wonderful! Now here are your tickets – your seats are at the end of the second row. You'll be just behind us, a bit to the side, but it's the best I could do. The taxi'll be here in five minutes.'

'Oh yes, Miss Alice – I'm so excited! I just can't believe this is happening to me!'

'Well it is, and you deserve to be part of it, after all the support you give me! Gosh, I hope that a producer won't take a fancy to you – I don't know what I'd do if I lost you to the silver screen!'

'Oh, no, Miss Alice, I wouldn't ever desert you!'

The Hollywood taxi drew up, Margaret kissed Alice and gently pinched her for luck, and Miss Tassie, almost crying with pleasure, but with a style and elegance as to the manner born, took her place alongside Margaret in the car to drive to Graumann's Egyptian Theatre.

Twenty minutes later a huge studio limousine collected Alice, who was escorted by Lloyd Hughes and Reginald Denny.

The clapping and cheering that followed the screening was still ringing in Alice's ears when she, the two leading men and the lovely, elderly Mary Carr took the stage. It was obvious that *Nocturne* was going to be the huge box office success of the season. Now, at the after-premiére party, the ball-room of the Taft Hotel was buzzing. Alice was surrounded by other stars as well as a select few invited members of the press. A reporter cornered Dayton.

'Mr Holt, you surely can't honestly say that Miss Townsend played the piano as well as danced? That must be your publicity department exaggerating, as usual. But how did you fake the shots?'

'No, Miss Townsend is as talented a pianist as she is a dancer! If you don't believe me, ask her.'

Dayton and John had prepared Alice for this kind of thing, and she was expecting to be approached.

Constance and Norma had congratulated her, as had Mary Pickford and Douglas Fairbanks, and now another pair of sisters who she admired but knew less well were chatting to her.

'My dear, Dorothy and I can't say just how much we enjoyed the photo-play. You were wonderful. All that dancing, and acting too – *and* you play the piano!'

'Thank you, Miss Gish. Yes, it was exciting, but I didn't have to be brave like you did when you were drifting down the river on the ice flow!'

'Oh my dear, that was years ago, now – but I must admit that I was rather frightened when I couldn't get up because my hair was frozen into the ice!'

Long before Alice had had thoughts of Hollywood she had admired Lillian Gish and her bravery.

Rather rudely pushing the two lovely women out of the way, the reporter approached.

'Miss Townsend, Mr Holt tells me that you actually played the piano on screen. Is that true?'

Alice was annoyed, and showed it.

'Yes, it is true. Mr Holt does not tell lies, any more than I do!'

The reporter looked her straight in the eye.

'Perhaps you'd like to prove it,' he said ironically.

Alice glared at him. She glanced over to where a group of musicians were playing pleasant background music. Her heart raced.

'Alright, I will!'

Head held high, as if about to ascend the throne of England, she crossed the huge, crowded ballroom.

The conversation of the guests died away, and they turned to watch her. Some stood on chairs to see what was happening.

Alice went straight to the musicians' platform. The pianist vacated the stool. She sat down and removed a ring, and a slave bangle from her upper arm. She placed her hands over the keyboard and faultlessly performed the Chopin Nocturne.

When she finished, a storm of applause even greater than she had experienced earlier filled the air, and Alice was all but mobbed by her admirers. The reporters rushed to the door.

Back at 'Sunburst' Miss Tassie hung up her special dress and going to the locked cupboard in the kitchen, took out the illegal medicinal brandy, put some in a glass, added water, and with the wonder of the evening buzzing around in her head, took it to her bedroom, and sipping it decided she would never ever forget this remarkable evening.

It was past three when Alice eventually got home. Margaret was waiting for her.

'Darling, it was wonderful. *What* a photoplay! I'm so glad I was there. You are terrific in it. But you should have seen Miss Tassie – how she cried in the sad bits. Oh, Alice! Millions of congratulations!'

Alice thanked her.

'Did you enjoy the party? I'm afraid I didn't get time to speak to you.'

'Yes, it was lovely. I made some good contacts, and a young German director who has just signed up with Paramount drove me home – but I made certain that Miss Tassie got her taxi, in spite of the crowd coming out of the cinema. I've been in for about an hour. I think Helmut will telephone me next week!'

'That's really nice! I'm glad you had a good evening, too.'

'I'll never forget how you played the Nocturne. That really made them take notice. It'll be all over the papers in the morning.'

'I already have seen them – we've had the early editions.'

The *Los Angeles Times* gave the photoplay a marvellous critique, and the gossip columnist made column inches of Alice's performance at the party.

'Please may I speak to Miss Townsend?'

Miss Tassie recognised at once the man's Italian accent.

'Of course, Mr Valentino – I'll fetch her.'

Putting down her bag of practice clothes, Alice went to the telephone.

'Oh, Rudy, how nice to hear from you! I'm just off to class!'

'Don't go, Alice. I've something I want to talk to you about. As you probably know I was away for your premiére and the party, but I had a private screening yesterday at United Artists. You were superb. May I come round and see you – right away?'

'Of course, and stay for lunch?'

He thanked her, and said he would be with her within a half an hour. Miss Tassie told the cook to prepare Italian antipasta and a light chicken Yolanda.

Rudy kissed Alice's hand, and once more congratulated her. Then he came to the point.

'Alice, I admire your work, it is, er . . .' he hesitated, searching for the right English words, '. . . really beautiful.'

She smiled, and rather coyly looked down into her lap.

'You know perhaps that for some time I shall be filming *The Son of the Sheik*, and I know that you have to go to Europe for the premiére of your film in London.'

She looked up. This was news to her, although not entirely unexpected. It had been mentioned. But obviously Rudy had been doing his homework in the last few days, and had heard more than she had.

'Now if all goes well, I'll have finished *Sheik* by the early spring. There may well be publicity tours, but then . . . well, Alice, I think you and I should work together.'

'You mean . . .'

'Why not? We shall ask Dayton to start looking for a suitable script. We can dance together. I've been told that I'm as strong as any ballet dancer, and while we couldn't dance the sort of thing you and Alex perform, well . . .'

'Perhaps we can work out some original, very modern movements that will suit both of us?' said Alice eagerly.

'You like my idea – yes?'

'Of course, Rudy. It'll be most exciting!'

Lifting a glass of fruit juice, she toasted, 'Here's to our partnership!'

They clicked glasses. When he left, after a somewhat hurried lunch during which they talked about their proposed work together, he lightly kissed her on the cheek. She would not see him again for some time, but she knew that he meant what he said – that he did want to work with her.

She had a lot to tell Margaret that evening. Margaret warned her again about losing her head over the great man. As a make-up artist, she heard all the rumours, knew everything that was going on in the studios. Alice re-assured her: the partnership would be strictly businesslike.

John Montgomery smiled at Alice from the far side of his desk, and gestured her to a chair.

He took a crisp folder from a drawer and, opening it, gave Alice a typed sheet to read.

'Leave Los Angeles Wednesday 2nd September.

'Arrive New York, Sunday evening, 6th,

'Sail for Southampton, Wednesday 9th,

'Arrive Southampton, Monday 14th.'

'Are those arrangements alright for you? As you see, you'll have two clear days in New York, where you'll be interviewed at your hotel and probably make a personal appearance or two.'

'Why, yes, John, that will be lovely. Er, what ship will I be sailing on?'

'We've booked a suite for yourself, and a separate room for your maid, on the *Mauritania*. We always use Cunard!'

A wave of memories flooded back – so powerful that they made her feel dizzy. She turned pale.

'Alice, are you alright? You look rather faint.'

There was no denying it. She asked for some water, and soon made a quick recovery.

'Oh John! I'm fine now, in fact I couldn't be better!'

With that she got up, rushed across to his side of the desk, and kissed him heartily.

'Thank you – oh, thank you *so much!*'

John gave an astonished grin.

'What, me go to London? *Me*, in London? Why, Miss Alice, I can't believe it!'

'But of course! I can't go without my companion, Miss Tassie.'

Her eyes were large in disbelief.

'And,' Alice went on, 'didn't you say your Mammy is in New York, and that you'd not seen her for sixteen years?'

'Yes, she's housekeeper to a wealthy family.'

'Well, you'll have time to see her. We have two whole days in New York before we sail. I've to do some publicity for *Nocturne*, but you can spend time with her, if her employers will let you.'

'Mammy says they're real nice folk. I'll write her, and perhaps Miss Alice if you could write to them . . .'

'Of course I will! Now, you'll have to get a passport. And I'll give you an extra clothing allowance. You must take your gold outfit – you're sure to need it.'

That was settled, but Alice had other things on her mind. Would she be recognised as the little cigarette girl who jumped ship? She didn't care if she was! After all, she would be occupying one of the most expensive suites on the liner . . . But she had much more important thoughts than that! If only, if only, *he* is . . .

She wrote a long letter to Philip, who she had learned, had told their parents that he had acquired an American pen friend – in case any letters with a United States postage stamp arose suspicions.

Alice and Miss Tassie were seen off, with an enormous amount of smart luggage, by Margaret and the Montgomerys. Alice was steeped in memories of her last journey on the famous train which would take them via Chicago to New York – but what a difference there was now: she felt extremely happy, and more than a little smug.

Her happiness was second only to Miss Tassie's, which gave her a great deal of pleasure. In New York, there would be a wonderful reunion between mother and daughter. What lay ahead of her where her own mother was concerned she knew not, and the thought of their probable meeting filled her with apprehension.

At the end of the long journey they were met at Grand Central Station by the Studio's New York publicity agent. There was a platform reception: cameras flashed, and she was bombarded with questions from reporters. After satisfying them and signing a number of autographs, the publicity woman – Maureen – took her to the waiting limousine, and she and Miss Tassie were driven to the Waldorf Astoria Hotel, where she was given the full star treatment and a very beautiful suite. Maureen told Alice that in addition to interviews she was to be photographed 'buying' outfits and cosmetics in Bloomingdales, and a piece of jewellery at Tiffany's. She would also be photographed with the manager of the Hotel for a new brochure that was being prepared.

Meanwhile, Miss Tassie would spend most of the time with her mother. It was to be a busy time for both of them.

Next morning, having rested in luxurious comfort, Alice sent Miss Tassie off in a taxi, and a little later she started her round of engagements with Maureen looking after her. The store presented her with a beautiful floral silk dress and a whole range of Max Factor cosmetics, and from Tiffany's she came away with a leather writing case embossed with her initials. Her second day was equally busy – but the management of the hotel attended her every whim.

It was a very happy Miss Tassie who accompanied Alice to the Cunard dock to check in for the voyage. They said goodbye to Maureen at the terminal, so familiar to Alice, and so full of sad memories. The porters took their luggage, some of which would go into the hold, they checked in, and were soon on board. The dazed Miss Tassie found it difficult to concentrate. She was in a dream – a happy, excited dream.

Alice's mood was quite different. She too was excited, but also apprehensive. As soon as they had been shown to their suite – one that Alice had glimpsed in admiration and longing last time she was on board – she made her way to the Purser's office. She did not recognise him, which was a relief.

'Can I help you, madam?'

'Why yes. Tell me, please, is Mr Ben Waterman still in the ship's orchestra?'

'Oh, madam, no – he left us about a year ago. He's joined a cruise line, that much I do know – but I did hear a rumour that he was about to form his own orchestra.'

'Oh, thank you.' Trying to smile, she added, 'I'm quite sure that your present orchestra is as good as ever!'

As she turned to leave the office a young woman of about eighteen approached, and said to the Purser, 'Can I check my stock, Mr Read, please?'

'Yes, Annie. Here's the key.'

Alice knew exactly what Annie had to do! She made her way to her suite, and did her best to rise above her disappointment.

Chapter 32

The softness of the late afternoon sunlight added a gentle sparkle to the Thames. The traffic flowed freely along the Embankment, and Londoners strolled along the tree-lined pavements.

It was good to be home, though it was strange to be staying in an hotel instead of the tiny flat in Chelsea or the comfortable Kensington home that Alice had enjoyed during her childhood and early teenage years. But all that was a long time ago.

Now, here she was in one of the very suites at the Savoy that had housed Norma and Constance almost three years ago. For a while, gazing at the view, Alice was lost in her memories.

The telephone rang. It was the receptionist.

'Miss Townsend, there's a Mr Philip Townsend to see you. He says he's your brother – is that correct?'

'Oh yes, *yes* – of course he is. Send him up at once please!'

'Miss Tassie,' Alice turned to her anxiously. 'How do I look? Am I tidy? What do you think?'

'Why, Miss Alice, you look wonderful! So wonderful that your brother'll wish you weren't his sister!'

'Tease! But quickly, go and open the door! Oh, *Philip!* Dearest, dearest Philip!'

'Sis, my God you look a real swell! How you've changed!'

'And how you've grown!'

After their long embrace they were standing holding hands at arms length as they looked at each other.

'Oh, Phil, this is wonderful! I can't believe it – after all this time!'

Alice was crying, and her brother, near to tears, just looked at her. They sat on a blue brocade settee in the boudoir. Alice wiped her eyes, and Miss Tassie, not altogether pleased at not having been introduced right away, came in and said, 'Shall I send down for some tea, Miss Alice?'

'No, I think some champagne would be more suitable! After all, Mr Philip and I ... Oh, I'm so sorry! – Phil, meet my companion, Miss Tassie!'

Miss Tassie became her usual cheery self again and grinned broadly at Phil. She was sure delighted to meet him at last. He returned her greeting.

The champagne arrived. They toasted each other.

'Now, dare I ask how things are at home?'

'Well, as I told you in my last letter, Mother's still very bitter, but Dad seems far more sympathetic – he always says reasonable things on the rare occasions when your name is mentioned. But you know, Alice, I'm sure that all this nonsense is coming to an end – and if it doesn't at the premiére, then it never will. I'm so glad that you were able to tell me the plans for the evening!'

'So what have you been able to do?'

'I've booked seats for the three of us, and for Uncle Eustace and Aunt Emma, and Rose . . .'

'Rose?'

'Yes – I . . . I *like* Rose, though she's only fifteen, and I'm afraid she likes me a bit too much. But she is a dear . . . I told you how we went to *Temptation*? It was wonderful! Well, anyway, I've booked for her, and for Stephen, if he's around. Sometimes he is, and sometimes he isn't – it just depends on his assignments. You know he's a professional photographer, these days?'

Alice had thought he might become one, and was glad to hear it.

'But – and this is terrific, Alice – I can't wait to tell you . . . You know Aunt Emma's sister Aunt Sarah – well, Lady Maitland?'

'Why yes. Go on!'

'She and Sir Lionel are home from Antigua for six months – until after Christmas. They're living in their house on Chelsea Embankment, I believe she's owned it since before they were married. Well, I had a long chat with her at a dinner party Aunt Emma gave. She couldn't stop talking about you – wanted to know everything!'

'And you told her – everything?'

'Yes. Oh, Alice, she's *wonderful*! Not a bit snobbish – not like Aunt Emma – and after she's got far more to be snobbish about! She's so understanding. She's the kindest and most sympathetic lady I've ever met – and she's still beautiful. I know you'll love her. She knew all about *Temptation*, and is following your career in every movie magazine she can get hold of. Isn't that sweet?'

Alice remembered how 'Aunt Sarah' – whom she had only met when she was very little – had sent her a cable when *Chu Chin Chow* opened, all those years ago.

'Well! Is she coming, too?' she asked.

'You bet she is – and Uncle Lionel! In fact we planned the thing together. Of course, Mother and Dad don't know where they're going, and neither do Aunt Emma and Uncle Eustace – but Rose is in on it, and she said she would fill Stephen in, if he turns up.'

'So what will happen?'

'I've told them I'm taking them to the Promenade Concert at the Queen's

271

Hall – I thought it would put Mother in a good mood. They're playing the last movement of the Emperor Concerto, she likes that!'

'But how will they get to the premiére?'

'I've booked taxis. We're all to have an early dinner at Queen's Gate, and then we'll leave, and there'll be a corking fuss when the taxis turn into Shaftesbury Avenue instead of going up Regent Street to the hall! I'll have to play that by ear. Oh, Alice, they are in for a surprise! I just hope it'll work out okay. Aunt Sarah said she would act surprised like the others, and she said Uncle Lionel will too. What larks, eh?'

'Phil, you're wicked! But all this has been expensive for you.'

'Well, I must admit it has cut into my allowance.'

'Never mind – here you are!' Alice reached for her handbag and gave him four crinkly white five-pound notes. Philip was delighted. They parted – he had to get back home otherwise he would be missed, having been out longer than he had said he would be.

The Russian Ballet had not long since completed a season at the Coliseum, and Alex was in London. They met for dinner that evening, and when the fuss of the premiére was over, planned to go to Astafieva's classes until Alice had to return to Hollywood.

During the next three days Alice was photographed by the leading newspapers, with the *Daily Sketch* publishing a long feature article about her, reminding their readers of the competition three years ago, reproducing one of Alice's photographs from 1922. She made a personal appearance at Harrods and another at Selfridges, promoting Max Factor Make-up, and there were large advertisements in every magazine and newspaper for the exciting photoplay which was about to burst forth on London's silver screens.

But Alice was very apprehensive. Was Philip doing the right thing? Should she instead just turn up at Edwardes Square?

It was difficult simply to let things happen, and enjoy her fame and the excitement of being so feted in her home town.

'You know, Philip, this really is awfully sweet of you, to give so many of us a night out.'

'Well, Mother, I feel I really want to say thank you. You and Dad, as well as Uncle Eustace and Aunt Emma, have done so much for me over the years. And the fact that I earned some money from those private German lessons I gave has helped.'

'But are you sure you really want to hire taxis? After all, Emma and the others could easily go in the Rolls . . .'

'No – I want to do this my way. It'll make a change for all of us.'

'Well, it's your party, dear.'

Smiling warmly up at her son, Lizzie went upstairs to change into a new knee length blue satin and chiffon evening gown.

'Robert, aren't you proud of Philip? I know this evening means so much to him.'

'Yes, darling – you'll enjoy that Beethoven, won't you?'

Robert was tying his evening bow.

'*And* I'll be playing every note with the soloist.'

'Well, you could always take over if he has a heart attack!'

'Robert, really!'

Robert drove up to Queen's Gate in his latest Wolesley sixteen.

In the taxi, after dinner, Lizzie gossiped with Emma as they drove along towards Piccadilly. She was looking forward to the Beethoven and to the numerous other items – songs, part of a symphony, a suite from *Carmen* . . . the programme would be a long one.

'I say, Robert, does the driver know where we're going?'

'Why yes, I think so, Eustace – but perhaps . . .'

'It's a diversion, Uncle Eustace. The road is being dug up!' Philip interrupted a little too quickly.

The remark diverted Lizzie's attention, and she returned to her conversation with Emma about the coming term's enrolments of new five-year-olds.

'Look, I say, old man . . .'

'It's alright, Dad . . . Listen everyone.'

The others were suddenly silent, having noticed that the taxi driver had not turned left into Regent Street but was now heading up Shaftesbury Avenue.

'What *is* going on, Philip?'

'Mother, and everyone, listen. I've planned a surprise. We aren't going to the Prom – but somewhere quite other.'

'Oh, *no* – I'm disappointed! We can't be going anywhere more exciting. Phil, really . . .'

Lizzie was perplexed and more than a little annoyed that she and her friends had been duped.

'Just wait, Mother. Aunt Emma, I don't think you'll be upset. In fact, we will have a lovely evening – I promise you.'

The taxi pulled up outside the Shaftesbury Pavilion. Philip got out and helped Lizzie out, then Emma, by which time the second taxi containing the rest of the party arrived, and Sarah and Lionel along with Rose, who was stifling laughter, joined them in the dense, fashionable crowd outside the cinema.

Lizzie was dumbfounded. She saw the still photographs. She saw Alice's name printed in huge letters, and the illustrations that formed the background to the posters which contained ballet shoes, a grand piano and two portraits of Alice, in each of which she looked slightly different . . .

'Oh no, I can't. I don't want to see her.'

'Lizzie, that's really a little bit silly, you know. Why, if you don't like the photoplay you can always leave,' remarked Sarah. 'Who knows, you might approve.'

'I don't think so, Sarah – do you, Emma?'

Emma was in two minds, but finally, perhaps a little reluctantly, agreed with her sister.

Upset and very emotional, Lizzie was hesitantly guided into the cinema, Robert on one arm and Philip on the other. Pale and shaky, she took her seat in the front row of the circle. She did not know what to expect. Nor how she would react to seeing her daughter on the screen.

The credits rolled. There were two shots of Alice – one as Angela, darning her ballet shoes, the other as Maria, leaning over the grand piano examining some music. Lizzie's heart missed a beat. She turned to Robert who was gazing at the screen smiling, but with tears rolling down his cheeks. She felt she could not distract him. But why should I? she thought. He'll realise in a minute what a fool his daughter's making of herself – oh yes, he'll see soon enough! And there she is, dancing again . . . Well, that doesn't mean much, though I suppose it's alright.

Lizzie glanced along the row to Emma, who seemed to be absorbed. The camera panned across from Alice dancing, to the piano. Lizzie could not believe what she was seeing: there was her daughter sitting at the piano – and it looked as if . . . was she? Was she actually . . .? But no, she couldn't be! Of course, she was just miming her performance. The orchestra had picked up the Chopin prelude that Alice was supposed to be playing. Lizzie thought, well, yes, she could act that well enough, I suppose – but she could never remember how actually to *play* it! The photoplay rolled on through its twelve reels. The plot developed, and was resolved. Now the photoplay was in its last five minutes . . .

On screen, the big charity concert in the Carnegie Hall New York was in full swing. Alice, as Angela, was starting her Nocturne *pas de deux* with her screen lover, who was being danced by Alex. They danced beautifully. The camera panned across to the piano . . . Still the orchestra played the Nocturne. Alice, as Maria, was playing on screen.

Suddenly a spotlight came on in the cinema, lighting a full concert grand piano at the side of the stage. The audience gasped – disconcerted at the interruption to the climax of the photoplay. Alice appeared in a dazzling white and silver gown. Lizzie bit her lip and gripped Robert's arm. Philip looked at his mother in anticipation. Alice sat down at the piano. The sound of the cinema orchestra faded. Alice picked up its last phrase and played the Nocturne as her character was playing it on the screen.

As the music finished, THE END appeared on the screen.

Lizzie was sobbing, her head in her hands. This was what she had so wished for – to see her daughter come out on stage and play to a huge audience. Her long lost dream was fulfilled at last. Her anger melted as tears of joy and sorrow about her long-felt resentment and stubbornness gushed from her eyes.

The audience stood up and cheered. Alice was joined by Alex, Lloyd and

Reginald on stage, and they took bow after bow. Alice moved a little forward. Lizzie looked up, and tearfully gazed at her daughter.

'Ladies and gentlemen. Thank you so very much for your wonderful reception of our photoplay. It is very moving for Reginald and myself to be so well received in our own dear town. And thank you, too, for tolerating my little intrusion at the end. But this was planned as a greeting for someone who is very special to me, and who is, I know, in the audience. Please forgive me, and thank you again.'

More cheers. More clapping.

'It's alright, old girl . . .' Robert put his arm around his wife.

'Oh, Robert, Robert, what a fool I've been . . .'

'She was wonderful, Lizzie!'

'Yes, I know – she *was* wonderful.' Lizzie was sniffing. He gave her his large handkerchief.

'But where is she? When can I see her?'

'I don't know – I'm as surprised as you are – as we all are . . . But perhaps Phil knows?'

'Yes, Mother, we've to go to the Manager's lounge . . .'

Philip led the way through the excited throng. Sarah, in animated conversation with Lionel, her sister and brother-in-law, smiled encouragingly at him and Rose. He had never seen his father look so relieved. Robert seemed to have shed years.

'You've done a marvellous thing, son. I can't thank you enough.'

'Jolly good, Dad – and look, here we are.'

Across the room Lizzie noticed a flash of shimmering white satin and sparkling silver beads. She rushed towards it. Mother and daughter were immediately locked in an embrace . . .

'Alice, I'm so sorry – and so *proud* of you! Can you forgive me, ever?'

Still clinging to her mother, Alice reassuringly replied, 'It's alright, Mummy, it really is. But can you forget my stubbornness?'

'Oh, you two – you're like two peas in a pod!' remarked Robert, attempting to lighten the highly charged atmosphere. There were tears and smiles.

'But please, Mummy, accept me for what I am, and allow me to be myself.'

'Yes, yes, Alice – I should have done that years ago. What a waste – a *waste* of nine precious years, when all I did was to harbour anger and resentment because . . . well, because . . . Why did I have that dreadful blind spot? I think I'm a reasonably nice person, but it all got the better of me for so long. To think that I didn't help you grow up into the beautiful young woman you are – so talented and famous.'

'Mummy, it's all in the past – and yes, we've both missed out on far too much, and it will take years for us to catch up on everything that's happened to us while . . . while, well, you know.'

'Look, you two, the others'll be coming in soon. Why don't you go to the ladies and repair your faces – you both look a mess!'

Philip had earlier told the Manager that his mother and sister had not met

275

for many years, and that she needed some time with the family. He had conveniently been looking after the other stars of the photoplay, the publicity people and a few special guests in another room. Philip had known that there would be an emotional scene which should not be witnessed by strangers. His plan had worked, and he was more than happy.

Mother and daughter went to the ladies' cloakroom and repaired their make-up, giving each other another long hug before they went out to join the other guests, who were by now chatting and enjoying liberal helpings of champagne.

After about an hour, during which everyone met everyone else, Alex called Alice aside.

'Old wounds are being healed, eh?'

'Oh yes, Alex. Thank God – after nine years. Silly, isn't it?'

'Quite mad,' he sighed. 'You know, we all have weird quirks to our natures – and who knows how they'll be expressed? But I must go now.'

She told him she would phone him in the next day or two. He kissed her on the cheek and left.

'Darling, I think it's time we all went home. Where are you staying? Can't you come home with us?'

'I'd love to, Mummy, and of course I will come over – but tonight I'll have to go back to the Savoy. Besides, there's someone there you will have to meet.'

'Oh, a boyfriend! Or are you . . .?' Lizzie glanced at the third finger of Alice's left hand.

'No, Mummy, not yet, and I don't think I will be for ages. But I do have someone with me.'

'Who on earth is it? Alice, please tell us!'

'She's lovely, Mother – *I've* met her!'

'Philip, what have *you* been up to?'

'Phil's the peace-maker, Mummy. No, this is my companion – the most practical, amusing and intuitive woman I've ever known.'

Alice promised to come home to Edwardes Square the following morning. Lizzie was beside herself with happiness. She had been right. Her daughter *was* good enough to perform in public, she *was* a talented pianist. But she now also recognised that Alice's first love was her dancing, and that nothing would change that – ever.

'Oh my, oh my, Alice dear, what a nice young woman you've become!'

Mrs Wilson had been waiting for their arrival with Molly on the pavement outside the house. She hugged Alice, who at once introduced her to Miss Tassie. Molly disappeared and brought out Lizzie and Robert with a jubilant Phil in the background.

'Welcome home, Alice darling! I just can't believe it!'

'Daddy, it's true, it really is! I can't believe it myself. And I want you to meet Miss Tassie!'

Grinning broadly, Miss Tassie kept repeating to everyone how pleased she was to meet them.

When the excitement had died down a little, they all went up to the drawing room and Molly brought in a tray of coffee. In her excitement she knocked over a jug of milk as she put it on the table.

'Here, let me help – I'll clear it up for you.'

'Why, thanks, Miss Tassie!' said Alice.

'Well, Miss Alice, this is your home too, and I want to help you and your Mammy and Pappy!'

'Come with me, then, Tassie,' suggested Molly, amused at the lively woman.

'Molly, we always call Tassie, *Miss* Tassie – it's a Hollywood tradition!'

Molly apologised, and the two of them went down to get cloths and more milk.

'She's such a character! Where on earth did you find her?'

'She came with the house, Daddy.'

'The house! Oh! So you own property, do you?'

'Of course I do. And a fantastic car as well!'

There was a surprised silence, the first of many that would occur during the next couple of weeks.

Alice went to her old room. She recalled the last time she had slept there on that fateful night so many years ago when, bundled up with clothes, she had slipped out into the dawn to make her own way. The room was thick with memories. She went to the dressing table. There was a clothes brush lying in exactly the same position as it had been on the day she had left. She smiled to herself as she remembered deciding not to take it. She opened the toy cupboard on one side of the fireplace. There were books, a set of solitaire with three marbles missing, and several dolls. They were a bit dusty, but she took them out and hugged them. She moved over to the wardrobe. Some of her clothes were still there . . . her Rosamund Academy School uniform, pink and white summer dresses, dark maroon winter tunic, two hats . . . So her mother had not had the heart to clear them out. She had thought that in her anger everything would have been stripped bare. A lot of things were missing – probably gone to charity – but, well, it was obvious that her mother nursed a few sentimental feelings for her in spite of everything.

Miss Tassie had unpacked for her, and put out her nightclothes. Just as she was about to turn down the familiar patchwork coverlet she noticed her teddy bear was in its correct, original position. She never went anywhere without him. She smiled. How did Miss Tassie know that was where he belonged? But that was Miss Tassie all over! He too had come home. Did she notice a little sparkle in his beady glass eyes as he looked up at her?

Emma, who was as relieved as Lizzie that the feud was over, gave a dinner party for Alice. Lionel and Sarah also attended, and Alice had just as warm a welcome from the staff.

The meal over, she was sitting by Stephen, who had been commanded to cancel any assignments – if he had any – and attend. The young man was more than impressed with Alice, who at once noticed his florid style and gestures, his identification with everything artistic. They had a lot in common, as Alice had expected they might. They were all assembled in Emma and Eustace's elegant drawing room as port, brandy and liquors were served.

'Of course Phil's told me so much about you!' said Stephen, amidst the babble. 'You really are a star, aren't you? I think that's ripping, after all the difficulties. You know, Alice, I don't have an easy time either. Mother and Father don't approve of me, *or* understand me. I've had really very bad times, so I keep my distance. But I couldn't resist coming to dinner tonight – I so wanted to meet you again, after all these years. Can I take some photos of you before you go back?'

'I'd love you to, Stephen.'

Alice was not surprised to hear that he too had had, and was obviously still having, parent trouble. She could see he was very different from Eustace and the ultra-conservative Emma. She told Stephen that she would get in touch with him later in her stay.

'Now, everyone, I believe Alice has some news for us', announced Robert.

Alice had decided that she would tell her family and the Beaumonts her future plans, but to ask them to keep them confidential.

'Oh yes, go on, Alice – tell us. I can't wait to hear, especially if it's to do with the movies.'

Emma glanced at Eustace and gave a little indignant snort.

'Thank you, Aunt Sarah. Well, yes, I do have something to tell you, but it really is essential that you keep it to yourselves. This is extremely important – the studios will make the announcements when they think the time's right to do so.'

'Now, Stephen, *you* remember this. No word to anyone – especially all those magazine friends of yours. Do you hear me?' Eustace sounded the schoolmaster that he was. His son blushed, and nodded with resignation.

'As if I would do that to you, Alice – you of all people.'

She smiled.

'Well, darlings, it won't take long to tell you. Just before I left Hollywood, Rudolph Valentino came to see me.'

'Oh, Alice, you *know* Rudolph Valentino! How wonderful! He's *so romantic!*'

'Rose – how *dare* you!'

Blushing the young girl apologised to her mother.

'He has asked me to be his next leading lady. He's still working on his present photoplay, *The Son of the Sheik*, and he'll have to do a great deal of publicity for it, then we're going to work on some dances and, well I guess that's it – but it will be exciting!'

Cries of congratulation buzzed round the room.

'And, I suppose, young lady, you'll be earning even more dollars than you are at present.'

'I expect so, Daddy.'

Her news had gone down well, which pleased Alice enormously. Most of the rest of the evening was spent in talking to Sarah and Rose, both of whom wanted to know every possible detail about their screen hero.

The evening was a great success, and Alice's confidence had been given a marvellous boost; now she knew that wounds had been healed for good.

'The front door bell is ringing, Madam.'

'Is Morgan there, or is he doing messages for Sir Lionel?'

'I think he is there.'

'Right, thank you, Lisette. But do go and greet Miss Townsend on the stairs.'

Sarah, wearing an oyster crepe-de-chine dress and relaxing in the first-floor drawing room of ninety-two Cheyne Walk, greeted Alice as she joined her for lunch.

'My dear, I'm so glad we can spend some time alone together. How are you, and how are things in Edwardes Square?'

'Remarkably happy! Oh, Aunt Sarah, it's been nine years – and all so silly! But I simply had to get on with my life in my own way.'

'And you did – from a very early age, didn't you?'

'Yes, I'm afraid so.'

'Alice, dearest, don't say "afraid"! You were brave, and yes, very stubborn. So was your mother, but your stubbornness consisted of sheer determination and ambition. I understood your point of view from the start – and your conviction about what you wanted to do. It's been a tragedy, and I'm sure Lizzie realises that too, but I give you full marks because it's exactly what I did – for different reasons – when I was even a little younger than you were. Because of the action I took then, I had a wonderful career as a dancer, and you know the final result – this home here in London, a wonderful husband, and a worthwhile role helping the poor of Antigua. We are both fulfilled women, Alice. But have you a lover? I so hope you have.'

Alice told Sarah about the two men in her life – her lost causes, as she called them.

'So, my dear, you've yet to fulfil that part of your life. A beautiful and talented young woman like you needs a really special husband. Be choosy, take your time – all will be well in due course, I promise you.'

They went on to talk about Alice's coming work with Valentino and Sarah became quite girlish in her admiration of him and her excitement for Alice.

There was a wonderful empathy between them. Alice enjoyed being in the beautiful room with its spectacular views of the river, elegant plaster ceiling decorations, and lovely furniture and pictures – with a huge portrait of Sarah by John Singer Sargent, obviously painted when she was in her late twenties, occupying pride of place.

At last, Lionel came in, and over lunch they told her about Antigua and their life on the Island as Governor General and first lady. They had hopes of entertaining her there one day.

Later that afternoon, as Alice took her leave, Sarah asked a favour.

'Darling, I would *so* like to watch you and Alex in class. Could I come along one morning when you go to Madame Astafieva? My dancing days are long since over, but I would love to join in – in my mind.'

Alice promised she would make the arrangements and left in the most contented of moods.

The rest of her stay could not have been happier. She spent a lot of time with Lizzie, often walking in Holland Park or Kensington Gardens, telling her mother as much as she dared about the years since she left home. She did not hold back in describing the hard times, but made light of them as much as possible, spicing her stories with anecdotes that had made her laugh at the time, and even more since. She entertained family and friends in expensive restaurants, she went regularly to Madame's class with Alex, where the day that Sarah joined them was special. She and Alex called on elderly Joan in Tryon Street, and had tea with lively Daisy Lloyd, who was doing well in musical comedy and pantomime. To the delight of Lizzie and Robert, Alice cabled the studios and asked if she could stay on until after Christmas.

Meanwhile, in early October the two families held a farewell party for Philip who was off to Cambridge. His first term passed quickly, and he was enthusiastic to tell of his experiences when he returned at Christmas.

Christmas in Edwardes Square and at Queen's Gate was very special. There was a poignant moment when Alice and Lizzie performed a piano duet. Robert and Phil glanced at each other across the room. It was something they never ever thought would happen. Lizzie was very tearful afterwards, and hugged her daughter.

On New Year's Eve, with Stephen, his friends, Alex, Philip and Rose (who was only allowed to stay until midnight – not dawn) Alice went to the Chelsea Arts Ball at the Albert Hall, to welcome in 1926, which she knew would be her year.

At last it was time to return to the States. In early January emotional farewells were said, Alice reassuring her family that the next time she would come would be in the following autumn – to launch her photoplay with Rudolph Valentino. (Rose almost passed out at the thought of possibly meeting him!) She and the now very popular Miss Tassie were to cross the Atlantic in company with Sarah and Lionel and their staff.

After two days in New York they went their separate ways: Lionel and Sarah were met by the Governor General's yacht, which took them down to the Caribbean. Alice and Miss Tassie, who had spent a little more time with her mother, went to Grand Central for the long train journey back to Hollywood.

1926–1927

Chapter 33

Miss Tassie had just given orders to the gardener when she heard the roar of a powerful car coming through the gates – a sound she recognised. She went into the studio, where Alice was going through her barre exercises.

'Miss Alice, Mr Valentino's just pulled up.'

'Oh, news gets around quickly in this place. Show him into the drawing room.'

They had only been back in Hollywood for four days. Putting a towel around her neck, and still wearing her pointe shoes and practice tunic, she made her way back into the house.

'I am so pleased to see you. You had good trip, yes?'

'Very, thank you, Rudy. It was wonderful to go home.'

'Ah yes, home . . . I still love Italy, of course . . .' He paused. 'I thought we might start, er, experimenting soon. What do you think? I see you've been practising.'

He looked down at her rather worn pink satin shoes.

'Yes. But I'll need to wear high heels for our work, won't I? Unless we're really experimental. What do you think?'

She became aware that he was eyeing her extremely closely.

'Can you tango?' he asked.

'Of course – since I was sixteen!'

'Why don't we try – now? Do you have a gramophone?'

'Why, yes – in the studio. Shall we go over there?'

'I'd like to very much, please.'

Alice found a record of 'Jealousy', which was perfect. Rudy took her in his arms and they started to sway to the hypnotic music. Their bodies moulded together. At once she knew she would feel secure dancing with him. But she felt other sensations too. He bent her back until her head touched the floor and as the music ended he held her hand at arms length, while she turned an easy double pirouette.

'Alice, that was marvellous. We'll be a sensation. Nineteen-twenty-seven will definitely be our year. Think of the publicity . . . Alice Townsend and Rudolph Valentino – together!'

The thought exploded in her mind as he spoke.

They left the studio, and she walked with him down the drive to his car.

'Alice, I know this is right for us. So exciting – and I'm quite sure we could do a little ballet together if you can work out some fairly simple moves for me. Or perhaps we could do something really modern, something jazzy, something that neither of us has done on screen before.'

'Mmm, the tango *is* very old-fashioned, although we would do it splendidly. And by the time our production is seen, I daresay the Charleston will be old hat. So yes, you're right, let's put it to Dayton and John that we plan to be totally new, and really original. Thank you so much, Rudy – I can't say just how thrilled I am!'

'Until tomorrow. I have two hours free at lunchtime. I'll come round, we shall dance some more, then go and see Dayton and the others.'

He took her hand and kissed it gently. She was impressed at his gentlemanly manner, but would have liked him to have held her hand much longer. She stood watching him manoeuvre the huge car down the drive, its chromium glinting in the strong sunlight.

She heaved a huge sigh of contentment. This topped everything she had done so far. This was the ultimate.

Their meeting next day went extremely well. The hunt would soon be on for a good scenario which, once accepted by all of them, could be developed into a script. They planned to start shooting in September – leaving time for the star to finish *Son of the Sheik* and promote it. Meanwhile, Alice spent hours in her dance studio listening to an ever-increasing pile of recorded music, some of which Rudy gave her to help her search for a very different style of dancing that would be modern, sensational, but not too taxing for him. While she was mostly practising in glamorous high heels, she wondered if perhaps there could be a dream sequence during the course of the action, in which they could dance in bare feet.

During this period she saw little of Rudy. On one or two occasions they worked on a series of movements and steps in her studio, and managed the occasional social outing. Meanwhile, Dayton searched for a likely scenario. As Rudy's shooting ended, during the several weeks of editing he had more time for their joint project, and became increasingly fascinated by Alice's highly original ideas. The rapport between them was extremely good – both when they were working and more personally. Like practically every woman around the globe, she found him increasingly irresistible – and she, unlike the others, was affected by his powerful physical presence as well as his dazzlingly handsome looks and perfect profile. His every move enthralled her. When their bodies met as they danced, she felt a return of feelings that had lain dormant in her for a very long time. When occasionally, he touched her off the dance floor, it was even more devastatingly arousing. She was swept along by everything about him, and try though she might – for she knew that his charm had its dangers – she could not help herself.

284

She knew full well that the vampish, smouldering actress, Pola Negri was living with him in his new home, Falcon Lair, and that after being with Alice he went home to her; but she just did not care. She felt not the slightest pang of jealousy towards Pola, though this puzzled her. She knew that next year their names – hers and Rudy's – would appear together on every cinema poster hoarding all over the world, so why should she worry? Her position was strong, and getting stronger all the time. To blazes with Pola, she thought to herself – and said as much to Margaret when they were enjoying one of their quiet evenings.

'Do you think you're falling in love with him?'

'Of course not. That would be foolish. But, well – can you blame me for being attracted?'

'No, but do try to keep it on a fun level if you can. At least, that's what I advise.'

Margaret had her reasons for giving Alice a warning hint. In make-up, she heard more gossip and news than any other workers at the studios, and she had recently learned that since Natacha had left, Rudy had collected quite a few ladies, in spite of his affair with Pola and alleged shyness with women. Indeed, he seemed to use his shyness as a challenge to his admirers.

Dayton eventually found a scenario, and the right person to work on it. He encouraged Alice and Rudy to finalise their ideas in order to enable the writer to build a story. This work was in hand by early July, and the new partners had about five weeks before Rudy was due to leave for New York to do some promotional work for *The Son of the Sheik*. Having worked together, they tended to spend more time enjoying each other's company. Often dodging inquisitive reporters by donning shabby clothes and driving an insignificant, small, elderly Ford, they would take off and enjoy a picnic lunch on a secluded beach. On one such occasion, as they were lying on some warm sand, sheltered by a high cliff, Rudy looked at her and moved closer. She gladly allowed him to gather her into his arms. His touch was gentle and full of tenderness, but it raised a tormented passion in her that wanted him ever nearer to her, wanted him to explore her body more deeply, more sensationally. He held her close and she pressed her parted lips to his muscular shoulder. His warm skin tasted of sun and sea. He turned her head and they kissed long and deeply, her hair caressing his neck. His touch was as passionate and deliciously disturbing as she had longed for it to be. As he broke away his lips lightly swept across her cheek. The sensation brought her more delight.

'Will you, Alice, please? Can we? Now?'

'Yes, Rudy, but not here . . .'

Not taking their eyes off each other they hurriedly flung on their clothes, and returned to his car.

Driving back from the beach he took a turning up a road she had not been before.

'Is this the right way, Rudy?'

'You will see.'

After he had driven for about a mile and a half at his usual breakneck speed, pushing the small Ford to the limit of its endurance, the road led them to the entrance to Falcon Lair. He expertly turned the small car into the drive.

A little later Alice was entering a huge drawing room which resembled a set from one of his films – high and spacious. Huge satin cushions were scattered over a massive fur rug, the furniture was heavily padded, soft and seductive. A tall vase of lilies and peacock feathers stood in one corner, while brass tables adorned with silver ornaments and drinking vessels added exotic detail to the setting. The light-weight muslin curtains fluttered in the late afternoon breeze.

He flung himself down on the pile of cushions.

'Come over here, Alice, and relax with me.'

He picked up a little bell from one of the tables and rang it. A handsome Nubian servant, straight out of the Arabian Nights tales, appeared, and very soon some delicious non-alcoholic drinks were placed in front of them, which tasted to Alice like a mixture of strawberry sherbet with oriental spices.

'Well, a little better than the beach? More to your liking?'

'Of course! It's beautiful – so spacious and airy. You have marvellous taste. But . . .'

Before she could complete her sentence he kissed her again. But even now, she had to satisfy herself about something else.

'Rudy, I terribly want us to make love. We share so much, and we're going to be sharing a great deal more. But I must ask you, where is Pola?'

She had not mentioned Pola's name before.

'Oh, Pola! She's not here. She's away. I dunno where she is, but she said she wouldn't be back for some weeks. Don't let's bother about her. She tries to dominate me. You don't. You're different . . . like spring in Italy. The first mimosa or bougainvilia falling over a wall, so beautiful, so sparkling!'

She glowed at his delightful speech, and desperately wanted to believe what he had said about Pola. Deep down, she didn't; but she didn't care. She was overcome by a surge of passion for this beautiful man, and nothing would prevent her from expressing it.

As if he were in front of the cameras, he picked her up and carried her upstairs to his enormous bedroom. The vast bed, covered with a crimson and white striped bedspread, was flung back to reveal black satin sheets. He laid Alice down, climbed over her, and started to release the buttons of her blouse. Suddenly he stopped, and, as if to excuse bold actions said, 'Of course, you know, all that business in *The Sheik*, when I was supposed to have carried off Lady Diana Mayo and rape her – that's not like me at all, Alice, you do realise that, don't you? I would never hurt you, ever. You are too fine and beautiful a young lady for that. You really are that English rose they all call you!'

She almost found the speech funny. She wouldn't have cared if he *had* treated her roughly – she would have enjoyed it – and her passions were now so aroused, she could hardly wait for him to enter her. The longing in her body had become a sensational ache. She approached him with complete abandon, with a breathlessness that she had not experienced before. Soon, bare of clothes, their bodies met, the whole length of her merged with him as their mouths unceasingly explored each other.

The sensuous feel of the satin sheets complemented her ever-increasing need for him. After the most glorious preliminary caressing and exploration, she encouraged him to enter her. His exciting firmness enabled her long-repressed feelings to explode. The wildness of the moment produced in her such magic that she experienced sensation after sensation with his every thrust. They climaxed together in one glorious moment.

She did not return to 'Sunburst' that night.

It was three o'clock the following afternoon before Rudy drove Alice home. They had two hours before a planning conference at the studios.

Miss Tassie made her feelings quite clear.

'Oh, so you're back. I can see you had a nice time.'

Alice was glowing. She realised that the intuitive Miss Tassie knew everything.

She went up to her room, bathed and changed into a fresh cotton suit to be ready and business-like for the conference that both she and Rudy had to attend at the studios.

She drove herself there, and was given a parking place just to the left of Rudy's huge Isola Fraschini. She was the last to arrive in the board room. As she entered she kissed Norma and Connie, and having shaken hands with Rudy, sat down at the table between Dayton and John.

Preliminary decisions were made about the production – as yet untitled. Shooting would begin in the Fall, and they discussed the timing of the announcement that Alice and Rudy were to appear together. *The Son of the Sheik* was important to him, and they agreed that they would wait until after he had finished his promotion work for it, and it was being shown around the world. That would be time enough to break the news, when shooting was due to begin.

Excitement at the prospect delighted all of them. Already at the pinnacle of their profession, everyone at the meeting knew that the sensation of this, their next work, would top everything they had previously produced.

Chapter 34

'Miss Tassie, could you spare me a minute, please?'

'Why, of course, Miss Margaret. What d'you want?'

'I'm stuck! I can't undo the back fastening on my frock – I think there's a thread caught round it or something.'

She was calling from upstairs to Miss Tassie in the entrance hall, who at once joined Margaret in her bedroom.

'Sorry about that! I just wanted to get you alone for a moment. I'm a bit worried about Miss Alice. I think she's going to spend the weekend with You Know Who. Well, that's lovely for her, but I don't want her to get hurt. Do you think that you could perhaps look at the cards?'

'I know what you mean, Miss Margaret. Yes, he's gorgeous – and so polite! But . . . we don't know whether he's two-timing Miss Alice, do we?'

'Exactly. So I wondered if we should warn her, just a little bit?'

'Well, let's see what the cards have to say.'

They went down to the drawing room.

'Hello, you two – and goodbye. I'm going away for the weekend. Have fun!'

'We will!'

Alice, with a surprisingly small suitcase in her hand, breezed out of the front door, and within minutes they heard her drive off.

Miss Tassie put out five cards.

'There's two warnings for her, Miss Margaret. There's the Empress – she always seems to represent Miss Alice – and there's the Knave of Swords that's him. And look, there's the Lovers – that's both of them. But the card's upside down, so the message is that Miss Alice shouldn't altogether trust Mr Valentino, and she must beware of rivals.'

'So we'll have to look after her, and try to warn her. She seems to be wearing rose-coloured spectacles at the moment!'

Miss Tassie let out a loud burst of laughter.

'Oh, Miss Margaret, I've never heard that before. That's real funny. But I know what you mean. Yes, you're right – so right . . . Now, what about *you*?'

Margaret was fascinated by Miss Tassie's predictions – that her future was brighter than it might seem, and that later on she would find true love.

Alice and Rudy's weekend was given over to lovemaking and the sheer pleasure of each other's company. They moved from the bed downstairs to cushions on the floor and back to bed. Night and day were one. They draped themselves in silk robes and then in yet another state of arousal would throw them off and fling themselves into more glorious sex, followed by sensual food and wine. Alice was experiencing passionate lovemaking the like of which she had never experienced before. But it was not an expression of love. She knew in her heart that she did not love Rudy, any more, probably, than he loved her. The emotion between them was quite simply lust, and because of it she was moving into a new phase of her life and development as a woman of the world.

Later, after their deliciously sensual weekend, when she was parted from him, her night thoughts would drift back to his glorious body, and the longing and the ache would return. She would caress herself to alleviate it and then drift off to sleep knowing that the next day would bring her closer to another encounter.

She came home around midnight on that Sunday evening. She was glowing, and deliriously happy as she waltzed her way into the drawing room where Margaret, who had entertained two girl friends for dinner, was waiting up for her, wasting time tidying up.

Alice was humming.

'You look pleased with yourself. You've obviously had a fabulous weekend.'

'Oh! I have, I have! He's wonderful. So kind, so passionate, yet so gentle. Just stunning. Life's going to be fantastic when we start work.'

'Alice, dear, are you sure you know what you're doing? You know, all the gossip about him and Pola.'

Alice turned on her friend.

'You and your studio gossip! Pola, Pola – always Pola . . . Well, she's not around, so there. *And* he's going to New York alone, so I can't think that there's much going on between them any more. He says she's a really nice woman, but dreadfully temperamental – and that's putting it mildly. They have flaming rows, and she's obviously not at all understanding of his sensitive needs. She doesn't appreciate him. He deserves better. But after this weekend I've nothing to worry about in that direction. So shut up, Margaret – you've just got everything out of proportion.'

'No, it's you who's got everything out of proportion. Please, Alice, be careful. You're right up on cloud nine, and while the sun is shining up there, that's fine. But don't forget that clouds can burst, and you might get very wet indeed.'

'I'm not going to get hurt. It's going to be wonderful.'

Alice's voice took on a dreamy tone as she continued, 'Me and my new screen lover! *The* screen lover of all time – don't you see? This is more than a golden opportunity, and if he happens to adore me, as I know he does, what's wrong with that? Especially as I adore him.'

Margaret sighed, knowing that Alice would take no notice of her warnings.

'It's your birthday soon, isn't it?'

'Why, yes! A few days after you leave. But how did you know?'

'Never mind – I just knew, that's all.'

Rudy smiled smugly to himself.

They were having a quiet dinner on an upstairs balcony with a stunning view over Falcon Lair's eight-acre garden on Beverly Hills.

'I'll not be here for your birthday, but I wanted to give you this.'

Alice, surprised and thrilled at the prospect of a present from her paragon could only utter a breathless 'Oh!'

He produced a pale blue Tiffany's box and handed it to her across the small table. Moving a champagne glass out of the way, Alice placed it in front of her, and undid the white ribbon bow. Inside was a black leather jewellery case. It contained a round, gold pendant hung on a heavy gold chain. A circle of diamonds formed the edge, in a very complex design. She could not see exactly what it was.

'Rudy! It's glorious! Thank you so much – such a beautiful piece. I never expected . . .'

'I'm pleased you like it. It was meant to be a surprise, and I thought I'd give it to you tonight – at our last meeting until I get back. Let me put it on.'

'What is the design?'

'To see what it says you have to look very closely indeed; but always remember that the hidden message is for your eyes only.'

He lightly kissed the back of her neck as he placed the long chain in position. His touch sent a thrill right through her body.

'But I can't see what it's meant to be.'

'Look at it this way.' He turned it round for her. 'Look, here is one symbol – see, it almost looks like a letter "K", but one horizontal stroke is longer and the down stroke crosses it, so that it makes a tiny triangle. That's a letter "A".' Then turning the medallion slightly he continued, 'Here's another triangle with a tail on the right hand side. That's a letter "R".'

'It's all very mysterious. What are these letters? They're obviously our initials, but in what language – Arabic? Chinese? No, they can't be Chinese. Perhaps they're Egyptian?'

He smiled, feigning mystery.

'They are early Phoenician Greek letters. And they represent us, in a very private – no, how you say? – er, personal way.'

His English let him down for once.

'How clever and thoughtful of you to have such a beautiful idea. Thank you so very, very much. It's our secret, isn't it?'

'Yes, our secret – for always, Alice.'

She repeated his words, smiling and nodding.

'You will wear it for me, won't you, Alice?'

'Of course I will, Rudy.'

'Let's make the most of tonight.'

'Alice, it's *beautiful*! What a stunning present! Does the pattern mean anything? It's very elaborate.'

'No. Rudy said it's just vaguely Arabian. He thought it would be nice for me to wear it to remind me of him.'

The gift had impressed Margaret, who was now thinking that perhaps she had less to be worried about for her friend. The pendant had obviously cost a very great deal.

Alice gave a large 'At Home' on her birthday on the following Sunday. She was awakened by the arrival of a huge box of orchids, which Miss Tassie brought in to her bedroom.

'Oh, from Rudy – how thoughtful of him!' She grabbed for the card.

But the message said, 'All love, Alex – thinking of you, missing you, but busy and happy. Have a lovely birthday.' A second box contained fifty pink roses from her family.

By noon her guests were arriving, and soon the beautiful garden was full of happy, chatting people, and the pretty pergola housed – just as she had dreamed it would, one day – a tuneful jazz band, the musicians dressed in pink striped blazers and boaters. The occasion sparkled. Security guards kept out reporters and potential gate crashers. After the elaborate lunch, Miss Tassie and the cook surprised Alice by wheeling in a huge birthday cake with one candle on it. The whole event savoured of richness and glamour, and had the frothy atmosphere that all Sunday parties under the Californian sun should have. At midnight Alice decided that although a year older – twenty-six seemed ancient – she had had a really gorgeous birthday.

Joe Schenck picked up the intercom.

'New York on the line, sir.'

'Okay, put them through.'

He listened, and a young starlet he was interviewing at the time heard the odd exclamation – 'Yes. No. I see.' Then, 'Is it serious?'

He looked grim. Putting the ear piece down he told the nervous seventeen-year-old, 'I'm afraid you'll have to go. See my secretary to make another appointment. Meanwhile, I'll keep these.'

He picked up a sheaf of photographs and waving them indicated that she must leave at once.

'Jesus!' he said to himself. 'Well, all we can do is wait.'

He picked up the private outside line and telephoned his wife.

*

Later that afternoon Norma arrived at 'Sunburst'. Alice was, as ever, pleased to see her friend.

'My dear, I thought you ought to know – Joe heard an hour ago. Rudy's been taken ill. He has some kind of septic ulcer or gall bladder trouble. They're operating on him. We don't know yet just how serious it is. It just depends whether they've caught the trouble in time.'

'Oh my God, how dreadful! He was fine a few days ago. I can't believe it.'

'No, neither could Joe and I. We can't do anything. Joe's keeping in touch with the hospital – the Polyclinic, in New York. Here's the number, if you want to keep in touch.'

'Is anyone going to New York? Do you think I should?'

'Heavens, no, Alice – that would cause such a scandal. Besides, remember that nothing's been put out so far. If you suddenly appeared, the press would have a field day, and the publicity for the film would be ruined.'

Norma went over to join Connie at Jean's. Alice was in a flurry of concern. She grabbed the telephone. The clinic's line was engaged. She tried at least twenty times, and eventually when she got through, a rough Bronx voice answered. She said who she was and that she was calling from Hollywood.

'Oh yeah? They all say that! Get off the line!' She heard the receiver slammed down at the other end. It was hopeless.

It seemed that Rudy was suffering from peritonitis. By the Saturday following her birthday the news was that he was considerably better. There was hope. They could assume that he was out of danger.

All over the world, that Sunday, prayers for Rudolf Valentino seemed to be being answered. The news of his illness had crashed into the headlines; people bought up every new edition as it came out. Crowds milled around the entrance to the clinic, hoping for news and willing their hero to pull through.

Alice was distraught and Margaret and Miss Tassie were distraught for her. An eerie stillness enveloped 'Sunburst'.

On the Tuesday morning, Alice decided she needed to be with Jean – Margaret had gone to go to work as usual. She drove over to the Montgomery's home, arriving there at nine-thirty.

Jean was on the phone. The maid showed Alice into the conservatory, where a latish breakfast was laid ready for the two women.

After a few minutes Jean came in. Tears were streaming down her face. She flung her arms around Alice, sobbing.

Alice held her friend.

'My dear . . .'

'Oh no, not . . .'

'I'm afraid so. John's just phoned. Rudy died about half an hour ago, at ten-past-twelve New York time.'

Breaking away from Jean, Alice fell back into the big cane chair. Turning, she thumped the cushion with her fists.

'I can't believe it! I can't believe it! It isn't true! It *isn't* true!'

Jean embraced her, their tears merging.

When their sobs had subsided, they broke away from each other looking dazed.

'It just doesn't seem possible, does it?'

They both spoke at once, and paused as they attempted to allow the shock to sink in.

They spent a seemingly endless hour hardly saying anything. Later that morning Jean had a call from Norma, telling her that it looked as if there would be a funeral service first in New York, then a further service and interment in Hollywood. She and Joe and Connie were due to leave for New York within the next day or two.

'Will you and John go? Shall I go with you?'

'No. John and Dayton have to look after the studio while Joe's away. Alice, quite honestly I don't think you need – it will be far better for you to stay here and attend the Hollywood ceremony.'

Jean looked at her seriously then added, 'I know you're in shock like the rest of us, but you do look a little tired, my dear. Perhaps you've been working too hard.'

Forgetting for a moment, Alice replied with automatic eagerness, 'Oh! Yes, Jean, I've been working out new movements and dances for our ... our ...' Realising what she was about to say, she stopped suddenly and bit her lip.

'I know, my dear. Now, you try to relax. Stay here for the rest of the day, and John'll drive you home and get a taxi back here. You're in no fit state to drive your car.'

Alice could not sleep that night, even though Miss Tassie gave her some herbal sleeping pills. She got up, pulled on a dressing-gown, and went down into her drawing room. For some time now she had owned the latest Rivard receiving wireless set. While it took pride of place in her drawing room, she had actually listened in very rarely, but tonight, hungry for any news, she switched on the centre knob. All she heard was a startling loud crackling noise which she hastened to get rid of, not wanting to disturb Miss Tassie or Margaret. She turned the right-hand nob, and eventually tuned in to what seemed to be a news bulletin. With fine adjustments the reader's voice became clearer.

It was a local Los Angeles station and she had to wait while there was a series of meaningless messages from sponsors. Leaning over the smooth mahogany top of the set, eventually she heard, 'The nation has been shocked by the tragic death of the world's most famous movie star Rudolph Valentino. There were scenes of panic at the doors of Campbell's Funeral Parlour in New York City today as a huge crowd of some thirty thousand people attempted to view the star's body as it lay in state. The doors of the parlour remained shut for many hours, and when they were opened many mourners were crushed under foot and had to be taken to nearby hospitals to have their wounds dressed.

'The parlour's ornaments, palms and furniture were smashed in the crush. The fans surged into the beautiful gold room where their hero was lying in state under the glass lid of a bronze coffin. Before the doors were open to the hysterical public Mr Valentino's fianceé, the famous film star Miss Pola Negri, knelt in respect by his coffin. It is believed that the funeral service will take place on Monday next at St Malachy's Church on West Forty-ninth Street. Dignitaries from the film world who are expected to travel from Hollywood for this sad occasion include Mr Joseph Schenck and his wife and sister-in-law, Norma and Constance Talmadge and Miss Mary Pickford. We will be keeping you informed of developments in future news bulletins. Meanwhile, we say good night from your favourite local Los Angeles station . . .'

Alice turned off the set. Her grief, which was mingled with an equal amount of disappointment, turned to anger. His fianceé, indeed! If only they knew what he really thought of her. She would have been just as domineering as Natacha . . . but then *she* really knew how to cope with him – just as Alice did. Oh God, what would happen now? Would John and Dayton be able to find her someone else to dance with? And no more loving . . . no more of those heavenly experiences she'd just begun to enjoy so much.

Her longing for the beautiful, gentle man she had got to know so intimately grew as she drifted back to the last time they had made love. That same memorable evening when he had given her the medallion. Her need for him became intolerable. She went to bed in a bad state. Grief mixed with unfulfilled desire, worry and concern for her shattered future merged with an uncharacteristic element of jealousy and fury that Pola – temperamental, passionate Pola – was being respected as Valentino's once future wife. Alice sobbed herself to sleep in a storm of self pity.

She awoke the following morning after a host of weird, indescribable dreams. As the morning wore on she gradually realised that her feelings for Rudy were not those of true love, but were memories of the deeply passionate sexual pleasure he had awakened in her. That would be no more; neither would the new screen partnership, she sighed.

'Are you quite sure you'll be alright today? You look pale again – not surprising, of course. Poor you, you're having a simply ghastly time.'

It was early Monday morning. Margaret, who was waiting for the car to take her to the studios, was standing by Alice's bed.

'Oh yes, I think so. Jean'll come over for lunch and we can commiserate with each other and listen to the wireless. It's already past ten o'clock in New York; there're bound to be newscasts later on. Oh, Margaret, do you think I should have gone?'

'No. Jean was quite right. There was simply no need for you to go. It'll be bad enough for Norma and Connie and Miss Pickford – and the train journey back will be horrid. Now look, don't hesitate to phone for me – I'm sure Dolores will let me come home if need be. We've only about ten extras to make-up today – Dayton says they won't need a great deal.'

'No, I'll be alright, I know I will.'

The friends kissed goodbye as Margaret's car arrived.

Alice and Jean listened to a live commentary relayed direct from New York. Dense, hysterical crowds lined the streets from the funeral parlour to the church. At times they broke through the heavy police cordon and the barriers that had been set up, slowing the progress of the procession down or stopping it altogether, undignified emotional scenes adding considerable distress to the many famous mourners. One commentator, placed at the entrance to the church described the congregation as they stepped from their cars, '. . . and now here is Miss Pola Negri, dressed in mourning robes which we believe, on good authority, to have cost three thousand dollars. She is being supported by two friends. Now she staggers, burdened down with grief. I can see here from my vantage point that she is weeping – in fact, if I turn my microphone . . .'

The atmospheric crackle coming along the lines prevented Alice and Jean from hearing anything more than the faintest hint of sobs.

Alice was attempting without success to hold back her angry reaction.

'She's all show! Three thousand dollars! Yes, *she* would!'

'Now, my dear, don't be too bitter. It's not like you to be jealous.'

'Jean, I'm not jealous. I just know what he actually thought of her. She's a real schemer. He didn't really love her, you know – he told me so!'

Sighing, Jean decided to be tactful.

'Well, perhaps you're right. At any rate I'm so glad we're not there, and that John and Dayton simply had to stay and keep things ticking over at the studio.'

Late that night, long after Jean had left and Margaret and Miss Tassie had gone to bed, Alice, once more wide awake, got up and made her way over to the studio. She was feeling calmer, but in limbo. She realised her life was on hold. It was totally empty. She could not plan for the future, and simply hoped that decisions would be taken for her. At least she knew she had the support of the studio and her lucrative contract, and was secure in that respect. She also had good friends. All that would see her through. It was just not knowing . . . and what was worse, she wondered just how long she would go on not knowing.

She crossed the studio and having put on several lights started to examine the pile of records that she and Rudy had collected. She felt that she could express her emotions in improvised movement, then perhaps, she would get some much needed sleep. She browsed through them, and was taken by surprise when she found one she had not seen before. It bore the Brunswick label. Reading the details she was amazed.

'Recorded 14th of May 1923. The Kashmiri Song. (Amy Woodforde-Finden). Sung by Rudolph Valentino'.

She had not even realised that he had made a record.

Hurriedly winding up the gramophone she put it on the turntable, screwed a new needle into the playing head, made the turntable spin, then placed the head and needle at the edge of the record to start the music.

Soon his voice came through the loudspeaker;

'Pale Hands I *loave* beside the Shalimar,

'Where are you *naow*? Where are you *naow*? . . .'

Alice was deeply moved. It had never occurred to her that she would never hear his voice again. She smiled gently to herself as his Italian accent, hardly discernable in conversation, was heightened by the recording of his light tenor. She slowly started to dance around the studio, making relaxed, sad movements to his music, and as the record ended and the needle scratched on the last grove, she got up from a dramatic final pose on the floor, to turn it over and listen to what was on the other side – a popular number, with Rudy playing the castanets as well as singing in Spanish, reminiscent of his famous tango dancing. She was comforted.

'Miss Alice, did I hear you playing records in the middle of the night?'

'Why yes. I found one of Mr Valentino singing, I didn't know he had ever made a recording!'

'I had my window open, Miss Alice, and as you know it's just above the studio, so I heard. Nice for you, eh?'

'Yes – very nice, very nice.'

'You . . . you're not too sad?'

'Well, I don't know. I am sad, and yet I think I could be a lot sadder.'

'Yes, you sure could be! You'll be better when he's bin laid to rest, proper.'

Miss Tassie looked at Alice in a knowing way. Alice was not aware that her companion was tuning in to her intuitive, psychic powers.

The large woman took a step back and nodded slowly.

'Why, Miss Alice, I think you've got that look in your eyes, I really do!'

She turned, and picking up the breakfast tray, quickly left the room before Alice could question her cryptic remark.

Chapter 35

Tuesday, September 7th

The route to the Church of the Good Shepherd in Beverly Hills was packed with quiet onlookers.

At ten o'clock precisely Joe Schenck had ordered filming, editing and associated work in every Hollywood studio to cease for two minutes. Stillness had enveloped the town, everyone hugging their own private thoughts and memories, many still in shock, in spite of the fact that several days had gone by between the death and the interment.

The solemn Requiem Mass was ending. The priest, giving a blessing, was embarrassed by the ever-dramatic Pola, who cried out in agonized grief, her features covered by a black veil.

As the mourners – mostly from United Artists Studios – left the church and came out into the dazzling sunlight they were confronted by banks of reporters, press photographers and newsreel cameramen, all hungry for interviews and impressions. Alice, Dayton and the Montgomerys were escorted through them by a rank of policemen who, arm in arm, held the crowd back to allow them to enter the fourth car of the procession. Pola was in the first, which now moved off along Santa Monica Boulevard towards the Hollywood Memorial Park. Even greater crowds lined the route, standing in respectful silence, the atmosphere, Alice and her friends realised, was very different from the hysterical behaviour in New York.

Suddenly they heard the buzz of an aeroplane engine. It sounded as if it was flying quite low not that they could see it from inside the car. Then they became aware of the strange sight of everyone in the crowd stretching up their arms and moving their fingers as if to grab at something falling from the sky. The plane was showering the route with rose petals, which the people were desperately trying to catch as the flowers descended. It was as if heaven itself was weeping.

Flowers were everywhere. Norma and Joe's carpet of yellow roses and orchids had been replaced by Pola's eleven foot coverlet of red roses adorned with her name in white rosebuds. Flowers also lined the path to the crypt where the final rites were said as Rudy's coffin was placed in it.

After the interment, Joe, surrounded by stars from the studios, was stopped by newsreel men at the gates of the Memorial Park. Choking with emotion he managed a few words.

'Rudolpho was the kindest and most considerate of all gentlemen. He has lost his last battle, but we must take heart, for heaven has gained an immortal. Ladies and gentlemen, this is the world's worst loss.'

The poignant moment was made even more emotional when someone started singing a song that had been composed during the preceding days. Constantly played on the airwaves, it was already well known, and the crowd joined in – a vast impromptu choir of thousands.

> 'There's a new star in Heaven tonight.
> 'That will never fade from our sight . . .
> 'There's a voice singing "Lead kindly light",
> 'With a smile that made the world bright
> 'Valentino, goodbye!
> 'But way up in the sky,
> 'There's a new star in heaven tonight.'

Those close to Rudy wept. Jean took Alice's hand, tears streaming down their faces once more. She noticed Alice was looking extremely pale, and with the help of a policeman broke away from the crowd and escorted the fainting young woman back to the limousine, which was parked not far away.

By the time Jean had settled Alice in the car she was in a dead faint, but soon came round.

'The crowd – it was so dense and it was so sad . . . and of course the heat . . .'

'It was a very emotional experience for all of us, my dear. I felt I was going to pass out myself. Look, here come the others. Thank goodness, now we can go home.'

Dayton and John joined them, and soon Alice was relaxing in the cool conservatory, after what had been a very heart-rending few hours.

'Miss Alice, you sure looks pale!'

'Well, you know, it's been a dreadfully wearing time for me, and I'm feeling more tired than usual – I suppose I'm totally drained emotionally. I've had so many different feelings to cope with in the last two or three weeks.'

'Yes, I know.' Miss Tassie was quiet for a moment, not quite knowing how to put what she knew she must ask; then her usual no nonsense manner returned, and she said in a matter of fact way,

'Miss Alice. I'm going to be very personal and I hope you won't mind, but I must ask you, are you late?'

'Late? For what? How can I be late for anything? It's almost bed t . . .' She stopped suddenly in mid-word, realising how stupid her reply had been.

'Oh my God, I see what you mean . . . my period.'

'Yes. When were you due?'

'Heavens! Oh no . . .! What with everything going on, I forgot.'

She thought for a moment, then said, 'Yes I *am* late – a week late.' Her tone became horrified. 'But that's nothing – I mean, er . . . that doesn't mean anything . . . does it? I've been late before. Oh no, Miss Tassie, you must be wrong, I've been late before.'

Miss Tassie sighed, and shaking her head as she turned to go about her business she muttered, 'Well, you've got that look in your eyes!'

'Don't keep saying that!'

'I noticed it days ago, and it hasn't gone away . . . I know what I know. My Mammy, she knew too . . .'

Alice picked up a book and threw it at her companion. Miss Tassie nimbly dodged it as she shut the drawing-room door.

Alice confided in Margaret.

'But didn't he take any precautions? Surely he did.'

'He was, well – sometimes, anyway – careful.'

'Alice, surely you know that simply doesn't mean a thing. Being careful isn't being safe. Don't you think you ought to go and see a doctor?'

'No, of course not. It can't be as bad as that. I'm sure to start tomorrow morning. The stress of everything is the cause, it must be. Now that's all over, I'll be alright again. I feel fine now.'

Margaret was unconvinced.

'Get a good night's rest. But if you don't really feel better, then you really should see a doctor, and the sooner the better.'

Alice slept very soundly – but the following morning she was horribly sick.

The immaculately uniformed nurse-receptionist showed Alice into a sumptuously appointed waiting room, where she tried to settle into a deep, soft leather arm chair. Attempting to look relaxed, she nervously thumbed through the latest edition of American *Vogue*. Sighing, she carelessly threw the magazine onto a nearby table, and started to pick at an imaginary chip in her red nail varnish. She seemed to have to wait ages, though in reality it was just a few minutes.

'The doctor will see you now, Miss Townsend.'

The crisp nurse showed her in through elegant double doors.

'I can take you completely into my confidence, can't I?' Alice asked apprehensively. In all the time she had been in Hollywood this was her first encounter with the Californian medical profession.

The smiling elderly man put her at her ease.

'Of course, my dear. You're English, aren't you? We have the same respect for our patients, the same code of practice, as yours. Now what can I do for you?'

Alice explained, not mentioning her lover's name.

'So you are over a week late . . . Well you know, you have had a very stressful time. Stress, being upset, too much hard work, can all effect a woman's system, and although you are looking rather pale, it is far too soon for us to come to any conclusions. I will give you a prescription for a light tonic – to bring those English roses back into your cheeks – and if your period does not occur when it is next due – in about three weeks, yes? – then come and see me again. For the moment, try to relax as much as possible. We have all been upset with the sad happenings in the film world, and as you are one of its brightest stars, it is not surprising.'

'Thank you, Doctor Gilchrist. I promise to relax.'

After he had scribbled the prescription they shook hands and she made her way back to her car which she had parked just outside his Pasadena mansion. Just as she was driving off an official stepped into the middle of the road and stopped her. A newsreel film crew had been set up at the gate of a huge house two doors down the street from the doctor. Alice saw a flurry of lightweight black silk catch the breeze. Pola in her sumptuous mourning robes was being filmed. She was cutting roses in her garden. They went for a take, but Alice heard the cameraman shout 'cut' at the lamenting star, who was sobbing her heart out as she clipped the blooms with hefty secateurs and put them in a trug.

She looked up at the cameraman, her face bad-tempered rather than heart-broken, and yelled at him, 'For God's sake what *now*? Do y'want more tears?'

'No, Pola – the light was wrong on your face, can you do it again for us?'

'Oh, okay!'

Within seconds she had turned on the tears again and the camera was rolling.

The shoot over, Alice was allowed through. Angrily putting her foot down on the accelerator she drove off at a speed which matched her seething reaction to the hypocrisy of the scene she had just witnessed. As she continued her journey rage gave way to tears. She tried to console herself by believing the doctor's comments. Yes, she had been upset and under stress, far, far more stress than he, or anyone – apart from Margaret and Miss Tassie – realised. She told herself she must not panic, and that should anxious thoughts spring to mind she must block them out immediately. It might never happen. She really had to be reassured by Doctor Gilchrist's comments and advice.

During the following week, Alice was called to a meeting with Dayton and John to discuss her future.

'We have decided to continue the search for a new dance partner for you. He must also be someone whose acting ability will match yours. We want you to show off your dancing talents again – the public love you for them – so while we know from past experience finding the right man will be very difficult, it will be worthwhile, don't you think so, Alice?'

Alice's attention had drifted. She blinked and nodded in agreement.

'There's no reason why we shouldn't go ahead with the planned scenario meant for you and Rudy – it is such a good one and would give you plenty of opportunity to display those new techniques you have been working on.'

'Yes, I suppose so.' Alice was biting her lip.

Dayton and John looked at each other in consternation. John got up, put his arms around Alice's shoulders and briefly looking at Dayton said,

'Dayton, Alice definitely isn't her usual self yet. After all, her disappointment is far greater than anyone else's in Hollywood. Let's postpone our meeting for a while.' Turning to Alice, he went on, 'Soon now you'll feel better, won't you? Do try to look to the future, which is none the less bright for you, you know. Have another week taking things easily, then we'll get back to work – and you always enjoy everything you do for us, don't you, Alice?'

Weeping, she nodded.

John's words rung in her ears: soon you'll feel better . . . your future is none the less bright . . . back to work next week. Next week she would know for certain.

'Your baby is due on or around the twentieth of April.'

Dr Gilchrist's words rang in Alice's ears. She was in a state of panic and ought not to have been driving, but she was anxious to get home to think and talk to Margaret. She narrowly missed hitting another car as she jumped some traffic lights, the driver tooting furiously as she swerved passed him. Not bothering to put her car in the garage, she ran into the house and flopped down on the settee in the drawing room.

Miss Tassie was waiting for her.

'So I was right . . . I'm never wrong in these matters – you didn't need to go to Doctor . . .'

'Yes, I know – I've that look in my eyes. Oh, Miss Tassie, what am I going to do?'

'You're going to lose that pretty figure of yours and you're going to give birth to a mighty pretty love-child, that's what you're going to do. How you set about it, well, I dunno, but I'll stand by you and help all I can.'

'Thanks – it's just like you to say that. I'll need all the help I can get.'

'And that little one's Pappy is with the angels, but he'll be looking after you, no doubt.'

'Oh yes, but I wish he were *here* to help.'

'Well, Miss Alice, all I can say is the Lord works in a mysterious way.'

'Yes, I know, I know.'

Margaret rushed in. Miss Tassie left them to talk privately.

'Well?'

'Yes, it's confirmed, I am.'

'Oh, you poor, poor darling! What are you going to do?'

'Heaven knows.'

Trying to make sense of the situation Margaret added, 'A few more people will have to be told, of course. But the fewer the better. I think you should go and see Jean right away. Listen what she has to suggest. Then there's Norma and Joe . . .'

'Oh, the Big Boss, he'll be furious. So will Dayton.'

Alice's voice became more despairing with every sentence.

'Perhaps you should go home and have it in London with your parents.'

'My parents! Heaven forbid! I couldn't. I simply couldn't put them through all that . . . the schools, Aunt Emma . . . I know Phil would be terribly supportive, but no, God no! Even although things are so good between us again – it simply wouldn't be fair on them.'

'Well, let's hope it doesn't get out who the father is – or was I should say.'

Alice was shaking all over and feeling dreadfully cold. She said, 'I can trust you not to tell, can't I? Please, Margaret. After all, it's only you and Miss Tassie . . .'

'Of course you can, darling – what sort of a friend would I be? After everything you've done for me? Why, if it weren't for you I'd still be in that poky little flat.'

She was quiet for a moment then gently sat down beside her friend. Taking Alice's hand, she said, 'Of course you could get rid . . .'

Alice snapped back, 'No, no, I couldn't, I couldn't – that would be too dreadful. After all, my baby is Rudy's only child.'

'We don't know *that* for certain!'

Alice had to agree, but hastily put the thought out of her mind.

'Go and talk to Jean.'

'I will – tomorrow.'

Then she had a very alarming thought.

'Tomorrow,' she repeated, 'Tomorrow – I've a meeting with John and Dayton – about my future . . . But now as far as work's concerned it's non-existent.'

She rushed up to her bedroom and fell into a turbulent sleep.

'Oh, my dear, my dear, I am sorry.'

'I'm desperate, Jean. In the first place, I've a meeting with John and Dayton at five o'clock about my future. How can I tell them? I've let everyone down so badly.'

'Don't worry about the meeting. I'll take care of that. Now, how much help can you get from the father? Is he free to marry you? Do you want to tell me who he is? No, don't tell me – there's no need. And from that I can gather that he is in no position to help you, is he?'

Alice smiled through her tears. She knew that Jean knew, but she was letting her off lightly. Not actually to have to say who he was, even to her older and very wise friend, was a help.

'My dear, your secret is safe with me, as I know it will be with Norma and Connie – they are the dearest, sweetest of people. They hate gossip as you know, and would never let anyone – especially you – down. Joe will have to be told of course, but don't worry, Norma will look after him!

'So you think that I can keep things very private?'

'Yes, of course, dear. But we will have to work out a plan for you. Let me think.'

The kind, motherly woman was quiet for several minutes.

'A few years ago I helped another young star like yourself who was in the same predicament . . . I'm just wondering if what we did then we could do again for you. Let me make a phone call.'

Alice opened her mouth to speak. Jean interrupted.

'Don't worry I'm not going to compromise you in any way. What I'm going to do is quite safe.'

She was out of the room for what seemed ages. Coming back she said, 'I've spoken to John. He understands, and of course he'll talk to Dayton. He said the studio can give you several months' leave of absence without any problem, so your contract is quite safe. We'll discuss details with him when you've finally decided what to do, but this is what I have to suggest.'

Jean told her that the young woman she had helped a few years back had left Hollywood for the last five months of her pregnancy, and gone south to San Diego. She had taken a suite in a large hotel, then as her confinement drew near, moved into a private nursing home, which eventually found a couple who wanted to adopt the child.

'Now, my dear, I would suggest that you do something like that. The nursing home we used is excellent – just the right sort of place to have a baby. What you have to decide is whether you want to have the baby adopted. To me, it seems the only possibility. You could not possibly continue your career, or expect eventually to marry, with a love child. The scandal would be too dreadful – you would be totally finished. And think of the disgrace it would bring on your family.'

'I've already thought of them. Margaret suggested I might go home, but I simply couldn't, Jean.'

'Of course you can't – I can understand your feelings. But equally, you can't stay here – at least not after you begin to show. However, you have a while before that happens.'

Alice was thoughtful. Jean was right. She could not stay in Hollywood when once what was happening to her was obvious, but the plan seemed over simple.

'What if I'm recognised in San Diego? People will know my name . . .'

'My other friend was as famous as you – she dyed her hair red and assumed a false name. If you dyed your hair black, or wore black wigs, I think you would get away with it.'

'But we'll have to put out some sort of a statement to the press. What? Oh, Jean, it's not going to work, it's not going to work!'

Alice broke down.

'It will work, my dear, I assure you. Early next summer you will be back

303

and getting on with your career again. We will put out a press release saying that you've been overworking, and are going to take a break from filming. Goodness knows, that's true enough; you're not just an actress but also a dancer, and carry a double burden. Quite often stars take a break and go off to a secret destination.'

'If we mention overwork, my parents'll be over here within weeks. They'll think I'm really ill, and take me home.'

'Well, that is a worry.'

At that moment John joined them. He smiled kindly at Alice.

'So how's our poor star who's got problems?'

'John, I'm so very sorry.'

'It's alright, he sure was a darned lucky fella!'

Alice hadn't thought of her situation like that before, his comment made her smile.

'Miss Alice is resting by the pool, Mrs Montgomery. I'll bring you some coffee in just a moment.'

Jean and Alice embraced.

'Now, my dear, I'm getting on quite well. The hotel has a pleasant suite available which you can rent for as long as you like. I've spoken to the matron of the nursing home. She says you can move in there as and when your gynaecologist suggests. They really are very nice people, and I'm sure you'll be happy there – as happy as possible under these most unfortunate circumstances. They also said that adoption can also be arranged should you wish it – I said that I thought that would be what you wanted. I haven't made any final arrangements, because I'm not sure when you want to leave Hollywood. You'll certainly be alright for quite a few weeks yet. You have very strong stomach muscles, and the present low, waistless fashions are an excellent disguise.'

The friends went on to discuss dates, working back from the approximate time of the confinement.

'You're just over two months on. I think you ought to leave us in early December. I don't think you can risk staying on for Christmas.'

At the mention of Christmas Alice's thoughts immediately turned to her family, and the very special one they enjoyed last year.

'Yes, I guess you're right. Oh, Jean, it's dreadfully sad. I said in January that I would try to be with them again this year. Mummy mentioned it in her last letter – she was getting excited already.'

Jean shook her head, her greying hair catching a shaft of sunlight.

'No, my dear, not this year. Incidentally, John said he would telephone us here after lunch, because he had a vague idea that could help you resolve that side of your problems.'

Later that afternoon Jean received the expected call and handed the phone over to Alice.

Chapter 36

The sound of Lizzie playing Chopin's C minor Nocturne greeted Robert as he arrived back from an after school hours coaching session with some of his sixth form boys.

Delighted to hear his wife's playing, he went up to their first-floor drawing room and kissed her on the forehead as she smiled and continued to play.

'That's a nice sound to come home to!'

'Yes, I love this piece – it's rather melancholy, just right for a chilly autumn day like this.'

'But you may want to change your tune, as they say, because here's a big, fat letter from Alice – it must have come with the five o'clock delivery.'

Lizzie broke off from the Nocturne, striking a bright C major chord.

'How wonderful! She must have a lot of news. What does she say? Oh, come on, Robert, open it up!'

Husband and wife sat down together on the settee, hungry for news of their daughter, their eyes darting from line to line of each page.

'Poor lamb, she must be so disappointed and like everyone very sad about Valentino's death – what a pity, just as things were going so well with her and him . . . It would have been lovely to see them dancing together, but that was not to be. At least the studio is obviously doing their best for her, which is quite something. Robert, we'll have to be very discreet, and only tell Philip and the Beaumonts what's happening. But I don't quite understand, do you?'

'Well, Alice's going to San Diego for a few months to help develop the new talking pictures. They particularly want her because her speaking voice is light and clear and she's so very articulate.'

Lizzie was puzzled.

'But why do we have to tell people – if they ask, that is – that she's simply resting?'

'Don't you see, it's because the studio don't want their secret plans be known to rivals.'

'That's understandable, isn't it? And look, at the bottom there she says that from the end of the first week in December we are to write to her care of

Mr Montgomery at the studio. While we can have her address in San Diego, we must not under any circumstances write to her there. They will be in direct contact with her at her secret location. It does seem a bit odd, but it seems that everything would be spoiled for her and the studio if it's known where she is and what she's actually doing – experimenting, I suppose, with different, um, what are they called?'

'Microphones, dear.'

'Yes, that's what they are. And as she says, the press and the gossip columnists in Hollywood would have a field day if they found out about all this, so we do have to be very careful.'

'Yes. You know, she'll get our letters only a day or so after they reach the studio. And then, as she says, in the spring she'll go back to make the new talking picture – we'll hear her as well as see her. They must like her English accent even more than I thought!'

He changed the subject.

'Now, Lizzie, what about the nativity play? Let's try hard to do something different this year . . .'

Chapter 37

'I do wish you could have stayed on for Christmas.' There was sadness in Margaret's voice.

Alice took Margaret's hand through the window of the car and patted it reassuringly, but sighed. Decisions had been made, plans laid, and the publicity department would soon issue a statement. She and Miss Tassie were off to spend a few months in a different environment. Alice would not be bored: the prospect of doing a certain amount of work at the experimental sound studio pleased her, and she knew that she could look to the early summer, when, after her child was born, she would return to Hollywood and work on the proposed talking picture, which would send her career off into a startling and exciting new direction.

With Miss Tassie at her side they made the short journey to the coast, and took the beautiful road south towards San Diego.

After they had been travelling for about a hour Alice smiled at Miss Tassie, and said, 'I want you to do something for me – quite soon, really.'

'And what's that, pray?'

'I want you to learn to drive.'

'*Me*, drive an automobile?'

'That's right. We'll need to be independent down there, and later on I'll probably not feel like driving – it mayn't be that safe for me, anyway. Don't worry, we'll find someone to teach you, it's not that difficult.'

'My, my, Miss Alice! Why, I just don't know!'

Miss Tassie was grinning to herself and tossed her head in pride. Alice could tell that her suggestion had gone down well. Turning a corner she noticed that her companion had begun to watch what she was doing.

They were quiet for a while then Alice went on, 'I know this isn't going to be easy for you, but I hope that every time you see me in one of those black wigs it'll remind you that once we arrive at Oceanside I'm not Alice Townsend any more. I'm Mrs Celia Newcombe. Do you like my wedding ring?'

'Why, yes, it looks about right to me, Miss – er, Madam. But how come you chose that name?'

'Well, Celia is an anagram of Alice – I mean it contains all the same letters. And Newcombe I thought would be easy to remember since it was my mother's maiden name.'

'And that husband of yours, where's he in all this?'

'Yes, I've thought that out too. He's in the British Navy, on loan to the United States Navy. He's doing an extended tour of duty in the far east, and while we live in England, he's based in San Diego at present, and will be returning there very soon after the baby is born, so that's why I decided to miss the winter in England and come to California to relax, and have my baby. Least, that's what I'm going to tell any hotel guests that ask questions. Can you remember all that?'

'Of *course* I can, Madam! And Madam lives in Kensington, doesn't she?'

'Why not? After all, you know that house very well, don't you?'

'I sure do!'

The two women fell into a fit of girlish giggles at the elaborate subterfuge.

They stopped for their packed picnic lunch at a beautifully quiet beach, where the surf was high and added a certain drama to the scene. It was late afternoon when they neared Oceanside, a sizable town which was about halfway to San Diego. Alice pulled the car over to the side of the road near a gate into a small paddock. She got out, and opening the trunk took out a hatbox. Among other things, it contained one of the three wigs Margaret had obtained for her from the studio – almost jet black, and cut in her own natural style. Propping up a small travelling mirror she put it on.

'How do I look?'

'Just fine, Madam, just fine.'

The dark hair suited her remarkably well. Grinning to herself in the mirror she decided that she would explore the gown shops in San Diego and experiment with a range of colours she never wore – turquoise and crimson as opposed to the clearer vermilion which suited her so perfectly as a blonde!

They drove on, and by half-past-four easily found the small hotel where a two bedroom suite, dinner, bed and breakfast had been booked for Mrs Celia Newcombe and her companion Miss Tasmania Duval.

On the afternoon of the following day they approached San Diego from the north and made the somewhat complicated journey to Coronado which, although attached to the mainland by a narrow strip of land, seemed to have the feeling and atmosphere of a separate island.

The air was clear, the sky blue, and it seemed a few degrees warmer than Hollywood. Alice drove up Orange Avenue and turned into a long, sandy drive, on each side of which were three rows of small, rectangular tents with thatched roofs. Beyond these, on the left hand side of the drive, they could just see an extensive beach and the sea.

'My it's beautiful here. But I don't much like the look of those houses – really poor – we're not going to have to live in them I hope. Especially in winter!'

'Oh no, Miss Tassie, that's Tent City. Mrs Montgomery told me about them. In summer a lot of fashionable people come and stay, and use the hotel, just up there, for their food and entertainment. It seems those little buildings were put up as a temporary measure, when the hotel was altered a while ago, and people liked them. But look! This is much nicer.'

By now they were at the main entrance to the hotel – a huge white wooden building with a round tower-like structure, striking red roofs, balconies and some beautiful gardens.

They got out, and Miss Tassie followed Alice into the rather dimly lit reception hall, its walls dark mahogany, thick luxurious carpet adding to a peaceful and expensive atmosphere. Alice went up to the reception desk.

'Good afternoon, I'm Mrs Celia Newcombe, with my companion, Miss Duval. We have rented a third floor suite.'

'Welcome to the Del Coronado Hotel, Mrs Newcombe. We gather you are going to be with us for several months. We hope you and Miss Duval will be happy here. You have a car, I take it?'

'Why yes, it's just outside – with some of our luggage. Three trunks will arrive in the next day or so.'

The smartly dressed receptionist clicked his fingers. At once a bellboy appeared, and taking the keys asked Mrs Newcombe and Miss Duval to follow him. They walked across to the large brass cage-like Otis elevator, and he drove them to the third floor.

'Step this way, ladies, please.'

He conducted them left, out of the elevator, and around a corner into a very long, wide corridor at the end of which was a smallish door. He un-locked it to reveal a sizeable glassed in sun terrace. From that, another door led them to the suite itself. It consisted of a large sitting room with a dining area, two bedrooms, a bathroom and a small kitchen. All the main rooms had superb views of the beach and the Pacific Ocean.

Alice looked at Miss Tassie and they grinned at each other approvingly. She gave the young boy a dollar; he saluted, smiled, and withdrew. Within a minute their luggage arrived.

Alice sat down.

'Well, what do you think? Will it do?'

'Why it's beautiful, really beautiful. It'll be just like being on one long holiday!'

'Yes, that's what I was thinking, and that's what we'll make of it – al-though as you know I do have some work to do!'

'But no getting up at five o'clock in the morning to be at the studio by six, eh?

'Definitely not!'

She looked around. Although it was towards the end of the day, the light was strong and the sunset promised to be spectacular. The overall colour scheme of the room was cream, with a certain amount of green. The settee and easy chairs were large, well cushioned, and upholstered in a dainty floral patterned fabric, white painted canework forming the arms and supports for the glass topped coffee table. In one corner stood a matching far eastern Emperor chair – more comfortable than it looked. There was a dining room suite with six chairs and a writing desk. Heavy curtains hung at the huge plate glass picture window which ran the whole length of the wall on the sea facing side. These could be pulled over at night to give the room a cosy atmosphere. The bedrooms, in blue and pink respectively, had a similar light, pretty, very welcoming atmosphere. Throughout the apartment several lovely watercolour flower paintings decked the walls, and the bedroom and bathroom doors were covered in mirror glass.

Alice was more than pleased. Soon Miss Tassie was unpacking the cases and settling in.

During the days that followed, in spite of the support that Miss Tassie was giving her, Alice began to feel lonely. She missed her equals – Margaret's lively chatter, the more sophisticated conversations with Norma and Connie, and the motherly cushioning that Jean had given her since she had moved to Hollywood. This, she realised, had been a godsend during the last very trying months; how would she have coped if it had not been for the older woman's experience and practical help?

But Miss Tassie apart, alone she was not. Every day she could feel a greater response from the ever growing little new life within her. Sadness struck her with each movement. Yet at the same time there was happiness, happiness in the knowledge that the famous father, who had been so cruelly struck down at such a young age, would live in his child, but sadness because Alice knew she could not possibly keep the child. She often had serious thoughts that she should do so, and tell the world who the father was – though it would mean sacrificing her career, her own life, being an outcast. If she did take that direction, she wondered if she would be believed. In all probability Pola – or someone like Pola – would say that Rudy could not have possibly been the father. That Alice Townsend was a liar and a cheat, that Rudolph had been with her (Pola) all the time . . . Alice knew her life would be blighted for ever.

While she was still in Hollywood, once she had up to a point accepted the tragedy of Rudy's death and the despair of her situation, and Jean had helped her plan her immediate future, she had been much calmer. But now, as she settled down to her sojourn in San Diego she became tormented. She had more time to think. The horror of her situation weighed more heavily upon her than it had done for some weeks.

She spent nearly all her time in the apartment looking at the beach, the sea, and the gardens from her window, or sitting on a recliner in the private sun lounge. For several days she stayed there as if in a dream.

Miss Tassie soon realised her distress.

'Miss Alice, why don't you take a walk along the beach or down Orange Avenue? You might see a smart dress shop. Then tonight, instead of having room service, you could take a table in that big restaurant, and maybe talk to some of the hotel guests. They look real nice people – I've seen lots of them – all ages and from all over. I guess next week they'll start getting ready for Christmas. You've been sitting around too much – not good for you or baby, especially after all that exercise you're used to taking.'

'Yes, you're quite right. I must get out, and anyway, I have to visit Doctor Wegeforth at the Coronado Hospital tomorrow.'

Alice felt better for her walk. She bought a pretty crimson cocktail dress in a very fashionable nearby shop, and wore it for dinner in the famous Crown Room – a vast edifice made entirely of wood, rather like a huge upturned boat. The lively atmosphere did her good. She was placed at a table with five other people, who were enjoying a short break from the bleakness of the Canadian winter.

The next day she walked the short distance to the Coronado Emergency Hospital where she was interviewed and examined by Doctor Arthur Wegeforth. He had already a considerable amount of information about her on file, from Doctor Gilchrist and an introduction from Jean.

'Now, Mrs Newcombe, I expect you would like to see the room we have booked for your confinement. Please come with me.'

He took her up one flight of stairs to a clinical but attractive and airy private room.

'We have only four such rooms, and this part of the building is extremely discreet.' He smiled warmly. 'Now you have decided that you child should be adopted, haven't you? Of course, we are speaking in the strictest confidence. We quite understand your situation, and we have already made the necessary plans and arrangements for the child. We have two couples – one who want a boy, the other a girl. They are wealthy, and your child will have the very best possible chance in life, I assure you. Both couples are tender and loving, and long for children. Their background is impeccable.'

Alice's heart had missed a beat, but he had reassured her. 'Will I meet them, when the time comes?'

'No, I'm afraid that's not allowed. They accept the fact that they cannot meet you. And I have to tell you that the amount of time you spend with your baby after he or she is born will be extremely limited. I know this may seem cruel, but the closer you and the child bond the worse it will be for you. This is something that, sad though it is, you must try to come to terms with, and the sooner the better.'

His hard words hit home and Alice started to cry. He got up, put his arm around her.

'I'm so very sorry, my dear. But believe me, it's all for the best, and you really can rest assured that the adoptive parents are lovely people.'

A nurse brought in tea. Alice calmed down and it was arranged that she should visit him for check-ups every two weeks, or at any time if she felt at all unwell. Fortunately the hospital was but a few minutes from the hotel.

Thinking about the interview with the doctor, she knew she would hate to part with the child. But she also knew that for others' sakes as well as her own she had to be practical, hard though it would be. She must either accept this solution or make life unbearable not only for herself, but her family. And although she was wealthy, bringing up a child without a father would not be good for the child.

Alice was resilient. She had had hard knocks before – though nothing like this, of course – and telling herself to be sensible and practical helped a lot. She called upon all her inner strength to see her through. It helped that her feelings for Rudy had been purely physical. He had swept her off her feet. It had been exciting and overwhelmingly rewarding, sexually, coming as it did at a time when she needed sex most – but she had not been in love with him. It was something she must cling on to. Rudy could have been her partner – on the screen as he had been in bed – but never her husband, in spite of the fact that she was carrying his child.

After ten days had passed, she was more or less her usual self, with only the odd hour or so when she slumped into melancholy. She had quite a lot to do, and made herself socialise – her acting ability stood her in good stead when dealing with hotel guests and some of the more senior members of staff.

But in the middle of the night she suddenly awoke and turned over in a gloriously romantic haze. Then, opening her eyes, she was immediately brought back to reality. She saw a shaft of moonlight through the curtains, and realised that she had been dreaming of Ben. They had been dancing together over a calm lake, their feet just touching the water. Her ecstatic dream brought back vivid memories. She realised that she still loved Ben, and as she tried to go back to sleep wondered whether she would ever truly love anyone else.

She had a visit from the owner of the Sabre Studio which was situated across the water in San Diego itself. During the whole of January she would be helping with their experiments there, and he gave her a pile of film scripts from which she was to read, making recordings under a variety of conditions. There were only three employees at the studio. To them she was just a well spoken English woman – Mrs Newcombe, whose husband ... The owner of the studio and inventor of the equipment had worked with Dayton and John in the past. He could be trusted, and knew who she really was.

She was now showing, but in that attractive way before the body becomes heavily distorted. Her pregnancy had brought a wonderful glow. She looked beautiful, and felt confident. She spent much time writing letters to her parents and the Beaumonts, and decided to take Alex into her confidence. As her oldest friend she knew he would not let her down, and it was good to pour her heart out to him on paper. She wished they could talk but that was out of the question, as he was in Europe. He had already written to her with his news and gossip from the ballet world which had intrigued her, but it increased her isolation from all that meant so much to her. She also had several packages of presents, Christmas cards and the usual piles of photographs to autograph sent down from the studios, as her fan mail continued to pour in – among it, messages from her adoring public hoping she would benefit from her rest. She missed dancing and the exercise and resolved to get back into practice as soon as possible once the child was born.

Over Christmas she and Miss Tassie joined in some of the celebrations in the hotel, and met a lot of interesting people.

At around noon on New Year's Eve there was a knock on the door of the apartment. Miss Tassie answered. Alice was apprehensive.

In walked Jean, John and Margaret.

'We simply had to come. We couldn't let you and Miss Tassie see the new year in with strangers!' announced Jean.

Alice hugged them all in turn. She could not have had a better surprise. They went to the New Year Ball and joined in the celebrations. Alice decided it would do her child no harm at all if she danced, and did so, with John as her partner, taking the floor for a tango. The Charleston she sat out.

Her friends stayed overnight, and Margaret and Jean spent the morning with Alice while John went to see the progress being made at the Sabre Studio. They said how well she looked.

Margaret had some interesting news. Her friendship with the young German director who worked for Paramount Studios was progressing. They had spent quite a lot of time together over Christmas and were falling in love. Alice could see the happiness in her friend's eyes and was delighted for her.

'Yes, he is a dear, I can't think that you've not met him as yet.'

'Well, that'll be something to look forward to in the early summer.'

Her friends had to depart, and she was sad to see them go, but considerably cheered by their unexpected visit.

'Thanks, I'll get a taxi from the other side. I'll telephone you when I'm about to leave the studio, and you can come down here and pick me up.'

'I certainly will, madam.'

Miss Tassie sat upright, and with remarkable self assurance for one who had only been driving for a few weeks, drove off to a wide corner where Alice watched her with unnecessary apprehension as she turned the precious car to go back along the straight private road from the ferry to the hotel. Meanwhile Alice boarded the ferry to take her across to downtown San Diego where she would be spending her first day at the recording studio.

The work was easy. She had learned some very different kinds of speeches by heart, and had an amazing and unforgettable day.

'Now, Mrs Newcombe, can you lean a little nearer that flower arrangement as you say, "I love you"? Then move back slightly, and in a more distressed voice continue with, "but *you* don't love me". We can then tell how sensitive the microphone is.'

Alice did as she was told but in leaning forward the chain of her medallion got caught up in the flowers and clinked against the vase. When it was played back it sounded as if she was breaking plates over the head of her imaginary lover.

'George, try putting that microphone just inside Mrs Newcombe's neckline.'

George did just that. It was cold and uncomfortable, and the experiment proved equally unsuccessful. All they could hear was Alice's heart beat.

And so it went on that day, and for the following four weeks. There were a great many laughs and a certain amount of tempers were lost. They brought in a male actor. His voice was too high-pitched. Another sounded like a grunting pig. Eventually, however, after four weeks of demanding but rewarding careful attention to detail and technical expertise, they made progress and found solutions which it was hoped, would cut down on costly big studio time later in the year. Alice's part of the work was completed as January ended.

She was now in the thirtieth week of her pregnancy, and went for her regular check-up with Dr Wegeforth, who was delighted with her progress. But she was feeling very heavy, and while her weight gain was exactly right, she began to think that her figure would never return to its former lithe, slim, flexible shape. He did his best to reassure her, but at times – especially late in the day, when she felt tired – she became depressed. She read a great deal, something she usually had little time for. She even did some embroidery. She longed to make baby clothes and buy a layette, feeling particularly upset when she was out in Coronado, for every mother she saw walking proudly with her baby in a pram, or a toddler by her side, added to the pain of what she knew she must face up to.

One morning Miss Tassie brought in a letter for her. It had been addressed to 'Sunburst' in a florid hand which she did not recognise. Its stamp, too, was one she had not seen before, the postmark obliterating the design, apart from a tiny corner which was obviously a section of King George the Fifth's head.

The back flap announced, Government House, St John's, Antigua.

'My God – a letter from Aunt Sarah, how wonderful.'

The bond between her and Emma's older sister was strong. She was delighted.

I wonder what this is all about, she thought to herself as she reached for her letter opener – the envelope was too thick to unseal without it.

Her first excitement soon turned to horror.

The letter began, 'Dearest Alice – how delightful to be in touch! I've some wonderful news for you. I hear that you are in San Diego, although I'm not quite certain where. And the fact is . . .' She read on. This was dreadful.

'Oh no, no – it can't be!'

'What can't be?'

Miss Tassie put a large bowl of flowers down on a nearby table while Alice awkwardly slumped into an armchair.

'Aunt Sarah and Uncle Lionel are taking an extended cruise. They are due to sail from the Caribbean today – travelling to Panama and up the coast. Their ship is stopping off here, and, of course, they want me to meet them. What on earth can I do? I suppose I'll just have to slip away somewhere during the time they'll be here, and pretend I've had to do some special location work or something.'

'That's one possibility. I guess I could tell some fibs for you.'

'Yes, that's the answer. But then, why would you be here without me?'

'Do you think you could possibly trust Lady Maitland? She seems to me to be a lovely lady, not prudish not like Mrs Beau . . .'

Miss Tassie stopped, suddenly realising that she had said more than she intended.

Her remark made Alice smile.

'I know what you mean – Aunt Emma really is a dear, but she is getting just a little, er . . . prudish in her old age. Aunt Sarah isn't like that one bit.'

'You know, you can do with all the support you can get in the coming weeks. I think maybe you should come clean and tell her. Think about it.'

Alice thought. In her imagination she worked out three scenarios. In one Sarah's response evoked sympathy and support, in another she was shocked and responded with an abrupt, 'of course you simply must tell your parents'. In the third Sarah was angry, telling her how sinful she had been. During the course of a very restless night – one when her child was obviously as wide awake as herself – she eventually dismissed two of them. She knew Sarah pretty well. Sarah had had many rich experiences in life . . .

'My dear, *dear* girl, of *course* you can trust me. In fact I feel very privileged that you've been so honest. Your secret is totally safe with me. You're doing the right thing. You must live your life to the full. You want and need your career – and I can identify with that. But you know, Alice darling, as we said when we were in London together, you also want and need real love, and you must be in a position to accept it freely when it comes along – whenever that is. That's my experience in life, and I've seen a great deal over the years as you probably know.'

'Yes, Aunt Sarah. Oh, you don't know what it means to me to have support from someone who is as near to being family as makes no difference.'

'I'm so glad you think of me in that way. You know, I feel as if you are a daughter to me – the daughter I never had. Now, my dear, is there anything I can do for you? You say everything has been arranged for your confinement and the adoption?'

'Yes, I have good friends in Hollywood.'

'I'm sure you have, just as I had good friends in the theatre, all those years ago. But, darling, are you sure that your medical advice is what it should be? Don't forget, Lionel is a doctor as well as a diplomat. I'd be much happier if he called on your doctor – just to make sure.'

315

'That's so kind of you both. You've made me feel much happier, and far more secure.'

'That's what we must always do – give support and real understanding when it's needed. Now, would it help if you wanted to tell me who the father is? You don't have to, but . . .'

'Only very few people know. The father himself doesn't know.'

'But, my dear, even if he's married to someone else he should be helping you.'

'He cannot. You see, Aunt Sarah, he's dead. He was very, very famous, and while I don't want to say who he was in so many words, he died in August of last year.'

Sarah gasped.

'You say he was very famous – *very* famous?'

Alice nodded, and was silent for a moment, knowing that Sarah had got the message.

She said, 'Now you see why I have to be so frightfully discreet.'

'Yes, I do see.'

Sarah's expression was full of sympathy, and more understanding than any other person Alice had told the news to.

She and the Maitlands dined together in the Crown Room. Alice felt much better. Her mood was bright, and the conversation was lighthearted.

'My dear, we know so much about this lovely hotel! David – I mean, the Prince of Wales – told us about it when he came to stay with us last summer. He'd been here a few years ago and enjoyed really scintillating company. Didn't he, Lionel?'

'Yes, dearest.'

The Governor General smiled beguilingly at his beautiful wife, then turned to Alice.

Patting her hand, he said, 'I've visited your hospital. I said I was your uncle and I'm more than satisfied with your doctor. You'll be quite alright, Alice. Let's hope that the next time we meet you will be back in shape and dancing again.'

'I fully intend to start practising as soon as possible.'

'Good girl,' said Sarah. 'You'll not lose your figure. Why, I've known dancers get their eighteen-inch waists back after babies – but then, waists aren't fashionable these days!'

The next day Sir Lionel and Lady Maitland rejoined their cruise ship to continue their holiday.

During the weeks that followed, Alice's mood fluctuated. At times she was relaxed and content, at others she suffered considerable depression. One dark and stormy spring day when the clouds were thick and grey, and the wind blew in from the Pacific, causing the breakers to crash against the rocks at the water line, she was looking out over the ocean. Her mood was as heavy as the weather, her body now almost unbearably heavy with her active, lively child. She had less than three weeks before the expected confinement. She told herself to snap out of her depression, that she was about to give life to someone who had a remarkable father, and even if she would never see her child grow up, or have the slightest chance of ever meeting him or her, she was giving the world someone very special. Would she have a boy or a girl? At least she would know that much. Would the infant be blonde like her or dark-haired? She could, at any rate, rest assured that the little creature in her – who was obviously not that little – was strong. She had no peace.

She decided to write to Philip. She wanted to tell him in more detail about the experiments at the little studio. She purposely had not done so before because she was afraid that as her pregnancy wore on she would run out of news! She settled down and took out her fountain pen, which she still used constantly. Looking at it in her right hand, her mind drifted back to that proud moment when she had signed her first autograph. Of the thrill she felt when Charlie, dear, long since dead Charlie, had given it to her.

How unfortunate I am in love! she thought sadly. To have two men in my life die, and the other might just as well have never existed.

Chapter 38

'Now, are you going to come today? You know you're due to?'

The only response from her child was the one she was quite used to – lively kicking. It was the Wednesday morning after Easter and Alice sat waiting for very different signs. She took a little light food from time to time, but towards evening she was feeling extremely fed up, and the food had made her feel slightly nauseous.

'I don't think baby will come tonight, Miss Alice. I think you can go to bed. By the way that child's been leaping around, I reckon he or she must be tired too. Try to sleep.'

Miss Tassie lightly tucked Alice into bed adjusting the extra pillows to make her as comfortable as possible.

It was almost six o'clock. Alice saw morning light, and a pretty dancing shadow caused by the sun glinting through a palm tree in the garden patio. She felt what she knew to be the first contraction. She called to Miss Tassie. They waited the thirty minutes until the next arrived. 'I'll get your things and telephone the hospital to expect you. The hotel limousine will collect us.'

The first stage of labour lasted for six seemingly unending hours. The second, about an hour.

The nurse wiped her brow for her, and the midwife said, 'Many congratulations, Mrs Newcombe. You have given birth to a wonderfully healthy baby boy.'

'Let me see him, let me see him!'

The baby was wrapped in a light-weight towel and was, as yet, unwashed. Alice held him momentarily, bloodstained and slippery. His hair was dark, long and very straight. Then the nurse took the child to wash him, while another gave Alice a blanket bath.

All the while, Miss Tassie had been waiting in the visitors room. More than relieved and delighted that all was well, she made a point of looking at the clock. It was fourteen minutes past one. She concluded that Alice's son had been born at five past one, on the twenty-first of April, nineteen-hundred-and-twenty-seven.

*

The following afternoon the nurse came into Alice's room holding the baby, who she was told, weighed eight and a half pounds.

'You can hold him for a while if you'd like to.'

'Of course I do! He's so beautiful, isn't he?'

'He certainly is, Mrs Newcombe.'

'Do let me feed him, my milk is beginning to flow.'

'Oh no, don't do that – we're taking care of his food.'

The nurse handed Alice her son, and left them together. She looked down at him. He was sleeping soundly. She was so proud of him. Her love was growing with every second they spent together. She examined and admired his perfect little hands and feet, counting the fingers and toes . . . He started to stir in her arms and was about to open his eyes. At that moment the nurse returned to whisk him away from Alice. She held on to him more tightly.

'I must take him now, Mrs Newcombe.'

'No, you cannot, and I won't let you. You must leave him with me for a bit longer.'

'But I'm not allowed to. It's bad for you, and it's bad for your baby too. Please give him to me.'

She bent down over Alice and tried forcibly to remove him from her arms.

'Go away. *Go away* this minute.'

'It's against the rules, more than my job's worth.'

'I don't care. You must leave him with me.'

'Well, for five minutes then . . .'

Very reluctantly the nurse turned away from mother and child. As she was leaving the room she said, 'Oh, don't worry about your milk. The doctor will give you something to take to dry it up.'

'Oh no he won't,' Alice muttered under her breath. 'Come here, my darling, precious.'

She put her son to her breast. He eagerly nuzzled and sucked her milk. She smiled down at him, and looked at him again more closely. He was so beautiful, so happy and contented. How could she allow that happiness and contentment be taken from her, and her son to live a life unaware of his real mother? She knew that he would grow up into the living image of his handsome father. Already she realised that she loved the child, that she could give him a real, warm love, in spite of the fact that he was the result of sexual passion rather than true love. That did not matter. She could make up for that. Her fame, her career now seemed unimportant. Within those few minutes she came to a firm decision.

The nurse returned and with sharp efficiency she announced, 'You really must give him to me now, Mrs Newcombe. You've had far too long with him.'

'I'm sorry, nurse, but I cannot. I've changed my mind.'

The almoner was talking to Alice.

'Mrs Newcombe, you do honestly know what this means? Are you quite certain? There's still time to change your mind. Why don't you give yourself a few more days really to think things through and talk to your friends? Remember, life won't be easy for you – it never is for any unmarried mother – and because you are very much in the public's eye, you'll have to make even more sacrifices.'

'Yes, I know – I do know, believe me. But I can't allow my child to be adopted. I really *can't*. It's cruel and immoral. I don't care about public opinion – what other people think. He's mine, and he will stay mine until he grows up and decides what he wants to do with his life – then the choice will be his. I must do what I know to be right.'

'You are a very brave woman, Mrs Newcombe. Brave and determined. But if you don't mind my saying it, also stubborn. You really should listen to what other people say.'

'My mind is made up, and I won't change it!'

'Very well, if that's the way you really feel, but . . .'

'No buts! Yes, it *is* the way I feel. I do want to go through with it. I want my son to have a real mother.'

'The proposed adoptive parents will be heartbroken – we have made all the arrangements . . .'

'Well, you'll just have to un-make them again, won't you?'

'I *suppose* that could be done, after all, you haven't finally signed the papers as yet.'

The almoner left Alice. Within minutes the nurse returned carrying a lace bedecked crib, and placed it by the side of Alice's bed. Alice leant over and looked at the downy dark head and the little wrinkled face peacefully sleeping.

'Why, Miss Alice, he's in here with you. I didn't expect to see him!' Miss Tassie rushed over and peered into the crib.

'Oh, isn't he lovely! The little darling!'

'Miss Tassie, you're going to be seeing a lot more of him – for a very long time.'

Miss Tassie drew in a deep breath and stared at Alice.

'You don't mean . . .'

'Yes, I do mean. Will you help me bring him up? Look, he's so beautiful, isn't he?'

'He sure is a beautiful baby; but, Miss Alice . . . no Pappy, and you're not a widow. Life is going to be so hard for you. It's not the done thing, you know. Why, young women in your situation always have their babies . . .'

'Oh, don't worry, Miss Tassie, I've thought all about that. If you think we'll need a nanny I can easily hire one, so that she can take over when I start shooting again . . .'

'Oh, when you starts shooting again . . .' She nodded thoughtfully.

'Yes, and I will, of course, as planned . . . In that new talking picture. I shall be so wealthy, I'll be able to give him the very best of everything . . .'

'You really think that, Miss Alice?'

'Why, of course . . . Won't I, darling?'

As she spoke she leant over the crib and picked up her precious bundle.

'Miss Alice, yes of course I'll stick by you and help – I know a lot about babies even though I was the youngest of our family. There were always the neighbours. We never had dollies – we always played with real live babies!'

Miss Tassie kissed both of them, and left. As she walked the short distance back to the hotel she was extremely worried. Yes, she knew that Miss Alice was doing the right thing by God, who had sent her the child anyway . . . but He was certainly going to make life tough, and she knew that Miss Alice simply didn't realise just how tough.

A week later Alice was back at the hotel and making plans to return to Hollywood. As yet she had told no one other than the people at the hospital and Miss Tassie of her decision. She wanted to surprise them. She was sure that if she invited Jean, Norma and Connie around to 'Sunburst' and then presented her baby to them, they would be so overcome by him that all would be well. She was excited and happy. She was feeding him herself and was beginning to take a little gentle exercise. But she also did a very great deal of shopping. She went out and bought a vast amount of baby clothes and a pretty baby basket, deciding she would not buy a pram until she arrived home. She did not feel quite strong enough to drive back even part of the way, so decided to stay on for another week; then with Miss Tassie doing at least half of the driving, they would make their way home, staying overnight en route, as they had on the way down.

She often sat on the sunny terraces with the baby in his basket beside her, and enjoyed the admiration of the hotel guests. She kept up her subterfuge: very soon she would be joining her husband. She also retained her dark wigs. However, once on the road home she decided they would be shed – for ever.

'Alice darling, you're looking wonderful. I gather all's gone well with you, and now you're looking forward to getting back to work. Look at her, Norma – her figure's hardly suffered at all!'

'Yes, Alice, it's wonderful to have you at home. I'll be reporting back to Joe. He and John have decided on the budget for the movie, and Dayton is really excited about making his first talking picture. Of course he doesn't know, as yet, whether it will be all-talking or just some scenes, but in any case, Alice, your lovely English voice will come over so well. They were delighted with the results of the San Diego tests.'

'Yes, it will be exiting, won't it?' smiled Alice.

She was entertaining Jean, Norma and Connie. She, Miss Tassie and the baby had been home for a few days. The first person she had taken into her confidence was Margaret, who, though shocked and very worried about Alice's future career, said she would do everything in her power to help Alice and to be discreet until Alice's future had been resolved. The staff were delighted with the infant, and had been sworn to secrecy over him until Alice gave them other instructions.

'Yes, I feel very well. I've even done a few barre exercises yesterday and today, so my dancing will soon, I hope, be reasonable again – just in case I've the role of a dancer in the new film.'

'Well, Dayton'll fill you in about all that. You have a meeting on Monday morning, I believe.'

There was a slight lull in the conversation. Alice was excited and keen to tell them her news, but deciding that actions speak louder than words, she said, 'Will you excuse me for a moment?'

She returned carrying her baby,

'I want you to meet my son!'

The three women were speechless. Being women they automatically got up and crowded round to see the lovely child. They admired him, but looked anxiously at Alice and then at each other.

'Alice, you're not . . .? You haven't decided to . . .?' It was Jean who spoke.

'Yes, my dears, I have. He's so beautiful, and I love him so much that I simply couldn't part with him.'

'Oh, Alice . . .' Jean sighed, and took the baby from her.

Connie let the infant's fingers curl around one of hers.

'Why he *is* lovely, and seems so happy and contented – but, my dear, do you know what this means?'

'Alice, it means that you'll never work again.'

'Norma's right, Alice,' said Connie. 'The studios . . .'

'Oh, the studios! Surely they'll understand? I don't see what difference it'll make. I can work as usual, I can bring him up. There's no need for any publicity.'

'Alice, that's not the case,' said Jean. 'You see, Hollywood stars are so famous, they influence the morals of young women all over the world. If it became known that you are bringing up an illegitimate child why, all over the world there would be a sad increase of unmarried mothers struggling to bring up their babies instead of getting them adopted in the proper manner. You would be accused of immoral conduct, and that would be very bad for the studio. At the moment you have an unblemished reputation. Think of the speculation about the father. The names of many of our male stars would be dragged through the mud . . .'

'I can't believe that, Jean – it's so stupid!'

'I'm afraid it's not, Alice,' replied Jean. 'And what have your family said?'

Alice hung her head and quietly said she had not told them.

'You can't keep it from them for ever, you know.'

'Yes, I know. That does bother me.'

The three women looked at each other.

'Look, Alice, Jean and I will talk to the menfolk. I'll try to convince Joe that it might be possible to keep things quiet, but . . . Well, we'll do what we can,' said Norma.

322

Jean handed the baby back to his mother.

'But he is a little dear. You're so right and brave in many ways, Alice, but you know most people would find you quite shocking. Have you given him a name yet?'

'No, I haven't. I'm thinking so much about that. It's difficult, you know, but he will be a Townsend – that I have decided.'

'Is the father's name on the birth certificate?'

'Yes.'

The three women gasped.

The next day, Alice had a phone call from John's secretary saying that the meeting planned for the following Monday morning had been postponed.

'I christen thee Peter Valentine Newcombe Townsend, in the name of the Father, the Son, and the Holy Ghost, Amen.'

Peter Valentine moved comfortably in the vicar's arms and cried gently as the water slipped over his head. The vicar handed the child back to Miss Tassie, who, with Margaret, promised as his surety to renounce the devil and all his works and to believe in God and to serve him and to see to it that – 'the infant be taught as soon as he is able to learn, what a solemn vow, promise and profession he hath been made by you, his Godmothers.'

Miss Tassie looked down at the baby with as much love and care as if she were his mother.

The small private ceremony ended with Alice, Margaret and Miss Tassie thanking the vicar and Alice giving him a generous donation to his church.

'Alice, do you just like Peter as a name or does it have any special meaning?' Margaret asked as they left the church.

'Peter was my mother's father's name. He was such a nice man, I loved him a lot. When I was a little girl he would tell me stories about his life at sea in the Royal Navy – years ago now, of course.'

'That's delightful. Besides, "Peter Valentine" goes well together, doesn't it?'

Peter Valentine made good progress. When Alice had a visit from Doctor Gilchrist to check on her own health and that of her son's, he also warned her that public opinion was very much against her. But certainly the child was in the peak of condition. He gave her advice about bottlefeeding him when she felt the time was right to stop feeding him herself.

Her only problem was that she knew that sooner or later she would have to tell her parents about Peter Valentine.

'There's a messenger here with a letter for you. He wants your signature for it,' said Miss Tassie.

Thinking it a little odd, Alice went to the entrance hall and signed for the letter. I expect it's a notice about the meeting, she thought. I'm surprised that

Dayton didn't phone and tell me. She tore open the letter. It was very formal, and signed by Joe Schenck.

'*I very much regret that as from Monday next, the thirty-first of May, we are terminating your contract. Until that date all monies will, as usual, be paid into your bank. Yours sincerely . . .*'

Chapter 39

Alice read and re-read the letter. Feeling totally hopeless she went into the drawing room, slumped down on the settee and started to cry. Miss Tassie heard her from the kitchen. Wiping her hands she came in to see what was wrong. Silently Alice handed her the letter.

'Oh dear, dear . . . do you think he really means it?'

'Looks like it, doesn't it? Why don't you ring that nice Mr Montgomery and see what he's got to say? Surely there'll be some way round it.'

'Yes, I'll do that right away. Can you prepare Peter's midday feed, please?'

Miss Tassie said she would, and Alice went to the telephone.

'I'm sorry, Miss Townsend, Mr Montgomery's at a screening. I don't know when he'll be through.'

She telephoned Jean. Her personal maid answered the phone, Alice asked to speak to her.

'Mrs Montgomery is at the hairdresser's. She said she expected you to call, and asked me to tell you that she would call over and see you later.'

That was a little more hopeful. Alice stayed in all afternoon but Jean did not turn up. When Margaret returned from work she said that it was all over the studios that Alice's contract was to be cancelled, but no-one knew why. All her friends knew that she lived with Alice and were hungry for gossip, but she said she knew nothing, which was, of course, the truth.

'Alice, it wasn't easy for me, but I'll never say a word, you know that, don't you? How's that godson of mine – has he been a good boy today?'

Peter had been fractious since lunch. He had not taken his feed as well as usual. Miss Tassie said it was because Alice was upset – and he felt it as she held his bottle for him.

Alice stayed at 'Sunburst' for several days, expecting Jean to turn up. She had failed to reach Norma and Connie, but then, they were always busy filming. About a week after she had received the dreadful news – a week during which she had experienced a great deal of anxiety, knowing that she would not and could not be in the planned talking movie – when she began to look haggard and feel unwell and extremely tired, Jean called to see her.

'My dear, I know this is dreadful for you – but, you see, you have only yourself to blame. Didn't you get sound advice from the hospital? Surely they impressed on you that this was entirely the wrong decision, that you would be sacrificing your whole future? I'm very annoyed about the whole situation, Alice. We arranged everything so carefully, and now you . . . well, all this mess!'

'Yes, the hospital did explain, and I'm so sorry that in many ways I've let you down; but Jean, you're a mother, and although your family is grown up, surely you can imagine just how it would have been if someone had wrenched your baby from you?'

Alice was crying as she spoke. Jean got up, put her arm around her and sat beside her holding her hand.

'Yes, I can; but, Alice, you're not married. And the father . . .'

'Oh yes . . . the father . . . Jean, this is dreadful, I know, but somehow I also know I've done the right thing.'

'As a woman and mother, yes, you have, but as far as the world is concerned you definitely haven't. You have behaved immorally and sinfully in far too many people's eyes. So you are an outcast, Alice, and you simply have to cope.'

'But, Jean, this is the twentieth century . . .'

'Yes, my dear, it is, but only very few people will condone your actions. I would advise you to move away from Hollywood. Maybe you should go home to London, and try to get your family to understand.'

'I know my brother would, but my parents . . . I don't think so. Besides, I've been the cause of so much trouble and unhappiness to them in the past that . . .'

'You cannot give them more trouble, is that it?'

'I suppose so . . .'

'And there's no other man in your life?'

'No, of course not!'

'Pity . . . Well, if you stay here for the time, you must not be seen with the little one. And remember you must not expect any invitations.'

'But, Jean, I'm *proud* of my baby.'

'I can understand that, but if what's happened gets out reporters won't leave you alone. Your story will top the headlines in all the movie magazines . . . Your family are simply bound to discover what's been going on. Oh, my dear, you have put a lot upon yourself, when you could be one of Hollywood's brightest stars.'

She hugged the young mother.

Two months slipped by. Alice hardly ever went out, and when she did she drove fast, wearing dark glasses and headscarves or a hat well pulled down, and never took her beautiful little son with her. Meanwhile he made good progress, and was happy and contented.

Alice continued to live comfortably, paying her bills and her staff. When she needed new clothes she had them sent on approval from Magnin's or another of her favourite stores. She thought she had good reserves of cash, but one day on receiving a regular statement she was horrified at how they had sunk. It was the end of July, and she realised that within a surprisingly short space of time she would run out of money.

She became very frightened. Thoughts of her early, impoverished days flooded back to her. The cheese shop . . . the awful apartment . . . being short of everything . . .

'No, no, that mustn't happen again, I couldn't bear it, I really couldn't – and now with Peter it would be far, far worse. Dear God . . .'

She had been thinking aloud, sitting on a recliner by her swimming pool. Peter in his pram was beside her. Tearfully she looked at him, so contented, sleeping after his morning bath. She looked across the pool to the outside of her dance studio . . . the garden, the little pergola . . . No friends called on her now, and she received no invitations – she only saw Jean very occasionally, and when she did the atmosphere was cool. She could not plan – or afford – to entertain in style. No musicians would make pleasant, jazzy sounds on her birthday this year, and if she arranged a party she knew that no-one would come. There was no doubt in her mind that she had to take some kind of action, but what?

Suddenly she saw Miss Tassie speaking urgently to the young gardener, half way down the garden path. The large woman grabbed a sweeping brush he was carrying and ran to the gate. Alice stood up. She could just see Miss Tassie wielding the broom, and a man cower before turning out of the gate, having been hit on the back by the obviously furious Miss Tassie.

Miss Tassie made her way up the path walking proudly and holding the broom upside down like a triumphant banner.

Alice was puzzled and looked tearfully up at her, 'What *is* going on – what have you done? You could have hurt that man seriously. What did he want?'

'He wanted to interview you. Said he'd heard rumours about you and why you weren't to be in Mr Dayton Holt's next movie. I told him to get out!'

'That was brave of you, but, well . . .'

Alice looked down at the crumpled bank statement which she was still holding.

'Miss Tassie, if we are not very careful I will have bad money problems, I don't think we can carry on as we are for very much longer.'

'Gee, Miss Alice, I'm real sorry. Look, if it'll help, I'll not take my wages for the time.'

'That's really sweet of you, but I don't think that'll make a lot of difference. As you know, I know what it's like to be poor – really poor – and I'm *not* going to let it happen again, ever, not for me or for Peter or for you. I'm not sure yet what we will do, but I must make a decision soon, while I've still got enough money to make a fresh start somewhere else.'

'Perhaps we should go back to London. Miss Alice. I like it there, and maybe you could do some acting in England.'

'But I still have my baby, and I'll still be an outcast – probably even more so. Oh, Miss Tassie, all this has brought it home to me – maybe I shouldn't have kept little Peter after all. He would have been better off in the long run with that nice San Diego family.'

She started to sob, pitifully. Miss Tassie sat down beside her and hugged her.

'No, Miss Alice, no, *no* – you did the right thing. God will look after you. He's already forgiven your sin of bearing little Peter out of wedlock – I'm sure He has.'

Alice smiled through her tears, but knew that she could all too easily sink lower and lower, and the threat of the snooping reporter added even more urgency to her situation. She spent most of the rest of the day in torment. She tried to practise, but her body would not respond to her instructions – she even fell off one foot when attempting a simple arabesque *en pointe* at her barre. She swam and showered, but she was restless.

However, when Margaret came home quite late that night Alice was distracted from her pressing problems.

'You look happy tonight – you're quite flushed – are you feeling okay?'

'Oh, yes, yes, Alice, I'm so happy. Look!'

Margaret thrust her left hand towards Alice, showing off a lovely five diamond engagement ring.

'Oh, my dear, I'm so happy for you.'

'Well, you see, Helmut has been offered his first thirteen reel feature film to direct. There will be some talking scenes in it, and of course he'll now be earning a great deal of money – so, well, as you can see, we're engaged. I do love him, Alice.'

'Of course you do, he is a very nice man, Margaret, you really deserve each other. You make a lovely couple, and you'll be chief make-up artist for his movie, won't you?'

'Yes, and for every one stretching for years into the future! Oh, Alice, after everything that's happened to me these last five years I'm now completely happy. I've been happy here with you, as you know, but this completes my happiness!'

The friends hugged each other. Margaret's happiness contrasted vividly with Alice distressing situation. She tried hard not to, but at that moment she broke down.

'My dear, I'm being selfish. Of course, you're missing Rudy. Then you've no work . . . I wish Helmut could employ you over at Paramount, but . . .'

'It's alright, Margaret, I understand. It's just that I've had bad news. But I don't want to spoil your happy day . . .'

'Whatever's happened?' Margaret persuaded her friend to talk about her problem.

'So you see I'll have to do something soon. But what? My immediate reaction is to go home while I still have a little money, and face the music with my family, but heaven knows how they'll take it.'

'Perhaps you should go to a different city at home – maybe start a dancing school somewhere like Bath. You could pretend to be a widow.'

'That's sensible – yes, that's a possibility. Just see my family, come clean, then before things get embarrassing for them go somewhere else – like Bath, or maybe Cheltenham. Thanks, Margaret – let me think about that. It'd be awful for a while, but I could make a fresh start, couldn't I?'

'Yes, darling, and you'll succeed. You've so much talent and skill. Any dancing school you open will be terrific!'

Alice lay awake until dawn started to break. Then, after about an hour and a half of very heavy sleep she woke up, and though red-eyed, felt better. She went into the nursery, where Miss Tassie was about to put Peter into his morning bath.

'I've decided that I must go back to England, and the sooner the better. Life is over for us here. You will come with me, won't you?'

The baby gurgled contentedly as his nurse carefully placed him in the baby bath.

'Of course I will, I couldn't leave you. So what will we do?'

'I've made no plans yet – just decided. Today I'll work everything out.'

She sat in the cool drawing room with a notepad and her pen, and made a long list of pros and cons.

The telephone rang. Alice answered.

'Alice, it's me. Can I bring Helmut around later on this evening? We're going to a preview after an early dinner. Say about ten?'

'Why, yes of course. I'm always delighted to see you together!'

Alice returned to her planning. There would be a great deal of packing to do. A lot of things could be sent by cargo ship. There was her car. Yes, she would take it rather than sell it – *if* the cargo charges were not too heavy. No, even if they were! She loved it, and besides, it would give her status at home and bolster her sense of pride! There was 'Sunburst', dear 'Sunburst'! Could she let it, just in case she came back? How she loved her house! How she loved her dance studio with its memories of happy hours dancing with Rudy . . . The pool, the garden . . . She would never have this kind of living standard in England. If she bought a place in the provinces, she might even have to put in a bathroom! She hated the thought. But she had to face up to things.

'Alice, dearest, have you had any more thoughts about what you want to do?'

'Well, yes, I have – thanks to our chat last evening. Why?'

Margaret moved nearer Helmut and took his strong firm hand in hers. She glanced lovingly up into his clear blue eyes.

'Well you see . . . Oh, darling, you say!'

'Alice, I want to buy a house for us. And if . . .'

'If I go home, you would like this one?'

Alice's voice was a little shaky.

'Yes, Alice, please. What do you think? Would that be alright? I do hope we're not being too forward.'

'Not at all. Why, you and Helmut were brilliant to think of it!'

'I love this house as much as you do, Alice, as you know – it's such a happy house. Then, later, when you want to come back for a visit – or work, perhaps, who knows? – you can so easily stay here. Even if by then . . .'

Margaret blushed and looked up at her man again.

'Well, even if by then we have our own little ones in Peter's nursery.'

'I don't want to sell, but I must. It will give me extra security while I re-build my life at home. I couldn't think of better people to buy it. This is a terrific weight off my mind – we can work out the business side of things in due course.'

'We don't want to rush you,' said Helmut.

'Of course you don't! But I really think I should go as soon as possible.'

The weeks that followed were sad ones for Alice. So much had been lost to her. She was, as her friends and the doctor had warned her, totally ostracised.

She wrote a long letter to the Montgomerys thanking them for all their kindness in the past, and telling them of her plans, and a similar one to Constance and Norma. Her friends replied, not unsympathetically, and told her to keep in touch – she was doing the right thing. They were still fond of her, but though so far there had been no speculation over her, if Hollywood heard her story opinion would be against her, and there would be much speculation about the father of her child. The sooner she went back to her family, the better.

Packing soon began and crates and boxes filled the rooms. There were special trunks in which to hang Alice's extensive wardrobe, cases for books and records, crates for pieces of furniture, which would be sent cargo. All those had to be labelled. That evening, when Alice had put Peter to bed and Miss Tassie was cooking their dinner, she went into the studio and labelled her gramophone, came back into the chaotic drawing room and labelled a pretty little antique writing desk she had acquired, then walked over to the wireless set. She labelled that too, and idly turned it on . . .

'And don't forget, folks, to stay with us until ten o'clock this evening, when we go over live to the Hollywood Hotel, where we will be bringing you direct from the beautiful ballroom the sound of Ben Waterman and his Twentieth Century Ballroom Orchestra.'

Chapter 40

'Pack up all my care and woe
'Here I go,
'Swinging low,
'Bye, bye blackbird . . .'

The vocalist came to the end of her number.

'Thank you, ladies and gentlemen, and listeners at home. And now for our next – get ready, everyone, let's *Charleston*! Right, boys! One, two . . .'

As the Charleston got under way Ben Waterman turned around to face the happy, dancing mob. Smiling broadly to couples as they whisked by him, he looked across the dimly lit ballroom. The mirrored ball turning in its prominent position at the centre of the ceiling reflected sparkling highlights on one particular dress of silver and brilliant white satin.

Still beating time, he looked again. The young woman who was wearing the dress was very beautiful. He wondered why she was standing in the corner of the room alone. Her man must have gone for drinks; no doubt he would return soon. Ben turned away, and for some sixteen bars concentrated on the band. Looking again, he saw the young woman was still in the same position, motionless and gazing at him. He blinked. Were his eyes playing him tricks in the indifferent light? No, they were telling the truth. Amazed, he at once turned back to the band and upped the tempo, causing the dancers to double their pace. The Charleston ended, and the couples returned to their seats exhausted.

Not breaking eye contact with Alice, he went to the microphone.

'And now, ladies and gentlemen, a change of tempo. Here's a lovely old number from way back – it's a favourite of mine, and of someone else who is here tonight in this beautiful ballroom. "You made me love you." Remember it, folks? Well, maybe you're all too young!'

He started the band, and had a quiet word with the pianist who took over. Walking straight up to Alice he took her in his arms and led her onto the dance floor.

'I can't believe it – though when I knew we were coming here, I hoped – oh God, how I hoped!'

'Ben! I can't believe it, either . . . I heard an announcement on the wireless earlier, and . . .'

'No, don't talk now, Let's just allow the years in between to slip away.'

She nodded. The pianist let the band play in slow tempo. Ben held Alice tight; the feeling of his strong arms around her was so familiar . . . It was just as if they had last danced together two or three evenings ago.

'What a really remarkable story! You've been through so much! To be at the top of your profession – and now all this. Darling Alice, you have suffered, haven't you?'

'Yes, I have; but the good times were spectacularly good, Ben. Now, sadly, everything's gone completely wrong again. I know I should have listened to everyone, and had little Peter adopted. But I just knew I couldn't – even though, as I said, I didn't really love Rudy. Oh, what must you think of me to have had a child by a man I . . . I only desired physically – and to keep him!'

'But you're his mother! You're a tender, loving person; you *couldn't* be so cruel as to give up your baby, even though you knew in principle you would have to make sacrifices.'

'I've had to make more sacrifices than I thought possible. But I still don't regret what I did. Oh, Ben, he's *so* beautiful!'

'He couldn't be anything else, with you as his mother, and with the father he had . . .'

He hesitated for a moment.

'When can I see him – tomorrow?'

Ben glanced out of the window of the penthouse suite of the Hollywood Hotel. He noticed dawn was breaking. They had been talking for hours.

'No, not tomorrow – I mean today!'

'You mean you want to?'

'Of course I do. Alice, I've found you again, I'm not going to lose you now.'

He stood up, and she joined him at the window. The first rays of the sun were creeping up the sky.

'I don't want to lose you, either and yes, I'd love you to meet Peter – today, if you like. But, Ben . . .'

He took her in his arms and they kissed.

'But, what, Alice?'

'You. What about you? Surely you have a wife somewhere?'

'No, Alice, I haven't. I've not been angelic, and there have been women – several in fact. But whenever I thought things were becoming serious, there always seemed to be something lacking. Oh, I've seen pictures of you in the magazines and I've loved all your movies. I thought *Nocturne* was marvellous! I've been waiting for the next one, and I thought recently that the wait was getting long . . .'

332

'And now you know why. But go on, what about your work?'

'I did a lot more crossings on the *Mauritania* . . . There was such a furore when you jumped ship that day, by the way! Then I joined a band on a cruise ship for a while, until my mother died and I came in for a small but useful inheritance. My brother suggested that I should form my own band, and that he should become my manager. We got the band together with some English boys and some Americans, and we've been touring the States on dates like this – playing ballrooms in big hotels, and doing quite a lot of broadcasting. Jim's in London at the moment, meeting the managements of one of the many smart new night clubs which have been opening there. He's just finalised a contract, and we open at the New Mayfair in September as their permanent orchestra. Maxine – that's our vocalist – is Jim's wife, they married not long ago.'

'For a moment while I was watching you, I thought perhaps she was your girlfriend.'

'Oh, no, she's definitely Jim's wife! You know, my life hasn't been nearly as dramatic as yours. I always had hopes, I always thought that perhaps we just might meet up again. Then, when you became so famous, it seemed most unlikely – I expected your engagement to be announced to some star or other at any moment.'

The sun was now well up. It was almost seven o'clock.

'I must go Ben. Miss Tassie will have given Peter his first morning feed by now.'

'So I can come and meet my son this afternoon?'

'Yes, of course.'

Alice turned to pick up her bag from a nearby chair and stopped dead in her tracks.

'Say that again, Ben, please.'

'I suggested that I should come and meet my son this afternoon.'

'Your son?'

'Yes, Alice, my son. Our son.'

'You really mean that?'

They stood looking at each other at each other, radiant with happiness and love.

'Alice, let's *really* make the years in between slip away.'

She nodded, and he put his arm around her waist. Without taking their eyes from each other, they walked into the bedroom.

Peter Valentine gurgled, and as he was picked up from the rug he put his little hand on Ben's face.

'You're right, Alice! He's terrific – aren't you, eh?'

He nervously held the child, and his inexperience made Alice laugh.

'Why, Miss Alice, I haven't heard you laugh like that for a very long time,' said Miss Tassie, who was standing by.

Ben handed Peter over to his mother, fearful that he might drop him.

'Well, you'll be hearing Alice laugh like that a very great deal more in future – won't she, darling?'

'I do hope so!'

They were sitting among the packing cases, which would soon be collected.

Miss Tassie took Peter from Alice, and left them alone together.

'First things first. There's something I must do right away!'

Ben got up from the settee and started throwing boxes, pieces of paper and books off the rug, making an exaggerated fuss to clear a space at Alice's feet. She laughed again; she could hardly stop. He knelt in front of her.

'Miss Townsend, I have loved and admired you for years. Will you marry me?'

She could not stop laughing and flung her arms around his neck. They rolled on the floor in a spontaneous embrace, caught up amid the boxes and paper.

'Mr Waterman, of course I will!'

Then, getting up rather abruptly and pushing her untidy hair back from her face, she said, 'But how, and when . . .?'

'Leave that to me. But it will be very soon – and I do mean *very* soon. As soon as I can possibly arrange it!'

'Let's keep it very quiet!'

'Yes, of course!'

'And you really like Peter, Ben?'

'YES, and if you agree, I'd love to adopt him, so that we can be Mr and Mrs Waterman and their son Peter Waterman – what do you think?'

'You honestly mean that? It would be so wonderful for Peter and me if you did. Oh, Ben, I'll never be able to thank you enough – if you're *quite* sure. After all, he's not . . .'

'I know he's not mine, but he is so nearly mine that I really wouldn't want it any other way. As far as he's concerned I will be his father. It isn't as though his real father is still alive, is it?'

'Oh, thank you so much for saying that!'

'Now, have I mentioned to you we have another two weeks here at the Hollywood? Our passages home are all arranged – for Maxine and myself and the band. When were you thinking of leaving?'

'Within the next few weeks. I'd have liked to stay for Margaret and Helmut's wedding, but they'll understand when they know you're leaving and we want to go with you. Of course, Miss Tassie must come too – I really couldn't do without her.'

'And there's no reason why you should. She seems a dear.'

'She's quite fantastic – half French, you know.'

'I am so pleased to see you again so soon. Your little boy, is he making good progress?'

'Yes, Vicar.'

'And Mr Waterman is now your husband. I'm confident that God will bless your union, and that all three of you will be very happy.'

They were in the vestry after the brief ceremony. Margaret and Miss Tassie were with them, Jean and John – who gave her away – and Norma and Constance. Maxine, Ben's sister-in-law, was also there, with Billy, the band's pianist, who acted as Ben's best man.

Alice wore a simple pale pink silk dress and matching hat; Miss Tassie and Margaret were in pale blue. Everyone was very moved by the quiet dignity of the occasion and happy for Alice and Ben. Jean was very relieved. Any anger she had felt was forgotten, and she gave Alice all her love and support. Norma and Constance felt the same: now that Alice had a husband, life would be much easier for her when she made a fresh start in London.

'Please sign here, Mrs Waterman.'

Alice went to her tiny handbag and took out her pen. As she unscrewed the top, the pen slipped from her gloved hand.

The vicar bent down and picked it up for her. Glancing at it as he did so he smiled, 'Ah! I see your pen is a Waterman too!'

Alice blushed, and nodded. She felt a light breeze blow through the vestry as she wrote her name in the appropriate place. She handed the pen to Ben, who added his signature.

'Oh, Alice, I'm so happy for you!' Margaret said delightedly. 'Things have worked out so unexpectedly and well! Give England my love, won't you? I don't think I'll ever return there.'

'Yes, of course I will. And I know you and Helmut will be happy here.'

'Oh, we will, we will! Pity you can't stay for our wedding – but of course you must go with your handsome Ben.'

'Yes, he is handsome, isn't he?'

'And a thoroughly lovely man, Alice – like my Helmut.'

The moment had come to leave Hollywood. The first cab, carrying Miss Tassie and Peter Valentine, moved off. The second, with Mr and Mrs Ben Waterman, followed.

They turned out of the drive into the road to make their way to the railroad station at the start of the long train journey to New York to join the *Mauritania* for Southampton.

Alice turned to look at 'Sunburst' for the last time.

'Don't look back, darling. Look to the future, our future.'

'Yes, of course you're right.'

Sitting under a palm tree on the promenade just below the Opera House Alex opened the long letter from Alice. To his surprise, the envelope had a British stamp and a London postmark. When he opened it, he saw it was on *Mauritania* notepaper. At the first sentence, he almost cried out loud with excitement. Alice was coming home. She and Ben were re-united. Alex could not have been happier. He sat for a while enjoying the warm sun on his face, allowing the good news to soak in. He had been very concerned for his friend, knowing all too well how difficult life had been for her in recent months. Now surely she had true happiness.

True happiness? Yes, but there would be something else that would make her life even more complete, and he, and possibly only he, was in a position to do something about it.

Alice had ended her letter: 'Write to me soon, Alex, and tell me you're happy for me . . . I so want your blessing.'

He went back to his apartment and wrote immediately,

'Alice, I know that life now has a lot to offer you, with your adoring husband, and beautiful son (dear wee thing). But do promise me you'll go back to class with Astafieva. Don't give up dancing *just* yet. I'm sure Ben will understand.'

From the bottom of his trunk, Alex took out several cans of film – a copy of their photoplay *Nocturne*, which he had arranged for Dayton to send him as soon as it was available. Then he went to Serge Diaghilev's hotel and asked to see him. He had something to show him, he said.

Chapter 41

Along with little Peter and Miss Tassie, Alice and Ben had comfortable staterooms on the *Mauritania* – very different from the staff cabins they knew so well in earlier days. Otherwise, the ship looked much the same, and they easily found their way around her. The staff were complete strangers, which they decided was just as well. As they sailed out of New York and passed the Statue of Liberty, Ben said, 'Look, I've something to show you.'

He took his wallet from an inside pocket and produced a very tattered snapshot. It was the picture of Alice he had taken on that last fateful morning.

'You see, I've carried it with me all this time.'

She smiled up at her husband.

'Yes, I can see that! It's so worn!'

'Stand over there, quickly, before Miss Liberty fades away completely. I want to take another picture of you.'

'And Peter?'

'Of course, and Peter.'

Alice picked him up from his pram and held him to face Ben's camera.

During the voyage home they gave a great deal of thought to a very urgent and pressing problem. And they decided that in order to be kind, they would have to tell a few white lies . . .

Robert read, 'DEAREST PARENTS STOP AM COMING HOME FOR GOOD STOP HAVE TWO IMPORTANT PEOPLE I WANT YOU TO MEET STOP ARRIVING LATE THURSDAY AFTERNOON STOP AM VERY HAPPY STOP ALL LOVE ALWAYS ALICE STOP

'Oh Robert! What *does* she mean?'

'You know, I *think* she means she's got married.'

'No, surely! Not in Hollywood! Why not here? Oh, she's got a lot of explaining to do!'

'Maybe, but she says she's happy, Lizzie, and that's the important thing, isn't it?'

'I wonder when she docks? The cable was sent from the *Mauritania*. Should we find out from Southampton?'

'If she'd wanted that she would have told us. No, let's just wait here. Perhaps she's just acquired a bigger entourage of servants, after all you can never tell with Alice, can you?'

Lizzie agreed. She was excited but very apprehensive.

They rang the bell at Edwardes Square, and were admitted by the ever faithful Mrs Wilson, who looked admiringly at Ben and muttered to herself what a nice man he looked.

'Mummy, Daddy, I want you to meet my husband, Ben Waterman.'

Lizzie turned very pale, but could see as Ben gripped her hand that Alice had made a good choice.

'Of course, you're most welcome, son,' said Robert, 'but why all the mystery? You know, you have taken us aback.'

'We're very sorry about that, sir, but the whole thing has been quite complicated.'

Alice took a deep breath.

'Yes, Mummy, Daddy, I know I've got a lot of explaining to do!'

She told them how she had first met Ben in the early days of 1923. They had constantly kept in touch and followed each other's careers with fascination, and in spite of their being miles apart, as time had gone on their friendship had turned to love. Blushing, she added that she had some wonderful letters from Ben, and took his hand as she continued their story.

Then, when she travelled back to America after the premiere of *Nocturne* they had met up again, fallen very much in love, and got engaged. But when the studios heard the news they were extremely upset. Big stars did not marry unknown saxophonists – their fans would not tolerate it – especially as, in Alice's case, the studio was about to announce that she was to star with Rudolph Valentino. So the plan was to to keep her marriage to Ben secret. They had married just two weeks later, and as her parents knew, Rudy had died.

'Well, darlings, in the cable I mentioned another person I want you to meet . . . Within a couple of weeks after Rudy's death I realised I was pregnant'

'Pregnant – oh, Alice . . .'

'Yes, Mummy. Of course, we had to stop the news being leaked to the public – who didn't even know we were married! I had some work to do in San Diego, so had my baby there. Oh, Mummy, Daddy, you have the most beautiful grandson! After he was born, the three of us – Miss Tassie, the baby and I, went back to Hollywood, and I had hoped to make the talking picture we'd done so much preparatory work on. But they had technical difficulties, and we couldn't go ahead. Meanwhile, Ben was . . .'

'I was touring America,' said Ben, 'and not so long ago I had an inheritance and was able to form my own band in America, though now it'll be permanently based in London.'

'My contract was coming to an end', Alice continued, 'and as Ben was

338

coming home and we wanted so much to be together properly – after only snatching time with each other for so long – I decided not to renew with United Artists . . . We were really both beginning to be homesick anyway. So here we are!'

'Oh, Alice, Alice! *Why* didn't you tell us all this? You could have trusted us.'

'Yes, I know, Mummy, but I simply could not risk it. Even letters get opened sometimes. Even if there were telephone links between Hollywood and England, *that* wouldn't have been really safe. I'm so sorry about all this, but we do hope you'll understand. If Ben had found a permanent home for the band in Hollywood, of course I would have told you right away.'

'Well, I understand, Alice,' said Robert, 'and I'm sure your mother does too – even if you have knocked us for six with all this!'

'Your father's right, Alice, and I agree. But where's our grandchild? Surely he's not outside waiting in some uncomfortable taxi with . . . well, who? Miss Tassie, I suppose?'

'No, Mummy, they're at the Ritz. Will you come and see him?'

'Wild horses won't stop me! Robert, get the car! I simply can't wait!'

'Alice, you really are the giddy limit, but I don't think I've ever seen you looking so very happy. Thank you, Ben, for turning her into a real woman!'

'It's been a pleasure, sir.'

'My little Alice – a mother! It doesn't seem possible!'

'You wait 'til you see him, Mummy . . .'

'I'm sure he's wonderful, but what's he called?' asked Lizzie anxiously.

Squeezing Ben's hand in the back seat of the Wolseley, Alice announced, 'Peter Valentine Newcombe Waterman.'

'Oh, Alice, *Peter* after my Papa – and Newcombe – how thoughtful of you!' She hesitated, and frowned slightly. 'And I quite like Valentine, too – a little odd and . . . well, unusual!'

That evening Peter Valentine was thoroughly spoilt by his grandparents, and the next day the Waterman family – along with the ever faithful Miss Tassie, moved into Edwardes Square. In due course Alice's husband and son would meet the Beaumonts and Philip, who would enjoy his new role as an uncle.

'My dear, Emma's just phoned. What do you think, Alice is married and has come home with her new husband and son!'

Lionel Maitland looked up from his copy of *The Times*.

'Her husband *and* son . . .?'

Yes, that's what I thought.' Sarah looked perplexed. 'Emma says he's a beautiful baby with straight dark hair, and both she and Eustace like the husband – he's a band leader.'

'So, she must have changed her mind about the adoption. Silly girl, but how brave!'

'Yes, Lionel, very brave.'

Sarah said nothing more for some time, then ventured, 'Lionel, now you've retired, do you want to go on living in London, or would you prefer to move to Plym Manor?'

'Dearest, you know I'm a countryman at heart . . . but I thought you . . .'

'If we restored The Manor, and as long as we could always come here . . .'

He smiled at his wife.

'Having been married to you for so long, I know how your mind works, my precious . . . You must do as you think best. This is *your* house. And of course it *was* a gift.'

'You simply can't mean it, Aunt Sarah. Oh, Ben, how wonderful!'

'But, Alice, we do. It's yours. This house was my home long before Lionel and I met – it was a gift to me as a young woman. I want to pass it on to someone who'll appreciate it as I have. We'll live in retirement in Lionel's family home in Devon, and if we can stay here during the London season, and at odd times, it will suit us very well. As you know, we've thought of you as our daughter for a long time now, and we can think of nothing better than you two living here with little Peter Valentine – and indeed with any more children you may produce in time.'

'But, Aunt Sarah, are you sure that Aunt Emma won't be put out? After all Rose and Stephen are your real niece and nephew . . .'

'My dear, I've already spoken with Emma. She doesn't mind at all. She's far wealthier than us, so there's no worry on that score.'

'Aunt Sarah, may I kiss you?'

'Thank you, Ben, of course you may!'

A flirtatious glint came into the elegant woman's eyes.

1928

Epilogue

It was the last night of a triumphant season, and Alice had come home to Her Majesty's Theatre. Nothing seemed to have changed very much since that distant time when she had been so very young, dancing so enthusiastically in *Chu Chin Chow*. There was still the same cream and green paint-work, the same familiar smells, the same harsh backstage lighting. But now, as she had had all season, her dressing-room was much larger – the star's dressing-room, near the stage, no more running up and down seventy stairs.

She was still in her tutu as she reflected on all this, and lowering her head to unpin her white *Swan Lake* headdress, with the feathers over her ears, she wondered if she would ever again experience another night of such triumph as this. She hoped so, but decided she would not mind when the time came to make way for a younger and perhaps even more talented ballerina. Sighing, she started to unloose her hair. As she did so, she suddenly felt cold.

'Hello, darling, you've made it! Do shut the door – there's a howling draught. Alex is ready, and I'll not be long.'

But glancing up at the mirror to smile at Ben, she realised that it was not her husband's reflection that she saw behind her, but that of a young man in his early twenties, in Army Captain's uniform. He gave Alice a huge smile.

'Oh! . . . *Charlie* . . . Charlie, I'm *so* happy!'

He nodded, and still smiling, vanished.

Somehow she knew she would never see him again.

Afterword

From *The Illustrated London News*, July 16, 1928:

'The famous ballerina Alica Tonsova is seen in our picture with her small son Peter, in the garden of the Chelsea home she shares with her husband, Mr Ben Waterman, the successful bandleader whose orchestra is resident at the fashionable 'New Mayfair Club'. This delightful photograph of Mother and Child was taken by the talented society photographer, Stephen Beaumont.'

You have been reading a novel published by Piatkus Books. We hope you have enjoyed it and that you would like to read more of our titles. Please ask for them in your local library or bookshop.

If you would like to receive details of new publications, please send a large stamped addressed envelope (UK only) to:

Piatkus Books: 5 Windmill Street
London W1P 1HF

PIATKUS

The sign of a good book